THE PACK: SECRETS

DAWN GRAY

ACKNOWLEDGMENTS

Special thanks to Jennifer R. Gaylord, who just loves to keep me in check and who hates my commas. All other errors are my own. We're only human and still miss some with multiple read-throughs.

Also, a shout out for the production cast and crew of "The Pack" trailer now up on YouTube and their dedication to the art of bringing worlds to life. It will be amazing to see what happens next.

To those who supported that filming endeavor, you have my many, many thanks.

Of course, my kids and parents, who have been nothing but supportive, especially this time around when not only did we write a book, but we filmed as well.

All my love to you, always.

PROLOGUE

"Plymouth Harbor, 1673"

HIS BRIGHT BLUE eyes scanned the port, taking in the massive amount of people that surrounded him, coming and going, yelling of their wares, trying to make a living. His tiny heart pounded rapidly in his chest as he held tightly to his mother's skirt, shaking as they made their way through the crowd.

He could hear his father talking, speaking in their native tongue, warning his mother to stay close, to keep a hand on the boy, not let him wander as they approached the front of the line. Where were they going? Why were they there?

The sixty-six-day journey on the boat across the ocean was taxing, held up in the hold of the ship as people lay dying, most never making it due to the cold, wet conditions. But they were the lucky ones. Their small family had survived, and the baby that grew in his mother's belly would thrive in the new world.

He just didn't know where he was.

"Andrei, keep close." His father's deep, authoritative voice broke though the waves of strangers' conversations, drawing his attention up to the deep red of his eyes hidden under the brim of his hat. Andrei nodded, the only thing his body would allow. It seemed as if he had lost his voice. "Good, we're almost there."

With his fingers clenching the fabric, Andrei shivered as they stepped up to the counter. His father removed his hat—something he never did—and lowered it in respect.

"Name?" The man behind the counter questioned, raising a pen and placing it on the paper.

"Vârcolac," he responded clearly, proudly.

The man in front of him raised his eyes, a sarcastic smirk on his face, and shook his head, scribbling down on a piece of paper. "Summerford."

His father seemed confused, angry, and glanced back at his mother, but her response was just to shake her head, and her hand went to Andrei's hand, taking it tightly in hers.

"Given names?"

"Iacob, Anastasia, Andrei."

But the response back wasn't what Andrei had expected as that pen started scribbling again. "Jacob, Anna, and Andrew." The paper snapped out from under the pen, and he handed it towards Iacob. "Welcome to the new world. Move along."

His dismissal was blunt, and Iacob took a hold of his wife, pulling them back into the deafening sounds of the crowd outside. That was it. It was done. Their past lives were left behind, their indiscretions hidden by thousands of miles of clear blue ocean, high mountains, and lifetimes of different languages.

They were finally free.

"Rosemont, Illinois - Present"

She closed her eyes against the cacophony of voices that filled the room. There didn't seem to be any one coherent conversation that she could follow to even voice her own opinion, not with the way that everything blended together.

She sat high up on the tier in an auditorium-type of room, surrounded by men and women of different designations, but no one appeared to be listening to the other. It was a free-for-all, and she was stuck in the middle of it, until—

"Mrs. Summerford!" The sound of her name was spoken with such annoyance... no, more like disdain... had her eyes wide open looking for the source of it. "*Alpha* Summerford. The floor is yours."

She spotted him, her blue eyes going right to the man in the middle of the mess. He sat to the right of the council, three men from the end, leaning into the microphone, and all other voices had seemed to stop. Silence filled the room as Juli Summerford stood from her seat, grabbed the black messenger bag from beside her chair, and headed down to the podium that stood in the center of the room.

With her gaze scanning over every person in the room, she drew in a breath, prepared herself for the scrutiny and onslaught of questions for what she was about to bring up, something that had been long overlooked and brushed under the carpet too many times.

At the stand, she dug into the bag and pulled out at least twenty manilla folders, placing them on the table beside her, spread out like playing cards before she flipped the one on top open for all to see.

The photograph inside was of a handsome man, not more than thirty, soft, mocha skin with a smile on his face immortalized in the candid shot printed on eight-by-ten paper. Beside him in the folder was a police report, stating plainly at the top in bold, black lettering that he was a missing person.

Juli ran her fingers gently over the photo before she brought her gaze back to the council before her.

"Whenever you're ready, Alpha," came a not so gentle push to get on with it from the right side of the collection of older people, this one a feminine voice with just a bit of impatience in her tone.

Juli couldn't tell which one it had come from, but the message was clear.

"Juli Summerford, Collins, Massachusetts." She stated for the record. "I'm here on behalf of not only myself but the packs that surround the territories in the state."

"We know what you're here for, Alpha Summerford." Thaddeus Malone, an older man in the very center of it all was dressed in a black robe as if he were some supreme court judge shifted on his *throne*, growing restless. "As we've told you before, there's nothing we can do. The FBI and Pack Division are the only ones allowed to look into any missing person cases within the jurisdiction of the county you live in."

"That's complete and utter bullshit." Juli's quick snap back had the crowd behind her in an uproar, whispering of disrespect and disbelief as she continued to stand there, unwilling to relent. "In the past few years, more and more pack members have gone missing from Hampden, Hampshire, and Worcester counties than any other in the entire state— No, the entirety of New England. There should be more that we can do as a whole than just sit back and wait for agencies that couldn't care less about our communities, to get their heads out of their collective ass and look into things."

"Your outbursts are unnecessary, as is your profanity. I suggest you watch your tone." Malone's words echoed over the crowd, vibrating the room, and all behind her grew silent again. He collected himself, straightening the robe as he again shifted in the chair. "I understand your frustration, and your pack isn't the only ones with missing members, but there are rules, procedures that we need to follow in order to keep the peace with those around us—"

"Keeping the peace is more important than the lives of our families, than the children that go missing, than the mothers and fathers that never come home?" The low growl in her voice caught the attention of those around her and the whispers began once more. "Forgive my arrogance, but before we came out to the world, there was a code among packs, to help keep ourselves safe. What happened to that?

Where has that loyalty to our people gone? Have we forgotten our roots? Have we conceded to live by rules suddenly placed upon us by those outside our collective? Are we regressing back to when we had to hide in the dark for fear of silver bullets, pitchforks, and fire?"

"You're being dramatic." The impatient woman who had prompted her before spoke up, once again catching Juli's attention, letting her lay eyes on the face that matched the voice. Margaret Lussier, an Alpha, and according to her plaque, from somewhere near San Francisco. "We're perfectly safe as a community. There's nothing to fear from humans or their politics. We've adapted. We've grown and just like our ancestors, we'll overcome any differences that integrating into society may cause."

"Now who's being dramatic?" Juli's eyes narrowed at her, a scowl present on her face as she closed the file and drew the stack from the table. "And incredulous." She grabbed her bag from beside her, stuffed the files in, and surveyed the council as well as the tiers behind her. "If you won't do anything about this then I will."

"Alpha," Malone barked, but Juli had already turned, making her way out of the room as the council and the auditorium burst into noise. "Alpha Summerford—"

But his call was lost as the door slammed shut behind her and Juli disappeared into the halls of the conference center.

CHAPTER 1

THE SOUNDS of the forest echoed in the night. It wasn't hard to hear the snap of the branch under the thin legs of a lone doe as she stepped out into the large clearing, or the way the leaves rustled while she dug down deep to find what she was looking for, grazing on the ferns and dark green of the grass that covered the forest floor.

She was preoccupied, standing alone under the nearly cloudless night sky, lit by the waxing moon, so much closer to full than not. Her concern was more about food than survival. So much so that she didn't even hear the breathing coming closer, or the bright red eyes of the predator that looked upon her.

Something in the night disturbed her, pulling her from the thought of food. Her body stilled, her eyes glanced over the area around her as her ears twitched, taking in the sounds of the forest.

Nothing.

Nothing but what she heard every night, the familiar chirps and croaks of the near-by wildlife, nothing but the nearly silent flutter of bat wings and hoots of owls. Nothing but sudden silence. Every sound around her stopped, and her tail twitched, body hummed with the sudden need to get away.

In the distance, somewhere in the darkness of the surrounding woods, came a low snarl. Her ears flipped faster, eyes pinpointed on the direction the noise emanated from, and she lowered her head just a bit, just as the sliver of cloud covered the moon, sending the clearing into a strange, ominous blackness.

Those red eyes stalked closer, stilled, and suddenly darted out from between the trees. The doe pivoted on fast, thin legs, and raced from the opening, moving swiftly as she darted through the forest.

It followed. Like a macabre game of chase around the twists and turns of trunks and broken branches. The night hadn't grown any brighter, the moon hadn't made another appearance as the doe snorted out its fear, racing into the night.

Behind it, the monster moved at an incredible speed, as if its height wasn't impeding it at all. The bulk of it was muscle, and there was no stopping it as it charged through the brush after its prey. Its vision was clouded with red, the edge of it lined with the color of blood, but it could see the doe no matter which way she turned, following her heat signature around large boulders and thick trunks.

And then it stopped.

The doe screeched to a halt, debating on the direction to take as she felt the danger all around her. Her eyes were wide as her heart thumped, blood pulsing quickly through her veins. Her ears twitched at the sudden silence, the weird stillness that overcame the night, and she was frozen. Her breath released in huffs, warm air hitting the chill, curling clouds around her nose. Her eyes scanned the area, her body grew stiff.

Nothing but silence.

Until there wasn't.

It jumped from the darkness. A large, black mass charging at her with such speed she had no time to react, no time to get away before its muzzle opened, and suddenly, its jaws were clamped around her throat, canines tearing into her flesh.

She made a noise, something unnatural, something full of fear, and it carried on the wind before the world turned to nothingness and the sound of ripping flesh, of shredding claws, became the only thing that filled the darkness.

Her body dropped from its claws, her head from its jaws as it rose onto back legs covered in black fur. It tilted its head back, long, blood-soaked muzzle to the sky, and the night was once again breached by a sound.

A long, deep howl.

"Collins, Massachusetts"

His eyes opened wide, staring up to the brightly lit ceiling as the streetlight just outside the window illuminated his room, and he bolted upright in bed, hand going right to his heart. He did everything he could to catch his breath, to slow his heart as the echo of the wolf filled his ears, but only time would slow those and make that sound disappear.

He let out a groan just knowing he hadn't been asleep nearly long enough to have it be anywhere close to six. So much for going to bed early.

Noel Summerford flipped the covers from his legs, sweat-drenched and shaking, and finally found the courage to close his eyes, only to find darkness behind them and not the bloody vision of the doe.

"Okay," he whispered to himself, needing something outside his head to focus on, "okay. You're okay. Just open your eyes. You're alright."

He forced them open, wanting nothing more than to go back to sleep, and looked around his room. He was home, not in the woods, and completely human. Flipping his legs off the bed, he dug his toes into the plush rug on the floor and let the feeling of the tickle at the bottom of his feet ground him before he leaned forward and set his elbows to his knees.

His head dipped forward as he ran his hands over his face, grossed out by the clammy feeling of the sweat that covered his skin before he curled his fingers and ran them through his dark, wavy hair. With a sigh, he gave a gentle tug, and let them drop to his lap, slouching forward.

His eyes traced the shadowed outline of his sneakers, taking in the strange way that everything in the room seemed to be monotone, then reached blindly for the phone on his nightstand. Noel cracked his neck, brought the phone close and tapped the screen.

It was only 9:47.

He sat up straight, scrubbed at the stubble that covered his chin, and sighed, dropping the phone on the bed.

"The fuck?" came out as just a huff, and he snatched the gray tee-shirt from the floor, standing as he tugged it on.

Dreams like the one he had just awoken from weren't new. In fact, they had been going on for almost a year and a half, more so since his father's death, but there was just something a little more... gruesome... about this one that still had him shaking while he yanked on shorts over his boxers.

He needed to get out, to run off some of the adrenaline he was feeling flow through his body, and he knew exactly how. Even three years after graduating captain of the track team, Noel recognized the size of his body's need for movement.

He grabbed the phone off the bed, and a pair of wired earbuds seconds before heading straight for his bedroom door.

THE SKY above the Donald E. Stephens Convention Center was overcast. A light drizzle slackened the roadway, the asphalt shining strangely from the years of accumulated fluid leaking from waiting vehicles in the horseshoe drive.

Douglas Payne scowled at the wetness below his loafers, as he stood patiently waiting, one hand holding the black umbrella above his head, the other content with playing with the strap to his messenger bag. He was swaying, trying to keep his mind occupied, and reminding himself that there was only so much whistling the guards at the door would take before they told him to beat it.

Of course, with Tom Wickery standing silent and still beside the black Lexus, looking just as mean as any bodyguard should. Doug doubted that any of the hired help around the center would actually tell him to do anything.

Tom was intimidating. The small flair of color, indicated by the crimson tie he wore, and the just-this-side-of-obnoxious fabric square tucked into the chest pocket, were the only things that set him apart from the usual black suited security. It still didn't make him any less threatening.

Having been part of the same security team that protected Juli and her late husband for years, he had become like a surrogate uncle to the three kids. However, when he was on the clock, Tom was all business. He straightened up when the door to the center flew open and the Pack Alpha strode out, determination in every step.

Doug turned at the shift in the bodyguard, dashing up to meet Juli just as she cleared the overhang, and held the umbrella above her. She moved without looking, fumbling with the zipper in frustration, only to stop long enough to glance at the waiting car. She halted, causing Doug to stumble and step back, keeping her covered from the rain.

"Alpha—" the young man started but choked on his next words as the woman beside him waved him off, wanting nothing to do with the title at the moment. "Sorry, it's just—"

Watching the assistant bumble through anything seemed to be one of Tom's favorite pastimes, and he gave a smirk as he moved to open the back door of the car, waiting patiently for the alpha to start walking again.

Juli closed the file folder with a snap and glared up at him. She wasn't angry with Doug by any means but what she just went through with the council, she really wasn't looking forward to another lecture.

"Whatever you have to say, please, stow it." And that tone of her voice had the man beside her nodding. "Good." She waved her hand at the open car door expectantly, but Doug didn't move. "Get in."

He paused again, unsure as if debating the whole idea, but didn't move to follow orders and Juli was not amused. With an exhale through her nose in irritation, she ducked in the door, disappearing into the safety of the car.

With one last glance around at the growing number of higher pack members trickling out the doors to the center, Doug collapsed the umbrella and scooted in beside her, the interior of the car cast into darkness as Tom closed the door behind him.

Doug waited on anything he might bring up. He could tell by the look on her face, the tense way the alpha held her body, that things didn't go exactly how she had hoped, but when she dug that file out again, he knew she's ready, and was about to interrupt her reading until he spotted the photograph.

Richard Scout went missing decades ago. It was a loss the pack had never gotten over, or forgotten, especially with the ties to Doug's family. He hadn't heard anything about the case in a very long time though, and while his mother had all but given up hope of seeing her brother again, Doug hadn't. It was still a shock to see his photo on the lap of the alpha across from him.

"Tom." Her voice had Doug blinking back to reality and away from the last time he had heard his mother crying over the loss of her brother.

Tom shifted in the driver's seat, just enough to see her through the rearview mirror. "Yes, Alpha?"

"Airport, please." He nodded, tapped the LED screen on the dashboard in front of him, and spoke quietly. Juli remained silent watching the directions pop up before she turned her eyes to Doug, who wore an oddly confused expression at her request. "Speak up."

"The airport? We're only three days into this summit."

He wasn't trying to get a rise out of her, but according to the itinerary he had quickly pulled up on his phone, a sudden change of plans could be costly. It was Juli's dismissive wave that had him more curious than the quick 180.

"It's a waste of time." Those words were spoken through clenched teeth, and he could see the frustration building, the way her body tensed. "God, they're such—" She closed her eyes, taking a second to center herself before she went on. "It's been ten years. Ten years of trying to climb out of this hole that one man dug us into. If Santana had just kept his mouth shut, we'd still be living exactly where we needed to be. There wouldn't be any of this secondary gender bullshit labeling. Packs were just fine where they were."

"Do you really believe that?" He had never seen her so amped up, not about what they were going through in this time where things were changing constantly, and it was strangely refreshing.

"Some of it. Packs ran themselves. We had an order, a system. We weren't above the law, we followed it, but we took care of what we needed to. But this BS about waiting around for the FBI and Pack Division to come in just to get some answers about missing people. They're *people*, not just pack members, and we should be doing more than sitting on our asses."

She closed her eyes, shook her head and waited just a moment before continuing, letting out all the anger from the meeting as she ran her fingers down the picture once again, smiling fondly at it and Doug wanted to know what that look in her eyes was. Why was she so emotional about one man?

"This was all just for show. The council was peacocking for the packs, and that's not what I came here for. I said my peace, I asked for help, and I got nothing. So, I just want to go home to my kids." At the mention of her children, a smile crept up on her lips, one that made even Doug smirk at the sight of it. "With them, three days more would have them at each other's throats if they're not there now. Noel's probably going out of his mind."

Making his way down the hallway, Noel's eyes were on the tangled mess of the earbuds he'd been playing with since he left the room, but his ears were trained on the noises within the walls of the house. He was checking for anything out of the ordinary, even with the distraction of the stupid wires and for the first time in a while, he inwardly berated himself for not getting the wireless ones his mother had offered.

He stopped dead in his tracks, and his thoughts, the moment he heard the loud thump from the bedroom door he had just walked by.

Noel took two steps back and grabbed at the silver handle to the door on his left. Narrowing his eyes, he waited just a moment, listening for anything else before he twisted the handle and pushed it open enough to crack it and peek in.

Beside his bed, shirtless and in a pair of shorts, stood Keegan. The eighteen-year-old was putting some dramatic effort in using the ten-pound weights as he huffed out something like "fifty" on each arm before he caught Noel looking in.

Keegan wasn't small, not in any way. He was built like the rest of them, made for track, but a hell of a fighter. He could hold his own in a tussle or in a full-on fist fight, so Noel knew there was no way in hell that ten pounds was going to make him even remotely sore.

Keegan dropped the weight in his right hand onto the bed, rolling his eyes in a fashion that told Noel exactly what the younger of the two was thinking, but the only thing that left his mouth was one simple word.

"Mind?" And it was said in a way that spoke volumes to Noel. His brother didn't want him in his room, that he got, but the growl underneath it gave him the feeling that Keegan didn't even want him in his life. Noel nodded, accepting the fact that Keegan, while just having turned eighteen a month ago, was still in that hormonal puberty phase. It was either that, or he was still angry. "Where are you going anyway?"

The question was out of nowhere, something Keegan would never usually ask, and Noel found himself stumbling.

"Out," he shrugged, trying to brush it off, "for a run." The narrowing of those hazel eyes served only to frustrate him more. "Try staying home tonight?"

Keegan *pffted*, rolling his eyes. "Not gonna happen."

"Fine, be home before six." Noel gave a quick salute and closed the door behind him with a click leaving Keegan to stand there, staring after the door.

The younger one clenched his jaw, holding in everything he wanted to say to the body that had just left his room, pushing down all he was feeling. It wasn't working. He cracked his neck, slowly placed the second weight on the bed beside the first before running his hands through dark, unruly hair.

He sat down on the bed, blinking away thoughts of Noel, of his dad, of his sister just down the hall, but most of all, Keegan tucked away the thoughts of his mother, and how she wasn't home.

"Fuck it." He stood quickly, grabbed a shirt from the back of the chair, slipping it on as he made his way towards the door hopping into a pair of sweats, and pressed his ear against it, listening to Noel stop not nine feet down the hallway in front of the youngest Summerford's door.

BITING HIS LIP, Noel paused, wondering if she were even awake, but the light that streamed underneath told him she was probably... most definitely... not sleeping. He rasped his knuckles against the wood and waited for only a moment. Pressing his forehead against the cold wood, he turned the knob and opened it.

Ellie paced the room, mumbling to herself as she made it from one end of the room, back to her desk in about six steps. Noel gave a smile as she paused, wrote something down in a notebook, turned quickly, and continued her pacing. The only real noise in the room was the high-pitched sound of the music that escaped her AirPods where they lay on the desk beside her Physics book.

Noel cleared his throat. “Hey, Ell.”

Upon her return towards the desk again, nine steps later, her eyes came up to meet his as Noel leaned on the door. She pushed strands of her long hair back from her eyes, tucking it behind her ear, and Noel smiled at the disheveled look when most of it fell from the ponytail she was sporting.

“Going for a run,” he continued once he had her full attention.

“Kay,” she shrugged, took three more steps and stopped in front of her desk, but she knew his eyes were still on her, and slowly she glanced up again.

For a moment, there was a look between them, a *where do we go from here* pause that had them both feeling uncomfortable about thirty seconds in, and Noel nodded before he started to back out.

“Don’t stay up all night, kay?”

The only thing Ellie could do was nod, because there was a good chance she would still be up figuring out whatever equation she was on before she gave up for the night.

Noel knocked gently on the wood, gave her a quick smirk, and closed the door behind him as he left.

He made his way through the house, thoughts of his sister and their emotional distance now on his mind. He got Keegan, they were both men of the family, they had both been taught to take care of their mother and sister growing up, they knew they needed to be strong for the family, but Ellie was just a mystery that Noel had no idea how to solve.

He would protect her with his life, do anything for her, but he had no clue as to where to start to even talk to her. She was smarter than both of them. Intellectually, Noel was nowhere near her IQ. Not that he was a slacker because most of the college classes he had been taking were levels that none of his friends came close to, but Ellie was a different kind of genius.

When they did speak to each other, Keegan and Ellie seemed to have a special way of communicating, but even then, it was only when she had an issue with an assignment that she would even approach him. They were like polar opposites, and it sucked because they weren't that way before.

Keegan was fiercely protective, to the point where it would become terrifying when he thought that someone had hurt his sister, but over the course of the last two years, and especially after Alexandru's death, he had pulled away from everyone and built-up walls that would block out the sun.

Ellie was quiet. She stuck with a few close friends, but she observed, she knew things. She never interfered. Not when Keegan got in trouble at school, and not when Noel and Juli got into it. They were like three strangers living under the same roof.

Noel stopped at the kitchen door, finally able to shake the earbuds loose and popped them in. With a deep cleansing breath, he took one more look around the house then tapped the screen, starting his music.

Inhaling enough to expand his chest, like preparing for battle, Noel grabbed the door and yanked it open. He let the breath out slowly before disappearing into the night.

THERE WAS silence in the car, letting the words that Juli had spoken sink in. The last ten years had definitely been an adjustment. The government had done a deep dive into their lives, scrutinizing pack dynamics and how they lived had been invasive, especially after centuries of secrecy, keeping their traditions close to the heart.

Who would have thought one tiny DNA test could cause so much damage?

It started in 1998, two years after the first release of the simple, home DNA test. It was a great thing, something everyone wanted to try, a way to find your origins, but it linked a lot of people, and the results had captured the attention of officials that really didn't need to be looking into it.

A marker, unknown to scientists until that year, was repeatedly found in those tested. Ten percent seemed to be linked to a specific species. To wolves. The packs had always known they were different. Bonded by blood and years of secrecy, able to keep their traits hidden except for those they trusted, and then a decade ago, one man high up on the political chain, came out as a beta, a strategist, and their world was blown wide open.

Not all of the packs were related. Like the different mythologies of old where men could shift into beasts, the pack lived in many geographical locations, made up of all ethnicities. Greek, Romani, Italian, Irish, Scottish, English, Russian, Asian, South American. So many of the world's packs weren't even connected except by one thing.

The Lupinus Marker.

That's what they were calling it. This little blip in genetics that set them apart from "humans," that gave them the ability to shift their eye color, to have different designations, or "secondary genders" as Juli had put it, to scent or be able to sense other members of their own pack and know when someone was not one of theirs at all.

One small marker in a larger DNA strand had put them on a path to... wherever they were headed.

Doug cleared his throat, finally breaking the silence, and Juli glanced up from that one particular file. "We might be waiting a while for the flight plan to clear."

That got her to close it. “It’s fine.” But her tone said it really wasn’t. “The council made their position on the matter perfectly clear. Pack relations in New England aren't on their list of priorities.”

“Let me make some calls and see if we can bump things up.”

“Please do.”

He noticed the way she turned towards the window, as if slowly getting lost in thought. “Straight home, then?”

Juli gave a chuckle, nodding against her fingers, as she ran the knuckles against her lips. “As fast as possible.”

It was the vibration of her own phone that shook her from her internal ramblings, and she pulled it quickly from the bag. A small smile formed as she looked over the name “Gustaf.”

“It’s not too late to book a commercial flight,” Doug interrupted without taking his eyes off the tablet on his lap.

“If it gets us out of here.” She laughed and finally placed the small device against her cheek just as the line connected. “Gus, why are you awake?

Gustaf Segal stared up at the ceiling, eyes on the shadows cast by the light of the moon across his room. With one arm tucked up behind his head on the pillow and the other held the phone tightly to his ear, his light eyes sparkled with a bit of humor even as he stared into nothing.

He could almost picture her sitting in the car, ankles crossed, one arm on the door with the phone against her ear, not quite a mirror image of what he was doing, but it made him smile to think of it.

“It’s only ten, I was just getting ready for bed,” he chuckled, “and you said you’d call as soon as it was done.”

She sighed into the phone. “It’s done.”

This got him to sit up just a bit, pushing onto his elbow. “And?”

“As I already told Doug, it's a waste of time.”

"That bad, huh?" He couldn't hold back the full grin with the annoyed tone of her voice.

"Worse. They don't care about missing pack members, not in Massachusetts."

Gustaf sat up completely this time, pulling himself back against the headboards as he scrubbed a hand over his mouth, feeling the need to shave already creeping up. He liked his scruff, but even he had his limits on how long he could let it get without looking like a mountain man.

"I don't get it; the numbers are rising." He pushed off the covers as he moved to the edge of the bed, sitting there under the light of the moon that flowed in through the window.

"Doesn't make a difference. We're simply not enough of a population to create concern."

"That's not true, and you know it."

"I know, and I'm also not the only alpha in the area, just the only one raising her voice."

Gustaf ran a hand through his hair, unsure of what to do next, what to *say* next to support her. "So, we send Rollins out to find them."

The scoff on the line told him everything he needed to know, pushing him up from the bed, to move towards the window. He knew right where she was, on the road in a different state, maybe going back to the hotel, but he hated that she was so far away. He always did. He was her Pack Second, her right hand, knew what he had to do in her absence, but that didn't make her being away any easier on him. He always felt stretched thin when she was gone.

"Rollins' force isn't big enough to keep all the packs in Western Massachusetts settled. We can only do that with help, and it doesn't look like we're getting it."

He knew that. He knew that way too well. They didn't have the manpower when one of the highest members of the Summerford pack went missing years ago, they certainly didn't have it now when so many have disappeared this year alone.

"I don't know," he sighed, closing his eyes even as he tilted his head up towards the moon. The light of it always helped calm him, but the pull of it the closer it got too full made him vibrate. Made him wish she were home.

Juli smiled at the silence on the line. She knew Gustaf was still there, he always kept her close, even when quiet, but she could feel his frustration too, because it was her own.

"Flight plan is secured, but we're looking at a few hours of waiting around."

Juli's eyes rested on Doug. He, however, was still looking at his lap. "Thank you."

"Leaving?" Gustaf's confusion was endearing, and hopeful.

"Coming home." She heard a relieved sign on the line. "Can you call our council members and arrange a meeting for three p.m.?"

"Are you sure you don't want to wait a day?"

Looking out at the flickering lights of the city, Juli knew her answer straight away. "I think this is important, don't you?"

One hand on his hip, the other still on the phone, Gustaf turned from the window and headed out of the bedroom towards the stairs. It's not that he didn't, he just thought... "I'll set it up."

He made his way quietly down to the den, just off the side of the stairway on the first floor, flicked on the light and slipped in behind the desk, starting up the computer.

"Go to sleep, Gus. I'll text you when I get to the airport."

He sat back in the chair, a soft smile on his face as he ran his finger across his lips. "You're awfully pushy for an alpha."

"I have my faults." Juli was smiling, that's what he wanted to hear, but he knew the minute it faded. "Are the kids okay?"

"They're fine." He glanced at the screensaver, a picture of the three Summerford children when they were younger, when they all smiled, and he rested his chin on his thumb, pressing his pointer into his temple, hoping to stem off the headache that threatened to form. "Noel's been doing exactly what you told him to do, taking care of the other two."

"And Keegan?"

"No calls from the principal yet, but it's still early in the week." He wanted to laugh at that, at the whole subject of Keegan's disciplinary actions, because the kid has gotten better, just not nearly enough. "I have faith in him, Jules, he'll be okay."

"I know, he's strong." The quiet moment between words, where it was just the sound of her breathing stretched on, until she whispered to him. "Goodnight, Gus."

"Night, Alpha." He closed his eyes. "See you soon."

He listened closely for a moment, waiting for her reply, but the line went dead. Tipping his head back, letting it rest on the chair, Gus placed the phone on the desk and closed his eyes, praying for a dreamless sleep.

CHAPTER 2

KEEGAN WAITED to hear that door close, to know that Noel was definitely out of the house before he swiftly turned, grabbed the waiting backpack by the window, and changed out of his shorts into a pair of black joggers. He did a quick scan of his room, making sure he hadn't missed anything before heading for the window, and paused.

Noel wasn't home anymore, why was he sneaking out? Why wasn't he using the door? Why was he hiding?

This wasn't his first time leaving in the middle of the night and it sure as hell wouldn't be his last. With that thought, he gently closed the window making sure to keep the lock wide open, grabbed his bag, and turned around, heading right out the bedroom door.

He tiptoed past Ellie's door, zeroed in on the way she paced the room before he picked up the tempo and made through the kitchen, unnoticed. With the straps over his shoulder, he hopped into a pair of boots, worn in over years of use, soft and fitted to his feet, before he grabbed the set of keys from the hook and reached for the handle.

In that one moment, he thought about turning around, of telling Ellie where he was going, but it faded as quickly as it came because

Keegan—in his paranoia—didn't trust anyone. Especially his little sister. Not because Ellie was a snitch, in fact, she seemed quite the opposite. She only told Noel the bare minimum when it came to hearing about him getting in trouble, enough to keep him *out* of anything major, but she still told.

He loved her for it, not that he would ever tell her or admit it aloud to anyone in his family, but he knew her intentions were good. His brain just had this way of thinking, a way that usually ended in him freaking out because it had concocted a story to serve its own anxious state, so he kept a lot close to the heart.

Most people thought he hated Noel. That was a lie. But if he let himself believe he could trust his brother, the only thing it would get him was more sleepless nights, and more blow-ups at school because of his excessive thought process.

It was better this way. For everyone.

With that, he tossed the keys once before catching them, yanked the door open, and stepped outside, making sure to lock the door before he disappeared through the garage and out to the old, trusty Jeep that sat waiting.

The thing was loud. Thinking he needed help keeping his concentration while driving, his parents had gotten him a standard, something sturdy and somewhat of a throwback to 1984, but it gave him the freedom and he loved the damn thing. As he started it up, he took a moment to look over the house, the quietness that surrounded his neighborhood, and with a grin, he threw it in reverse and backed out of the drive.

He was respectful, knowing most of the residence for years now. He also knew that they could recognize him and the old CJ-7 just by the sound it made, so he took it easy down the street before flooring it at the stop sign. It was definitely a good night to get away.

Ellie glanced up from the notebook, having heard the Jeep over her music, and shook her head. There he went again, but knowing that Noel was out on a run, she was left with the whole house to herself.

She clicked off the music, dropped the pen, grabbed her phone and headed for the kitchen to raid the pantry. Juli kept the good snacks there but when it was just the three of them, Noel had a habit of portioning them out.

To hell with both the boys, it was time for her to enjoy herself a little.

Grabbing Cosmic Brownies, Funyuns, a package of crisp apple Pop Tarts, and Swiss rolls, from the back of the pantry, Ellie juggled the small plastic packages as she made her way to the counter in the room. Dropping them down, she turned to the refrigerator and yanked open the door. There wasn't much in there.

Scratch that, there wasn't much in the way of junk food drinks in there, but it was completely full. Her oldest brother was definitely in charge of the shopping and Ellie wrinkled her nose at the number of healthy fruits and vegetables, lunch meats, and drinks that filled it. No soda, and that was exactly what she was looking for.

Grabbing a few hidden Capri Suns from the bottom drawer, and a pudding cup, her own little stash, she closed the door and added them to her pile of goodies, then proceeded to find a shopping bag. She was sure she wouldn't make it to her room with all of that in her arms.

It was as she was huddled down under the island, rummaging through the cabinet doors, that her phone went off and Ellie immediately stilled.

For a moment, she expected to hear Noel's voice from the living room, or Keegan's nosy question from the den, but the silence in the house reminded her that she was alone and stood quickly to retrieve the vibrating device.

A smile played on her lips as the name flashed on the screen and she tapped the banner without a second thought bringing up a text thread between her and Mitch Rollins as her cheeks turned a light shade of pink.

Mitch: *You up? Need help with this history question.*

Ellie bit her lip for a moment, worrying on it just enough for it to darken before she stuffed as much as she could of the snacks in every pocket she could, and headed for the room, both juice bags between her teeth, freeing up her hands.

Ellie: *One sec...*

Once she was safe behind a closed door, she dropped the bags on the bed, emptied her pockets, and sat down in the plush bean bag in the corner.

Ellie: *Sup?*

She expected a text back, but instead got an incoming call message on her screen. Taking a deep breath, she slid her thumb across and brought it to her ear.

"Your dad's not gonna give you hell, is he?" Keeping her voice low, as if she weren't the only person in the house, Ellie pulled her knees to her chest.

"If he were here, sure," he huffed out, but there was a smile on his lips that could be heard in his tone. *"And I'm sorry."*

"You haven't done anything yet to be sorry for." She returned the smirk, before suddenly growing worried. "Have you?"

The phone vibrated against her cheek, and why wasn't she surprised to see a video chat request on the screen? She gave it a minute, made him think that maybe she wouldn't accept, before doing exactly that and the face of a blonde-haired, sixteen-year-old popped up, that same smile that his voice held was widely spread across his cheeks.

"I lied." Mitch admitted into the camera, getting Ellie to simply roll her eyes. *"I don't have history homework, I just wanted to talk to you."*

"You could have waited until school." She wasn't at all upset, in fact, just the opposite. "But I'm glad you called. Both my brothers are gone... somewhere."

"Knowing Noel, he's out for a run." Mitch shrugged, rolling over on the bed, giving Ellie a clear view of his ceiling. Her only reply was a nod. *"And Keegan?"*

"Who knows." She slipped down further onto the bag, getting comfortable, before she grabbed a nearby blanket and draped it over herself. "Where's your dad?"

"Don't know, took off sometime this morning for parts unknown, and hasn't been back. Mom says it's "Pack" business."

"Mine's out of town and Gus has been locked up in the meeting-house all week. We haven't heard about anything new."

"Do you think he'd tell you what's going on?"

"No, but he'd tell Noel."

Mitch thought about that for a moment, bit his lip and nodded. *"Right. And Noel would—"*

"Talk about it to Keira, which means—"

"The whole house would know. Gotcha." He gave her a quick grin but shook his head. *"You have a very weird family."*

"This coming from a guy with a half-finished basement and used to think it was haunted."

"Hey, we all have our secrets, Summerford, and you swore you'd never use that against me." His teasing was cute, and it made her feel strangely warm inside. It always felt that way when the two of them were able to be in the same space, even if it was just on the phone. It was... easy. *"So, tell me about the rest of your day, after science. I never get to see you before you leave."*

So, she did.

Juli put the phone down, turning once again to the passing lights outside the car as she ticked away the moments with her finger against her lip. Tom hadn't said a word the whole trip after verifying their destination, but Doug was sighing as he scrolled through paperwork and business emails across from her.

"Doug." She spoke his name quietly, almost inaudibly, before turning towards him. "Douglas."

"Hmm?" He sat up straight at that and turned towards her. "Sorry, yes?"

"I know it's late, but could you message Illy and ask her to take over my classes for at least one more day?"

"For today?"

"I meant for Monday."

"Will do."

"I'd like to spend some time with the kids, maybe take them away for the weekend after the meeting. I don't want to rush home. Besides, it's my family's money... Alex's money that keeps the department open."

Doug grinned, though he shouldn't really be laughing at the situation. "You really don't have to explain to me, but it's totally understandable." Juli's gaze stayed locked on his as he pulled up a contact on his phone and brought it to his ear. "Hello, Illy. It's Doug..."

When she looked away, it was to the folder on her lap and the man staring up at her from the photograph. She had last seen him when Ellie was just a baby, not more than three months old. He had come to the house to check on her and the infant, to see how Keegan and Noel had taken to being older brothers, but when he left, it was the last smile she had seen from him, the last kiss on the cheek, the last "see you tomorrow" she would ever hear.

She flipped the folder closed, catching a glimpse of Doug before he looked away.

"How long?" She hoped to break the tension in the car, but the man only shrugged.

"Fifteen minutes."

And they fell back into that strange silence.

Keegan pulled the Jeep around the side of the small building. It looked just like any other generic coffee house, but this one was different in the way that he never had to pay for a cup of coffee.

He idled at the backdoor, tapping on the steering wheel for less than two minutes before the door opened and a head peeked out.

“Thought that was you.” Dillon propped the door open and made his way towards the Jeep, large coffee in hand.

The door opened wide, and Alesha Greenway, a perky brunette, stuck her head out, grinning as she stared at Keegan. She wiggled her fingers in greeting as Keegan returned the wave.

“Hey, Lesha.”

She all but giggled at his attention and sighed a sultry, “hi Keegan,” before ducking back inside.

“Man, you gotta stop that. She’s drooling over you all the time, and besides the fact that you’re my cousin, the only thing she knows about you is that you drive this shit box.” Dillon rolled his eyes.

“Hey, never speak ill of the ride.”

“Whatever you say, dude. So, sneaking out?”

“Nah, gonna go see Paige, too much shit at home.” Keegan accepted the coffee gracefully and put it in the cupholder as he glanced around the lot. “What time are you out?”

“Shift barely started. You wanna come back for six-ish, that’d be cool.”

Keegan gave him a nod, both looking up at the red Z28 that made its way through the lot. “Really?”

“Someone you know?”

“Dumb jocks.” Keegan nearly growled, but it wasn’t in anger, just frustration. “Like I can’t get away from them. If it’s not school, it’s home, or here. Fuck! I need to get out of here.”

“Dude, the year just started, maybe take a minute, lock it down, and just concentrate on graduating.”

Keegan's eyes were set on the car, the way it pulled over under a streetlight, distracted him from his cousin, at least until Dillon hit him in the arm. Keegan whipped his head around, glaring at Dillon with bright golden eyes.

"S'up, Beta? Smell something?"

Keegan let his eyes fade, angry at himself for being caught. He pushed it to the background, and pressed his foot to the clutch, hand on the gearshift. "Like I said, just a dumb jock." He shifted into first and raised his brow. "Gotta go, can't leave a lady waiting."

"Right," Dillon laughed, stepping back. "Enjoy that coffee."

"See you at six." Keegan stepped on the gas, released the clutch and took off, away from the curb, turning into the parking lot, but cut the lights and made a U-turn towards that Camaro.

Stalling out, he let the Jeep glide in beside it and waited, shifting it into neutral before he pulled the e-brake. He hadn't waited there more than a minute before the door opened and Daniel Payne stepped out. His eyes glowed a bright red in the night.

Keegan let out a breathless sigh as he smirked, "hey, Alpha."

Daniel slipped into the light, red eyes fading. His mocha skin glistened with sweat as he stood there in a loose tank and shorts. It was unusually hot for a fall night, but the way he looked, curly, black hair shining, Keegan knew Daniel had been out at the track.

He walked over to the darkened side of the Jeep, away from prying eyes, or any plain asshole that happened to drive by, and put his hand out against the frame. "Sneaking out?"

"Maybe." Keegan scanned over him, taking in the way his muscles flexed on his arm as he clenched the cold metal. "Maybe I'm just out cruisin' for anyone that might tickle my balls."

"I think you have a girlfriend for that." Payne grinned, looking around the lot, but even in the darkness, Keegan could see the emotions in his eyes, the way they became lust blown.

"Maybe a girl isn't what I'm in the mood for."

"God," Daniel shook his head in disbelief, and stepped back, putting some room between him and the man in the Jeep. "You're unbelievable."

"And insatiable." The grin on his face was wide, not only a challenge but an invitation to the man just steps away. "Come on, Alpha, don't you wanna take me for a spin?"

Daniel rushed the Jeep. He stepped up on the footrest to gain leverage over Keegan as he dominated the space and locked him into the seat with one hand on either side, one pressed against the cupholder, nearly knocking over the coffee, the other gripping the seat belt.

"You're pushing your luck, little beta." Daniel's words were more whispers than threats as his dark eyes moved from Keegan's hazel ones to his lips and back up.

Neither moved, they didn't dare. The tension between them was thick and pulled so tight one wrong move would send them crashing into each other. Which was why Keegan did it. His fingers came away from the steering wheel, rested gently on slick skin just below the hem of Daniel's shirt, on exposed flesh and the alpha above him growled.

Keegan licked his lips, catching Daniel's attention even as his muscles tightened, and he let his finger slide along the ridge of his abdomen. "Want me to stop?"

"Only if your intention is to actually make it to Paige's house tonight." Daniel huffed out, swallowing hard at the feel of Keegan's fingers. His eyes drifted shut when Keegan flattened his palm along his side, running it up his ribs. "Probably not the best place to do this."

"No, but it's the most fun I've had all day." Keegan grinned, eyes still locked on Daniel's face, enjoying the feeling of having him so close, but he knew when his time was up, and let his hand fall away, letting out an exasperated sigh. "You're right."

Daniel took a moment to compose himself, inched back away from him, and opened his eyes only when his feet were flat on the ground. Keegan's head was back against the seat, his gaze up towards the stars, but there was a glistening in them that had Daniel worried.

"It won't be for long."

Keegan scoffed at that, turning his head, eyes locking on the alpha's. "Come to Paige's."

"Not gonna watch you and your girlfriend make out, Key. That's weird, and I draw the line at weird." Daniel stuffed his hands in those short pockets, brow lifted.

"I've seen you do some weird shit, so your version of the word is a little askew, Payne." He laughed, reaching for the keys.

"I know." Daniel ran a hand over his head, shaking off the way being close to Keegan made him feel and rounded the front of the car, stopping at the passenger's side. "I'll see you tomorrow."

"Today," he joked.

"Whatever. At school?"

"Sure." But the smile fell from his face as Daniel made his way to the driver's seat and slipped in.

Keegan knew what "at school" meant. They were going back to pretending, to being in separate cliques, to resenting each other, and Keegan hated that more than anything. He started up the Jeep, slammed it in first, and chirped the tires taking off out of the parking spot. It wasn't until he hit the road that he turned on the lights.

THE ONLY THING Noel could hear was the thumping of his own heart above the music that blared out from the earbuds. The things he could feel were a little bit more. The burning of his lungs as he kept up the brutal pace he was trying for. The way his calves cramped as he lengthened his stride, and the hard pulse of his chest that caused him to press the heel of his palm to it.

He was beating himself up. He wanted to feel that pain, to keep that pace going. He needed to.

Life after his father's death had not been the same. He had spiraled down a dark hole, thoughts going to places he never dreamed he would venture. The feeling of not belonging, of survivor's guilt was real, but Noel fought his way back for two specific reasons, and right about now, neither of them seem to have a fucking clue.

He couldn't leave Keegan to figure out this world on his own. He never would. His younger brother was his responsibility, had always been, but he wasn't a burden. He was just Keegan. There was so much the kid needed him for, especially when his ADHD went wild, or more to the point when Keegan went wild. He was hyper, which got him into more trouble than he needed, not being able to get the crazy thoughts from his head, to separate what got in from what was going out. Noel helped him with that the best he could, and that was one of the reasons he fought his way out of the darkness.

The other was Ellie. She was so young. She had already lost her dad; she didn't need to lose Noel too. He needed to be there to help her, to show her what being cared for was like. No matter how much she pushed him away, or shut him out, he would never leave her alone, and the fact that he had been so close to doing just that had scared him enough to bring him back to reality. Noel couldn't be selfish, he had to stay for them.

And he did.

But there were times like these when he needed to feel that burn, to erase all the bad thoughts and sudden nightmares that invaded his mind. Werewolves. Why werewolves? The nearly full moon above him might be a clue, but he had always felt its strange pull.

As an alpha, it was in his blood. They were leaders, so he was told, they helped lead the pack, and usually made their way up the ladder pretty fast, but Noel didn't want it, he didn't want that responsibility, he just wanted to be a big brother. To keep his siblings safe.

He wasn't even sure if he could do that right.

Keegan pulled up beside the curb, glanced over his shoulder at the house behind him, at the one light that remained on in a second-floor window, and slowly slipped out of the Jeep. He made his way over, checking the area just in case, and stopped next to the side of the building.

The only way up was the trellis attached to the side of the house, not a dangerous climb, but with it still covered in the leafless, thorny, vines, it definitely was going to hurt. Keegan stepped back, slipped his pack over his shoulders and waited for it to open. It didn't take as long as he thought, before Paige stuck her head out, blonde hair cascading down as she grinned at him.

Keegan's eyes shifted to a gold so bright it was almost the only thing visible on him, and with a smirk on his lips, he headed up towards her.

Ellie gazed down at the dark screen. Mitch had hung up only moments before, but already she could feel the vast emptiness of her house.

With a sigh, she stood, collected the forgotten snacks from her bed and headed for the desk. With a well-coordinated hop, she managed to get her toe under the handle of the small drawer at the bottom of the cluttered desk, and pulled it open, only to dump the treasure in it and close it tightly. Bounty for another day.

She closed the notebook with the pen still trapped inside, shut the textbook on the page she needed and clicked off the lamp before heading towards her bed. With one last look at her phone, she slipped under the covers, nestled down on her pillows and typed out a text to Noel.

Ellie: *Going to bed, come back soon.*

And she sent it off before shutting off the light beside her bed. She turned over, never seeing the screen light up moments later.

Noel: *Omw.*

And the house drifted into silence.

Juli's gaze was drawn from the window as they pulled up to the gates to the small hanger just outside of Chicago. It was a private strip, one used mainly for pack members. Tonight, it was quiet, almost empty and Juli pulled out her phone.

She quickly opened a text thread, and typed, eyes still on the field as they approached the plane.

Juli: *At the hanger, coming home earlier than expected. See you soon. Love you.*

And she sent it off to Noel before she closed the app and tucked the phone into the messenger bag beside her, storing the file folders as well. Doug collected his things, filling his bag as well, but she noticed he was looking around, confusion written on his face.

"What's wrong?" She hated when things were left unsaid.

"Something's not right," was what he came back with, but that was all he said, not elaborating further.

"I'm sure everything's fine."

Doug nodded, trying to put her at ease, but the way he shifted had her suddenly on high alert.

Noel slowed to a jog, something easy enough that he could pull the vibrating phone from his pocket and still move. Ellie's text about going to bed was right there on the banner, and it didn't take him long to reply, this time coming to a halt at a stop sign, the perfect place to turn around.

It's blinking bright red, the LEDs that surrounded the octagon shape reflected against his skin, turning everything a blood red, and he flashed back to the way the crimson liquid covered the doe. He swallowed hard, put his hands on his hips and struggled to catch his breath.

That's when he saw it, parked under a blown-out streetlight just down the road was a darkened SUV. He could see them in the dark, the shadows that moved in it. There were at least three, one in each seat and one crouched between them in the middle. It was the red of its brake lights that illuminated the cab, giving him a clear view of the occupants.

That color! That flashing, blood red, addictive color had Noel's heart racing. He closed his eyes against it, but even behind his eyelids, it came and went, drawing him back into that dream, letting him feel the predatory nature of the beast, and he ran his tongue along his teeth.

Noel rolled his neck, cracking it as he stretched, hoping to release the tension in his body, but the moment he opened his eyes, he could see the slight tint along the edges, and he knew his nature was showing.

THE CAR ROLLED TO A STOP, and Juli grabbed her bag, watching Doug do the same, as the door beside her opened and Tom peeked in.

"Take your time, Alpha," he whispered politely, but Juli had had enough of the car ride and climbed out with Doug right behind her.

Tom guarded her from one side, and Doug from the other as they moved towards the small, twin-engine Cessna 340 that waited for them.

Noel clenched his fists, feeling the unsettling rage in him grow, as the lights on the SUV came to life, blinding him with the white glare from its high beams. He raised his hand, blocking out what he could as he started to take a step back.

There was something really wrong with this.

As they made their way down the asphalt, Tom's eyes were on the surrounding area, observing, but it was Doug that was trying to distract the tense alpha by letting her know exactly what was going on, when take-off was, and their estimated arrival time in Worcester's Regional airport.

She heard none of it though. The white noise that filled her senses took over even her hearing as warnings tingled up her spine. Juli stopped dead and turned in her spot just as headlights speeded towards them.

The engine revved, and Noel knew it was time to go. He turned on his heels and shifted into a sprint as the SUV stomped on the gas, peeling away from its spot, gunning for him. And they're gaining.

Noel leaned forward, throwing more weight towards the front of his body, and embraced the burning in his thighs as he pushed to go faster. He ducked and weaved through front yards, and gates, but the SUV kept coming, following him around a corner when the houses ran out.

Her eyes were wide when the window rolled down, the tip of an automatic weapon shined beneath the streetlights that filled the tarmac, and suddenly shots were fired. There was no time to hide, or cover, except ducking down behind a small two-seater plane, but that didn't stop the bullets as the car passed, whipped around, and came back again.

Doug was between the car and Juli, and she watched him go down, eyes wide as he lay there on the concrete, the color fading as the pool of blood grew around him. Tom grabbed her arm, yanking her away as they made for the Cessna.

But they weren't quick enough.

The rat-tat-tat of the gun unloading had Tom spinning, putting his body between Juli and the bullets. He was the human shield that protected her from death, but in the end it killed him, and his weight brought her down with him to the tarmac.

Noel moved the best he could, but he was running out of reserves, and stumbled over a root that pushed up an unkempt sidewalk. He tumbled onto the dew-drenched yard in view of the corner of a street. As he landed, his face barely missed the ground and the heavy stockade fence. The SUV swerved around the corner with Noel in its headlight.

Juli pushed herself out from under Tom, coated in his blood, a split on the side of her head from where she hit the concrete. She was dazed, making it a struggle to her feet, failing as she suddenly found herself back on the ground when her legs refused to listen to the command of "get up and move."

The lights of the car were centered on her, and she spotted two silhouettes coming closer. One carrying the semi-automatic that took out her two trusted allies, and the other a form she knew. The way he held himself, the gait of his walk, even the roll of his shoulders is familiar, but the way he adjusted his fingers on the handle of the gun really tipped her off.

She knew him well. Butcher Thaygen.

She scurried back on her hands, trying to get away, to put space between them, but when she's able to focus, she saw the malice in his eyes.

Noel tried to move, to back away from the edge of the street, but there's nowhere to go, no entry through the fence on this side of the road, and the SUV pointed right at him. He let his eyes glow, let the anger rush at him just as they stepped on the gas, gunning right for him, and Noel prepared for the end.

At the last second, they swerved, and disappeared into the darkness.

He took a breath, eyes following the motion of the car, and slowly let it out, hoping to catch his heart. When they finally disappeared, he fell back on the grass, hands going right to his face, and just laid there for a moment. He focused on his breathing, hoping the slow in-and-out would stop the painful pounding in his chest, but made him aware of the vibration of the phone.

Quickly digging it from his pocket, he looked at the banner that took up the middle of the screen. It's a text from his mother. The first communication with her in nearly twenty-four hours, and he couldn't help but laugh.

Juli: *At the hanger, coming home earlier than expected. See you soon. Love you.*

Noel scoffed out a laugh, dropped the phone to the ground and ran his hands over his face. He'd just be happy for today to be over.

He smiled down at her, not caring that he stood in a growing pool of blood. Juli raised a hand, hoping to negotiate, to plead with him, but as fast as her hand went up so did his aiming the gun at her chest.

There was no pause between the aim and when his finger pulled back on the trigger, but the strange sound that came from it threw her off. It wasn't a bang, or the ignition of gunpowder, more of a whoosh of air, and the pain of whatever hit her wasn't anything she felt before.

She raised her hand and pinched at the spot. Between two fingers, she plucked the dart from her skin, and glanced at it only a moment before it fell from numbing fingers. She was pissed, as angry as she could get, even as the drug flowed through her body and her eyes turned bright red, glaring up at the man who stood above her, not much older than Doug had been.

His cocky smile took over his lips before her arms gave out and she fell back to the hard surface below. He tucked the gun away, glanced left, then right and backed out of her fading view. The last thing she heard was his voice.

"Put her in the back of the car. Let's go. We don't have much time."

And darkness and silence cascaded over her.

CHAPTER 3

"Day 1 - 5:07 a.m."

In the darkness of the woods, just before the sun began to rise, the sound of footfalls running over crisp fall leaves broke the silence. Heavy breathing filled the night as branches snapped, and brush rustled with the passing movement.

Luca Morrin's brown eyes filled with fear, and just the edge of gold around the rim, tripped and stumbled over hidden rocks and down trees as he made his way through the dense woods. His body ached, but he pressed on as his heart thumped painfully in his chest. He needed to get as far away as fast as possible.

He'd been on the run for days, moving west, heading away from Worcester. He wasn't even sure where he was, but he needed to escape.

His body was littered with scars and newly opened wounds, things that were recently closed by stitches had broken open overnight. His shirt was covered in blood, but he didn't feel anything, he just knew that he had to keep moving.

His face is covered in dried blood from a long gash along his hairline, and his right eye was swollen shut from a bruise that's still dark purple, something new. In the darkened forest he tripped, unable to rely on his depth perception, going down as the breath was knocked out of him. The blackness took over his vision as white dots floated in front of his eyes, for only a moment before it came back into focus.

He's up again. The sounds of angry voices, whistles, and the snapping of branches seemed right on his heels, but the growl of the dogs had him back on his feet. He moved, pushing up off the ground as he checked behind him, trying to see how close they were, gauging his chance of escape.

He made his way forward into the growing morning light.

Pushing through the trees, he stumbled out into the road, falling to the gravel with no thought of saving himself the impact, but he rolled, covering his face with his arms as he came to a stop in the middle of it. Blood seeped from his side, coating the gravel and dirt with dark blood.

His eyes were on the approaching light, two high beams in an otherwise empty darkness and silently he prayed, hoping for safety but knowing if it was *them*, it wouldn't be a quick death.

The truck horn blared as it approached, brakes screeching as it slowed. Luca didn't have it in him to move, the only thing he saw was red. He reached out towards the silhouette that exited the vehicle, but it blurred into nothing recognizable. His head dropped to the ground, eyes rolled back in his head, and he let out a moan.

The man stepped closer, cautiously kneeling in front of him, before he reached out and placed a hand on Luca's shoulder.

"Hey," the gentle voice of an older man broke through the darkness threatening Luca. "Hey buddy."

He let go, falling into unconsciousness. He didn't even feel the shake the old man gave him, but he could hear the muffled conversation around him.

He sat back on his heels, glanced into the woods, and quickly dug his phone out of his pocket—an old flip phone—and dialed 9-1-1 before he put it to his ear. He placed his fingers to Luca's throat, feeling the thready pulse, and didn't even wait for the dispatcher to talk before he spoke.

"Help! I need help! A guy just came out of the woods, and I can't wake him up." He went silent for a moment, listening to the instructions the person on the other end gave him before he leaned down and placed his ear to Luca's chest. "Yes, he's breathing, but he's bleeding. You gotta send someone. Hurry."

"Chicago, 4:10 a.m. CST"

THREE BLACK ARMORED SUVs pulled onto the asphalt, passing the quiet, black Lexus before coming to a stop in front of the open hanger doors. In the bright light of their high beams, the bodies of Tom Wickery and Douglas Payne lay motionless surrounded by blood.

As if in unison, the doors opened and men and women dressed in black exited, all carrying semi-automatic weapons, but it's the man from the passenger's side of the second car that stepped up to the bodies as the others scattered.

He stopped beside Tom, eyes scanning as he placed his hands on his hips and surveyed the scene. Gil Drake couldn't say what happened, but he knew it was bad, and it was his job to figure it out, but from the looks of things, that wasn't going to be easy.

"Mallory, give me check-in, find the surveillance footage, and call in a coroner." He spoke aloud, only to have the chirp in his ear indicate the devices they wore.

"*Yes, sir,*" was the only response.

The last man from the car, a young soldier who was new, stepped up beside him, glancing over the bodies with a little green in his cheeks. Drake grinned, shaking his head.

"You gonna puke, you do it over there." He ordered, raising his brows at the kid, but all Fellahin did was give a solid "no" without turning his head too much. "Good, sweep the parameter. Give me a count on how many planes we got. I wanna know the schedules of every take off." Fellahin nodded, backing away. "And get me the incoming and outgoing call logs."

"Yes, sir!" And the kid was gone.

From the other side of the bodies, Parson, an older man, stepped up looking down over Doug. "We got nothing. No signs of forced entry through any of the gates. What were they doing here without security?"

That statement had Drake glaring at him. "What?"

Parson held out a rolled-up paper. "Logs."

"Already? I just sent Fellahin to get them."

"They were right on the seat." Parson pointed back at the plane. "Nothing was verified, no flight plan, no staff. This thing hadn't even been fueled up. Bet if we dig deeper, there won't even be a reason for it to be out of the hanger."

Drake rolled the paper, handing it back to the man. "Good work, see what else you can find. And get in touch with ATC, find out what the fuck's going on."

"On it, Sir." Parson turned and disappeared once again.

With one more look around at his guys, Drake squatted down beside Tom, looking over the bullet wounds in his chest.

"Oh, Tommy boy, I told you getting close to an alpha would get you killed." He reached out his fingers, headed right for Tom's open eyes, but paused, knowing the protocol, and he drew them back. "Sleep well, my friend." He stood glancing over Tom once more before his eyes went to Doug, and the messenger bag that lay beside him, untouched. "Parson!"

"Yes, Sir," came the reply from the steps of the plane.

"Get me Simmons." He raised his eyes to meet the older man. "We need to scan for electronics. Cell phones, laptops, anything."

"Sir?" Parson made his way down the steps, curious as to where it was going. Drake pointed to the bag on the ground.

"We're missing something." Parson got the point and took off towards the car, talking into his earpiece.

Drake stepped back, taking in everything, from the position of the plane to the bodies, and suddenly his eyes caught something small. He moved to the space between Doug and Tom, reached into his pocket and pulled out a glove, just to slip it on. Between his fingers, he plucked a dart off the ground, holding it up so he could see it more closely. Putting it back exactly where he found it, he pulled the glove off and pressed the button on his neck piece.

"Get me Control. We have a problem." He closed his eyes, counted to ten and opened them again, gaze going to the open gates. "Okay, Summerford, which way did you go?"

"Undisclosed location."

JUST BEYOND THE haze of the drug-induced dysphoria, Juli could feel the hands on her, the way they strapped her down to the gurney, and the weight of the belts across her chest, waist, and legs. She didn't have the strength to move as it was, so the use of the restraints was a bit of an overkill. Her mind was fuzzy, her vision, when she could open her eyes, was blurry at best and she had no idea where she was.

In her disorientated state, she groaned, capturing the attention of the person to her left. He leaned in close enough for her to make out some of his features, and the neutral combat uniform he wore.

The muffled voice above her from the man to her right spoke up, clearly annoyed. "Sir, she's waking up."

The one that crowded her view of the narrow world around her scoffed, straightened, and spoke quietly to his partner but Juli had already started to fade. It was the sound of a walkie chirping, echoing off solid walls that made her jump.

"The doctor will meet you in the room." Whoever's voice that was set off something in her, a hint of familiarity, but it was just on the edge of her reach.

The motion of the gurney continued with the sound of an elevator opening. She struggled to keep her eyes open, to hold onto that small stream of consciousness and instead of looking around she began to count the lights she passed under. Bright, fluorescent lights that spanned the width of the hall, making it nearly impossible to see, but she counted, until she couldn't, and the vast darkness cascaded over her.

The door to the quiet cell opened, illuminated only by the light of the hallway, and the two men slipped in. They never bothered to turn on the overhead light, though the room itself seemed as dark as the hallway they had traveled through.

The bed pressed against the corner wall was barely a bed at all, more of a cot with a near paper-thin mattress, a threadbare blanket, and a flat pillow. They unbuckled the restraints, first at her waist then at her chest and legs at the same time, pausing to see if there was any movement before they lifted her gently, one by the shoulders, the other by the legs, and laid her down on the mat.

Neither moved to cover her up, or even looked back as they latched the straps on the gurney once again and turned to attention at the man that stood in the doorway.

Butcher was almost happy she was out cold again, that the dart was strong enough to keep her from fully regaining consciousness. He hated to see what the angry alpha could do to a couple human soldiers if provoked, but he wasn't worried about himself. He nodded at them, gesturing them out of the room as he moved aside to let them pass before he was right back in the way, guarding it.

Behind him, an older man in a white coat stepped up, glancing in before clearing his throat. "The boss would like to speak with you."

"Hmm, I bet he would." His bright blue eyes lit up the room, and a menacing smirk crossed his lips as he turned, allowing the doctor in, and while he probably should have moved out, headed towards the main office, he stood instead, watching as the next dose of the sedative was administered. “Set up an IV.”

“What?” The shock in the man’s voice only got him to smile wider.

“An IV. You know what that is, I assume?” Which only got a nod from the doctor crouching beside the bed. “Well, set one up. She’ll be out for a bit before we can move her upstairs, so fluids, vitamins, the whole nine. He needs her healthy, not half out of it.”

With one more nod of acknowledgement, Butcher turned, leaving the doctor to his duties, as he made his way past the guards and through the darkened halls.

Butcher stepped out of the elevator directly into the brightly lit office space of his benefactor.

It was a corner office that would soon be lit by the natural glow of the morning sun. Two of its sides with floor to ceiling windows overlooked the near-by city. The middle of the room was occupied by a large desk, uncluttered and well organized and currently occupied by Ancram Lagos, one of the founding members of Lagos Pharmaceuticals.

He sat behind the desk, facing the window, at least until Butcher knocked on the wall beside the elevator and rolled his eyes as Ancram waved him in, turned the chair around, and twirled the pen in his hand, not saying a word.

He hated that, hated waiting for acknowledgement, but he stood at ease, folding his hands together behind his back and shrugged. “She’s secure.”

“Very good.” Ancram dropped the pen and stood, fixing his coat. Butcher observed with disinterest as Ancram made his way towards the sidebar, one that held a carafe of coffee, and poured himself a cup. “However, you weren’t supposed to kill the other two. That’s why I gave you the tranquilizer gun.”

“Collateral damage.”

Ancram chuckled. “I think you underestimate the Summerford Pack.”

Butcher shook off the military stance and crossed his arms. “I doubt some small-town pack is going to track me down for stealing their alpha.”

“You don’t know Gustaf Segal as well as I do, my friend. He’s not just Pack Second, he’s retired military with some very interesting connections.” Ancram made his way back to his chair, set the mug down, and unbuttoned his jacket. As he sat, adjusting the chair, his eyes landed on Butcher. “Make sure everything is ready. We’re going to move this along a little faster than the others.”

He nodded and turned back towards the elevator, pressing the button. “I hope she’s worth all of this.”

“If her bloodline is what I suspect it to be, her and her children are the answer to everything.”

Butcher shook his head, not bothering to look back and stepped in without another word. The doors closed behind him, blocking out the bright light of the room.

“Segal Residence, 5:30 a.m. EST”

In the quiet of the morning, the only thing that could be heard was the sound of Gustaf’s stomping as he made his way down the stairs. He didn’t sleep much after the phone call with Juli. He never slept much when she was away, not when he had kids to look after, or a pack to take care of, but mostly it was because of his concern with her being so far away that kept him from actually falling into some useful sleep.

He ran his hands over his face, and back through his hair as he entered the kitchen, beelining it straight for the coffee pot. Five-thirty was his usual time, this way he could get up and make sure he was caffeinated enough to deal with three kids. He put his hands on the counter and realized his mistake.

Noel wasn't a kid anymore, hadn't been for a few years now. He was twenty-two, a college student, and well on his way to being a great alpha, but Gus couldn't let go of the image of his face at his father's funeral, the one that told him Noel really didn't have it all together. It didn't help that he had seen the darkness Noel had slipped into over the year and the way his walls had come up to shut out that threat. He just couldn't get the kid to talk about it, to help him with it and that might be the reason he couldn't let go of it.

Letting out a long sigh, he grabbed the filters and the coffee and started to prepare the pot before yanking the sprayer from the sink to fill the reservoir. It was going to be a long day that needed a larger than usual amount of something, anything. He slammed down the lid and flicked on the machine before he turned and headed for the basement door.

The yellowed light that illuminated the underside of his house was his only saving grace in the early hours. It didn't hurt his eyes as much as the fluorescent ones that seemed to occupy every lamp in the damn house, so he actually liked being down there. That, and it was his hidden sanctuary, his *art* room.

In the middle of the floor sat his handcrafted table, one too large to get up the steps and too much of a pain to get out the bulkhead without help, so most of the time he ignored it, like now when he headed towards the workbench instead.

There, wedged between two C-clamps was a new table leg, one he was designing for the meetinghouse, an upgrade from the two-thousand-year-old table that his stuff was currently scattered across in the middle of the meeting room floor. Beside it, a little way down the table were two of its mates, already completed and waiting. It was the table top itself that he hadn't decided on yet.

Further down was a two-by-four piece of wood, nearly four feet in length, partially carved to look like the others, but this one was in a lathe, waiting to be worked on. It was the one he was aiming for.

Taking his phone from his pocket, he set it down on the dusty counter, and picked up a chisel. It would be hard to hear it from the noise, but he would see it once the phone went off, lighting up the screen. Grabbing the stool, Gus made himself comfortable, and placed the edge of the chisel next to the wood, his finger reaching for the power.

That was when the phone pinged, and he jumped. Maybe he would be able to hear it over the noise after all. Glancing over at the banner, he slowly lowered the chisel and reached for the device because what was on the screen made absolutely no sense.

Doug: *Arrived safely at Midway. EDT one hour.*

Confused, Gus tapped the screen, opening the text.

"That doesn't make any sense." But upon opening the phone, he found multiple banners for email, messages, and several other apps that Keegan had installed, and sighed. "Right. Do not disturb."

He closed the screen, flipped the ones with the multiple apps he didn't use until he found settings and went through the steps that Keegan had shown him to find the setting he was looking for. "Do Not Disturb: 12:00 to 5:00."

"That explains it." He clicked out of it. "I hate technology."

Leaning forward on the bench, he scrubbed his eyes with his fingers before wishing the coffee was complete. He knew it wasn't, but he couldn't help the wishful thinking. He reached for the chisel and hammer again, this time also stretching his toes out to flick at a toggle switch and smiled with the machine powered up before switching that foot to a pedal.

With a gentle press, the machine started up, and the smile got bigger. It was old, not very large, but the piece of wood began to spin, signaling the beginning of a new day, at least for him. And then a thought hit him. He put down the hammer, grabbed the phone and quickly scrolled through again until he found the alarm setting.

After a moment of looking at it, of debating whether to actually wait until they called, he set up an alarm. "Noel, 6:00 a.m." It's not that he didn't trust him, but in his eyes, Noel was still a kid.

Dropping the phone on its back, screen up, he slipped on a pair of safety goggles, then the hammer, letting the noise of the machine clear his mind.

"Summerford Residence, 5:30 a.m. EST."

THE MORNING SUN filtered through the window, giving Noel's room a light-yellow glow. It was cluttered, like any normal kid's room, filled with discarded clothing, sports equipment, books, a television that looks as though it was used more as a picture frame than what it was intended for, and in the middle pushed up against an angled wall, was a full-sized bed.

On the nightstand beside it, a cell screen lit up moments before the sound of a foghorn broke through the silence. From the piles of blankets pulled up around a body, feet sticking out the end of the bunched-up comforters, a hand reached for the device, patting along the dark cherry top until it could grab ahold, and tap the screen, finally making the noise stop.

Frantic movement was the only indication of how tangled Noel really was before he finally tossed the fabric down from his face and stared up at the ceiling. The time between falling asleep and waking up was not nearly long enough to satisfy any need for rest, and he scrubbed a hand down his face, inwardly debating on getting up, but he reached for the phone again.

Bringing it into his eyeline, he glanced at the time. Five-thirty a.m. and another day begins.

He tossed the phone down beside his leg and kicked the rest of the covers off, laying in the chilled air of the fall morning, windows opened, abandoning the warmth of his *nest*, and mentally counted to ten before he finally rolled out of bed.

The adjoining door to the bathroom was never locked on his side, but the fact that it was *unlocked* within the room told him that neither of his siblings were awake, and that was helpful in only one regard. He didn't have to fight for his shower this morning.

Once cleansed of the night before, the run and the aftermath of nearly being run down by a van scrubbed from his skin, Noel stood before the mirror contemplating shaving the light stubble that graced his chin. After a few moments of mentally making a checklist of what to do next, he turned the water on, and moved to grab for the shaving cream, only to pause.

He just didn't have the energy for that kind of self-care this morning. Instead, he splashed the cold water across his face, giving into the shock of it after the heat of the shower and opened his eyes, only to see gold shining back at him.

That was his only flaw, or so other people thought, other pack members. Noel was an alpha, at least that was what his genetics told him. He would grow up to be a leader, help run companies, take on those roles that would decide how other people lived. It was their way, their customs in the pack to give into their natural order of things, but Noel was different.

His eyes weren't red.

Each designation had a specific eye color, or their secondary gender presented as one. Alphas were red, a sign of power, of position. Betas—like Keegan—were gold, a step just below and mostly strategists, the thinkers, those that could get in and out without being seen, and Keegan lived up to his designation. The last were Omegas, blue-eyed peacekeepers and diplomats. They were sent in to negotiate, to come up with ways to help, to avoid the conflict, to mediate, but that didn't always work.

Noel blinked, letting the color disappear before he was staring at his natural blue "human" eyes, another genetic trait passed on by most family members, and he grabbed the towel, wiping away the water.

He was an alpha like both his parents.

Noel huffed. He didn't feel like either of them, didn't feel like he was born to lead, which was obvious by the color of his eyes. He wasn't normal by any means, no matter how much he wished he was, and apparently that bled into his pack life as well. Whoever heard of an alpha with golden eyes?

Tossing the towel down on the counter, Noel yanked open the bathroom door, and flipped off the light. Even if he didn't know where his place was in pack dynamics, he knew where he landed at home... in charge of his siblings and the keeper of his mother's "rules," and those started every morning just like clockwork.

Noel made his way towards the door on the left, grabbed the handle and turned, pushing the door open wide.

Rule number one should have been pretty simple. Get Keegan up and make sure he stays out of trouble.

But nothing was ever truly *simple* with Keegan.

The room was dark and empty, completely void of anything that would signal his younger brother had been home at all in the hours between midnight and that moment.

Noel sighed, closed his eyes for a moment, and shook his head. "Jesus, Keegan."

Not much else to do but wait.

KEEGAN'S CHEST rose and fell quickly, as if he were running in his sleep, eyes moving rapidly back and forth behind his lids, with parted lips. He wouldn't remember what he dreamed of, he never did, which could be a good or bad thing, but he always felt drained of every ounce of strength when he woke up from them.

Like now.

The light knocking on the door had his eyes wide open, staring at the strange little porcelain dolls that took over a plush chair in the corner of Paige's bedroom, pink and purple curtains, bedspreads, and pillows surrounded him, but he wasn't sure if what woke him was the dream or...

Three loud bangs echoed through the room causing him to jump as his heart raced. He wasn't imagining it and pushed the blankets aside. Paige groaned from behind him, hand reaching out to run along his bare back.

"What time is it?"

Her gruff tone had Keegan smiling. "Five-forty."

"Paige, are you awake?" The muffled sound of Mrs. Pierce filled the room, attracting Keegan's attention as Paige huffed.

"Every morning," she mumbled, tucking her face into the pillow Keegan had just abandoned.

He faked a smile as he looked back on her, pushing her blonde hair from her face, and leaned down, kissing her gently on the temple. He always admired how she couldn't care less about her mother catching him there because she knew it was right. That's how Paige was, she operated on what felt good to her, part of her omega make-up, keeping the peace, keeping Keegan's peace.

"Yes, I'm up!" Sometimes, Keegan wondered if she were really a beta with how aggressive she could make her tone, but he knew she just wasn't a morning person.

"I have to go," his whispered words were against her ear as he kissed her softly.

"You could stay." She grinned as she rolled over, bright eyes taking in the disheveled look she loved when he just rolled out of bed, but he just shook his head.

"Nah, gotta make it home in time to piss off Noel." He winked, slipping from the bed, and made his way towards the window. Three more knocks on the door had him up and opening it a little too hard. The thump against the frame seemed to shake the house.

"Paige, what's going on in there?"

Paige got up from the bed, met him there, hand raised, stilling his movements. "Nothing, Mom. I'm trying to put on pants, tripped over a book."

Keegan grinned at that because her floor was immaculate. There wasn't a thing to trip on anywhere in sight, not even the edge of a throw rug.

Shaking his head, he quickly grabbed his clothes from the floor, not caring about the fact that he had brought his backpack. He had planned to be dressed and ready for school before going home, but that was out the window.

The silence from behind the door was broken again by Mrs. Pierce's voice. "Breakfast is ready. Hurry up or you'll be late for school again."

"Yeah, okay, I'll be down in a minute."

Waiting on her to walk away, both paused to listen. When they were greeted with nothing but silence, Keegan made his break for it. Boots, pants, shirt... backpack, they all went flying from the second-story window. Keegan turned, slamming his forehead against the frame.

"Son of a—" he growled low, placing his palm against the bump on his forehead.

"And good morning, Keegan," came the voice from beyond the barrier once more.

She hadn't moved? She was still waiting outside the door?

Keegan's eyes went wide as he mouthed *"what the fuck?"* to Paige, who's only answer was to stare at him in shock. "What do I do?"

"I don't know," she shrugged, panicking as she looked around. "Answer?"

Keegan looked around, there was no escape. Well, there was no *other* escape but the way he intended to leave anyway, so what the hell? He cleared his throat and prepared himself for the backlash. "Morning, Mrs. Pierce."

"Use the front door next time," was the only reply given, that and the retreating sound of footsteps had both barely breathing.

"Holy shit," Keegan mumbled, heart in his throat as he pressed one hand against his chest as he slipped one leg over the sill to straddle the window. Paige laughed, hard enough that she could barely contain herself, but it wasn't at the expense of Keegan, just the insanity that happened moments before. "She's going to kill me one of these days."

"She has to get through me first. Out...before she changes her mind."

He gave her a quick nod before ducking out the window and onto the trellis, still close enough for her to lean out for one last kiss.

Hopping down the last few feet, Keegan landed gracefully on his feet, knees bent, and with a smile, he glanced back up at her. Gathering his clothes, he makes his way towards the Jeep, towards his freedom and one of his greatest getaways.

NOEL WAS ABOUT to turn away, to leave the door open and let Keegan bitch about it when he got home, but that's when he noticed something peeking out from under the bed. Curiosity was a bad habit of his, especially when it came to his brother, so without a second thought, and after calculating how much time it might take the middle of three to get home, he pushed the door open further.

And regretted it as the scent of the teenager assaulted his nose. Part of their makeup came with heightened senses and right then Noel wished that smell was not one of them. Something about being in another person's room put him on edge no matter who it was, but when you invaded what would be considered another's *den* or their safe space, it was worse.

It smelled like Keegan, and everything he had ever done behind closed doors, leaving nothing to the imagination.

"An air freshener or opening a window once in a while would be nice, Key," he mumbled as he breathed through his mouth instead of his nose. He hoped it would keep the headache he could feel coming on at bay for just a bit because this was something he was curious about.

He glanced out into the hallway, listening for Ellie to make her presence known for just a moment before he took the edge of the gold and blue shirt between his thumb and pointer. There wasn't a name on it, but it was definitely a football jersey. It was the number "17" that had his interest piqued.

"And who do you belong to?" Curious because there was no way Keegan was playing sports of any kind. He hated them all with a passion.

It could have been anyone's, and Noel would have thought maybe one of his friends, but Keegan didn't have many that he knew of, at least that would have come over. With one last look at the shirt, he dropped it and nudged it back under the bed before he took another glance around.

The room was a pigsty. The walls were covered in band posters, littered with black clothing, most T-shirts had obscure band logos on them, and Noel wondered if he had made them himself, and there were random things everywhere.

He had to get out before Keegan knew he was in there. And the kid would, he picked up on everything. All Noel wanted today was to avoid a fight. For just one day. With a sigh, he stepped out of the room, thought twice about it, and reached in pulling the door shut behind him.

Keegan slowed as he pulled around the back of the same cafe that he had stopped at earlier that morning. He paused before putting it in park and smiled. Cafe West wasn't his preferred morning drink, but hey, free stuff was sometimes the best stuff, and he shifted into first, making his way around to the drive-thru speaker.

“Welcome to Cafe West, can I take your order?” Dillon’s voice barked over the speaker.

He smirked, debating for a moment on how much of an ass he was going to be and decided to go with it, changing his voice, pitching it up a bit. “One caramel macchiato with seventeen sugars and some high-grade cocaine, and... add a little Karo syrup.”

The pause was just what he wanted, to shock them into silence. Dillon’s response was exactly what he was looking for.

“You’re an asshole.” He could hear the sound of one of his co-workers in the background, a little, high-pitched giggle that told Keegan his cousin hadn’t worked alone. “One double-x douchebag with extra whip. Seventeen-twenty-four, please pull around.”

Keegan rolled his eyes. “Hurry up and clock out, I was supposed to be home ten minutes ago.”

“Yeah, yeah,” cracked over the speaker before he shifted it into gear and made his way around the building again, this time stopping at the backdoor.

He took a minute to enjoy the music playing over the speaker outside the building, knowing that Dillon was the one who chose it, but that peace didn’t last as long as he hoped when the door suddenly opened and the man himself stepped out into the growing sunlight.

Dumping a black trash bag in the garbage on his way by, Dillon made for the passenger side of the Jeep, hopping up without preamble and handed Keegan a creamy iced drink. Glaring at it in confusion, he accepted the bribe, set it in the same cupholder as the previous hot coffee and put the Jeep in gear.

It was Dillon’s glaring that had him finally snapping a look in his cousin’s direction as he pulled up to the light. “What?”

Dillon continued to look over the lack of clothing that Keegan wore. “You lose your clothes somewhere?”

Keegan turned back to the road, shifted as the light turned green, and took off. “Had to duck and run.”

“Tsk, tsk, thought I taught you better than that.” There was a smile in those words that had Keegan grinning, but he didn't look over, just poked back.

"Thought I taught you how to avoid the cops, now look at you, bumming rides."

"Yep, the things we do for pack."

That had Keegan glancing at him, shaking his head. "Not pack, Dill, family. Pack can be a lot of things but..."

Dillon reached over and messed up his hair. "I know."

Noel made his ways towards Ellie's room, ears tuned into the noise behind the door and smiled at the scratching sound he heard. She was awake, which told him she probably hadn't had a great night of sleeping either, but she wasn't pacing, and her music was off.

That was one of the benefits of heightened hearing, being able to figure out the situation before stepping into it, but Ellie didn't have that yet. She hadn't gone through the presentation of her secondary gender, which usually happened between the ages of fourteen to seventeen. The boys found it better to tiptoe lightly around her since they didn't know which designation she would be, because sometimes she could be exactly like an alpha.

It was like hitting puberty all over again and while they say it's easier for boys to go through it, Noel hadn't witnessed a girl presenting himself but if Keegan was anything to go by as far as boy's presentations, well, they were in for a world of hurt if Ellie's was even remotely difficult.

Rule number two of Mom's law wasn't particularly trying, and easy enough because she was usually self-reliant. Get Ellie to school on time.

He rapped his knuckles against her door, waiting on the muffled answer before he opened it slowly and peeked inside. She was at her desk, bent over the notebook, scribbling down some sort of math problem as if she hadn't even heard him, but he saw the moment she became uncomfortable with his leering and picked her head up to glare right back.

"Breakfast," he whispered, because there was no need to be rough with Ellie. In fact, he barely ever raised his voice at all.

She shrugged at him though, almost rolling her eyes, as she wiggled her pen. "Homework."

Noel pressed back against the sill, opening the door a little wider. "Come on."

She huffed out her irritation, stuffed the pen in her book, and stood, scooting by him in the hall. With a smirk, he released the door and followed, listening to the heavy footsteps that disappeared into the kitchen ahead of him.

THE LIGHT in front of him turned red and Keegan slowed the Jeep to a stop, eyes focused on the road and the music. His thoughts were all over the place. Paige, Daniel, his mother, they were divided onto a thousand different trains all speeding towards one end, a concrete wall, but Keegan couldn't drop any of them, skipping from one to the other.

Until the music shut off.

Glaring at Dillon, Keegan reached for the volume control only to have his cousin's hand on his. "Dude?"

The calm tone of voice Dillon used was the only reason Keegan wasn't going off the rails. "What is it?" Letting his hand drop, Keegan shook his head. "It's that kid, isn't it? The one from this summer?" But his answer was again, the same. "You know I don't care about that stuff, right? You can talk to me about him, about Paige? Who you love is who you love?"

Growling, Keegan snapped his head up, bright gold eyes on Dillon. "You know we're in a Jeep, Dill. No windows, no sides—"

"So?"

Keegan cracked his neck, slowed his respirations as he clenched his teeth. "So? Keep your voice down." At the change of the light, Keegan shifted, stepped on the gas and took off. The town was empty, people were still sleeping, but as paranoid as he was, he couldn't risk anyone hearing. "Besides, that's not it."

Dillon shifted in his seat. "Oh, good, I kinda like that kid."

"You would." He cracked a smile as Dillon laughed quietly. "It's Mom, I just..."

Dillon reached out for his arm, giving it a little squeeze. "She'll be back before you know it."

"Every time she leaves all I see is Dad's car."

"You really need to talk to someone about that, pal. It's going to keep tearing you apart if you don't." He gave him a gentle pat before he took his hand away to stare out at the rising sun, but Keegan stayed quiet. Keegan put it in park as he pulled up to the curb and pushed on the e-brake. Dillon jumped out, but didn't leave right away, instead he just looked at the younger man. "You gonna be okay?"

"Sure, Dill. I'll be fine." He grabbed the gear shift without looking at him.

"Do me a favor," and this got his attention, "find your friend. You smiled more around him."

"Nah," Keegan laughed, thinking about the jock the night before, "I'm good."

"Sure, you are. Us betas, we gotta stick together." Dillon patted the hood of the Jeep. "Tell Paige I said hi."

"I will." He waited for Dillon to back away before he released the brake and pulled away from the curb, heading towards home.

CHAPTER 4

CATCHING the shine of the screen out of the corner of his eyes, Gus removed his foot from the pedal, toggled the switch to off and instantly regretted his decision on the blaring alarm choice. It's 6:10 and it's been going off for nearly ten minutes without him knowing.

Frustrated, he yanked the goggles from his face and set them down on the table as he scooped up the phone and fought to fight the volume, finally ceasing the noise. Debating on whether to call first or to wait on Noel, he picks up the hammer again, but his peace and quiet has already been disturbed, there was no way he was going back to it now.

Grumbling to himself, he set the tool down gently, aware of his own strength, and grabbed the phone again, this time rising from the stool as well, as he flipped to his contacts and searched for the number.

NOEL SEARCHED THROUGH CABINETS, opening one than the other before he settled on a door on the bottom row under the microwave. He reached into the back and yanked out a new container of coffee, not the best kind, but coffee was coffee and that morning he really needed it. When his phone vibrated on the counter above him with that certain ringtone, he knew his morning had just gotten times more fucked than before.

Rule number three: check in with Gustaf every morning. Even on weekends, which it didn't happen to be, but Noel hated anyway.

Rising to his feet, Noel shot a quick glance at Ellie, who had seated herself at the breakfast table and was fully invested in the bowl of cereal in front of her, missing the murderous gaze in his eyes as he grabbed the phone off the counter and put it to his ear.

"Morning," he snapped out, nearly slamming the container down on the counter.

He grabbed a reusable K-pod cup and clicked open the top with his fingernail. At least that was easy enough, but he fought with the container, hoping the seal would give a little before it ended up all over the floor. When it opened successfully, Noel counted it as a win for a moment before searching for the scoop.

HE COULD HEAR the tone in Noel's voice, the one that told him this might not be the best conversation to have with him, but it had to be done. He made his way up the stairs, shaking off the sawdust and dirt before hitting the kitchen.

He grabbed a cup from the counter and moved up to the pot, placing the phone down. It took him less than a second to hit that speaker button because he hated holding the damn thing to his ear. It was too small and didn't weigh nearly enough.

"You're late." His tone was flat, almost unimpressed and while he didn't really need to speak to him that way, the interruption of his time still had him on edge. He grabbed the handle of the pot and poured his own cup.

"By ten minutes! I was doing my job," Noel bit back, and Gustaf could hear him turn on the faucet.

Without missing a beat, the alpha sighed and continued without acknowledging Noel's tone. "Your mother will be getting in about three. I'm guessing she sent you a text?"

NOEL HUFFED AS he fought with the top of the machine to get it closed. "Yeah, she texted, said she was at the airport last I heard. What's going on?"

Finally, it clicked shut and he locked it, hitting the flashing large cup icon. Noel peeked out the doorway into the driveway. Still no Keegan, and that would be an issue if Gustaf knew. He didn't have time to worry about that now, he just wanted to wake up.

"I'm not at liberty to discuss it right now, but I expect you'll all be where you need to be?"

Noel dropped his chin to his chest, counting backwards from ten before he closed his eyes tightly. "Just like clockwork."

"Excellent." Noel shook his head at that one word because Gus sounded like some kind of mad scientist. Apparently, he wasn't the only one who had the thought as Ellie mimicked him with her pinky against her lip. When she noticed him, she only smirked and continued with her breakfast. *"The rest of the pack leaders will be there as well. She's called an emergency session."*

That had Noel's attention. "Something wrong? She never does that."

"One of life's great mysteries is to understand why women do anything." Not that Noel was going to argue with that logic but the

scowl on Ellie's face told him better not agree out loud. "*Anything to report?*"

Ellie raised a brow, still not saying a word as Noel glanced down the hallway, unsure of what to say before his eyes went back to the empty driveway.

"No, they're good, awake and getting ready."

THERE WAS something in Noel's answer that had Gus pausing with a scoop of sugar just over his cup. It wasn't his tone, which was believable but the silence just before it. He dumped the sugar in and let it go, giving the coffee a quick stir before bringing it to his lips.

He cringed at the taste, grabbed another two spoonsful, and mixed again before trying it one more time.

Perfection.

"Good, we'll see you at three."

And without waiting for a reply, he hit the end button before he stuffed the thing away and headed towards the bench by the window.

This was going to be a long day.

NOEL GRABBED THE PHONE, raised it up, threatening to toss it down, but paused as he took a breath. "I hate when he does that."

"No one likes being hung up on," Ellie whispered, bringing the spoon to her mouth, but she glanced over at him. "Mom's coming home?"

"She sent a text last night, but I haven't heard a damn thing about it since."

"Maybe she's still on the plane."

Noel stuffed the phone in his back pocket and pulled the cup from the machine, before turning towards the island in the middle of the room. He leaned against it, nodding. How was he supposed to tell her that trips from that particular airport should only last three hours, if that and he got the text almost eight hours ago? He crossed his arms on the counter hoping that whatever the hell happened had nothing to do with his mother.

Ellie moved up to the counter, pushed her books aside, and set the empty bowl across from him. Noel knew exactly what she wanted and grabbed the box of cereal from under the counter, sliding it over to her as he reached for the fridge, grabbing the half-gallon of milk.

Just as he set it down, he paused as the familiar sound of the Jeep was pulling to a stop in the driveway.

It took less than a blink for the door leading out to the garage to fly open dramatically, slamming back against the cart and the trash barrel that buffered it from the wall, and for Keegan to step in, dressed only in his charismatic boxers and multicolored socks. Ellie choked on the cereal she had just taken a bite of, but Noel paused his cup on the way to his lips.

Keegan waggled his eyebrows at his brother, strolling in with a certain swagger in his step and dropped his backpack, clothes, and boots by the door.

"You're late," Noel scolded as Keegan grabbed an apple from the island bowl, giving it a good toss before catching it, his eyes on his brother the whole way by.

"Am I though?" He swung around, smirk on his face, and raised a brow waiting for the next move. Ellie shook her head, walked by them both and closed the kitchen door, kicking Keegan's boots out of the way.

"We're leaving in twenty minutes, and you're riding with me." Noel placed the mug on the counter beside him, preparing for the backlash that little tidbit was going to cause. Keegan didn't disappoint, even if it did start off slowly.

"Why?" He crossed his arms over his chest, puffed it up to look bigger, but Noel outweighed him by nearly twenty pounds.

"We need to be at the meetinghouse by three, Mom's request, and I don't need to go looking for you." Noel wasn't about to posture but Keegan stepped just a bit closer, looking up at the three-inch height difference, still glaring.

"I'll take the Jeep."

Noel stepped just a bit closer, eyes glowing a bright gold. "You'll ride with me, Keegan."

Ellie turned back to her bowl, over whatever dramatics her brothers were creating but slipped to the other side of the counter in case it got physical, but even her brows went up when Keegan backed down.

"Whatever." He waved him off, and with a dramatic bow, he punctuated his statement with a huffed out "Alpha."

He took a bite of the apple, maintained eye contact for a moment more, before giving him a shit-eating grin and headed down the hallway.

Noel rolled his shoulders, easing the tension as the door slammed shut, and his eyes landed on Ellie, who's only gesture was to give him a shy smile. He really wished he understood what the hell was going on with his brother.

He could hear Noel, just the way his brother moved through the kitchen, worried, frustrated. He could smell him too, but what the hell was he going to do about it?

Keegan gripped the marble counter hard, leaning in on locked arms, taking in the noise of the shower, and closed his eyes tightly. The steam brought out the scents on his skin. Paige and the night they spent together wrapped up in a cocoon of blankets, then Daniel and how he had pressed against him in the Jeep, trying to show his dominance. Or at least Keegan hoped that was what he was doing.

There was a plus side of being bisexual, you could have both gentle and rough if your partners were okay with it, and Paige was definitely okay with Daniel. It was the football player that wasn't exactly sure what the hell to do with him yet.

Opening his eyes slowly, he took a moment to look in the mirror, to gauge himself, right all of his trains one more time and get them back on track. That was when he caught the strange lack of a bump or bruise where he had clearly had one after slamming his head at Paige's. He just shook it off before yanking off the socks that would have to be thrown away since jumping from the trellis had caused a rip in the bottom of one. It wasn't the first incidence of things mysteriously healing lately.

The violent buzz of his phone had him pause by the sink, slip the phone from the pile where he had wrapped it in a towel, and blink at the banner on the screen. A text from a contact simply called "Bye Boi" had Keegan scoffing, debating on ignoring it as he flipped to Spotify.

Picking the loudest, most annoying band listed in his library, he pushed the button, synced it to the shower speaker—because a silent bathroom always freaked him out even as a child—and let the music blare.

His boxers slipped to the floor as he stepped into the shower and closed the sliding door. Keegan grinned, started out singing to the music in a soft voice but once behind that glass, his voice raised, off-pitch, and for a moment, he felt... normal.

Gus's moment of silence was broken by the unfamiliar tone of his phone. He was sure he had set something for each of his contacts, another suggestion from Keegan when he upgraded the damn thing, but that tone... he didn't know it.

"Better not be those pain in the ass kids," he grumbled, grabbing the phone. He didn't mean it; he just had no clue who else it could have been. The "unknown number" that scrolled across the screen confirmed it. Clearing his throat, he brought it to his ear. "Hello?"

"Is Mr. Segal available?" No other words, just that spoken in a pleasant, feminine voice, much to his surprise. Enough so that Gus pulled it away from his ear to peek at the screen again.

"Who is this?"

"This is County General Memorial Hospital and I'm looking for Mr. Segal. Is he available?" Still pleasant even after his barking tone, Gustaf was definitely confused.

"This is."

"We have a situation."

Gus placed his coffee down on the table, almost empty anyway and cold, and rose to his feet. "Go on."

"Since you're listed as the next contact in case of emergency when Mrs. Summerford is unavailable, and her voice is going to voicemail..."

"I get it." He paused in the doorway, glancing at the coffee pot. Maybe he did need a refill if this was how this conversation was going to go. He was trying to be civil, he really was, but if she... "She's out of town on business. You called the right person; how can I help you?"

"As I said, we have a situation here at the hospital."

Gustaf rolled his eyes, heading up the stairs towards his bedroom. She's stalling, she has to be, why else would she... "Who is this?" But his answer was only silence on the line. "Your name, could I please have your name?"

"Marie Penn," the shy reply came, and it sounded as if she were moving away from her desk.

He grabbed his jeans from his bed and hopped into them as the click of a door became evident. She was hiding, and he stopped, shirtless and jeans undone, worried about the woman on the line suddenly. "Are you in trouble?"

"No, no, I'm fine. Thank you, but this is sensitive information." She kicked something, a cart maybe, and swore lowly.

"What's the situation?" He had to keep her talking until he could get out the door. Placing the phone on speaker, he dropped it on the bed, finished his jeans and grabbed a shirt. She needed to start talking just a little faster if this was sensitive stuff. "Ms. Penn?"

"A man was brought in only five minutes ago through our emergency department."

"And the reason this has to do with me, or Mrs. Summerford?"

"Sir, he's a..." *Oh, here we go.* "He's a beta, at least from what we can determine. Blood typing has him matched with that designation, but something about the tests is off. And there's something else."

Like pulling teeth. "Go on."

"It seems he's having some sort of amnesia."

Gus shook his head, rubbing his fingers back and forth across his brow before he pinched his nose. *How convenient.* "I'll be right there."

With that, he hung up, mostly dressed anyhow, and tucked the phone in his pocket as he headed for the stairway. He should really call Rollins, or even Noel, but there were kids to get to school and classes to take. Rollins would be his last call if things became violent or some sort of movement had to be made.

He slipped on his boots, grabbed the keys and his jacket and paused at the front door before going into the kitchen. He clicked off the coffee machine, wondering for only a second if he had time to make a travel mug of it, but he needed to sort this out before Juli got home.

With a sigh, he darted for the door, firm in his decision to get this done and over with, because he still hadn't contacted the pack leaders yet and that was going to go over about as well as a fire in a hay field.

KEEGAN STOMPED INTO THE KITCHEN, making as much noise as he could, glancing over at Ellie, who stood against the island with a backpack on and three books on the counter, before going to Noel, who stood by the back patio door. He had purposely found a shirt that would piss his brother off, a black one with a band logo, simple enough—a hand with a middle finger pointing up, the words *"f*ck *ff"* printed in the background surrounded by a square—but just enough to get a reaction.

Ellie slipped from the room, almost unnoticed except by Keegan who noticed her every step, protective and curious.

"You can't wear that to school." Noel's words were more like sighs.

Keegan hid the grin on his face as he yanked the fridge open and pushed around bottles and containers looking for anything that might set the older sibling off. "Watch me."

His hair was still wet, the ends dripping from his shower but not overly so that the fall air would give him a chill, besides, he liked the messy look. He grabbed a bottle of orange juice, just a single serving size and stood, breaking the seal as his eyes stayed right on his brother.

This had to be his favorite past-time because Noel gave him what he wanted. His full attention. He drank down all of it in one go, Noel's blue eyes locked on his, and pulled it away with a satisfying *"ahh"* before tossing the empty bottle into the trash.

"Funny." Keegan was curious about that tone because Noel wasn't usually one for the brush-off he had just given him. This was a thing, *their* thing.. This morning routine, as much fun as it was for Keegan, but Noel usually responded...better? "I'm serious. I don't need to pick you up for a dress code violation when Mom's on her way home."

Well, that explained the tone, but wait... "She's coming home today?"

He leaned on the counter, curious about this new development and why he hadn't heard anything about it, but as Noel made for the breakfast nook again, arms crossed, Keegan's curiosity grew. Maybe he could push it a little.

"Wonder how long it'll be for this time?"

Noel's growl was cut off by Ellie grabbing her backpack from the counter. Her books, the three large volumes that sat beside them, tilted and Keegan reached out to snatch the top one out of the air before it fell to the floor. With eyes on his sister, and a small "thank you" on her lips, he handed it off before his gaze focused back on Noel. Ellie didn't need any of his shit, that's what big brothers were for.

The younger of the three looked between them. "Are you two fighting again?

"Nope," Keegan winked, but it was the jarring "no" from Noel that had her annoyed.

Keegan headed for the discarded clothing he left by the door and slipped on his boots, taking his jacket from the rack, but it was when he looked up at the key hooks that all playfulness disappeared and he turned, golden eyes glaring at Noel.

"Give me my keys." His only response was a shake of Noel's head. "Seriously? I'm not really in the mood to play—"

"I need you to be there when Mom gets home, Key, and I—"

"Anyone ever tell you you're a dick!"

Noel got to his feet, ready for his brother to charge. "I can't chance you taking off on some stupid—"

"Fuck you, Noel, if you think I'd do that to Mom!" Noel's eyes shifted, matching his brother's but as Keegan watched, the color changed to a strange orange, which did nothing but confuse the younger of the two. "What was that?"

Noel let out a long exhale before taking one in again and let the power fade in his eyes, raising a brow to Keegan. "I'm sorry."

He scoffed, grabbing his backpack from the floor. "Whatever, can we go?"

He didn't wait for Noel, or Ellie, just grabbed the handle, yanked it open, and ducked down into the garage.

Noel ran a hand down his face, frustrated and unsure that what he just did was the right thing before his eyes landed on Ellie. She hiked the straps over her shoulder as she hugged the books to her.

"It's going to backlash on him."

Noel nodded. "I know. Just..." Hell, he didn't know what to do anymore. "Let me know if—" He gestured to the retreating back unsure of how to word his concern.

"Kay," she whispered as she walked by, following Keegan out the door.

Noel glanced around one last time before digging his keys out of his pocket. He grabbed his bag from beside the door and headed out, closing it behind him.

THE LIGHT ahead of him turned red just as he approached, and Gus let out a huff. Of course, that would be how his morning was going to go. More red lights than green and he wasn't even close to the hospital yet.

His eyes wandered to the Cafe West sign at the insertion, and while he really didn't need another cup, the idea of being a little more awake for whatever he was walking into sounded like a great idea.

Until he happened to glance over into the parking lot.

The backside of the cafe was littered with cruisers and one familiar unmarked. He knew the whole stigma of cops and donuts, but this looked more like work then snack. Flipping on his directional, he pulled into the right-hand lane and headed in.

In the middle of the commotion was an old green beater,

possibly a Cavalier by the shape of it, but definitely one he knew. Pulling up to an open spot on the other side of the small median, he shut the car off and headed over.

Morgan Wells, dressed in plain clothes, looked up from the uniformed officer he had been talking to, his eyes landing right on the new arrival, and he shook his head. "No." It was low enough that only the alpha could have heard before Well's got just a little more edgy. "You can't be here, Gustaf."

The alpha rolled his eyes, and crossed his arms, waiting for Wells to get a little more in-depth with his explanation. It didn't take long. Leaving the officer behind, he marched towards Gus with purpose, only to stop short and cross his arms.

"You can't be here," Wells repeated as he blocked his view of the scene.

"So you said, but you haven't told me *why*." Gus wasn't so easily put off, and he had known the Detective for years, so just a little bit of reverse psychology always worked. Just like this time.

Wells grabbed his arm, tugged him further away from the scene and the onlookers before they stopped out of view behind Wells' SUV. "A kid's missing."

"A kid?" Gus blinked, a little confused about why it would stop him from behind on scene, until— "Wait. From here? Dillon?"

"No," Wells cleared his throat, took one quick look around and finally exhaled. "A girl. We think she left her shift this morning and never made it to her car."

"Okay, that sounds suspicious. Why am I not supposed to be here again?"

He debated a moment, frowning, before he just let it out. "She's part of your pack."

"What? Who? And if she's pack, you're wrong. I need to be here." Gus moved to shift around him, to make his way to the scene, but Wells just grabbed his arm.

"I can't," he finally got him to stand still. "You know I can't tell you that."

"Morgan, come on."

"The Chief will have my head if you get involved."

"You said she's one of mine. That makes me involved."

"Look, all I know is that she worked with Dillon, and we're trying to get a hold of him."

"Okay." Gus took a step back, closed his eyes a moment and shook his head. "Okay, I'll call his mother, but he usually works the late shift, so he might be sleeping."

"Thank you." Wells shifted and was about to turn, but Gus grabbed his arm. "What?"

"You have to put out an alert."

"It's too soon for an Amber Alert."

"You don't understand. Pack members have been going missing."

"What? Why haven't you called the station, or even reported a pattern?"

"You just told me that I can't get involved. We're trying to figure it out ourselves without the CPD getting tangled in it, but this girl... She makes four in the last week and a half from the area. If you think there's something weird about the scene, then we need that alert out as fast as you can."

"All right," Wells nodded. "I'll put it out."

"Thank you!" Gus pulled the keys from his pocket and raced to his car. He slipped in, hit the call pad on his dash and dialed out.

The feminine voice on the line sounded confused and concerned all at once. *"Gus?"*

"Jenn, hey, are you home? I need to talk to Dillon."

"He's sleeping."

"It's important."

The pause on the line only managed to stir up the strange anxiety over the loss of the girl.

"Okay, I'll wake him up."

"Good. I'm going to have a detective call in the next few minutes. Just keep him awake."

"What's going on? Is he in trouble?"

"No. He's a good kid. Wells just has some questions."

"All right, he'll be up."

The phone disconnected, leaving Gus to sit there in the quiet of his car. He hesitated only a moment before grabbing the phone off the seat. He sent out a quick text to Wells, telling him to call Dillon and supplied the number before dropping it back down.

He started it up, and headed out of the parking lot, right back on the road to County General. There was only so much he could do at a time and a rogue beta might be a clue as to what happened to the girl.

THE OLD PICK-UP pulled up beside the curb, and Noel shifted into park, eyes going toward his brother as Keegan stared out the window. He had been quiet, not even really paying attention to the conversation between Noel and Ellie, and while it was normal for him to ignore his siblings, his quietness, his stillness was a bit unnerving.

Without a word, Keegan pushed open the door and grabbed his backpack from the floor, but Noel's hand on his arm stopped him. Keegan glared, not saying a word, and kept his expression otherwise calm.

"Two-thirty, kay?"

Yanking his arm away, Keegan gave him his best go-to expression, a little smirk. "Yeah, I got it, bro."

He slipped out of the truck but stopped the instant he saw the crowds. He stepped back against the truck, a small anxiety response, and grimaced, hoping Noel didn't notice. It didn't work, his brother was always too observant. He took a few deep breaths, praying he could just walk away but...

"Hey, Key?" *Of course not.* Keegan turned, albeit slowly, and moved around the truck to the driver's side window. No sense letting the man yell. Keeping the distance, he paused about a foot away from the old machine. "What's going on?"

Keegan's eyes shifted to Daniel, still with that sweat-shined look in the morning light, but this time dressed in the gold and blue letterman's jacket befitting the captain of the football team. He stood among others, back against the wall, surrounded by his adoring fans and, in an inappropriately timed thought he wished he could just push him up against it and take what he wanted, show the others who Daniel belonged to. But he masked the thoughts with a small shrug and a smug look before responding.

"Nothing."

"Really? Do you need me to come in? Speak to the coach?"

That caught his attention, drawing him completely away from the jock, away from his thoughts of Daniel and he glared at him. "Why the hell would I want you to do that?"

"Look," Noel shifted in the seat, facing him, locking eyes with his younger brother. "Something's going on, I can tell."

"Dude," he scowled, "keep your schnoz to yourself, I'm fine."

"Who the hell says schnoz?" Ellie laughed, gaining Keegan's ire, but while it had him legitimately smiling, she never looked up from her book.

"I'm just looking out for you." Noel's words brought him away from the humor in his sister's profile to the man in front of him.

"I finally get out from under your thumb and now you wanna look out for me?" The laugh he gave was full of sarcasm as he shook his head. "No thanks. Later, Ell."

She looked up this time as Keegan walked away. He didn't head for Daniel, never really intended to, but beelined for Paige, who was now waiting just down the sidewalk for him. With a grin on his face, he wrapped his arms tightly around her and kissed her passionately in front of the whole world. If he couldn't have one, he would certainly lavish attention on the other.

THE ELEVATOR DOOR dinged moments before it opened on the fifth floor of County General. Gustaf, still uncertain as to why he was there except for the unverified fact of an amnesic beta, cautiously moved from the confines of the box onto the bustling floor. Nurses and MAs moved in and out of rooms, pulling blood pressure carts and holding charts but he didn't see any guards, which was the first thing that struck him as odd. With a seemingly dangerous pack member on the floor, he thought there'd be at least an orderly, but nothing in the way of security even floated around.

Stepping up to the counter, Gus stood for a moment, looking over the three women at the desk, totally ignored before he cleared his throat and the woman in front of him glancing up, annoyed.

"I'm looking for Ms. Penn." He put on a sweet smile, or at least that was what Juli called it—he was pretty sure she was yanking his chain—but it had the desired effect, and the cute blonde in front of him pointed down the counter at the last woman, who was frantically scribbling notes into a chart. "Thank you."

He made his way slowly, as to not startle her, but her eyes were on him the moment he paused in front of her.

"Ms. Penn?" Her eyes went wide with fear and her body locked up. Not something he had expected before her gaze lowered as if she were being disrespectful. That wasn't at all right, she was human, wasn't pack. "Ms. Penn, you don't need to keep your eyes lowered."

"I'm sorry, Alpha." Even her voice shook, and Gus couldn't hold back the slight giggle.

"What's your designation?" Because that always threw them off.

Those bright brown eyes of hers came back up in confusion. "I... I don't have one."

Just as he thought. "You're not part of any pack?"

"No, sir. I'm..."

"Human?"

"Yes, Alpha."

Gus really did smile that time. It had been a while since anyone that pretty had called him that and he tried not to preen at it, or the feeling of power it gave him. *Shit!* He shrugged it off. "What do you know about our rules?"

"Only what I read online."

"Well." *This was new.* "Thank you for taking the time to look that deep into it, but unless you have a designation, you don't have to lower your gaze for an alpha." Her expression brightened with a shy smile, as her cheeks grew darker with a blush and she really did look at him this time, giving him a nod. "You called me down here for a rogue beta, could you please show me where he is?"

She snatched the cart from her desk, glancing down the way at the other two nurses, before nodding. "Of course." He had never seen anyone so nervous. "Right his way, Alpha."

"Gus," he smiled. "Gus is fine."

Her eyes sparkled as the smile grew at his flirtation tone, and she gestured towards the room at the end of the hall. Gus ducked his head, placed his hands in his coat pockets and followed, trying to make himself as small and harmless as possible. An alpha in a hospital this big, especially since it wasn't their usual place for medical treatment could be seen as a threat by anyone.

Marie slipped into the room, her keycard the only thing that unlocked the door, and he suddenly understood the reason for the lack of guards. She was one of only two nurses allowed in, something her knowledge of pack dynamics came in handy for, as slight as they might be.

Glancing at the man on the bed, the first thought in his mind was questioning how he was even alive.

"I don't think he's a rogue, though he came through in pretty bad shape." She turned up the lights, giving him just a little more to work with as far as evaluating his condition.

On the bed, hooked to a heart monitor, IV machine for fluids, and with a nasal cannula hooked around his ears blowing oxygen into his nose, was a pale man, even with his dark skin he looked ashen. The bruises on his face alone told Gus about his fight and how desperate he was to get away from those that held him.

"From the looks of him, I think I agree with you but if you could keep that on your report, I'd appreciate it." Gus glanced back at her as she moved towards the monitors, taking in his vital signs on the chart in her hands, but his request confused her.

"That he's rogue?"

It seemed the hospital was looking out for their safety as well as the injured man's. His wrists were tied down, his legs strapped by cuffs, nothing that would hurt him or cause more injury to him, but as a means of making sure he didn't flee. They even had one across his waist.

Gustaf gave a slight nod as he inched closer to the bed, taking in the man's scent. Definitely pack, though he was unsure the stranger was part of his. There was a familiarity to it but something on the surface was changed.

"It will keep away unwanted guests. Most humans won't come near anyone with a designation if they're injured, more so with someone marked as a rogue. You're very brave."

"I don't understand." And she really didn't, Gus could hear it in her voice.

Smiling, he turned to her. "Think werewolf movies, feral beasts that hunt in the night." Her expression dropped, but her eyes were more questioning before she scoffed at him. "It's good to know you don't fear us."

"You're just people." While he had turned away from her, he could almost picture her rolling her eyes in some annoyed way. "My job is to help anyone who's injured, pack or not." She tapped him on the arm, handing him her chart and an extra key card. "This is usually for family members, but I think you're the right person for him. Don't lose it, they track them."

"Thank you," he slipped the card away, but kept his eyes locked on hers. "I need you to do me one more favor. Tell no one."

"Of course."

"Do you understand why?"

"My best friend in high school was part of a pack. She hid it from me because she said it was dangerous for me to know things. If you're asking me to keep his secret, I know why and I understand it."

"You're a very special woman, Ms. Penn." She blushed at his words before heading towards the door. "Could you mark this room as solitary?"

"It already is."

He gave her a slight nod, and Marie glanced over at the man on the bed once more before slipping out of the room.

He grabbed the rolling stool from the corner, making himself comfortable next to the bed as he flipped open the chart.

"Now, let's see who you are." His eyes went to the face of the man, to the gauze wrapped around his head, and the large bandages visible on his arms, wrapped tightly around his lower left. His eyes then traveled down to the blood spots on his gown, and the shape of several large four-by-four patches under the thin fabric.

Gus looked away from the IV wires, to where the tape held the needle in, and the monitor cords that peek out from under the gown. Whatever happened to him was severe, but it was the large bandage on his right side that got him. He shifted the johnny, looking over the six inches of tapped down gauze, dropped the chart to his lap and crossed his arms.

"At least, it looks like you put up a fight." He unhooked the strap, sliding his arm from the soft material and leaned in, bringing the man's wrist to his nose, before inhaling deeply.

The hint of his run through the woods was clearly foremost on his skin, but underneath was pain, fear, and again something familiar but faint. As gently as possible, he slipped it back in, tightening the strap only enough that he would acknowledge it was there before he picked up the chart, stood and paced the room.

His wounds were many, as were the lists of his condition. "Beta" stuck out first, knowing they had typed him before calling him, but the multiple stab wounds had his stomach turning. "Laceration to the abdomen" explained the larger gauze. "Head trauma." Gus glanced up at the bandage around his head, which might explain the amnesia, before he went on to read "dehydration and malnutrition."

"What happened to you, my friend?"

His eyes rested on the wide brown ones of the man on the bed who did nothing but draw in the alpha's scent. His sight was focused solely on Gus, but only for a moment before his whole body relaxed, and he groaned in pain. It took the alpha not moving, for the fear of harm to pass for him to start tugging on the restraints, his eyes glowing gold for only a moment before it faded, too weak to keep it up.

"Where am I?" His voice cracked, frantic.

NOEL FOLLOWED Keegan's movements through the crowd as he connected with Paige. She was good for him, always had been, and being an Omega certainly helped keep him calm. That was the other thing that confused him, the real question of who the shirt in the room belonged to? His eyes went to the group of jocks that Keegan had been staring at, observing as they shifted, grouping up as couples or little cliques to move inside the building.

It was the moment their back was to him that Noel sat up a little straighter. There, on one of the jackets, embroidered in blue and gold, was the number "17." *What the hell?* Maybe he wasn't as observant as he thought he was.

Noel sat back, let his head fall on the rest behind him and took a moment before turning towards Ellie. "Your turn."

The two shared a smile before she slipped over to the door and opened it slowly. She scanned the quad, looking for someone specific and spotted Mitch the moment he moved out from behind a tree with his hands in his pockets smiling at the truck before Reagan Taber ran up beside him, placing her hands on his shoulder.

Noel saw the moment Ellie locked eyes with the boy, and she slipped from the truck, shrugging on her backpack as she grabbed the three books from the seat, but it was the expression on Noel's face that stopped her from moving.

"Don't be paranoid," she whispered, and it was almost like hearing his mother.

Noel smirked but shook his head. "That's the Rollins kid?"

"You know it is, Noel, don't worry. He's safe."

"Still, Ell—"

"Listen, no one's going to disappear on you. We're right here." Noel bit his lip, nodding. Leave it to the sixteen-year-old to give him a piece of her mind and call out his fears. "I'll see you at two-forty-five, okay?"

"Okay." It was the only thing he could give her, at least at the moment. His mind wasn't wrapping around anything that morning, it was just going on its own course, and he began to wonder if this was what Keegan dealt with every day.

Ellie gave him a reassuring smile, backed up and closed the door. With a wave, she turned and moved towards Mitch and Reagan, who each grabbed a book, but it was the last look back from her that really set him at ease.

They were both safe, and now Noel had to face his own day ahead.

He put the truck in drive, looked in his side view, and pulled away from the curb, into traffic.

Maybe he'd stop at Cafe West, he could use a little more of a jumpstart before classes began.

The pull of the needle, the sting of pain as she shifted was the one thing that brought her back from the brink, teetering there for a moment before she forced her eyes open. But there was nothing, even when she knew they're open, she saw nothing. Groaning at the thumping in her temples, a side effect she knew is from whatever drug they injected her with, she let her head loll to the side, and startled at the movement in the corner.

"Juli," his sweet voice whispered to her, a voice she hadn't heard in a year, one that she longed to hear again, and that movement began to come into focus. The room around her brightened as he stepped out of the shadows and into the light.

She was in a hospital bed, arms free of any IVs, body void of wires, but that didn't explain the uncomfortable pain, until he got close enough. In his arms, bundled tightly in a white blanket, with a blue and pink footprint pattern on it, was a newborn.

Alexandru was a mess. His tussled, wavy, brown hair was in disarray, but the smile on his face and the sparkle in his blue eyes was pure joy and he sat down beside her on the bed, managing not to move her too much as he shifted, facing her so she could see the little one's face.

"He's beautiful," she whispered. Her fingers danced over what little dark hair graced his head, pushing the hat back just a bit for a better view.

"He is. He's perfect." Alex chuckled, offering him to her, but letting Juli sit up in the bed before she accepted the tiny human. "I can feel him already, Jules. He's going to do amazing things."

She let him settle the newborn in her arms, placed a pillow under him for more support, and just watched him. It was Alex's gaze that brought her away from the child, and the small smirk on his face made her grin.

"At least wait until he's a few years old to tell me you want another one," she laughed, but that didn't change the way he looked at her. "What is it?"

"Nothing." It was barely-there reply, and that strange look was wiped off his face. "So." He moved to sit beside her the best he could, and he held her hand as she caressed the little one's face. "What are we going to call him?"

She had thought about it, in fact, they both had thought about it a lot, but nothing clicked. Not one name matched what she felt while carrying him through the last nine months, but now, the name just came to her.

"Noel." She spoke it softly, with a smile on her lips, and the infant in her arms opened his eyes, bright blue like his father's.

"Well, look at that," Alex chuckled. "He likes it."

But Juli glanced up at him, uncertainty in her expression as the man continued to smile down at his son. "Are you sure?"

"It suits him."

"What if he hates it?"

Alex kissed her temple, leaving his lips against her skin, smiling. "Then we give him a little brother to focus on. Trust me, his name won't matter anymore when he's got annoying siblings to chase after."

Juli laughed. Leave it to him to make light of a situation. "Then Noel it is."

She brought the baby up, kissed him gently on the forehead, and held him close just to take in his scent as her memory faded into darkness.

NOEL PULLED AROUND to the drive-thru, eyes on the caution tape that formed a small triangle around a green Cavalier and stopped at the speaker. He knew a couple of the uniformed officers that stood around it too, but he just swallowed down his curiosity and waited for the greeting.

"Welcome to Cafe West, how may I take your order?"

That was not a voice he recognized, but Noel didn't have time to wonder just what was going on. He let a smile cross his lips, hoping to sound pleasant to the person on the other end and gave his order, eyes still on the abandoned car, before vaguely hearing the cashier repeat it back to him. He didn't have a clue if it was right or not, he just rattled it off from memory, and waited to see when he got there.

With a strange feeling in his gut, Noel gave it a little gas and just moved onto the next window, the abandoned car disappearing as he rounded the corner.

CHAPTER 5

GUS TOOK A MOMENT, letting the beta before him work out the fact that he wasn't getting out of the restraints before he held his hands up and shushed him quietly, like a parent coddling a child. He lowered the chart to the bedside table and approached with caution.

Betas were known for their strength among other heightened senses. With that knowledge, there was no telling what this man could do in his state. However, he simply cowered back, fear setting off the monitors around him, and the noise sent his heart rate spiking.

Taking a moment to breathe calmly through his nose and out through his mouth, Gus let off nothing but the sense of safety, which the beta instantly picked up on, settling as Gus turned the machines away and lowered the volume of the alarms. For a moment it was nothing but peaceful in the room.

"Alpha, please," his voice shook even as his body started to relax. "Where am I?"

"Be patient," Gus whispered as he rolled the stool over to the bed, and slowly sat down, eyes still going over the one before him. "You're on Summerford lands." He observed the confusion, saw the moment it turn to something like fear before it faded altogether. "Who are you?"

"What?" The question drew him from the blank stare he had fallen into, fingers tugging on the sheet that covered him, and his eyes set on Gus. "I..." He shook his head, debated a moment, and suddenly they lit up. "Luca." He spoke that one word with confidence, nodding to himself. "Luca Morrin."

The name sounded familiar, but like his scent, it was clouded, not anything Gus could pinpoint, but he made a mental note to look into it. There were other questions that needed answers first. "Why are you here, Luca?"

He jolted at the sound of his name repeated back to him, but the only thing he could reply with was, "I don't..." Gus raised his hand, quieting the man who started to once again shiver, words stumbling out of his mouth before he shook his head and made eye contact once more. "I don't understand. How did I get here?"

He took the chart from the table, showing him the report, but it only seemed to confuse him more. It was time for a different tactic.

"Before I get to that, I'm going to need you to answer a few more questions." The shiver became violent, almost as if Luca was terrified, and Gus moved towards the closet, grabbing a second blanket from the shelves. He needed to get the man to calm down, to trust him. He unfolded it and spread it out across his legs before pulling it up to his chest. "Do you understand?"

"Yes," he groaned. "Yes, Alpha."

"Good." Taking the seat, he waited, watching as the shivering stopped, and Luca took in the room, and him. "Where are you from?" There was a long pause, a moment of contemplation before Luca responded with a simple shake of his head. "What pack?" The fear began to spread again, reaching his eyes as he tried to remember, but once more, he said nothing. "You know your last name but not the pack you belong to?"

He shook his head violently, as the monitors started flashing, and Gus thanked the gods above that he had taken the time to turn them down, but he could see the way Luca strained against the cuffs.

"Okay." He raised his hands just before slowly reaching out. Luca stiffened as if preparing for a blow, but Gus gently wrapped his fingers around Luca's wrist, giving a little squeeze. "Just relax, no one here is going to harm you."

The beta's muscles loosened under his touch, his body settled, and Gus gave a smile when the monitors stopped. Luca's own fingers open slowly, the color returning to his knuckles as he sank into the pillows.

"Let's start with something a little easier. What do you remember?"

Gus could see the moment he slipped back into the memory, but he waited, fingers closing on the wrist below his touch. There were many aspects humans didn't know about pack abilities, about their heightened senses, and there were things many pack members didn't know about themselves. This was Gus's secret, that memories could be shared, that he could see their most recent ones if they were strong enough.

He could hear Luca quietly speaking, verbally telling the story, but in his mind, he became that person, experiencing what they had, and he was drawn into the last thing Luca remembered.

In the darkened forest he tripped, unable to rely on his depth perception, going down as the breath was knocked out of him. The blackness began to take over his vision as white dots floated in front of his eyes for only a moment before it came back into focus.

He was up again. The sound of angry voices, whistles, and the snapping of branches seemed to be right on his heels, but the growl of the dogs had him back on his feet. He moved, pushing up off the ground as he checked behind him, trying to see how close they were, gauging his chance of escape.

He made his way forward into the growing morning light.

Pushing through the trees, he stumbled out into the road, falling to the gravel with no thought of saving himself from the fall, but he rolled, covering his face with his arms as he came to a stop in the middle of it. Blood seeped from his side, coating the dirt a dark crimson color. His eyes were on the approaching light, two high beams in an otherwise empty darkness.

Luca was shaking when Gus slipped back, releasing his wrist. The alpha sat quietly for a moment, taking in everything he had seen and crossed his arms, not shielding himself from Luca, but mulling over the facts he now had.

"I don't know who was following me," Luca's voice pulled him from those thoughts, and Gus made eye contact with the beta, giving him his full attention. "I don't know who... I just... I know I had to get away."

There was nothing to say to that. Gustaf knew it was true. He felt the fear, his desperate need to run. Luca let out the first real calm exhale since he had entered the room, but as the beta stared at the ceiling a tear slipped down his cheek before his brown eyes were back on him.

"Alpha," he choked back a sob. "What happened to me?"

Keegan closed his eyes, pressed up against the metal lockers, his own door wide open so he could see the space inside. It was actually very organized, unlike everything else in his life. Books and notebooks were together by scheduled times, so he only had to grab and go, and they went back in that order as soon as he was able to get back to the locker. A place for everything... yada, yada, and today was like any other day.

Predictable.

It had been an ongoing, well-rehearsed act since the day before school began, and while he was always ready for a good fight, he really could have taken a pass on today.

He heard them the moment they were in range. Daniel and his

friends. To Keegan they were more like groupies. The three seniors followed him around like puppies just waiting for a treat from their master. None of them were even pack, they were human. Weak. Little. Humans.

Greg was the weakest of all, just a follower, just a sheep. So were Patrick and Steven, all part of the football team, but still none were a match for Keegan on his worst day. Today might be just that.

He shivered the second Daniel was by his side, his body heat close enough to wrap around him like a blanket. The scent of him was intoxicating and he hated the alpha for it. He hated the attraction, the fact that he couldn't get away fast enough, and more than anything, he hated that he wanted so badly to be touched by him, even if it was in a mock fight that they'd both walk away from. It never got to physical blows, at least none that would leave a mark, but he'd give anything for that contact.

Out of the corner of his eye, Keegan could see the predatory look on the other senior's face, not at all immune to how being so close to Keegan was doing the same thing to him, bringing out the animal nature, and for a moment, time stood still.

Until it all rushed in and the sounds from the hallway invaded his space.

"Well, well, well." Daniel's voice was low, mocking, but a whisper that seemed to sooth Keegan's own inner wolf. As Daniel shifted closer, his shoulder brushing intimately close, Keegan clenched his fingers around the spine of his history book. He never took his eyes off the gold-leaf lettering, grounding himself against the urge to reach out and touch, or rip it apart. It was the warmth breath against his ear that brought him back to the reality of the situation. "What do we have here?"

Releasing a slow exhale, something meant to keep him from giving in to the act of swinging, Keegan let his shoulders drop. His mind sung out to him; "*all part of the act, just stick to the script*," and without looking he swallowed and replied. "Don't you have something better to do?"

Wrong choice of words, at least with how Daniel leaned in, the weight of him settling against Keegan's back. "Maybe... If you're willing."

That was not at all what they agreed would be in the conversation.

Keegan slowly turned his head, unsure of what to do or where to go with that little bit of teasing, because he knew Daniel's "crew" didn't have the heightened sense to hear that offer. He swallowed back the reply, quieted the voice inside his head that screamed *"yes, yes, yes"* before making eye contact.

The flirtatiousness in Daniel's words were gone, his expression showed nothing of the desire Keegan could almost smell on him, and he scowled. The three backup dancers behind him waited on the captain's next move and knowing full well people were there for a show, Daniel didn't disappoint, as Keegan continued his stare.

"You might want to submit, little beta." Spoken with a deep, gravelly voice, the nickname quickly had Keegan bristling. It wasn't meant as the taunt it sounded like, but a plea for him to back down. Daniel dropped his chin only enough that the man in front of him would notice but his voice lowered with his next words. "Staring at me like that is only going to get you beaten."

Keegan dropped his backpack, still unzipped and half-full of books. The sound of it hitting the floor echoed even in the crowded corridor, and not breaking the stare, he stiffened, standing just a little bit taller. This was a game he could play, *wanted* to play, because sexual innuendos were just too much fun.

"You offering to get me off?" His voice went sultry, and the only one who would pick up on it was Daniel, whose cheeks flushed, and pupils blew wide. "You're not my alpha, Dick." And that itself had several meanings, one that Daniel quickly picked up on, especially when Keegan pressed his chest against his, clearly unafraid of the height and weight difference as he tilted his head back to stare up at Daniel with a smirk on his face. "Why don't you move out of my way before I show you...again...what this little beta can do to you."

It was Daniel's time to lead, like a dance, first one than the other, and he took half a step closer, leaning into Keegan, getting him to press back against the lockers. His breath caught, having blocked the beta in enough to see that line of his throat tighten, the thump of his heartbeat along the cord, and Daniel shifted. He flashed just a quick shine of his eyes, a fade in of the red behind his brown before it disappeared, enough to get Keegan's golden eyes glowing.

Daniel hated this part, the nasty stuff he had to say to really get Keegan going. "You might be one of the oldest packs, Summerford, but you're nothing without your brother."

Keegan cringed at that, even with the repetitive thought in his head that *"it's all a scam, he doesn't mean it"* but there was a saying amongst siblings, that they're the only one allowed to do or say bad things about the other but should someone outside the pack try... Keegan took that to heart. He and Noel might not be on the best of terms, but he'd put himself between him and danger in a second.

"Who do you think starts and ends it?" And he wasn't lying. He was the one with the temper, the issues, not Noel. He placed his hands against Daniel's chest, and at first, it was just to center himself, to get a moment of contact, but then he shoved, getting the alpha to take two steps back. "Here's a hint, it's not him. He's only there to mediate." Keegan pushed himself away from the locker. "Unlike you, he knows his place, and he knows I can take care of myself, but if you're feeling froggy..."

Keegan winked at him, gave a sarcastic smirk, a small gesture of *come on and try* was front and center, and while he knew Daniel wasn't truly going to make a move, the way the alpha rolled his shoulders, just for a moment, Keegan wasn't sure.

"Go on! Get to class!" The crack of Principal Hebert's voice boomed over the crowd, and just like that, it was over. Keegan hated the guy but was never so happy to see him in his life as he was at that particular second. Hebert, a rather robust man in what looked like a tweed jacket, complete with vest, stepped through the dispersing wave of seniors and juniors alike, his sights set squarely on Daniel and Keegan. "Do we have a problem, gentlemen?"

"No, sir," Daniel answered first, breaking eye contact with the man in front of him just long enough to pat Greg, the closest groupie to him, on the chest. It was Greg's glare, the blatant hate or misconstrued lust gleaming in his eyes, that had Keegan rolling his. "We were just leaving."

Keegan's gaze didn't leave their backs until Daniel, who continued to glance back at him, Greg and the other two varsity nobodies rounded the corner, disappearing with the rest of the crowd. It was only then that he reached down, grabbed his bag and turned back to his locker where he snatched his math book out and stuffed it down.

"Mr. Summerford—"

He scoffed at that, knowing that tone all too well.

"Don't bother." He closed the locker, twirling the combination with a little too much force, and turned, a fake smile planted on his face as he zipped the bag and hiked it over his shoulder. "I don't need your help."

"As a favor to your mother, it's my job to keep you from getting suspended, Keegan."

"Oh, still kissing ass? That's awesome." He shook his head, less than impressed with anything done for him in his mother's name, and he had heard that one plenty of times before.

"And if that keeps you from taking out the captain of the football team, well..." The smile was real this time, and maybe he had underestimated Hebert.

Maybe he really did understand Keegan just a little bit...or what Keegan could do when he swung. He slipped his arm into the waiting strap of the pack and hiked it up. "I'll tell her you said hello."

"Please do." Hebert slowly turned and headed down the hallway in the opposite direction, leaving Keegan to wonder what the hell just happened, before he himself moved into the thinning crowd.

He didn't see Paige, who stood in the doorway of the stairs, watching everything that had gone on. He didn't notice when she slipped away behind him, following but not engaging before she ducked into the hallway to the right, one filled with more rooms as Keegan continued straight and he sure as hell didn't see her walk right up to Daniel.

THE PAIN at the base of Ellie's neck wasn't anything new, it's where all her headaches started but this was just a little different. It had been going on nearly a week, and she was happy for once that she had a lower locker. She sat with her legs crossed on the cold floor in front of the door, having swung it wide open and unzipped her bag.

It was a backwards scheduled day, something the school thought would help fight off boredom, but Ellie hated it. Figuring out which books to grab with a tension headache slowly climbing your skull was a less than wonderful way to start your morning. She drew in a breath, glanced at the mirror in the back and went still for just a moment.

Her normal, deep blue eyes weren't at all normal, and they certainly weren't that deep ocean color. Right this second, they were Omega blue, enhancing the natural color in them with just a light glow. However, as soon as she leaned in to investigate them more, they faded. That might explain the headaches if her presentation was starting—finally, but she thought she'd have more signs.

Huffing, she grabbed the science book in front of her, and the bag, and stood way too fast to be recommended. The room swam, her focus blurred and for a second, and she saw black. The feeling of a hand on her lower back steading her, had her spinning this time and she pivoted, coming face-to-face with Mitch.

"Hey," his greeting was accompanied by a shy smile that Ellie thought bordered on sly.

"Hi." She stuffed her book into the bag, less than eloquently, and laughed when the zipper stuck. Mitch gently took it from her hands and finished zipping it as Ellie closed the locker. "Thanks, but what are you—"

"Listen, my dad—"

"Oh, God, are we doing this whole "we can't be friends" thing again, because I can't. I just have too much—"

"Okay, okay. I wasn't going to say that. Just give me a second, all right?" He held out her bag, a gesture of good faith that she wouldn't run away, and when Ellie took it, she saw the uncertainty in his eyes before she slipped it on and waited. "I miss you."

That was it, that was the emotion in his voice the night before, just this weird need that she couldn't pinpoint. "I miss you, too."

"I know we talked last night, but that was... I don't want to sneak around and wait for him to not be home to talk to my best friend. I want us to *be* best friends. It's stupid, and honestly, I don't care what my dad says." He paused a second, eyes wide that he had let that all slip, but what he got back in return was a beaming smile from the girl in front of him.

"We are still best friends." She slipped her fingers between his and gave him a gentle squeeze. "And thank you for last night. I needed that too."

The wide grin on Mitch's face made him look twelve instead of almost seventeen and he laced their fingers together. "Good. Me too. I mean...You don't know how much that means to me."

"I do," she sighed, as the headache eased just a bit at his contact.

"Good." His fingers slipped away as the bell tone echoed through the hall. "Walk you to class?"

"Sure."

Sitting in the cab of his truck, Noel's eyes focused on the phone in his hand, and the unanswered, unread text messages to his mother.

He has sent two since the incident with the SUV. One asking for an updated time of arrival, and the other was simply three question marks. He didn't understand why she wasn't replying. They had Wi-Fi on the plane, *any* plane, and he should have gotten something back by then.

Noel's foot shook to the point where the truck seemed to be vibrating, but he couldn't stop looking at it, even as he pulled at his fingernail, ripping it just a little. The pain of that nail breaking away from the skin was what brought him back to the present.

"Ow!" He waved his hand, as if that would stop the pain, but when he looked up and out the windshield, the waving halted.

From a park bench just across the green from him, Noel could see Keira. Her back was to him, her arms were going a mile a minute, which was usually what happened when she was talking passionately about something and for the first time that day, Noel actually smiled.

He slipped out of the car, hooked his bag over his shoulder and dug out his earbuds. No use bothering her with the odd doom and gloom the day had cast down on him. So, with those in and the music playing, he moved away from the truck, and his girlfriend, hoping to quietly slip into class unnoticed.

It didn't happen.

"Noel!" He could hear her just over the music, almost sensing her as she ran up behind him, grabbed onto his shoulders and tried as hard as she could to hop up.

If he wasn't so quick on his feet, he would have been taken down, but he managed to grab her by the back of her thighs and hold her up, giving her a short piggyback ride to the closest bench. Her touch seemed to brighten everything, lifting the haze he felt he was trapped in as he turned in her arms to wrap his around her waist.

"Hey," he grinned up at her.

Keira was beautiful, dark hair, bright hazel eyes, radiant in everything including her personality, which seemed to attract everyone, including those who he probably shouldn't be near, but she was also human and pack dynamics didn't apply to her.

Approaching footsteps caught his attention as Adin Michaels, who stood just as tall as he did and maybe a little wider, moved in their direction with a small group. He paused far enough away that Noel couldn't scent him, couldn't tell his intentions and that shouldn't have mattered. The college campus was neutral territory, there were no *packs* on the grounds, however, Noel couldn't help but feel the threat from Michaels, the defiant way the beta smirked at him.

That was Juli's next rule, to stay away from other packs if he could help it.

Things were fine, quiet among pack relations, but he knew there were those outside his own that would be out for Summerford blood, or at least their position on the World Council. It didn't help that Keira was friends with all of them, because she was friends with everyone. It was the way that Michaels looked at him, the way he stared defiantly, knowing Noel was an alpha, that got to him.

He couldn't help the flash of gold towards the beta, but it faded just as fast as it appeared. Michaels, as if he had just won some sort of unknown bet, smirked, glanced between the two of them, and turned away, taking the rest of the group with him.

Noel ducked his head, not giving away what had happened, but with a tired sigh. Taking it as a sign for comfort, Keira slipped her hands over his face, pressing her palms against his cheeks as she brought him in, kissing him hard.

Like a jolt of electricity, Noel felt every nerve in his body respond to her touch, and his hands gripped her shirt, pulling her in tighter as her kiss took over, tilting his head just a bit to capture her lips more, to pour everything into it.

Breathlessly, she slipped back, her forehead to his, with a wide smile on her face. "Maybe I should go away for the weekend more often."

"Oh, please, don't do that," he whispered, fingers still clenching, searching for something more than her sweater. "It was total hell, and with Mom gone..."

"I know," and she had the gall to giggle about it, "but we do have a free period, and my mom's not home."

Noel backed away at that, looking down into her eyes, hoping to find exactly what he did. She missed him too. "Tease."

"Oh, I'm not teasing," she laughed, going up on her toes as she wrapped her arms around his neck. "Far... far from teasing."

"We could always miss a class or two." Noel debated on just going home anyway. "Drive out to the lake house. I know where Mom hid the key."

"Tempting." She pushed him back, getting him to look her in the eyes. "But we already missed class Friday with that little stunt you pulled with the flat tire."

"Me?" He laughed, genuinely laughed. "How is that a stunt? It really was a flat tire."

"Ah-huh," she giggled, grabbed his hand, and jumped down from the bench, tugging him towards class. "What was that? With Adin?"

Noel glanced over the students that surrounded them, most just hanging out on the quad, sitting in groups, alone, or as couples. His eyes landed on a girl who leaned against a tree with a thick textbook in hand, and he shrugged.

He couldn't let go of the feeling that crawled along his spine, the tingling sensation of something behind them, and he rubbed his neck before looking back. Noel stopped again, there wasn't anything there. No threats, no one walking behind them. Nothing but students, but her hand on his arm had his eyes on her once more.

"What's going on with you? You're awfully jumpy."

Noel shrugged, giving her what he thought would pass as a debonair smirk, but the twang of a guitar string brought his eyes to a group sitting in a circle. He couldn't hear what the guitarist was singing, but with each pluck of the string, it grew louder, even off-key at points. It was nerve-racking, and he could feel himself cringing back, but again, her touch seemed to calm everything, and without even knowing he had closed them, he opened his eyes only to be locked on hers.

"I don't know." He let his forehead touch hers gently. "Full moon, maybe? You know I get itchy. Hormones?"

"Hormones?" Her laugh was like a balm, soothing over the frayed edges of his nerves and the sound of the people around them faded off to nothing but her scent, her heartbeat, just... Keira.

"Can we go somewhere private?"

"No," she scolded, not picking up on any of the signs that he was slightly on edge. "Class, remember? We just talked about this."

"Right. Sociology." His least favorite class.

"The full moon's three days away, right?"

He nodded. He knew when it was full every month without having to look at a calendar. It was in his make-up to *feel* it.

Noel kissed her forehead, took her hand in his again and moved down the sidewalk, hoping to get as far away from that guitar as possible. "I know, I'm just still hoping to get you alone."

"Keep trying. The semester's almost over, you just have to make it through a couple more weeks of him."

"One more year until graduation." He looped his arm over her shoulder, pulling her in close before kissing her head. "Until we can get away."

"You really want to run away?"

"I don't want to stay in Collins my whole life, that's for sure." Stopping outside the Wells building, a massive structure that held more auditorium classes than any other, Noel gently took her hands, bringing them up to his lips. "I want to go to Europe. I want to see the world, and I want you to go with me."

"After graduation." She punctuated with a smile, and that got him to chuckle.

"Of course, this place is too expensive to drop out now."

She gave him a playful swat before tugging on his hand, pulling him towards their first class, and the asshole of a professor that he's hated since his freshman year, mainly because Wilkes had it out for his father's position.

"Come on, Alpha, let's get today going. The faster we get there, the faster we can disappear."

Noel didn't let her see the way he bristled at the title when it fell from her lips. Lately being an alpha meant being pissed off more than anything, and at that moment he wished he was anything but, because he was starting to find out that alphas could be pricks.

Daniel stood by the open doorway with Greg, Paul, and Mark, three of the most annoying people Paige had ever met and she couldn't care less if she stepped on toes when she walked straight for them. Daniel had been watching the hallway, had seen her turn and beeline for him, but hadn't bothered to move until she pushed Greg out of the way.

"Hey, watch it." The human jock scowled

She turned; her whole five-foot-two frame turning towards the jock and glared up at him before whipping back around to put that look right on Daniel. Paige knew Greg was about to speak, to say something inappropriate to her when Daniel raised a hand, stopping it before it even came out of his mouth.

"It's cool." He grumbled as he wrapped his fingers around her upper arm and the two of them stepped away from the group, moving further down the hallway to a small alcove. Daniel kept his eyes forward, like a guard on watch as Paige slipped into the small space, back to the wall, knowing nothing would happen to her, not while he was there. The moment of silence stretched before Daniel couldn't take it anymore. "What's going on?"

"What the hell was that?" Clearly, she was upset, and Daniel knew he was in trouble. He raised both hands in defense.

"Look, I—" and she slapped him on his bare arm. It stung,

almost like a thousand bees had stung at once, and he shrunk back. “Ow!”

“He’s got enough shit going on, he doesn’t need the theatrics from you.” Daniel pinched the bridge of his nose and shook his head because he should’ve seen this coming. “It’s been six months, just come out of the closet already.”

He wasn’t even sure how to start this conversation.

“I want to, but—” That alone had her silent, which was new because Paige was never silent about anything that had to do with Keegan. “He doesn’t.”

“Why would he not—” She really was at a loss for words, and all he could do was smile.

“As if I could explain Keegan. You know him, and you’re the reason we’re doing this whole thing to begin with.” He didn’t mean to throw it at her like that, but it wasn’t a lie. He would have never pursued the beta if she hadn’t encouraged it.

“I told you to figure it out, not toy with his emotions. He’s on the edge as it is.”

“Yeah, I noticed that last night.”

“You saw him?”

“Before he went to your house. He asked me to come over.”

“Why didn’t you?”

“Because how would it look if two of us were jumping out your window at five-thirty in the morning?”

“I really don’t care.”

Daniel sighed. It was like they were the same person, Paige and Keegan, not caring about anything but each other... and him, which was what made it so hard. “I do.”

“That’s your problem.” She reached out and gave the raised red mark on his arm a gentle brush. “Just go easy on him.”

“I can’t promise anything,” he smirked, knowing she meant one thing while his brain went completely the other way. “We kinda have a thing.”

"Well, your *thing* sucks! And I mean it, Payne, today is not the day."

She slipped out of the alcove, into the suddenly empty hall, and Daniel peeked his head out. "Do you know why?" That question only got her to pause, confused. "Do you know why he's..."

"His mom? The Moon? PMS? Who knows, but... be gentle."

The only thing he could give her was a nod before she disappeared the way she came.

With a sigh, he leaned back against the alcove wall, and pulled out his phone. The text thread he searched for was listed under "Lil Beta," no real names and part of their plan, but he wasn't sure he wanted to keep playing this game anymore, he never intended to feel that way.

With a quick tap, he typed out *"I'm sorry,"* before hitting send and slipped the phone away as he headed out towards the classroom door.

CHAPTER 6

Noel paused at the door to the auditorium, curious about the lecture hall sign that read “Sociology: A Study in Pack Dynamics.” It wasn’t because of the title, he had regretted signing up for the class the moment he stepped into the room on the first day, but because the word “Dynamics” was covered by a piece of masking tape with a hastily scribbled word written across it. “Mythology.”

That can’t be good at all. No one knew their history on this campus better than his father, which was his expertise, his main field of study, so why did Wilkes, the asshole of assholes, think he could teach something like that to kids who were less than willing to even accept pack members to begin with.

“Oh, fuck,” Noel whispered as Keira tugged him into the room.

They made their way towards their usual seats, three rows down from the top, almost directly at the end and Noel plunked down in the seat, raising the tray up to set his bag on. He kept his head down, and eyes on the growing crowd as the room started to fill, thanking everything above that she was sitting beside him.

As the noise grew, and the seats were taken up, Noel could feel that itch under his skin, the way that being around so many people put him on edge, but he stretched out his fingers, hidden away by the chair, to brush the tips of them down Keira's leg.

Contact.

He hated that he needed it but at the same time loved that he craved it from her, and he closed his eyes, drawing in her scent, which for a human was fairly unique.

Raspberries, vanilla, just a hint of petrichor on a warm spring day. Every pack member was good at something, better at it than most, but Noel hadn't found his niche yet, he just kept being bombarded with all sorts of changes.

Sometimes it was his hearing, which ramped up so much he could hear a bee a thousand feet away. Or his sense of smell, where he could pinpoint his siblings across a football field in a crowd of people. His ability to focus on things further away heightened the closer the moon came to full. While it had its advantages, most of the time it made sunny days and brightly lit rooms uncomfortable, and the need for sunglasses had people assuming he was hung over. Noel tended not to drink for that very reason, he didn't need to actually experience a hangover, not if it felt like that.

Speaking of scents, he caught a very familiar one that had his head turning as Michaels stepped into the room. His sly, asshole-like smirk was plastered his face as he caught Noel's gaze for just a moment before heading back towards the furthest seat away from the alpha. Noel closed his eyes tightly, swallowed back the growl in his chest, and grasped onto Keira's fingers. In response, she simply laced her delicate ones through his and gave a gentle squeeze.

They were best friends growing up, neighbors at one point, and Keira spent most of her pre-teen years running around Noel's backyard, swimming in the pool with him and Keegan, but her family outgrew the house and suddenly they found themselves across town, away from each other.

Sneaking out at night became a thing, and when Noel hit fifteen, and his alpha side became apparent, her family tried to force them apart, to tell them that now that they were different, they weren't allowed to associate. That didn't stop them, not in the least, in fact it brought them closer together.

Keira knew every secret Noel had, every bad experience he had been through, and she was by his side every step of the way when his father died. It didn't matter if she was human, Keira was as much pack as anyone in his life, and Noel intended to keep it that way for as long as he could.

Ellie slid into her seat, eyes rolling as she glanced up at the board. Today's lesson: "Pack Dynamics."

Great, just what she needed.

Her hand went to the back of her head, rubbing at the tender spot at the base of her skull and sighed. She couldn't get rid of it, even the nurse's suggestion of an ice pack was less than helpful, especially now that it was just sitting on the edge of the desk like a squishy paperweight, having lost its chill ten minutes into using it.

Ellie crossed her arms on the desk and let her head drop down, cradling it as she closed her eyes. She just wanted to make it through one day. *One* day. That, of course, was a wish ungranted the moment she was bumped on her left side.

Turning her head, she came face to face with the smiling, bright-eyed expression of her other best friend, Reagan. Her red hair was all over the place, even with it pulled up in a bun, and the table shook as the girl tossed her bag down on it.

"Hey," she smiled, completely oblivious to the fact that Ellie was definitely having a moment, but she did her best to keep the girl in a good mood and sat up.

"Hey," she shrugged, unzipped the bag and pulled out her notebook.

"So," and that was a little more drawn out and dramatic than it needed to be, "I saw you with Mitchie this morning. You guys back together?"

"We were never together," she grumbled, hoping *that* rumor never got out. They were friends, best friends, and while Ellie could hope, she was sure they would never be more than that. "His dad and my mom just don't seem to see eye-to-eye. Ever."

"But that's what the classic love stories are made of." Reagan pawed at her arm, and Ellie's first thought was how much like a puppy she really was. Reagan was human, completely okay with the whole pack thing, but she couldn't see what all the fuss was about, and why Tobias Rollins was the biggest jerk in the history of parents. "Forbidden by feuding families, their love linked them forever."

"You know Romeo and Juliet died, right?" She scoffed, glancing at her before they both glanced up to see Mr. Heon step into the classroom. He was dressed in a button-up with a vest on, looking not quite as old as Ellie thought he might have been. Of course, at sixteen, everyone was old. Noel was old and he was twenty-two.

"Way to burst my bubble." Reagan crossed her arms, sitting back in her chair, as Heon moved towards the board, his mumbles of "good morning, class" was lost on the pair. "I'm just saying, I'm holding out hope that he figures it out. You'd be perfect together."

"It's high school, not a dating pool."

Both girls turned towards each other at the same time, and slowly the frowns on each face turned into a smile, as Reagan leaned in just a bit closer.

"Did I detect a bit of deflection in that tone?"

Ellie felt the blush on her cheeks, the way her neck heated up, and while she debated on denying it completely, she finally gave in. "Look, I'm not saying he's not..." She bit her lip for a moment. "I'm not saying he's not hot, but he's my best friend and that could go really bad."

"You won't know until you try." Reagan made a good point, a valid point, and Ellie sat back, nodding. "See, so next time you're with him, you just take him by the shirt and give it to him."

"Ms. Taber," Mr. Heon's voice had them both looking up, wide-eyed and embarrassed. "While your antidotes are more than enjoyable, class has begun, and today..." He turned away from them towards the board, raising the piece of chalk in his hand as he underlined the two words Ellie was already dreading. "Our topic is pack dynamics. There's a lot to cover, so let's get started."

Ellie closed her eyes, crossed her arms, and slipped down in the seat, already feeling the weight of the topic pressing down on her, but it was Reagan's sympathetic look that had her sighing.

This was going to be a very long day.

KEEGAN SAT in the back row of the classroom, closest to the window, eyes focused on nothing but the way the clouds started to roll in outside. The phone in his hand had already buzzed once, but that was more of a reminder than anything else. He just needed to wait it out. He knew something was coming, he just didn't know what.

In the background, above the humming in his ear, something that happened when he sank into his own little world, he could hear Mrs. Lemitts speaking, or mumbling. It was like one of those adults from an old Charlie Brown special that his mom loved to make him watch on holidays, but he wasn't paying enough attention to figure out *what* she was mumbling about.

It was the rolled-up ball of paper hitting him on the side of the head that finally caught his attention, and he whipped around to look at one of his close friends. Keegan didn't have *best* friends, he didn't think, he just had friends, and Mike Deluca was one of them.

The seventeen-year-old's animated face and big brown eyes had always interested Keegan, and by interested, it meant that he could spend hours looking at him. Keegan never thought of him sexually, which was good because Mike would pretty much take his head off if he had any inkling that he was interested, but there was just something about the already perfect lines of his face that Keegan was drawn too.

That and the whole expression of *"what the hell, dude?"* written on it at the moment. Keegan shook his head, going back to sky gazing. This time when the ball hit him, he kept his cool, but scowled at the other man before shaking his head. He was on edge, which was typical for him, he was always that way, and the meds never really helped, but as he tapped the edge of the phone on the desk, his eyes went to the math problem on the board.

As a feature, the tapping lit up the screen, and with a quick glance down. Keegan could see the text banner that took up a sliver of the home screen. "Bye Boi" was highlighted in blue and while there were words that followed, he hadn't opened it yet, not knowing what it might say, or what he hoped it might, but he was too wound up to chance it being something else.

Distracted by the screen, Keegan's thoughts opened him up to the sounds around him, including Mrs. Lemitts' voice.

"Okay, now we're going to try an exercise. On page two-twenty, I want you to do the exponential equation in logarithmic form." Her eyes landed on Keegan and the lack of books on his desk, giving him a frown before she went on. "But I only want the odds. You can work together in pairs. Long form, people. No cutting out steps and I want to see your work." Keegan followed her eyes to the clock as he reached for his bag. "You have fifteen minutes."

Shouldn't even take him that long. He pulled out his book, flipped it to the page, and was glancing over the problems just as Mike bumped his desk against Keegan. His hazel eyes settled on his friend for just a moment before Mike handed him a blank piece of paper. Keegan huffed at it, accepting it without a word and they worked quietly together.

For a moment anyway.

"What's wrong with you?" Mike's words shook him from his focus, and he didn't bother to look up, knowing that the other boy's gaze was locked on him.

"Too many people asking me what's wrong with me, that's what's wrong."

Mike's hand on his, stilling the motion of his pencil, had him sighing, but he shook it off. "You challenged an alpha in the middle of the hallway—"

"It was against the lockers."

"You could have gotten your ass handed to you."

That had him looking up, glaring as he put his pencil down. He laced his fingers together as he set them on the desk, his own way of keeping from reaching out, and let the smirk rise on his lips.

"You really think that little fucker could have taken me? Football player he might be, but he's far from a true Alpha." Mike's silence had him picking up the pencil again, hoping the topic was dropped, but just as he hovered it above the paper, his phone vibrated on his thigh. "I'm not exactly a weakling."

"You rely too much on your designation, Keegan."

Ignoring the jab, Keegan flipped the phone, and took in the new banner on the screen. "Bye Boi" again, this time the text is clear, and Keegan tapped it to open the thread.

Bye Boi: *You okay?*

Just above that were two words in their own little bubby. *"I'm sorry."*

He hated how it made him feel, how much he wanted to run to him, to tell him it was okay, and that Keegan wasn't affected by it, but it would have been a lie because he hadn't been able to shake off the feelings of Daniel being so close even after so long. He flipped the phone over, raised it to the desktop and slammed it down, albeit carefully. The noise muffled was by the low chatter in class, as he gave a low growl of frustration.

"Payne outweighs you by a good seventy-five pounds—"

"It's not even that much," and he knew because he remembered every moment of being pinned under his weight, but he shook it off. Trying hard to forget, he picked up the pencil, ignoring Mike, and scribbled out the equation.

"Not to mention he has his lackeys as back-up."

Fuck! Keegan grabbed the phone, unable to ignore it anymore, and quickly typed out *"fine"* before sending it. He poised to slam it down again but paused and instead did so gently. His gaze came up to meet Mike's, the worry in his friend's expression made his heart thump hard in his chest, but he just shook his head.

"I'm not afraid of them."

Mike shrugged that one off, eyes going to his paper. "Never said you were."

He couldn't concentrate, it was gone. Something in Mike's demeanor, the way he's been grilling him suddenly had Keegan all worked up, and he snapped. "What's your point then?"

Mike placed the pencil down, sitting back in his seat. "Your mom wouldn't want this."

Keegan grinned, not at all friendly, and leaned towards him. "My mom's not here." He glared, dropped the pencil and gathered his books, stuffing them in his bag. "She's never here." Mike's eyes grew wide as Keegan stood, snatched the completed paper from the desk and left him sitting there as he made his way to the front of the room. Mrs. Lemitts gave him a gentle smile as he slipped the paper on the desk. "Can I have a pass to the nurse?"

Looking over the work, she nodded, writing out a hall pass. "Not feeling well?"

Keegan glanced back at Mike, at the defeated way his friend looked down and away. "I've been better."

With the pass in hand, Keegan slipped from the room, almost silently as the door closed behind him.

AT THE FRONT of the class, Professor Wilkes made his appearance by stalking out of the shadows. Noel bristled at the way he scanned the class and headed right for the podium. There was just something about him, something off that made the animalistic part of him unsure, but it might just come down to the fact that Wilkes was nothing more than an ass.

The doors to the auditorium closed behind him, clicking shut, and as Wilkes stood there, the voices in the class started to quiet down until you could almost hear a pin drop if it wasn't for the racing sound of Noel's own heart.

It's the moment that Wilkes stepped back from the podium that really got Noel's attention, because the small, black device in his hand only meant one thing. The sudden noise of the white backdrop lowering from the ceiling sent chills up his arm and he shifted forward, anticipating the need to run.

"Lights, please." Wilkes's voice boomed through the wide-open space, and as they lowered, a picture of two battling wolves filled the screen. Blood and fur, bared teeth and claws filled Noel's vision as he stared, but he shrank back at the same time, trying to become smaller, to not feel the eyes on him. "Last class, we started the section on pack dynamics and how it's changed our way of viewing the world when it comes to political standings. Today, we're going to change it up a bit. Pack history, or more to the point, pack mythology." He gestured towards the screen. "Anyone care to recap for those who missed the last lesson?"

Right up front, two rows from Wilkes, Noel's eyes trained on the young woman who raised her hands. His eyes widened, the room came into full view even in the dim light and he could almost see the blood pumping through her veins, like the nightmarish werewolf in his dreams.

"Ms. Carmichael," the professor grinned as she stood, "what do we know?"

"We know packs make up less than ten percent of the population, but the majority of that ten percent control some of the highest-ranking positions in the United States alone."

Noel blinked at that one. That wasn't right. He didn't remember that from the last class. Packs tried to stay hidden, to blend in, to live under the radar. There weren't even enough of them in Congress to blink at.

"Very good."

"No," the voice inside his head screamed. *"Totally wrong."*

"But what do we know about their history?" Behind Noel, up closer to the wall, a hand rose catching his attention. While *Ms.* Carmichael sat down, Wilkes pointed at the hand. "Mr. Faraday, care to give it a whirl?"

Noel shifted in his seat, focusing on the thin, young man in the back who nervously pushed his glasses up further on his nose. Not pack either, just like the girl, but his eyes went right to Noel. The alpha licked his lips, curled his fingers, digging into his own palms and Noel could almost smell the blood he drew as he took a breath, then faced Wilkes again.

"I have more of a question."

"Ask away."

"Why history?"

Noel shook, turned away from him and slipped back down again, hand searching for anything to hold onto.

"Excellent question," and he pointed right up at the violence on the screen. "Know thine enemy."

"But they're not—"

"It's just a figure of speech," Wilkes stalled his protest, getting the twitchy man to sit back down. "However, it still rings true. If you recall not ten years ago, we knew nothing, or the world knew nothing, of our friends. Our little corner of paradise had always suspected, but the world—" He started pacing the stage, eyes going from one known pack member to the other, including Noel, who he zeroed in on holding his gaze. "Luis Santana wasn't the first to step forward when the controversial findings of the Lupinus Marker came to light."

The sound of the class rose at that, and Noel shook, holding back his own thoughts. They were controversial, they were against the law. People never even knew that their DNA was being studied, not when they purchased the test, not when they submitted it. They were only looking for connections to the past, not knowing they were giving scientists what they needed to find abnormalities in the strands.

"No, no. He was just the first in Congress to open his mouth and address the fact that hidden among us was a race we hadn't known about, would have never known about if it weren't for that test."

"Illegally obtained information," a voice from the back spoke up, deep and irritated, and Noel—like Wilkes—searched the crowd. "That doesn't mean anything."

"Mr. Myers, please stand up."

Confident in himself, Devon Myers stood, arms crossed and relaxed as his eyes went right to Noel before landing on Wilkes. He wasn't intimidated by the size of the class, or the fact that they were outnumbered, but he held Wilkes's stare with unwavering cockiness.

"Let's hear it again."

"The information on the Lupinus Marker was illegally obtained. The Supreme Court ruled on it and people were compensated. The only reason it was leaked to begin with was because of Santana. These people have the right to live in peace, just like the rest of us. And how do you know this is true at all? Whatever history you're coming up with? How do you know this is all true?"

"How do you know it's not?"

The murmurs in the room grew, causing Noel to flinch at the sound, but Myers met his gaze and slowly sat back down having said his piece. He didn't believe a word of it, and Noel gave him a small nod, something that echoed back as Myers raised his chin just a bit.

"History. It's not whether you believe in it. It's what's written down for us to learn." A bullshit line if Noel had ever heard one, but when most of the class hung on his every word, Wilkes seemed to be able to get away with anything. "Anyone else?" The room fell into silence once again, the only noise was the hum of the projector. "This is going to be a very boring class if I'm the only one dragging on about this. Participation is seventy-five percent of your grade."

Noel ran his hand down his face, pinching his nose to stem off the headache that was beginning to grow between his eyes, and he wondered how fast he could get out without being seen.

THE CLICKING of the chalk against the blackboard did nothing to help ease the tension at the back of Ellie's head, even with her hands over her ears, but she toughed it out. She never missed class, as much as she would love to drop out of this one because the guy at the front of the room was a jerk. She didn't think of most of her teachers in that light, but Heon was definitely the one that held that honor above the rest.

"Alpha, beta, omega." The three words that graced the board were spoken aloud in his muffled voice before he turned to the class, waiting. Ellie must have missed something when a hand went up in the back of the room. Jeff, a gangly kid who she was sure she recognized from her neighborhood, raised his hand with an impatient grimace on his face. "I haven't even asked a question yet."

"This isn't about designation or dynamics, but—this guy, the one that wrote the book? Was he even part of a pack?"

Oh, maybe she hadn't missed anything, and the question had her sitting up just a bit straighter.

"It doesn't mention it, but what's your opinion on it?"

"I don't think he knows anything."

She tried to hide the smile that crept up on her lips as the class erupted into less than quiet chaos, and Jeff's eyes met hers before he quickly looked away.

"Care to explain?"

He closed the textbook on his desk, hand gently caressing the cover as if the art on it would give him some inspiration before shrugging and turned his eyes to the teacher in the front of the room. "Okay, well... He stated in this book several times that the duties of an omega are, and I quote "to ensure the happiness of an alpha." Pretty sure that's wrong."

Ellie knew for damn sure *that* was not the case at all.

Lindsay, the pretty blonde cheerleader from the front of the room, cleared her throat expectantly and answered, "wrong how?" It was said more as a scoff, like her little human brain could wrap itself around pack dynamics better than anyone else in the room, and Ellie rolled her eyes. "No matter who wrote it, these are the facts. Unless a pack member," and her eyes narrowed in on Jeff, "comes forward and corrects it, which doesn't seem to be something they want to do, this is what we have."

She wasn't necessarily wrong, but the fact that they were discussing something that shouldn't even be in school was getting on Ellie's nerves. Pack dynamics, while not sacred or a secret, was something no one outside a pack was ever going to understand.

"And it's bullshit," Jeff concluded with such force that Ellie smiled.

She turned away, covered her face with her hands to hide the smile, and slowly lowered her face to the book. She was done with class, done with everyone trying to figure out the structure of her family, and certainly done with the argument that was now going on between Jeff and Lindsay.

She sat back just a bit, grabbed her phone from her hoodie pocket, and scrolled through her text messages, finding Noel's without issue before she typed out a text and hit send.

THE VIBRATION of the device in his back pocket had Noel suddenly shifting in the chair, surprised by the force of it, and he dug it out quickly to find Ellie had texted, which was odd because she barely sent him anything unless he was out, and she needed something from the store.

Quickly opening the thread, he gave a small smirk at the frustrated message that graced his screen.

Ellie: *They're arguing about pack dynamics, and I don't want to be here anymore.*

With a quick look around, he let his thumbs do all the work as he replied: *"Me either."*

"All right, all right!" Wilkes yelled above the cacophony of noise in the room. "Let's get it together. We're all semi-adults here, so, what do we know about packs now?"

Noel rolled his eyes as Carmichael stood again.

"Alphas are annoying, overbearing, and authoritative."

"Wow," Noel shook his head and mumbled, "bitch."

Keira's giggle eased the growing tightness in his chest as the student up front continued.

"They control the rest of the pack, right down to the omegas."

"That's not—" He started to say through clenched teeth, but Keira's hand against his chest had him second guessing throwing anything out there.

Wilkes waved her off. "Thank you for your opinion, and for the segue into our history lesson." He turned to the screen, the little black device in hand, and clicked to the next picture. A seemingly innocent pack of wolves running through the woods. "Packs, or more specifically, where they come from in regard to mythology."

The small *click, click, click* as Wilkes scrolled through each picture grew louder, enhanced as Noel took in each picture, gradually becoming more and more violent. Wolves covered in blood ripping apart a deer. One with a white coat saturated red. Two wolves, one black, one chestnut, going for each other's throat.

"The one you feed..." His father's voice echoed in his mind as his body started to shake, and his thoughts rolled with the images of the way things looked on that dreamscape. The dark greens, blacks, and grays. Night vision zeroed in on the doe staring at him before he rushed it. *"The battle between two wolves..."*

A low growl emanated through the room, and Noel struggled to find where it came from, only to see all eyes turned to him. Keira tried to take his hand, but he shook it off as he shrunk down again.

"Shit."

KEEGAN MOVED DOWN THE HALL, away from his math class. There's no one else around, won't be for several minutes, which was good, it gave him time to get away. He made his way towards the gym, flinging open the door, only to pause at the sight of the empty basketball court, one that took most of the gymnasium floor. *Perfect.* Pulling the straps on his bag tighter, Keegan headed for the door at the furthest edge of the court, and with a not so gentle push, he stepped out into the cloudy morning air.

Turning right, he slipped around the building, heading towards the loading docks behind the cafeteria. He'd be safe there; he just needed a minute to get his head on straight as the morning events caught up with him. He climbed onto the dock, took a few deep breaths, and pulled the phone from his pocket.

There was still a thread open, still those words from *him* on screen, and Keegan debated, thumbs hovering over the keyboard for a moment. He had no idea what to write, how to respond, how to ask, and quickly he tucked the phone away, eyes going to the clouds.

"Fuck!" He whispered, wiping the side of his hand across his eye, preventing the emotions from forming as he rested his elbows to his knees. Maybe he should just go home.

The blessed silence of the outdoors soothed him, at least for a moment. Eyes closed, taking in the scents. From where he sat, he could almost imagine himself in the middle of the woods, under the falling leaves as the breeze slipped through the trees. The fall chill on his bare skin while he stood at the top of the quarry, shirtless, just soaking in the sunshine.

But the peace never lasted, at least it was always interrupted, and this time it was the pulsing noise of an alert from the phone in his pocket that shook him from it. Rushing to draw the vibrating thing from his jeans, he fumbled it before finally getting control, but while he expected one thing, what he got was completely unexpected.

He stared down at the screen, at the Amber Alert banner that took up most of the middle of it, covering the lock screen picture. *Alesha.* The name on the screen was Alesha, and it described her perfectly.

He could see her, head poking out of the doorway, little fingers waving at him in the glow of the overhead security light, grinning.

Keegan tapped the screen, pulled up the details, and froze.

She was last seen leaving Cafe West after her shift, described as wearing her uniform with a black backpack. Her car was still in the lot when the manager arrived just a little while ago.

"What the fuck?"

He closed his eyes tightly, held back the scream that threatened to rip out of him, and clenched the phone tightly. He had to breathe but couldn't get it out. Had to calm his racing heart but there was nothing stopping the pounding in his chest.

The sound of the bell was the only outside stimuli that made him move and he knew exactly where he needed to go.

His eyes were golden when he opened them, focused on the crop of maples across the field, and with a sigh, he grabbed his bag, jumped down from the dock, and headed back the way he came.

KEIRA'S EYES CAPTURED HIM, forcing him to shake off the feeling just under the surface.

"You, okay?"

"Yeah," he nodded, feverishly, "fine." So, why was he sweating?

Keira didn't buy it, not for a second but Wilkes's voice caught their attention.

"Let's talk wolves—"

"Oh, God, let's not," but that plea was just a whisper.

The feeling of Keira's eyes on him once more was not something he could ignore. "Are you sure?"

But his only answer was a nod as Wilkes finished his statement.

"—Specifically, werewolves."

It was as if the whole class was looking right at him. Noel curled his fingers into his palm, hoping to hold on for just a little bit longer, as he stared down at the professor. He needed to keep his cool, needed to not freak Keira out, but it was growing harder by the minute.

"We'll start with Greek Mythology."

The *click* vibrated through him as the screen lit up with the depiction of a naked man running through the streets, his teeth and chin covered in blood, a wild look in his eyes. Lycan, the story of the first werewolf.

Whatever the professor was spewing turned into incoherent, muddled words as Noel stared at the screen. The only thing he could really hear clearly was the beat of his heart, and then the screams. They came out of nowhere, women and men alike and the black and white drawing in front of him became covered in crimson.

"—Narratives that transformed to what we know today as a story of a man who could turn into a wolf..."

The sound of the *click* shocked him, his whole body jolted with it and the next slide was met with the rise of bile, something he fought to keep down, as the long black muzzle of a wolf sank into the neck of a woman. Not just a wolf, a werewolf.

"... But werewolves themselves are believed to be of English origin. A creature of the night that shifts into a beast, not necessarily true wolf form, which feeds on humans, corpses, and animals..." But the next slide is one of modern times, of people speaking to one another in a group, which has Noel completely confused. "Who during the day is a normal human."

Oh, that explained it.

Wilkes turned back to the class, and the lights rose just a little to illuminate the room. "Who can tell me the difference between Lycanthropy and Therianthropy?" As the students whispered amongst themselves, Wilkes grinned, as if an actual wolf in sheep's clothing, eyeing over his prey. "I see I have you stumped."

Noel sat up straighter at the next slide, split down the middle with a man in a straitjacket on one side huddled in the corner and a screencap from *"American Werewolf in London"* on the other. "What the hell?"

"Clinical Lycanthropy is the definition of someone who *believes* they can shift on a full moon."

Carmichael raised her hand up front and even Keira shook her head this time. "Therianthropy is the ability to shift into any animal. Like Skinwalkers."

"Very good, but partially wrong. Navajo legends are a completely separate topic. However, yes, it's the ability to shift into any animal. Ten points to Google."

She quickly sat down as the next slide continued its gory story.

Noel closed his eyes, the sounds of the heartbeats in the room began to magnify as the feeling of heat in his chest grew. Wilkes's voice seemed to fade again into muffled sounds, and Noel reached for Keira's hand, letting her hold it tight, begging for it to ground him.

As she whispered softly in his ear, he could feel her breath against his skin, but there was nothing but the heartbeats, the rush of blood pumping through veins. He couldn't control the shaking anymore, or the sweating. His shirt was soaked. He was losing the battle.

Ellie plugged her ears, tired of the fighting in the room, the escalation of voices, and she tried her best to block it out, until the bell rang.

"Okay, shake hands, kiss and make up. Remember homework is due tomorrow at the start of class."

Ellie grabbed her bag, thankful that this one was done, and headed towards the door, praying the next class wouldn't be as bad, but she yanked her phone out and sent a message off before she even hit the threshold.

With a shaking hand, Noel pulled the phone from his pocket, relieved for the distraction as he opened his eyes just enough to see the text from Ellie.

Ellie: *Thank God, that class is over.*

Wilkes' words echoed through the room. "Okay, let's go about this another way."

And the tension in the back of his neck pulled on the muscles in his shoulders as he stiffened at the picture on the slide. A full werewolf, head back, claws stretched out, howling at the moon.

His vision blurred as he was dragged back into the nightmare, standing up on two legs, blood dripping from its mouth, surveying the forest. Silent. And with a deep inhale, its chest expanding in the chilled night air. It tilted its head back to the sky and let out a long, mournful howl.

Noel bolted upright, grabbed his bag, and kissed Keira on the head before he darted from the room, leaving nothing behind but the sound of the door slamming shut behind him.

It was as if the world had come crashing in. Juli sat up, eyes wide, bright red, and clear as day, but at the same moment the sharp pain from the needle ripping out of her surged up her arm. Instinctively she slapped a hand down to cover the bleeding, but it only slickened her hand.

Her alpha red eyes gave her the ability to see in the dark, or at least as much as she could with what little light streamed in through the bottom of the door. The gap between the floor and the bottom of it was at least an inch, and with that she could filter enough light in to make out anything else in the room.

The IV bag hung on a hook above the cot. There was a small sink on the other side of the room, but she doubted there was running water. The metal toilet in the opposite corner was not something she would normally use, but the empty bag told her she had soaked up at least a thousand milliliters of some sort of solution. With that much liquid, there was no holding back the uncomfortably full feeling in her bladder.

She stood on shaky legs, pushed herself to stand, and used the wall to find her way around the room. She was groggy, hungover from probably a second dose of the sedative, and her body was protesting the movement in all ways possible, but nature was nature.

When she was done, while shivering from the chill the fluids had caused and happy that there was at least toilet paper available, she fought to make her way back to the cot, having exerted all her energy just to make it to the toilet. She wished for water, or hand sanitizer, and kept her hands away from her face, but it still didn't sit well with her.

Who the hell were these people? Why was she there? *Where* was she?

It all came back to her as soon as she sat down on the cot. The way he stood, the aim of the gun, the sound of the dart whooshing from the chamber, and while she knew who had taken her, she still didn't know why.

She remembered the summit, the way she spoke up in front of so many leaders, the words that tumbled from her lips. *"In the past few years, more and more pack members have gone missing from Hampden, Hampshire, and Worcester counties than any other in the entire state— No, the entirety of New England. There should be more that we can do as a whole than sit back and wait for agencies that couldn't care less about our communities, to get their heads out of their asses, and look into things."*

She was positive whoever had taken her didn't like what she had to say at the summit. She was getting too vocal, too close to the cause of the kidnappings, and while she hadn't said anything to those who happened to surround her, she had a sneaking suspicion she and Gus were closing in on the person responsible for it.

She leaned forward, elbows to her knees, as she tented her hands over her nose, breathing in to stem off the chill. She had done this to herself, and now she had no idea what to do next.

CHAPTER 7

"County General - 10:15 a.m."

THE CONSTANT BELLS and whistles of the hospital floor seemed to drown out the words of the physician even with how close he stood to him. The medical terminology wasn't new to Gustaf, he understood the diagnosis perfectly, he just didn't care.

He needed to move the beta in the room to a secured facility, that much was apparent after speaking to Luca, but to go against medical advice without knowing the full scope of his injuries wasn't the best plan. He had to get these people to understand the urgency required for this move.

There were only a few things that sunk in from the long-winded speech the doctor had given him. Luca may never regain his memories of what happened to him, or even who he was apart from his name, and that put him in more danger than the physical damage done to his body.

Ten-thirty and no word from Juli, or Doug, which bothered him. He knew it was an unscheduled flight, and Doug had been the one to call and set it up. He also knew it took time to get a flight plan secured and approved, but it still shouldn't have taken this long to get some sort of update on a three-hour flight.

Glancing back at the sleeping beta through the security windows, Gustaf scrubbed a hand down his face and back through his hair. He was still cuffed to the bed, hooked up to more monitors than Gus would like, but it was quiet, and all signs show that he wasn't in any pain. On the plus side, the IV bags were gone, so he was no longer in danger of the effects of dehydration.

After a moment of stillness, he drew his phone from his pocket, and tapped the screen, searching through his contacts for one specific person, Tobias Rollins. Before beginning the call, he checked the handle, making sure the door was secure, and headed away from Luca's room.

Pressing the call button, Gus placed the phone to his ear, and waited for the call to connect. It only took three rings.

"Alpha," the gruff voice on the other end of the line cooed, which made Gus roll his eyes, *"such a pleasure."* The fake excitement was just a bit more annoying than his regular greeting, but he didn't have time to scold the man in formalities. *"And what a surprise to hear from you. To what do I owe this honor?"*

Gus paused in the hallway before answering, standing in front of an office door, and with one quick look in each direction, he grabbed hold of the handle and yanked down, breaking the lock. He ducked inside, made sure to tug it closed, and glanced around at the tidiness of the room.

"We have a rogue," was his only response as he moved behind the desk, plunked down in the chair before letting the little edge of exhaustion take over.

Rollins sat back, rocking as he shifted, and smiled, pen against his lip. It always amused him to push the man's buttons but the growl

on the line told him that he wasn't playing around. He sat up straighter, dropped the pen on the desk, and waited.

"A rogue what?"

"A rogue member, you idiot." The bark in the man's voice had Rollins at attention, something Gus seemed to be the only one able to do, but he was determined not to let him in on his reaction and cleared his throat.

"I'm well aware that you're referring to a pack member, Alpha, however, I need to know their designation."

GUS TIPPED his head back on the rest, blinked a few times to clear out the red haze around his vision, and unclenched his jaw.

"Does it matter?" He stretched out his hands, uncurling his fists to relieve the ache caused by clenching them so hard, and waited. Talking to Rollins always had him on edge.

"Not in the grand scheme of things, no. However, if I send someone out and your rogue is another alpha, there are precautions that need to be taken."

He pulled the phone away knowing that Rollins was not wrong and grumbled. "There's a rogue beta at County General, I need him moved."

THE SMILE CREPT up on his face once more, as his body relaxed, the hold the alpha had over him dissipated, and Rollins once again sat back in his seat.

"Of course, Alpha." He quickly pressed the red button on his landline phone before continuing. "Is there any specific place you'd like me to bring this beta?"

The question was met with an angry rumble over the line. *"You know where,"* and the pause had Rollins smiling wider. *"Get it done."*

The sound of the disconnect was never as much fun on a cell phone as it used to be. He had known Gustaf for ages, and it seemed a routine for the alpha to slam down the receiver when tethered to a landline, but this new age of hand-held devices just lacked the abrupt click and the following dial tone Rollins always loved.

He placed the cell down on the desk, less than satisfied, and scowled when the quiet knock on the door accompanied it opening. The man that slid in was almost silent, despite his size, and he folded his hands in front of him, waiting for the man behind the desk to speak.

"Assemble a team." Rollins slipped the chair back as he stood and moved to the window, taking in the warmth of the sun that filled the room. "We have a guest to pick up at County General." The lack of verbal response had him turning to eye over the man. Smith gave a nod. "Three should work."

"Yes, sir. Will you be joining us?"

"No, I have an appointment on campus. I'm sure you know what to do with our new friend."

Smith once again nodded, reached back for the knob, and slowly slipped out. Rollins grabbed his jacket, buttoned it against the fall weather outside, and slipped his phone off the desk, tucking it in his pocket as he grabbed his keys. With a smile, he too slipped from the room.

In a darkened corner of the library, Keegan huddled up, his knees pulled to his chest, eyes closed tightly, nearly gasping for air. His fists were clenched, pressed firmly to his chest as the world around him seemed to sway. His jaw ached at the tightness there, trying to get it to relax, but he was in the midst of an anxiety attack, and nothing seemed to be working.

His coping mechanisms were useless. Five things he could see... it just wasn't working.

He couldn't believe Alesha was gone. He just saw her! How could she be missing? What about Ellie? Where was Ellie?

He drew out his phone, quickly typed out a message, and hit send, shaking while he waited for a response. What he got back didn't ease the anxiety, but Ellie was safe.

Ellie: *I'm in class, what do you want?*

He didn't return the message.

Everything had been leading up to this, he knew it, but he hadn't stopped it and purposely left his meds at home. He hated that he was tethered to them, that he hadn't found a way to get it to stop without them, but this... this feeling of uselessness, of being unable to stop his own reactions to things angered him and made it worse.

He could hear the sounds of people, the indiscernible chatter outside the walls of the library, but even with putting his hands to his ears, it only grew louder, and the elephant on his chest became a crushing weight. He tried to become smaller, to huddle in more, but nothing worked.

Until the sound of a bird twittering silenced everything.

On the ground beside him, his phone lit up, the screen blindingly bright against the darkness of the space he had put himself in. With a shaking hand, he reached for it, bringing it closer, holding it between his knees and his chest as his vision blurry with tears, and he focused in on the screen.

It was a text message.

Bye Boi: *Where are you? Class started ten minutes ago.*

He wiped his eyes, the tension in his chest released one respiration at a time, and with shaking thumbs he replied. This could be it, the salvation he needed.

Library, he answers, *having trouble.*

The bubbled reply came not seconds after his was sent.

Bye Boi: *Need me?*

Keegan chuckled because how funny was that? He never wanted to admit he needed anyone but suddenly, there it was, written on the screen. All he had to do was say... *Yes!* And he sent the text out. He struggled to catch his heart as he dropped the phone, prayed that he made the right choice, prayed that he wouldn't show up and hand Keegan his ass, but even that would be better than feeling this helplessness.

It didn't take as long as he thought to hear the library door opening, the tell-tale squeak of it closing on a rusty hinge. It was the click of the lock that had Keegan on his feet, eyes wide as he breathed through his nose, backing up into the corner.

There wasn't time to fight, or even to compose himself before he was pushed back further against the wall, blocked in by a body, by a weight he knew well, craved even, and he did his best not to panic when warm, strong hands cupped his face, touched his neck, wiped away the tears instead of bringing on more.

The wetness of lips pressed against his, and he let his eyes slip shut, giving into the feeling of the heat that followed that kiss. The tender way they showed dominance even with the rough tug as the collar of his shirt was pulled aside, and he let his head drop back the moment they left, trailing down over his neck, sucking on the skin at the curve of it, thumbs tracing the muscles there.

He was lost in the moment, the feeling of them holding him up, gripping his shirt, giving him the contact he needed, longed for, bracing him in, and suddenly, panic took over.

His heart raced, his eyes flew open, and his hands came up to push at the broad shoulders of the man in front of him.

"Wait, wait, wait." He shifted against him, fingers clenching, pushing but pulling at the same time, his eyes golden filled with emotions, and everything slowed as Daniel backed away.

Confusion written in his expression, his dark eyes roamed over Keegan's features, taking in the brightness of the power in his gaze, but as his hand landed on the beta's neck again, the panic registered and Daniel shifted back, giving him space, more worried than before.

"Jesus," his words were soft, comforting, nothing like he had been in the hallway. "You weren't kidding." The panic seemed to ease, and suddenly, Keegan was smirking, his defenses slipping up, and he tensed, ready for a fight. "I didn't—"

"It wasn't you," the smaller of the two confessed, but Daniel didn't move. He knew this tactic, had learned it well over the last six months, maybe longer if he was honest with himself, but he only gave a huff. "It's fine."

"It's not fine, Key, stop—"

And his protest was halted by the feeling of a bruising kiss as Keegan gripped his shirt and pulled him in tight. Daniel grabbed his hands, slipped his thumbs between Keegan's white knuckled fingers, prying them loose enough to slip back, only to find the beta's eyes shifting from his lips to his gaze.

"I just need..." There was something in those words that Daniel couldn't decipher, he could hear it, but didn't understand the emotion. "I just need this."

He lowered his hands, letting Keegan have his shirt as he slipped his arm around his waist, bringing him closer while backing him up, blocking him in again. He was bigger than him but not by much, and the fact that the angry man between him and the wall was allowing this was something that tugged at Daniel's heart. Keegan wasn't the easiest person to care for, fought him at every turn, but this...

"This I can do," and he leaned in slowly, drawing back when Keegan tried to connect before he was ready, getting the low, frustrated sound he was counting on, feeling it rumble between them and, oh, so gently, he brushed his lips against Keegan's. Once. Twice, and then smiled at the sigh that finally escaped the beta as he closed the distance.

Keegan needed this to be slow, not a fight between them, not him being an alpha and dominating everything. He knew Keegan needed to be shown gentleness, and he intended to give it all to him.

Gus's light eyes scanned over the borrowed room, taking in the neatly organized office before he rolled his shoulders, tucked his phone away, and ducked out into the confusion that filled the medical floor.

The space in the small hallway grew less and less the closer he came to the nurse's station. Shift change was upon them, and Gustaf was stuck in the middle of the chaos. He watched as folders changed hands, one station was traded for another, and unfamiliar faces filled his view.

He honed his power, blocking out the rest of the unnecessary noise to focus on the one person he was trying to find. He could hear her heartbeat, had memorized it for just this occasion and no matter how many other nurses, men and women alike, offered their help, his focus was only on her.

Marie glanced up from the chart in her hand as she approached the desk, her pen pausing on the paper, and she paused in front of him. "Is everything alright?"

Thrown off by the concern in her voice, Gus only smiled and nodded, slipping his hand gently around her elbow as he guided her to a small alcove away from prying eyes, before he exhaled slowly. Human hospitals were too crowded for him. They held too many scents, too much noise, and the effort to block it out put him on the wrong side of pleasant.

"Ms. Penn," he whispered, drawing on the fact that she was not like him, and had been more than helpful, to keep his attitude in check, "I need a favor. I have several pack members coming by to help escort Mr. Morrin to one of our facilities—"

"He's not stable enough to leave."

Gustaf raised his hand at her protest, giving her the best smile he could before he nodded. "I realize that, but he needs to not be *here*, not with what he's been through. Our facility is better equipped to deal with," his eyes went to the door before he continued, "pack members in Mr. Morrin's... condition. I would hate for you to get hurt helping him. Would you be so kind as to get him ready for transport?"

"Mr. Segal, against medical—"

"I know, but that's not up to your doctors to decide if he can leave or not. He's volatile, and I'm afraid he might hurt himself or others giving his care if he's left in the hands of people who—" He scoffed, shaking his head. He didn't know how to be gentle, not like he needed to be. "Your safety, Ms. Penn, that's my main concern. As Pack Second, it's in my right to have him moved."

"You're the pack emergency contact."

"Precisely, which also gives me power of attorney should this specific occasion arise. I'm sorry to go above you."

"No," she glanced around at the people passing by. "I understand. Is there anyone I should contact?"

"No one at all. I've already made the calls and have people on the way." Marie nodded, though the disapproving look in her eyes told Gus she didn't agree with it at all. "Could you have an ambulance waiting to help transport him? We'd use our own drivers and return it as soon as he's relocated."

"Is that part of the power of attorney?"

"No," he smiled at the aggravation in her tone, almost proud that she was voicing it at all since most people hid from anyone with pack affiliations. "It's more of a favor."

"Of course." Her small defiant smirk had the grin on his face widening. "I'll do my best."

"They should be here within the hour."

She gave a curt nod and with a quick glance right into his eyes, squared her shoulders, and stormed off.

Gustaf didn't hold back the smirk as he watched her go. She wasn't the first person outside the pack to stand up to him, or give him even a little bit of hell, but she was definitely the prettiest.

He pulled the phone from his pocket, ducked out of the corner they had occupied, and headed down towards the elevator, dialing out as he went. It rang only twice before a low voice on the other end picked up.

"This is Segal. I need to know what you can find on Luca Morrin." He eyed the way the scrub-covered wave of people seemed to fold together.

"Moran?"

"No. Morrin... two R's and an I, N."

"Got it. Any other information?"

"No, no other at this time." The door slid open revealing an empty elevator, giving him only a moment to step in before the doors began to close.

"That's not much to go on."

"Just get it done and call me back!" He yanked the phone away and ended the call as the doors closed, shutting out the sounds that assaulted his ears.

The door swung open, banging back against the brick of the building's exterior as Noel made a break for the sidewalk. He never heard Keira's voice behind him, never even sensed her presence in any way, his hazy vision and sole mission was locked on getting as far away as possible.

It wasn't until the feeling of fingers wrapping around his sensitive skin that he even realized anyone else was nearby, and he twirled to face them, gaze glowing a deep orange. He held back the growl that threatened to rumble from his chest when he noticed the eyes on him. Keira's angelic hazel eyes. And she was less than happy, especially with the theatrics.

"What the hell, Noel? What's going on with you?"

He shut his eyes tight, squeezing them until light burst behind them, and tried to will away the twitch just under his skin. He inhaled deeply through his nose, taking in her perfume as his nails dug into his palm. Between the fresh air and everything that made up the woman in front of him, Noel's racing heart slowed.

"I'm just." He finally looking at her, smirking as if he were just shrugging it off. "I'm just a little off today."

"A little?" She giggled as he fought for control, focusing on the pain from the rips in the tender skin. His gaze went to his fist, clenched tightly, and suddenly noticed the cramping, the way his knuckles had turned white. He stretched out his fingers, instantly noticing the blood beneath the nails, and swallowed back bile. Her hands on his cheeks took him away from the crimson color and brought him back around, drowning out the rest of the world under her touch. "You need to reign in your alpha."

Noel smiled because she was right, and he let the warmth of her palm draw him in, letting his eyes close as he stuffed his hands in his pockets. "I know. Annoying and overbearing."

"Some of your finest traits." She stepped into him, closing the space between them. He placed his forehead against hers as his hands slipped to her waist. "Is that what this is about? What that witch said? The bullshit Wilkes was spewing? You know a lot of us don't believe that. Hell, most of the people in that class only took it for the credit. This community is well aware of what you are, but sweetheart, no one's going to understand packs like you do."

He slid his hands away, stuffing them in his pockets. "It's not about that. Not about him."

She grabbed his shirt before he could get away. "Then what is it?"

Noel shook his head, gaze going to the surrounding area, scanning for anything out of place, any foe. She stepped back, taking the warmth of her hands from his face, confusion present in her eyes. That caught his attention, bringing him back to her, and he fought to stand still and not take off running from the strange feeling that crept under his skin.

With a long, tired exhale, Noel scrubbed at his eyes with the tips of his fingers before shrugging, still avoiding her scrutiny.

"I told you, it's just the moon." His deflated words were followed by another shrug of his shoulders, at a loss for any other explanation. "It heightens everything."

"Ah-huh."

The little noise was spoken with a slight turn of her lips and Noel took just a small step back away from her, putting enough space between them so he could pace. He ducked his head low as his eyes lit up against his will. He didn't need to show his other side to Keira, didn't like doing it at all. She was human and shouldn't have to deal with any ornery alpha bullshit but here he was being exactly what *those* people expected.

He clenched his fists tightly, rolling his fingers in, and he could feel the bite of his nails once more. He needed to do something, needed an out, needed...

She grabbed his wrist, yanking him to a stop, or maybe it was him letting her take over control, because he was about to lose it and there was no way he'd come back if he did. His chest expanded with every deep breath, taking in her scent again, calming him, and she closed the space.

"Maybe you need a break." She wasn't kidding, and he wasn't taking it as such. She knew just where he was, how close to the edge, and with a slow release, he blinked away the red. Noel tucked his arm around her waist and dared to pull her in against his body. "Maybe you need some release."

He wrapped both arms around her, one hand settling at the small of her back as the other traveled up her spine to rest at her neck. He closed his eyes as he ran his thumb over her skin, tucking his face to her neck where the scent of her was the strongest. For a moment, he just relaxed.

"Maybe." His word was warm against her skin, but the pull to keep her safe had his eyes wide and alert.

"Come on, there's a place I want to show you." Her fingers carded up through his hair, nails scratching against his skin, and Noel nearly melted at the feeling of that little bit of pain. He nodded, slipped back, and took her hand, following her blindly as she turned and moved down the sidewalk away from the Wells building.

THE LOCK on the library door clicked and opened slowly into the empty hall. Daniel slipped out, pressed his back against the wall, letting it close as quietly as it opened, and yanked on the collar of his jacket, straightening it as his eyes scanned for witnesses.

His dark eyes squeezed tightly shut for a moment as he composed himself, expression changing from worried to cocky in an instant before he pushed away from the chilled brick behind him. With a glance down the hallway, he headed right, disappearing without so much as a sound.

Long, dreaded minutes passed without a sound, before the loud shrill of the bell echoed through the hall, and doors swung open. It filled with waves of bodies that poured from classrooms echoing in the small tunnel of two walls. The click of locker doors and metal-on-metal clashing assaulted Keegan's ears the moment he pushed open that heavy wooden barrier.

He paused only for a second before ducking his head and stepping into the crowd, hoping to get lost, to just become one of the faceless people. He followed it to the left, away from the direction he knew Daniel would go in, away from Paige and their next class to a spot he knew would be completely empty at that moment, and for most of the day.

He halted at the cross-section of a hallway, watching the ease in which the movement of the bodies merged. He didn't think of them as people, most of them he didn't know, even having grown up in town, and it didn't matter, he probably wouldn't have liked them anyway. For a second, he felt his heart thump hard in his chest before he pushed away from the wall and beelined for the dark room directly across from him, one labeled "computer sciences."

The room was dark with the shade pulled low, opened just enough to give the room a bit of light. It also meant no one would be looking in. He knew the schedule, that it would be unoccupied for at least another hour, but just to be safe he locked it.

Moving towards the furthest computer, Keegan slipped into whatever sunlight streamed in, hiding behind the large screen, just to feel the warmth. The clouds had gone, the sun was shining, and the heat was a nice break from the chill in his bones that hadn't left since the car ride home.

He wiggled the mouse, bringing the screen to life and smiled as he tapped the escape, F10, and control keys consecutively until it went black again, but this time, it gave him a prompt, and Keegan started typing. His fingers flew over the keys, tapping out codes that most people his age wouldn't know, and just as fast as he started, he stopped.

A smile rose on his lips as he looked over the lines of green coding before him, snapped up his bag, and was gone from the room in a blink. The door closed softly behind him, and it fell back into the silence that filled it before.

At the very bottom of a screen filled with codes, and words that wouldn't make sense to most people, were three little lines.

"11:00 a.m. Emergency Fire Preparedness Drill. All halls. Evacuation measures readiness."

In an empty office space, or more of an uninhabited one, free of dust, books, and files, the sounds of passion filled the air. Noel's lips caressed over exposed skin, kissing, nipping his way up from Keira's navel, her hands in his hair.

This was the distraction he needed, the release he was looking for, if only for a few moments. To feel her under him, around him, above, tightly in his arms. They were soulmates, at least in his eyes.

She knew everything about him, kept him sane, kept him level-headed and in these moments, she let him relinquish control. He didn't have to think, he just had to be there.

With a sigh, one content release, her head tipped back exposing her neck. Noel knew the world would one day be righted again, and he let his lips rest against her pulse, a warm, wet kiss just to taste her when he finally came to rest as the lethargy took over.

Sweaty but still heated, he covered her like a shield and slipped his arms around her, pulling her in as his ear rested against her chest taking in the sound of her heartbeat. She ran her hands down over his back, tracing the muscles in his shoulders before gliding down once more.

He finally relaxed, the postcoital haze setting in, and he tried not to think.

"We could stay here all day," she whispered to him, hoping to keep him calm, to offer him a solution out of the odd madness that had taken over him.

"I wish." His words were no louder than a soft brush of air, but he didn't move, just focused on a spot on the wall, a place emptied of a frame, one lighter than the wallpaper around it.

"Will you tell me what happened last night?"

He chuckled. Of course, she would know him well enough to pinpoint when all of it had started, but Noel just gave a minute shake of his head, one she barely felt before voicing his reply. "Couldn't sleep. Nightmares. They just had me up and moving, and even after that it was hard to get back. I'll catch up tonight."

"Okay." She didn't push him, would never think of prying if he didn't want to talk about it, but she didn't believe him, and he didn't need to be a supernatural lie detector to know that.

Noel pushed up on his elbows, releasing his weight from her body, and smiled down at her, projecting as much love as he could, and kissed her, as gently as possible. "I promise, I'm fine."

He sat up, scanned the room for his clothes, and found his jeans about three feet away, pooled in the middle of the floor with his boxers. He rubbed his forehead, hoping to help ease the headache that was suddenly forming and while his intention was to get dressed, he found that he didn't have the energy to move, resting his elbows to his knees as he wrung his hands together.

"I'm sorry." He scrubbed over his face, suddenly on his feet, and he snapped the rough denim from the floor, still not looking back at her. Keira shifted, reaching for her clothes as Noel yanked his own on. He turned, jeans up over his hips, button undone as he leaned back against the desk. "I feel like an asshole."

"You're just having an off day."

"I've been having an off year. I don't know how you put up with me." He crossed his arms over his chest, trying to keep her out, trying to keep himself together, but he knew it was a dick move, signaling her that he didn't want her touch, not yet, and she knew him well enough to not even try. "That's no excuse, you deserve more."

"Hey," on that she did move, coming close enough to put her hands on his arms, gaze locked on his. "You're right, you've been off, but you got help, Noel, and I'm proud that you did. You're doing so much better, and Dr. Kelson said if you ever needed him again, his door was wide open. I don't want you to go into that dark place again. I never want to lose you like that."

Noel glanced down at the small spot where her thumb caressed his skin, at the tattoo that was barely noticeable, just a small scar, a reminder. "I'm in a good place." He leaned in and kissed her forehead. "And his numbers on speed dial if I need it."

"I really wish you would tell your mom." She backed away, continuing to collect her clothing as he ogled her, taking in the movements she made before his shirt connected with his face and her giggle filled the room.

Noel grinned as he slid the fabric from his skin, brow raised in a challenge, but she wasn't even looking as she slipped on her own jeans. He tugged the shirt down, and scanned the room for his sneakers, ones lost in the frantic need to disrobe.

"She knows, sort of." He grabbed one from under the desk, the other by the door, and pushed into them, not bothering with the laces, eyes still on her. "She gets the bills, remember?"

"That's not telling her, Noel, and you know it."

Oh, he knew, and while the good doctor had told him that he would keep it confidential, the threat of "telling his mother should Noel become a danger to himself" was always hanging over him. He really was in a better place, and he wanted to stay there. He just wished he knew what the hell was going on with his body.

"Come on," he smirked, holding out a hand for her as he grabbed his bag from the floor. "Let's go grab something before our next class."

Keira slipped her hand in his. "You always say the sweetest things."

"Part of my charm." He pulled her in, kissed her softly, and the two ducked out of the room, peeking down both ways before disappearing into the empty halls.

CHAPTER 8

THE CAMPUS QUAD was always crowded, from the coffee cart that was parked outside the library to the small canopy tents lined up for new students and visiting potential. The cafe itself was packed with people. It was staffed and supplied by the culinary department, which was not only a plus for students who frequented there for the baked goods, but hands-on training for the hospitality management majors and some of the top up-and-coming chefs this side of Worcester.

This was the part of college life that Noel loved, the normalcy of it.

The community college was not his first choice, not with UMass Amherst so close, but it was the best choice in the end. His mother and father both taught there, with his dad heading up one of the largest departments focusing on pack history in the state. Financially, it was a great decision, they didn't need to pay tuition, but Noel wished he was just a little further away where he could really hide, be normal, *not* be pack.

Among the masses was where he found it. With most students

not even realizing who he was, this was his normal, but there was always that off chance that someone recognized him.

"Hey, Summerford," came a chipper greeting from somewhere on the quad.

Noel shook himself from the daydream he had slipped into just people watching and looked for the hand that waved at him. Turned out it was some guy from his Eco class, and while he remembered the face, he couldn't match the name, but gave a friendly wave in reply.

Keira's sudden presence at his side startled him, her hands filled with two cups of coffee from the cart which, in his opinion, was the best damn brew ever made. He held in the shock as he accepted the offered bribe of caffeine in place of a real meal and smiled when she presented him with one of the "voted #1 in the state" scones from the cafe.

"Thank you." He leaned down to kiss her temple.

There were some advantages of being tall, nearly six feet in height, he could protect her the way he saw fit, and there was always that smidge of happiness he felt when she blushed at that gesture. Her eyes would look around, as they were doing now, and her cheeks would pink, warming under his lips as he also rubbed his nose against her hair, humming at the smell of her shampoo. Yes, he loved to embarrass her.

She would sigh, as she did every time, as if completely put out, but there would be a spring in her step that told him he was doing it right. Today, it was the addition of the little smirk on her face, which kept the smile on his.

They were quiet as they walked along the edge of the bustling campus center, taking in all the people out lounging the odd warmth of the mid-December day. It hadn't officially become winter yet in New England but the sun shining without a blustery cold wind was definitely a treat. Leaves still clung to the trees, and the grass was mostly green, so the fact that bodies took up spots just to soak it up was a sight to see.

Noel scanned the crowd, the earlier itch had faded to almost a light tickle, but he stopped dead, eyes going to where they had just left as he caught the sight of someone familiar. Keira halted beside him, confusion on her face as she fought to focus on what he was looking at. She grabbed his hand and gave him a tug.

"Wait," he whispered so softly that Keira's first thought was whoever he was spying on was close.

"What is it?"

Across the green, walking with purpose, was Rollins, and from the strides he was taking, he was on a mission. Noel slipped behind her, leaned down to her level and guided her eye to the man in the tan three-quarter jacket.

"That's Rollins, one of the council leaders."

"So?"

"I've never seen him on campus before."

Keira twirled in his arms, glaring up at him as if he might have gone insane. "Maybe he's meeting someone."

"Maybe." He wouldn't believe it unless he saw for himself, and without taking his eye off his target, he slipped his hand around hers. "Come on."

They moved down the sidewalk, back towards the cafe, but shifted to the left when the sidewalk curved, following him towards the library as Rollins navigated the crowd. Noel scrutinized his every move, could sense the man even as he trailed him, but in a blink, Rollins had disappeared around the corner of the building.

"Dammit!" He scowled, still in hot pursuit, but faltering when they swept past the corner only to see that the alleyway was empty.

With his shoulders slumped in disappointment, Noel continued around the walk, fingers threaded with Keira's, a little more relaxed. It wasn't until they were a good distance away that she finally broke the silence they had fallen into.

"So, who's Rollins again?"

"Part of our security force." He wasn't really sure how to answer that, pack laws were completely different than most of the judicial system, though they worked in tandem most of the time. "He's the guy Gus goes to when he needs something done."

"Like a mob hit?"

Noel stopped dead, unsure whether to be offended or not by the question, but his lips slowly turned up into a smile. "What?" He laughed, unable to hold it in any longer. "No, Gus isn't a mobster." But it would make sense when he thought of what the Pack Second did at his alpha's instruction. "At least, I don't think?"

"That's not funny, Noel. My uncle—"

"Is an asshole?" His smirk widened, there was no love lost between Noel and Ancram, not over the many, many years Noel had been coming around. They just didn't click.

"Okay, yes, but I think he really is one. Ancram's into some really strange stuff."

Noel pondered that one over a moment. "Maybe him and Rollins should hook up."

"Ew!" Her face twisted to match her words, as if the images filling her mind were just as bad as he thought.

"Not like that," he chuckled as she pretended to gag. "I meant they're both kinda creepy jerks, they'd make great pen pals."

"Pen pals? From where? Separate maximum-security prisons?"

"That would probably be the best option."

Keira gave him a gentle smack across the arm as they moved along then wrapped her hand around his bicep. The growing sound of multiple voices, all chanting above the other filled the air, becoming nothing more than a ringing in Noel's ear.

"Our campus, our rights. Our campus, our rights!"

It was clear what was going on, and Noel steadied himself for what he was about to walk into.

Just off to the right of the walk, a large group gathered. In front of the growing crowd, three women stood on boxes, or some sort of platform and from where they stood, he couldn't make out which, but they were right there, dead center. Above them, strung up between two trees, was a colorful banner that read "Campus Society for Humankind," and while he wasn't positive, he was sure that Carmichaels was the woman on the right.

Signs, both printed and handmade, stood stuck in the ground all around the stage in plain view of the walkway. It reminded him of the slides from Wilkes room, the hateful depiction of two wolves fighting, bloodied and tearing each other apart. There were some with propaganda against those with the Lupinus Marker, against those like *him*, and he suddenly wished he was somewhere else.

The leader, whoever she might be, a faceless hatemonger, spewing nothing but unfounded lies to rile the crowd, screamed into a megaphone. Her words were mostly unintelligible, but whatever she was saying was followed by cheers. The only thing Noel heard, above the hum, was the high-pitched noise from the speakers, and a ringing in his ear.

He winced in pain, nearly doubling over as his hand went to his ear. He barely heard Keira's voice breaking through. "Noel, can we—"

She must have seen the state he was in because he was suddenly being pulled away. His heart slowed the further they traveled until it was back down to static white noise. Noel shook it off, dropping his hand, only to check his palm to see if he was bleeding.

"What makes them so hateful?" His question was to anyone, anyone who could answer because he just didn't get it.

"Some people will never change. They need something to rally against, something to focus their anger on. Most of us accept packs because we've grown up with them, you know that." She tried to catch his gaze as he dropped his chin to his chest and sighed. "There will always be people who don't. You don't have to prove to them that you belong, that you're no different. You just have to be yourself."

His eyes shifted back to that stage, to that woman as she continued speaking, not that he could make out her indistinguishable words from that far away, but the crowd only grew louder. Keira tugged on his hand once again, knowing he needed to move.

"Noel, please."

He nodded, eyes still focused on the people, even as he moved in the opposite direction. His campus, his rights, too. His right to live in peace, to not fear being at school, but the vast number of people in that crowd made him realize just how small the population of pack members around him was. Whether Juli knew it or not, Noel had found out about the kidnappings, and the fact that their numbers were slowly shrinking.

THE INTERIOR of the small Honda was silent, which wasn't unusual, but this time, as Gus pulled up into his parking space right along the side of the meetinghouse, there was a reason. Once in park, he shut off the engine and let his head fall back on the rest.

His eyes were tightly closed, going over everything that he had seen at the hospital, everything Luca had told him, and he made a mental note to stop by the facility later that night to make sure the injured beta had gotten settled.

He had phoned the physician in charge and explained everything, even managed to convince the doctor at County General to release their findings and the treatment plan they had suggested, faxing it all over in order to have somewhere to start without putting Luca through it all again. The beta should be set, he should be comfortable, but it was nearly eleven and he was late getting anything else done, like the meeting Juli had asked him to schedule.

Taking the five minutes he could afford to gather his own thoughts, Gus finally snatched the keys from the ignition, swung the door wide, and got out. He knew there was stuff he needed to do, but a coffee would be great.

Flipping through the master keys on his ring, he finally found the one he was looking for. A regular house key with the picture of a howling wolf on it, something Juli had found funny when she presented it to him years ago. She didn't seem to realize just how much he treasured it now.

Unlocking the door, Gus slipped in, flipping on the lights as the door clicked shut behind him. It was like any other meeting hall built in the 1800s. A foyer that housed the bathroom, a coat room, and the entrance to the kitchen before the inner doors that would open to the actual meeting room.

He never liked the color, some odd salmon shade that made the whole thing look pink, but he loved the fact that straight ahead was a large stage, usually blocked until they celebrated some pack event, and above them a horseshoe-shaped balcony that overlooked the main floor.

Under the cover of the balcony floor stood glass cases filled with the memories and achievements of the pack members. It ranged from little league game trophies to old photographs from its early days. Within its protective hold, Collins' beginnings and the Summerford pack was laid out for the world to see.

In the middle of the floor was a huge, mahogany table, surrounded by chairs of the same color and design that seated twelve comfortably. It was where every pack meeting was held, from the time it first opened its doors to that very day, but currently it was covered with a project that Gus wished never had to see the light of day.

The file folders of missing pack members.

Gus stopped at the edge of the table, his fingers going to the most recent one—excluding Alesha—was a young woman not more than twenty-five, with raven hair and bright blue eyes staring back at him.

"It's getting worse." Gus looked up quickly, staring down the memory before him, more solid than anything his imagination could come up with. He remembered this conversation from sixteen months ago, the way Alexandru stood, arms crossed, eyes down at the files, a pile smaller than what it was now, almost a dozen less. "Three more in the last month."

"And the council's turning a blind eye to it," Gus replied,

standing straight as he closed the folder, one of a young man no older than Noel was now. He yanked out a chair, plopped down into it and ran his finger along his lips, more pissed off than anything.

"There's got to be a way to get their attention," but the Summerford Alpha was just as stuck as Gus was.

"Unless you rub their noses in it, there's nothing we can do. They're just going to ignore it because they have more important things to worry about than a small pack community like ours."

And that was the reason Juli was at the conference, because something *had* to be done.

The doors flew open at that very moment, like a dramatic gust of wind had blown them open, but the one standing there was certainly not some Greek God of the North Wind, it was Keegan. He had slid into the room like a child in socks on a newly polished floor.

The grin on his face faded when he met the eyes of the two men in the room, and his shoulders hunched, making him look smaller but only for a moment before he found his bravado and straightened, the smirk coming back in full force.

"Keegan," Alexandru's voice was low, strict, authoritative, and Gus held back the smirk because Alex was neither strict nor authoritative when it came to the middle one of his tribe.

"Oh, hey Dad." The beta grinned, eyes glancing at Gus, who gave more of a lecture than his father and tucked his hands into the pockets of his coat.

"Any reason you're not in school?"

"Free period?" There was just something in the boy's voice that had Gus on edge, like a fear hoping to never come to light.

"Ah-huh," Alexandru nodded, "gym?" Gus held back a growl when Keegan's eyes lowered and the only response he gave was a slight nod. "Go sit in the office, we'll talk."

With one quick glance at Gus, Keegan darted off to the back office to the right of the stage, and the two men in the main room locked gazes until the door clicked shut.

"You're too easy on him." He wasn't trying to be an ass; he was trying to pry some sort of information from his best friend about his adopted nephew.

"He's going through some things, Gus. I'm not going to discipline him for something he can't control." Neither would he if Alex would just let him in on what was going on with the boy. "Let me take care of this and we'll finish our conversation." Alex turned and walked away from the table, and Gus faded from the memory.

It was the vibration of the phone that broke the sullen peace in the room, making him jump at the feeling of it before he dug it from his back pocket.

On screen, a text banner lit up against the background photo of the three kids, Juli, Gus, and Alexandru were five words he was hoping not to see or hear today.

Ellie: *Keegan's having a bad day.*

He ran a hand down his face and set the phone down. With a quick glance at the clock, he realized it was only closing in on eleven.

"Great," he growled, speaking to no one at all but himself. "It's not even lunchtime."

He stuck the phone in his pocket and headed back out those two inner doors, headed right for the kitchen and the coffee pot.

THE ART ROOM WAS QUIET, not silent, but quiet, with the soft sounds of the brush strokes or scratch of pencils on canvas. The beat of music —something not recognizable through the earphones but there nonetheless—was familiar, and brushes twirling through water before being tapped to start something new, made it all very... tranquil.

Paige could feel the unease in the room, though, like a vibration in the air. Her body shivered at it as she scanned the circle of classmates all concentrating, more or less, on the vase filled with bright flowers in the middle of the room. She homed in on it, where the emotion was coming from, hiding behind an easel almost directly across from her, and slowly she rose.

She threw a quick glance at Ms. Williams who was deep into the trashy romance novel she read specifically during this class, as she made her way around the edge of the circle of students and stopped behind the man she had cornered that morning.

They'd been in class for more than twenty minutes, long enough for most to be halfway through the project, but before Daniel sat a blank canvas, his eyes set on nothing, and she could feel the uncertainty from where she stood not three feet behind him.

This was the reason omegas were the peacekeepers. They had the uncanny ability to zero in on those vibrations in people and work around them, ease that tension, and release that emotion that clouded their judgment.

With a gentle sweep across his shoulders, Paige stepped up, crowding against him as she leaned in. He was the only other pack member in the room, no one else had heightened abilities, no one else would even hear her words with how low she spoke, so she knew what she said was safe.

"Not even going to try it?" She put a smile on her lips, which reflected in her voice, and she saw the way he shifted, looking up to the vase and back at the canvas.

"Not really in the mood to paint flowers."

That was when she noticed it, the light familiar scent on his skin, and that fake smile turned real. "What happened? You smell like Keegan and—"

It was the shake of his head that made her pause, cutting off her line of teasing and turned her humor into worry. Daniel was serious. Looking down, she followed his lead to the phone in his hand.

On screen, open to a full text thread, were the ones sent from a contact listed under "Lil Beta." Paige knew that nickname, and she reached down to touch the screen, scrolling down to the last lines.

Lil Beta: *Library. Having trouble.*

Paige didn't need to see the rest. "Is he alright?"

Daniel tucked the phone away, ran a hand down his face, and scratched at the back of his neck, as if trying to keep calm. “It was bad but—”

It was as if both had heard someone calling their name, as their heads turned simultaneously towards the door. It was a pack thing, the feeling of being watched, of a member being close, and there, in the small four-by-eighteen window, was the grinning face of Keegan looking right at them for just a second before he slipped away.

“Great,” Daniel dropped his chin, shaking his head. “What the hell did he do now?”

Seconds after the question left his mouth, the fire alarm blared with an ear-piercing pulse and the bodies around them started to move, some happy for the interruption, some complaining because of the timing.

Paige’s grin had the alpha sighing because she was laughing at the situation. “I’ll go find him.”

He rose to his feet, snagging the varsity jacket off the back of the chair. “Good, ‘cause he doesn’t need any more trouble.”

Paige gave him a light pat on the shoulder before running her hand over his heart. Her lighthearted smile eased some of the tension in him while she grabbed her jacket and followed the crowd out.

He wished he knew what was going on with him, why everything suddenly seemed so much more intense. He slipped his bag over his shoulder, glanced in the direction she had headed, and forced himself to go the opposite way. The beta didn’t need any more issues, and Daniel going to his side would just cause more than they could handle.

Keira stopped on the first step up to the building behind her, finally eye level with the man who was slipping his arms around her, and she smiled, narrowing her gaze at him. With a sly smirk, he leaned forwards, kissing her gently before pulling away, but she didn't let him get that far, hands going to the collar of his jacket.

Her lips are warm against his, keeping out the world around them, and he found himself content to stay there soaking in the sun at his back, but the peace didn't last.

The blare of a high-pitched car horn went off as if he had his ear pressed against the mechanism itself, and he quickly flinched away, covering his ears, startled. Wide-eyed, he looked around, hoping to find the source of it, but the continuous pulse only told him that an alarm was going off somewhere.

"Noel?" Her voice was muffled, as if he were underwater fighting to get to the surface. The rev of an engine filled the space between her words and the horn, rumbling through him as if he were sitting on top of it, not a half-mile away from the parking lot. His breathing picked up, as his heart raced to keep up with the adrenaline going through his body, and his hands pressed harder. It was her hands on his face that made him focus, nearly yanking him around to face her. "Noel, look at me."

He fought to find the strength to block out the noise, shaking as he locked his gaze on her, and just as suddenly as it started, the world went quiet.

"Sorry. I'm sorry, I—" He fought against her hold, hoping to find something, anything to explain it, but there's nothing.

"What was that?"

With a deep inhale and a slow release, Noel willed his heart to slow. "It's nothing." Lies and more lies, that's all he felt like he was doing to everyone, but he didn't have the answers. His fingers traced up her arm to the small, gentle hands on his face, and slowly, he removed them, leaning in to brush soft kisses on her lips. "I gotta go."

"Okay," she relented, dropping her hands as she stepped back one more time. "Come find me after history?"

"Yeah, definitely." The curt nod he gave was the one sign that told her he had no intention of going to history at all, but she said nothing. "Love you."

It was quick, barely audible, but she had caught those two little words before he turned and nearly raced away down the sidewalk. Keira watched after him for only a moment before she headed up the stairs, glancing up to find Adin standing near the door, confusion on his face as well while watching after the retreating alpha.

It wasn't until Keira stepped up beside him that Adin smirked. "What's with him?"

Keira shrugged. It wasn't like she actually knew, but she certainly wasn't going to tell him. "Bad day."

"Ah," was his only reply as he reached for the handle, pulled the door open, and gestured for her to enter.

He glanced one last time at Noel, just as the man disappeared around the corner of the building. He would never understand the Summerfords, mostly Noel, because there was just something about them.

Noel dug out his phone as he moved, hoping to get somewhere safe, somewhere quiet, before whatever the hell that was happened again. He could feel the sweat pouring down the side of his face, and his fingers slipped, barely registering with the thumbprint security, before it opened up and he scrolled through the phone.

Opening the text thread labeled "Mom," he let his fingers fly over the keys.

Noel: *Text me when you land. Something's going on. Mom, something's wrong with me.*

With a quick tap on the send button, he moved to tuck the phone away, pausing as it vibrated in his hand, but his eyes were on where he left Keira and the fact that she had already moved onto class. The knowledge that she was in the building eased the tension. Her safety was all that mattered.

He debated looking at the text, couldn't take any more bad news right at that moment, but his thoughts shifted to Juli and the possibility that it was her finally checking in. Bringing it up, he knew he made the wrong choice. There, on screen, was a text from Ellie.

Ellie: *Someone set off the fire alarm. Two guesses who.*

Noel closed his eyes, counted to ten, and put the phone away.

"I can't right now," he whispered to himself, but the next two words came out as a low rumble of frustration. "Dammit, Keegan!"

The growl in his words echoed off the buildings that surrounded him, and he stuffed his hands in his pockets, hoping to look small as he moved across campus. He needed to get away, maybe just end the day and go home, but as he followed the way the sidewalk twist, his eyes caught the one strange thing he never understood.

While the college mascot was the dragon, the one gracing the green he was now passing was... weird. It stood tall, wings spread wide as it stood on its hind legs, eyes to the sky. It wasn't that the pose itself was strange, but the fact that there were others on the grounds that looked nothing like it. The weirdness of it all always threw him off.

He shook off the urge to find out what exactly was going on with it, because he was sure there was a plaque somewhere, and headed straight for the furthest building on campus.

KEEGAN SAT MID-BLEACHERS, high enough in the stands to see anyone coming, but just low enough to hide against the fence that saved him from the twenty-ish foot drop. He could hear the hustle and bustle of the students leaving the building, the sounds of the approaching fire trucks, and with his elbows to his knees, he grinned.

The field in front of him was empty. This hour seemed to be the only one where people weren't running or kicking around a soccer ball, so he was all alone, finally. The overwhelming scent of the overcrowded school usually didn't bother him, but today, everything did. All the voices. All of the touches when he tried to get by someone. The sound of the coat fabric brushing against itself as people moved. It was all so much. He liked the quiet, he liked being lost in his own world.

In his hand, gently folded in half and held with love, not frustration or anger, was a picture of his family, the three of them and his parents, all smiling, probably the only time in the last year and a half that he could remember really being happy.

That wasn't true. Daniel made him happy. Paige made him happy, but this was different. Their—dare he say it—love helped with a lot of things, but he missed his siblings, his mother, and no matter how much he tried to ignore it, he missed his father.

"Keegan!" His name echoed through the stands causing him to sit up just a little more, to fold that picture and tuck it away into the inner pocket of his light jacket, eyes going to the blonde woman who was now making her way up the stairs.

It didn't take her as long as he thought to find him, which was a blessing and a curse. They had been playing this game for years, so it didn't surprise him that she knew him so well. She sat down beside him, a small smile on her face, before she leaned in and gave him nothing more than a quick peck on the lips, but her smile faded when she noticed the expression on his, the little scowl hidden by his usual smirk hadn't changed.

Her eyes narrowed as she took his hand, brought it up to her lips and kissed over his knuckles, a gentle sweeping of her lips that relaxed him, and she grinned when she heard him sigh. Her next move was to crowd him, to press against as much of him as she could before her lips found his in a deeper kiss, and Keegan seemed to melt against her.

"I'm not going to ask if you're okay, I can smell that you're not."

The words were spoken with her lips still against his, and Keegan let out a chuckle.

"Damn omega heightened senses." It was a joke, and it wasn't. He knew she would feel what he was, that she could scent it on his skin. His anxiety, his sadness, but he pushed it away the best he could.

"It gives me some advantage." Her fingers ran through his unruly hair, curls flopping any way they wanted when she gave them a little tug and released them, but he didn't pull away. "I'm not going to lecture either. I know what happened, and I know this..." Her eyes went to the arriving fire trucks before landing back on his. "This is your doing. So, I'm just going to sit here until you want to talk—"

"Which will never happen." He shrugged, giving her a wide Joker's grin.

"We've been together for three years now, I think I get that part of you."

Keegan agreed, only because he knew she wouldn't push, and he shifted away from her, elbows once again to his knees, even though her hand was still in his, their fingers linked together.

He hated her reverse psychology and let out a loud sigh. "Sometimes I wish it would all come out."

"It could," she shrugged, passive in her answer.

He scoffed. "No, I don't—" He peeked at her quickly before looking away. "She wouldn't understand."

"Your mom?"

"Yeah."

"I think she'd surprise you."

"Sure. Let's go with that and how she's totally going to be okay with "hey, Mom, I'm poly or at least bi, and yes, I do have a girlfriend. Oh, and a boyfriend, who happens to be the *brother* of your assistant." That will go over well."

Paige giggled, covering her mouth with her hand, which had Keegan smiling. He didn't know how he got so lucky, but he leaned over and kissed her on the side of the head.

"You're insane," he whispered softly in her ear.

"So are you," she winked. "We're a matching set."

Keegan nodded and let the feeling of her leaning in on him relax him. Minutes ticked by. The trucks pulled away, and the crowd moved back into the building, leaving the two of them to sit in silence, at least until the bell rang.

"Lunchtime," Keegan announced with dramatic flair, jazz hands and all.

"Not really, but we can go with that."

"Okay," he laughed, giving Paige's hand a tug as he grabbed his backpack. "Lunch for me, science for you."

She leaned in, giving him one more kiss before the two made their way down the bleachers, headed for the still open door of the building.

NOEL MADE his way over the green, finally arriving at his destination, a blind path from where he had left Keira right to the administration building where his parents worked. On the lawn, directly in front of the door, stood a four-foot statue of a wolf, the only one on the property, and Noel headed straight for it.

He crouched down, looking up at the way it stood on its hind legs, much like the dragon statue, front paws out as if it was about to attack, jaws open wide in a snarl. He got why it was there, what it represented but it was the plaque on the bottom that he made a habit of reading every time he came by.

The gold lettering against a black background read: "The Defender - 1919." The next line was something he knew, something he had been taught since his early childhood. "In honor of the gray wolves, last gracing our state in 1840." He had heard all about it, how they had been driven north or killed off, making them nearly extinct in New England, but it was his father's name in memoriam that always made his heart thump painfully in his chest.

He ran his fingers across Alexandru's name, gently brushing off any stray grass or leaves before he stood and moved away. There were so many things on campus that reminded him of his father, but that one thing, out in public, was the most heartbreaking.

Inside the building, it was easy to find his way to his father's office, which was still filled with his belongings. He shied away from the other students, some TAs that passed him in the halls, and two professors who nodded their greetings at him, but he wasn't in the social mood, so he only returned their nod while faking a smile.

At the end of the second-floor corridor, just to his right, was a locked door with a large, frosted window. The golden words were scratched and peeling at the edges, but his name was still legible.

"Dr. Alexandru Summerford," Noel whispered, as if speaking it out loud would bring him back. "Department of Mythology and Archeology."

To his left was a door much like the one he stood in front of, but behind the glass, the light was on. More than likely Illy was settled in behind her desk, organizing his mother's classes, or the material for when she returned, but Juli's name graced the door as well, a professor instead of doctor title before her name.

Knowing full well the door was locked, Noel still grabbed for the handle like an odd force of habit, giving it a little jiggle before smiling. He dug down deep, pulling his truck keys from his pocket, and flipped the large bronze key out from the other four. It looks like an old skeleton key, something his dad had pride in keeping, because what would better suit a man that delves into the past than a key like that for his office.

He slipped it in, took a moment to brace himself, and gave it a gentle turn, always afraid that it was going to break, but the lock clicked, disengaged and Noel grinned as the door popped open.

With one last glance in both directions, he removed the key and stepped in, dropping his backpack as he flipped on the light. With a quiet exhale, he turned, shutting it quietly behind him.

Ellie felt the vibration of the phone in the front pocket of her hoodie. She glanced around the room, hoping no one else had heard it since it rested against her keys, but no one in the math class even bothered to look up. Placing her pencil down gently, she pulled it from its hiding place, and glanced at the screen.

It wasn't a text, though she had been expecting one, but an alert from the security system in her father's office. "Main door" was flashing in bright red. It took her only a second to dig into her pocket again, find her wireless earbuds, and slip them in place. They were always connected, but she checked just in case before clicking the banner.

A video feed with an angle from high in the corner of the room, showed the contents of Alexandru's office, but it wasn't that anything was out of place, it was that Noel was standing in the middle of it. He did it often but always forgot that there were other people watching. She exited out of it, accepting the alert, which shut the notifications off, and tucked the phone away.

What Noel did with his time was his business, as long as he was safe. With another glance around the room, she hid the earbuds, picked up her pencil and went back to the problem in front of her.

With the steaming cup of coffee in hand, Gustaf paused just inside the inner doors, hearing the ping of his phone and he rolled his shoulders. Whatever that was, it couldn't be good. Pulling it from his pocket, he noticed the new banner, the way it flashed red, and the words on the screen.

"Summerford office. Main door."

With a small shake of his head, he clicked it, knowing what he would see when the video feed opened. Noel was moving through the space, touching the desk, the chair, and his father's jacket, one Juli couldn't bear to bring home. He observed as the boy move though the wide filing cabinet, making his way down the five-foot counter to take in the photos that lined it before he paused, tapped one particular photo, and moved away, headed for a door that Gus knew was marked private.

"What are you doing, kid? You gotta stop torturing yourself."

Shutting the video down, Gus tucked the phone back in his pocket and headed straight for the office to the right. There were things he had to get done and chasing down Summerford kids who just loved to give him a migraine was not on the schedule today.

Inside the office, finally tucked behind the chair, Gus placed the coffee down carefully. There were way too many things in front and beside him to risk spilling coffee on, but he needed to get some work accomplished. He rubbed his hands together, opened the laptop, and paused at the screen.

The screensaver was the same one as his phone, him and the Summerfords from nearly two years ago. Gus yanked the phone from his pocket, clicked on the text thread with Juli and stared at the fact that there was nothing. No response, no updates, and he placed it down hard on the desk, scrubbing his hands down his face.

"Come on, Jules, where the hell are you?"

In the right-hand corner of the screen, the email icon blinks with several new arrivals. Gus slid the mouse along the screen and clicked the icon, allowing the Outlook page to open. The first two new emails were spam, the next one was the minutes from the summit the night before.

He knew she had given them hell but reading the minutes from the session she was in angered him more than he realized he'd be.

They just ignored everything that she was pleading for. It was for help, any kind of help, to stop the disappearances of pack members not only on their pack lands, but the New England area as well.

Flexing his fists, stemming off the need to punch something, Gus reached for his landline phone, dialed out, and placed it on speaker. It rang twice before a familiar voice picked up.

"Alpha?" Quinlan Gervais answered, a loyal member of the pack and a beta for her own was curious about the phone call.

"I'm calling a meeting," he huffed, sitting back in the chair.

"We're already set to arrive at three, Juli's assistant sent out a message last night."

Gus nodded. Of course, Doug would be on top of it. Not that Gus was complaining because it saved his ass since the whole thing with Luca threw off his plans, but that wasn't why he was calling.

"Now."

The older beta sighed, as if completely put out. *"I'll pass it along, but it's a little unorthodox."*

"Well, looks like we're going off book. Call the meeting, Mrs. Gervais, this can't wait."

"Right away," was the only answer he got before the line went dead.

He wouldn't usually go above Juli's head, but the silence and the minutes in front of him was starting to get under his skin. He sat back, folded his hands in front of him, and took a calming breath, his eyes still on those words.

Something needed to be done, and with Luca's appearance, something needed to be done *now*. It couldn't wait another four hours. He picked up his phone, dialed out and put it to his ear.

It didn't even ring but went straight to voicemail.

"You've reached Juli Summerford, please leave a message after the tone. I'll return your call as soon as I'm able."

"Juli," Gus snapped, "where the hell are you? You should have landed hours ago." He closed his eyes, let the frustration and anger drain from his voice and shook his head. "I'm worried. You can't still be in the air, can you? Maybe a layover somewhere? It's a private jet, you should be— Call me back." He pulled the phone away, tapping the red disconnect and pressed the back of his hand against his lips. "Fuck."

Luca couldn't remember much about the transport. He knew the alpha had left him, he knew the nurse at his side had spoken to him with a soft voice, something caring, treating him almost like a human, but after she dosed him again with some anxiety meds, or what she claimed them to be, he didn't recall much else.

There were rough hands on him, shifting him from the bed to a gurney before his hands were strapped down with rough restraints. A hard yank felt like it ripped at the stitches across his stomach when they strapped him in. The tightness across his chest was enough to cause his heart to race, and for the panic to rise up, but he couldn't move to make them stop what they were doing. He vaguely remembered the words leaving his mouth, begging them to stop, but that all faded to blackness the moment he started moving.

Wherever they had taken him, at least, the vehicle—a large van or maybe even an ambulance—was warm, and he was covered by a blanket. They had managed to get him into some scrub pants, and a heavier johnny, but other than that, he was naked.

It was the move from the interior of the transport to where he found himself next that was jarring. It was cold out, the sun was hiding behind the clouds, and the chill of the late fall afternoon was starting to kick in. His teeth chattered with the sudden drop in temperature, but the downward angle that he was now at, headfirst, brought on the nausea and vertigo.

He was pretty sure if he had anything in his stomach, he'd be sick, since the disorientation of the drugs and the decline were so dramatic. But when they stopped, when he was unbuckled and hoisted from the bed, he found that it wasn't a comfortable room that he was placed in, but a dirt floor cell lit only by the small window at the top of it.

And it was freezing.

The mat was on the floor tucked into the corner. The window itself, while barred, was wide open and the breeze that came in was colder than the exposed air outside had been. He was dumped on the mat, unceremoniously so, but the blanket was tossed at him, giving him some protection. The men, two or three of them, Luca wasn't sure, didn't say a word, never even looked back at him as they pulled the gurney from the room, shut and locked the door behind them.

He could feel the blood running from the bandage on his side, but he was pretty sure the wound hadn't opened. He was at least lucid enough to give himself a rundown of his injuries but while everything hurt like a bitch, he knew he'd survive and not bleed to death. Becoming a bipedal popsicle was something altogether different.

He curled up against the wall, pulling the blanket around him tightly as he closed his eyes, wishing he hadn't believed the alpha that had visited him. He might not have remembered where the hell he came from, but he should have known not to trust anyone when it came to his own self-preservation.

Relaxing was hard, especially with the footsteps above, but he knew these rules. Don't say a word, don't make a sound, don't bring attention to yourself and you'll survive. It's how he made it through the last decade without losing his life, though the torture he had been through, at times, had been enough for him to wish he had died.

Luca curled up more, dipping his head down towards his knees as he huddled into himself, and let his own body heat keep him warm as the drugs dragged him down into darkness again.

CHAPTER 9

KEEGAN CAME to a screeching halt outside the cafeteria doors, another place he *hated* to go.

Not only was it filled with the stench of body odor, unwashed teenagers, and whatever dime-store perfume the girls' thought was hot that week, on top of it was the smell of whatever the hell they thought would count as cooking—he was pretty sure it was a butchered version of American Chop Suey.

He tried not to breathe in too deep while also calming the nerves that tingled just under the surface of his skin, and turned to Paige, who's eyes betrayed her feelings, filled with worry. She wrapped her hand around his upper arm, giving it a gentle squeeze as Keegan raised a brow.

"Don't worry," he smirked, giving her his best wink, "I'm not gonna run through the room knocking over trays and jocks."

"Hmm." She let her lips brush his. "Maybe one jock."

He turned, slipped his hands up to cup her cheeks, thumb gently caressing her skin, as he leaned in to get a better angle. "Knocking him over is not exactly what I plan to do with him."

"Take pictures," she teased, going up on her tiptoes to close the distance, before brushing her hand over the zipper of his jeans. Keegan nearly choked on his next breath; eyes wide as she backed away. "One of these days, you'll have to invite me along."

"Jesus, who are you?" His tone was light, filled with laughter and the sultry smile on her face had him blushing. "I'll see if that can be arranged."

"Mmhmm." The vibration of her lips made him shake, in a good way. He thought of pulling her down a few vacant corridors to the empty closet on the second floor, but he knew better than that. He slipped his hands down from her cheeks to her shoulders and held her there as he took a step back. "See you in English?"

"Maybe."

"Be good, Key," she chuckled.

"I'm not the one giving me visuals about..." He glanced into the room, towards the far end of the hall, focused on Daniel for just a second, and licked his lips. "Okay," he cleared his throat, shifting his weight, "maybe waiting would be a good idea."

"Love you." Her kiss was chaste, but sweet, and he smiled at the way her hair swayed as she walked away, but it quickly faded.

With a long sigh, he hiked up his bag, and headed into the room, beelining for the table, and Mike. He slipped in across from him, keeping silent as Mike glanced up for just a second before going back to his food, giving him a half-smile. That was Keegan's cue, his *in* for actually speaking, but he waited. Instead, he opened his backpack, pulled out a lunch bag, and slipped out the sandwich Noel had managed to tuck into it.

The noises in the room seemed to fade away as Keegan counted the seconds. He knew he should say something, apologize, admit to anything just to make sure one of his only friends wasn't mad at him for the way he left, but he fiddled with the bag instead, drawing out one half of the PB and J that he found oddly appetizing.

He took a bite, chewing on it for a moment before looking up. He was done waiting, he couldn't take it anymore and swallowed what was in his mouth, before speaking.

"I was an ass," he admitted, only to get a scoff in reply before Mike took the time to shrug and meet his gaze.

"You usually are." Keegan huffed, a smile on his face, and took another bite. "You pulled it, didn't you?"

This could be bad. He knew Mike's favorite class was during that time of day, and that the girl he was crushing on was partnered with him for lab. He slowly lowered the food, and crossed his arms on the table, staring off at nothing for a moment until he decided to rip the bandage off.

"Programmed it, actually."

Mike grin was not what he had expected. "Nice."

"Really? I thought you'd be pissed."

Mike sat back, mimicking his position, and contemplated for a minute before shaking his head. "Nah, Cora met me outside and the two of us...we talked. Got a date Friday night."

"Well, then you're welcome."

"So, what was it?"

Keegan scoffed, ran a hand through his hair, and shrugged. "I don't know, man. The moon? Mom? I guess she's coming back early."

"I figured." He reached for the soda beside him, but only twirled the can, watching the way the white swirl on the label rose and fell. "You usually act like a fucking idiot when she's on her way." His eyes landed on Keegan, on the way the beta suddenly fought for control, like there was a shift in everything. He could see his hands shaking, and Mike leaned forward. "Hey, Key, I'm not trying to be a jerk, but seriously, you need to really think about what you're going through. I mean, you haven't even gotten over—"

Keegan's eyes snapped to his bright beta gold, as his lips twitched, curling back just a bit. "Don't." The warning was simple, a low growl that had people surrounding them looking in their direction. Mike didn't even flinch at it, in fact, his stare never wavered as he waved it off. "My dad isn't up for discussion, so, just drop it!" It seemed as if he knew his mistake the instant the words came out and he punctuated it with a quiet, "please."

"You sure you're not an alpha?" He sat back, arms crossed, and he cocked his head a little to the side, looking him over. "'Cause your attitude reminds me of the damn jockstraps on the football team!"

At that, Keegan focused on the table across the room, the blue and gold jackets, the familiar back of Daniel's head, surrounded by teammates and cheerleaders.

Keegan could tell the instant the alpha felt his eyes on him as he turned slowly, connecting with Keegan's gaze. He had his phone in his hand, that much he could see, but he wasn't sure what Daniel was doing, or if it was even him the football player was thinking about, but it was a bit too much.

Keegan finally broke the connection, shifting away, finding it hard to concentrate because his reaction to Daniel was always that strong. He shook it off, eyes going to the half-eaten sandwich, and he pushed it away, leaning in, shrinking down to make himself smaller.

"I'm not—" His thoughts were racing, unsure on how to go about it, but he finally huffed. "I hate school."

"Everyone hates school, Keegan. It's a thing. No one *wants* to be here." He had a point, Keegan could see it, but he didn't respond. The bell shrilled overhead from a speaker somewhere to the left of them, and Mike hopped up from the bench. "Gotta go!"

Just like that, the man was gone, and Keegan was left to clean up. He waited until the room was almost empty before he gathered the trash from both meals, tossed it out, grabbed his bag, and headed down to the locker room.

Luca's quiet reprieve, the warmth and safety beneath his blanket didn't last as long as he had hoped. It was the creak of the lock on the door sliding back that brought him back to half-consciousness. The shock of the cold air on his skin that had him fully awake and aware, and the bright glare of the light shining in his eyes that had him ducking further into the corner.

He knew the shapes of the men who had left him in the cell, could make them out by their silhouettes alone but it was the new man, the one slowly sitting in the chair being placed a safe distance away that he didn't recognize. He was wrapped in a warm coat, knowing it would be freezing down in the cells, which only made Luca wonder if he was the one the footsteps above belonged to.

"Hello?" Rollins snapped his fingers twice. "Eyes on me." It wasn't like Luca had even looked away from him, in fact, against all his conditioning, he was staring the man down. He could feel him, sense his designation from where he sat. His captor was only a beta. "You might be wondering why you're here."

The pause was for Luca to beg, or agree, or even move, but he held as still as he could.

The man before sighed. "All right, let me explain. You..." He pointed to him as if he were an idiot. "Are on the wrong pack lands, my friend. We don't deal well with strangers, and our alphas are not the kindest in the world."

That got Luca to shift just a little because somewhere in his damaged mind, he remembered the alpha's touch, how it calmed him, how he made no attempt at hostility. He had even stayed to talk to the doctors, which Luca only knew because he faked sleeping just to see what the man would do.

"Oh, that got something from you, didn't it?" The man in front of him leaned forward, elbows to his knees as he laced his fingers together.

Luca froze, eyes wide at his own misstep.

"Well, let me tell you how this is going to go, *friend*." The man smiled, but it was full of cruelty and malice, something Luca knew well. "I have to be at a meeting in thirty minutes to report on your condition. So, we're going to start with a few questions, and if you answer them, you might get rewarded, if not—" He looked at the big men that surrounded him. "Now..." Luca tensed, preparing himself for what came next. "Let's begin.

THE INTERIOR of Alexandru's office is an organized mess, something that hadn't changed at all since before his death. Juli wouldn't allow it to change, she needed everything to remain as it was. Like a tomb or a shrine in his memory.

Noel hated it.

There were books everywhere, not only stacked haphazardly on shelves, but also on the desk, lounge chairs, floor, there were even some on the windowsills crowding the plants, which were—weirdly enough—well-watered and vibrant. Most of the books were research ones, thick and well-worn, and nothing Noel would ever think of touching.

An open planner lay centered on the desk but wasn't set on the last day Alexandru was in the room, it was up to date, set on the last week his mother had been in town. A blue suit jacket, without an ounce of lint or dust on it, covered the back of the chair, and the only plastic plant in the office sat on the corner of the desk. Noel was sure it was supposed to be some sort of flower, but he knew his dad liked to pick at things and had probably removed the petals long ago.

To the right, beside the door, was a wide, metal filing cabinet, maybe five feet long and filled with picture frames. Of them, three were larger eight-by-ten frames that held family photos, while the smaller ones were more individual and trio shots of the kids together, but those main ones were like looking through the years.

The oldest was right after Ellie was born, when their family was complete, the middle when she was nearly eight, and the last was the Christmas before he passed away, when all five of them staged a reenactment of the very first, with Juli trying to cradle Ellie in her arms. That was the one Noel focused on, the one he slipped up to, and reached out, tapping his fingers on the glass.

It brought him back to the last time he saw his father alive and the very last conversation he had with him. It was a year ago, the end of Fall semester, when late entry acceptance letters for Spring sessions were still coming in.

Alexandru, who looked like an older version of Noel, was on his way out the door, ready for a day of teaching, but he was one of those professors who wanted to be approachable, so the Doctor title was dropped for either Alex or Mr. Summerford, and he tended to dress the part of someone not of his standing.

In jeans, a dress shirt, and an old sports jacket, he stepped out of the house and headed down towards the driveway. Last one in, first one out. They had a garage, but it was used to hold the kids' seasonal equipment and the Jeep when the top wouldn't go on correctly, otherwise all four cars were in the driveway.

Noel was usually home first, since classes ended at random times, his truck pulled up close to the house, Keegan's Jeep was behind him, only because of the teen's tendency to run out at any given point in time. Juli's Crosstrek was up beside Noel's and Alexandru's Kia finished out the pattern.

With his keys in hand, Alex stopped at the driver's side door, and hit the unlock button, adjusting the worn leather satchel in one hand as he tugged open the door.

Just as he tossed the satchel in, Noel made his presence known, bolting out of the front door and down the steps.

"Dad!" Alex smiled as his oldest approached, but the grin didn't seem to reach his eyes. "Hey, you said we'd talk about my acceptance letter to UMass this morning."

"Sorry, Kid," he did his best to be gentle. "I'm running late, can we do it over lunch?"

With the door pulled open wide, Alex stepped around, one foot on the floorboard as Noel stuffed his hands in his pockets, shivering from the chill of the air.

"The deadline's tomorrow for transfers."

The silence between them spread, and while Alexandru had hoped to let his son down easy, he knew it was now or never. "I don't think you should go to UMass."

"But, Dad," Noel shook his head, trying to figure out how to argue that. "It's a great college, why would I not want to go, and the commute is only another thirty minutes?"

"It is. It's really good, but—"

"You think I should stay here and play alpha while you and Mom run off to do your stuff?"

"Noel, your mother and I—"

Noel remembered the laugh, the sarcastic smile on his face as he stepped back, away from his dad's outstretched hand. "Save it." The smile fell, and he rolled his shoulders. "I know how this goes. You have a dig to get to, and Mom has pack relations to take care of, so," he cleared his throat. "I'm just the built-in babysitter."

"That's not true."

"Funny." He stepped back again. "It seems that way. Whatever." He waved him off. "It's fine. I got class to get ready for." Noel turned away, headed for the house and without looking back, he gave a curt wave. "See you at lunch."

He remembered hearing his dad get in the car, the slam of the door shutting, and the revving of the engine, but he was already inside, the front door closed and locked behind him. There was no fixing that conversation.

The memory that came next would haunt him forever, cementing that last conversation as something he could never take back. He was out the door not twenty minutes later, after arguing with Keegan about taking Ellie to school, and on route to the college when he came up on a small Kia surrounded by fire trucks, ambulances, and blocked off by cruisers.

He wasn't going to stop, with the flames that high it was too dangerous to even think of it, but it was the license plate, the white and red one tacked to the back of the tailgate melting that made his heart, and his truck stop.

Noel parked just beyond the line, jumping from the cab as soon as the engine had stopped, and he raced towards the scene. The plate, six red letters, barely visible from the smoke and orange flames, which read "SMRFRD," disconnected from the plastic hatch of the car, clanging to the asphalt as the water from the trucks tried desperately to douse the fire.

He knew he screamed, that he headed straight for the fire, uncaring on whether or not it would burn him. He had to get to his dad, and silence blocked out the sounds of everything. His voice, the sirens, the loud flow of the pressure from the hoses, everything as he made out the shape behind the wheel.

A cop wrapped his arms around Noel's waist, picking him up off the ground, holding him back. It wasn't an easy feat since Noel was high on adrenaline, but it didn't take long before two more joined the effort to keep the boy back, to keep him safe. The world around him began to blur with tears, and the blissfulness of unconsciousness.

Noel drew his hand away from the picture, feeling the heat of those flames again, and swallowed down the bile that rose in his throat. He could still smell the smoke on bad nights, still hear the muffled cries out for Alex, his own cries, but he could ever shake himself out of it.

It had dragged him down into a personal hell, into a darkness so thick that he barely made it out. They tried pills to help him, therapy, but there was no coming back, at least he thought. It was six months later, while on a camping trip with the family, anything to get away, that Noel couldn't fight it anymore.

The water was cold, as it usually was so far north because while summer temps were up in the eighties in Westmore, Vermont, the temperature in Willoughby Lake rarely got up past sixty in the shade of the mountains, even colder the further down into its depth. Noel had agreed to go out on the lake with his cousins, something that they usually did, but when he stopped the boat far offshore, his thoughts weren't to swim back, it was to *not* come back.

He had filled his backpack with rocks, knowing once he hit a specific depth, his muscle control wouldn't be enough to unclamp the chest strap, and when everyone else was in the water, splashing and fooling around, he slipped that bag on, clipped it tight, and jumped in.

He didn't remember how long he was under. It had worked just the way he thought it would, sinking down into the darkness, growing colder as the sun became nothing but a spot above him.

But as his mind grew fuzzy and his lungs screamed for air, Noel saw Keegan. He saw Ellie, and he saw their life without him and how much losing one more person would affect them, his brother especially. Keegan was barely holding on, being reckless, doing things he really shouldn't, and Noel had been there at every turn to put him right back on track.

His heart thumped, his fingers fought to find the latch, slipping and catching on the sharp corner of the plastic, slicing a line across the side of his wrists, and by a twist of fate he was able to free himself from the weight, even as the blood from the cut turned the water a deluded pink around him. It was the teen himself that appeared next, this time swimming through the water like a fish, and his arm wrapped around Noel's waist, holding him tightly. He had never been so happy for a touch, but when they breached the water, the two parted ways without a single word.

Keegan was furious, evident in his eyes and the way he scowled at his older brother. He just released him, scoffed, and swam back towards the boat without a sound. Noel watched him go, treading water as he gulped down the oxygen his body needed to right itself. When he was settled, still shaking and cold, he followed him, surprised that no one else noticed, none the wiser to his plans or his rescue.

Except Keegan, whose glare continued to this day, as if that one pissed off look would keep Noel from doing anything so stupid again. And it did.

He got help. He confessed his plan to his doctor, he worked on a treatment, and the world got brighter. He even accepted Keegan's hostility, but he knew it couldn't keep going. He needed his brother back.

The click of a lock had him whipping around from the photo, eyes wide as the door, one that separated Juli's office from Alexandru's, opened wide and Illy, a studious blonde with a pixie cut, entered the room without even looking up, at least until Noel shifted.

She gasped, eyes locked right on him, and slammed the book in her hand closed, other hand over her heart. "You scared the hell out of me, Noel. What are you doing here?"

He hesitated a moment, thinking of a lie, a good one because even though she wasn't pack, or even genetically linked to a wolf, she could spot a lie a mile away.

"I need a book for Sociology. We're doing pack dynamics and well, Wilkes is an asshole who likes research. I think I remember Dad having a book about it in..." He pointed at the room marked private behind him.

"Well, that's why we keep this stuff in here." She moved to the shelves, swapped out the book in her hand with another and headed back towards the door. "Lock up when you're done." Noel gave a quick grin and a nod, but Illy paused in the doorway. "Tell Keegan to bring back the one he borrowed two weeks ago, okay? I was looking for it the other day for your mom's class."

"Keegan took a book?"

"Yeah, he's always looking at them." Her reply seemed to be filled with confusion, and it was justified, because Noel had no clue. "Just... don't touch his notes."

"Got it."

Illy closed the door behind her, leaving him in the silence of the office.

With an exhale, one that released all of his emotions, Noel drew his eyes from the picture in front of him and scanned the room one more time. Not a speck of dust on anything, like Alexandru was still here, and his eyes landed on the door beside the cabinet, one marked "private."

It was a place he was never allowed to go before. In fact, it was usually locked, but something today made him curious, and he stepped up, grabbed the brass knob, and twisted. The door popped open, the interior lights automatically clicked on, and with one quick look around, Noel stepped through.

The chattering in the main hall was what pulled Gus from the files on the computer. On his way out, he yanked the papers from the printer, and entered the room where five pack members waited. They were chatting amongst themselves, unaware of his arrival but that was fine. It was Rollins who entered from the inner doors that caught his attention anyway.

The beta nodded at Gustaf, moving up towards his seat beside the head chair and with a roll of his eyes, Gus moved to stand at the end, dropping the stack of papers with a loud thwack that caught the attention of the others in the room. He checked his watch, then glanced up at the clock on the wall, as the remaining five moved to the seats. Seven, seven of them at a table that seated twelve.

"Is it done?" His voice was low, directed right at Rollins, and the beta gave him a curt nod.

"He was transported a little over an hour ago to the requested secured location."

"Good," Gus shifted his gaze to the others in the room. Quinlan Gervais, the black-haired beta in the business suit was to his left. Kevin O'Leary, a seventy-five-year-old ornery man stood beside her. James Mason, middle-aged and annoying, took up the end. Talia White, one of the higher-ranking betas at her corporation, dressed in designer attire stood across from him, and Shain Lee, foreman of his construction company, was in the middle between White and Rollins. They were all quiet, waiting for him to start, and he felt every eye burrowing in. "I realize a meeting was called by our alpha for later this afternoon. However, certain events have come to light that made convening earlier necessary."

"What would be so important that we couldn't have waited for Alpha Summerford to arrive?" That was Gervais, and while she wouldn't usually question his actions, Gus could tell there was something just under the surface of her tone that was different.

"In her absence, the protection of pack lands falls to me. This morning, an unknown beta entered the territory and was taken to County General." The whispers that filled the room were something he expected, so he waited as patiently as he could for them to die down, until they didn't and he raised his hand, silencing the group. "Whoever this beta is, he was held against his will and tortured."

"Tortured? On pack lands?" O'Leary's tone was complete disbelief as if he hadn't been around in the times before pack laws were enforced, when it was the betas in his position that took care of getting the information needed to keep the pack safe. Gustaf kept his poker face, maintaining as neutral an expression as possible.

"I don't believe so, but that doesn't stop my fear that someone might be out there looking for him."

"So, why not send him back out where he came from?" That did get a response as Gus glared at Gervais and let a rumble of disappointment flow through him.

"We do not harm those who come to us in need," he reminded her. "And there's a problem with that train of thought."

"I see no problem with tossing a packless beta back out in the world." Rollins' smug comment had the Pack Second shaking his head.

"If this man is who I believe him to be," Gus paused, hoping to keep his composure. "He's not packless, he's missing."

The voices in the hall rose as Gus placed his fists against the table, took two seconds to compose himself before praying for strength. He really was trying, and thank God Juli wasn't there to see his patience quickly coming to an end.

He raised his hand, closed his eyes, and opened his mouth to speak just as the doors to the left of the table opened and Nicholas Fogerty, a nervous, wide-eyed young man entered in a state of panic. He was an intern, only there to do the books usually first thing in the morning, so when he came skidding to a halt right beside him, Gus was curious.

He waited a moment, eyes flitting over the betas in the room before he landed on Gus and gave a slight bow. He was terrified, Gus could see it in the way his hands shook.

"Alpha?" The shake of his voice had the word going up an octave before Fogerty caught his breath. "There's news."

Gus turned towards him, taking in the stench of fear from the kid, and narrowed his eyes.

ROLLING HIS SHOULDERS, Noel took in everything about the mysterious room that he could. Each shelf not only held books, but artifacts, some he recognized from discussions his father would have with them during dinner, some just as mysterious to him as they looked. Most of them had to do with wolves, werewolves, general mythology, or the regions the lore came from.

He found statues that were crafted out of jade, small bone wolves with intricate designs struck a chord in him, and paintings encased in class that resembled tattoos on skin, but while most were black, somewhere bright with color.

Noel cringed at the thought of it being actual human skin and pulled his hand away from the frame faster than he thought his reflexes were capable of. A full-body shiver went through him, causing goosebumps to crawl up his skin and he stepped back. He recognized things from Greece, Romania, and something he believed was Celtic, but he wasn't positive. Even the books themselves were strange but inviting.

In the middle of the room sat a long table filled with more old books, and some that were a lot newer than Noel thought was possible, all on the mythology of werewolves. Most were open to the last pages Alexandru had flipped to, and the older ones contained hand-drawn depictions of the beasts, some dating back centuries.

His fingers caressed the pages as he looked over them, shifting books out of the way to see the passages under them, then gently slipping them back into the same position they had been, as if he didn't want to disturb the flow. In the back, tucked down in the middle of a u-shaped collection of open tomes, was a small space void of anything but a legal pad, and Noel leaned in close in the dim light to see if he could decipher any of the shorthand notes that graced the page.

He remembered some of it, a few of the words that his father had taught him one summer, years ago when Noel was still curious about what his parents did for a living, but without more time, there was no way he was getting down to the bottom of it.

He glanced to his right, caught the names printed in gold along the spines of the books that rested in two, four-foot sections. They were thin, not more than three-quarters of an inch wide on most, black, leather-bound books and those names on them, they were pack names of those not only in the immediate area, but the surrounding states as well, and they all had one thing in common.

They had once been part of the Summerford pack.

He ran his hands down the spines, repeating the names in his head as he touched them, until he came to the very last Summerford name. Gently, he removed it from its spot, turned to the table behind him, and opened the book carefully to some random page, but they were all the same.

A list of names. They were in no way alphabetized, not even in chronological order. Most were the first, middle, and last name of a person, followed by parents first names only, then birth dates, death dates, and curiously followed by the secondary designation. This particular volume, or at least the page he had landed on, started sometime in the late 1800s.

Noel knew his father was one of the top researchers of Lycanthropy, and Therianthropy. It was why Wilkes' little lecture had gotten under his skin, beside whatever the hell was going on with his biology at the moment but knowing his dad's work was being spoken by that asshat had only served to piss him off more.

This. This was totally different.

Noel grabbed the legal pad from where it sat, glanced around the room until he found a small desk lamp and shifted it to the table, before flipping on the light. That was when he noticed the little notation on the edge of each line of documentation. It stated how many children each person had.

Noel grabbed the chair, swung it around to the side of the table where everything was set up and sat down. With a pause, just to steady himself, he licked his lips and reached for the edge of the page. He knew a lot of the names further into the book, recognized cousins from his childhood, great aunts and uncles, even a few of *their* grandparents, but it was the shifting of the penmanship that really had his attention.

His father had written some of the last pages, or rewritten, Noel wasn't sure, but from 1936 on, it was all Alexandru's fluid strokes. Noel sat back, unable to turn that last page, knowing what he would find there, and in that moment, taking a break from the entries, he noticed something he hadn't before.

In the middle of the table, stacked upon the books, new and old, was one volume with a name written in a language he recognized but didn't know. The name on the very battered, very old book was "Cei Dintre Noi," and there was an extra-large Post-It sticking out of the pages.

The instant his fingers touched it, a cold draft wafted through the small room, and his bright eyes shifted to find the source. Spooked and uncertain, he continued his mission, this time achieving it by yanking the paper from between the weight of the pages.

The handwriting was fluid, legible, and matched the ledger entry to a tee. Alex had been writing both. Noel sat forward, holding the new paper under the light to better see the words, and the title.

"Symptoms of lycanthropy," he whispered, as if he were in the middle of a crowded room. "Heightened sensitivity to noise, aches in the gums from extended canines, bouts of heightened vision, for example, possible white out flares. Blood under the—" He stopped, swallowed back the sudden fear as he glanced down at his fingers, at the dark, dried blood that had been caught under the cuticle, something he would need a scrub brush for, and willed away the heat on the back of his neck. "Under the fingernails and nail beds from nocturnal shifts. Anamorphic shifts during the full moon?"

Noel stood straight, his eyes going to the legal pad that now sat below the ledger. The words he recognized, the ones he immediately knew. They were just like this, they matched *this*. He knew his dad spent a lot of time looking into their history, into their family line, but he never knew why.

Not until now.

Noel dropped the paper, flipped that final page, and ran his finger down it until he came to the last few names that Alexandru entered. Theirs. It was his name, Keegan's, Ellie's and beside each one was their designation, with a blank space under Ellie's.

His eyes went back to the last line of the note paper, finger now on it to make sure he could understand what he was looking at.

"Most common triggers," his voice was low again, cracking with the energy that vibrated through him. "Stress during heightened times of crisis in one particular designation. Most notably, an—" He stopped. His gaze went back to the family page one more time, landing on his name, in his father's handwriting. He dragged the note paper down, placed the last word above the designation beside his name. "An alpha."

Noel dropped everything, stood straight and tented his hand over his nose.

"Holy shit!" He barked out in a panic as he paced the small area between one end of the table and the other. "Holy shit!"

Noel reached out quickly, grabbed the edge of the family ledger and slammed the book shut.

"He thinks we can shift."

Gus wasn't sure what to make of the fidgety kid who suddenly stopped talking and stood quiet and still. He knew he had to approach with caution, the omega in front of him was seconds away from passing out.

"Go on," he urged.

"There was a call that just came in." His eyes went from one beta to the next before Gus stepped in front of him blocking his view, getting him to focus right on him. "From the security team at the airport." Gus crossed his arms, keeping his gaze locked on the kid. "The plane...it never left Midway."

He was pretty sure he heard that wrong.

All the noise in the room stopped, all the air was sucked out at the same time a blast of heat felt like it was lighting him on fire, and Gus was dumbfounded.

"I'm sorry." He blinked, once, twice, before he narrowed his eyes. "What did you say?"

"Sir, Alpha Summerford's plane never took off."

Behind him, the six people at the table whispered amongst themselves, their voice growing louder with each passing second, but Gustaf only had to raise his hand to silence them, his eyes locked on Fogerty. "Repeat."

"She never boarded, and the plane never departed."

His heart nearly stopped. This wasn't happening, this was some sort of joke, Juli was planning on—

His eyes began to glow, the bright red shine of his power was at full intensity, and he could feel every person in the room.

But his voice stayed calm. "Do you have more information?"

"Mr. Payne is unavailable as well. No one can reach him."

He would have admired the kid, how even his voice sounded in the presence of an angry alpha, but he was too busy trying not to rip out his throat. Gus turned to the table, eyes closed, and slammed his fist down against the wood, rattling everyone in the room. Fogerty's bravado instantly faded.

"Get security on the phone." The low growl of the words flowed in Fogerty's direction, but the man did nothing but tremble. "*NOW*!"

The omega was quick to take out his cell, dialed the number he had just hung up with and made his way through the instructions to get to his contact. All the while, Gus paced, his back to the six as he went over everything from the night before.

He could feel the moment Rollins stood as the omega held the phone out to Gus, but he didn't make a move when the alpha snatched it away and gently put it to his ear. He didn't know who's on the line, he didn't care, he just wanted to know one thing.

"What the hell is going on? Where's my alpha?"

He never dreamed; never fell into the memories of the places he had been *before*. Never thought of what happened, or how he came to be where he was, but he could see it now, like the beating had jostled something loose. It was all so confusing.

His face hurt. His eyes swelled with the bruising. The tenderness of the flesh on his cheeks smarted, but it wasn't anything close to what he had endured in the time before. That was what he was going to call it, "the time before" because anything was better than where he had been.

But he never dreamed.

Not until now.

He could feel the sun, the warmth of it on his skin, and not just his arms, but his chest and back, and the coolness of the water that surrounded him. He was swimming, at least he thought he was, it had been so long since he thought of water being something other than a torture tactic, but yes... swimming.

His vision filled with the beauty of a tree lined lake, as his ears picked up the laughter beside him. He was young, his hands were wrinkled by prolonged exposure to the water he stood in, and as he turned around, he could see the reason for the sound.

She was petite, dark-haired, and stunning, but she wasn't alone. Beside her, with a good foot of height towering over her, was a man, familiar in such a way that his heart ached when he looked at him. Luca focused on his wavy hair, unruly in its attempt to fall in his face, both of them wet from swimming, but that wasn't all he noticed, at least, not about her.

Her belly, though not overly large, was round, as if she held a small beachball hidden in her suit, and in his arms was a boy, wide, blue eyes and a scoff of curly black hair on his head, not more than a year and a half. The little one was squirming to get out of his father's arms, to get away while laughing hysterically, but it was the way the child was reaching that got him.

His little hands opened and closed, beckoning him to come get him, to hold him, and while he could feel his movement in the water, he never got any closer. The boy only giggled, crying out something like "unca" or "uncle" but he couldn't reach him, even as he brought his arms up to close the distance.

That sun faded, the heat that surrounded him disappeared and he was left in the dark, cold and panicked beneath a black hood. He could feel the ties on his ankles, the ones that held his hands behind his back, and his heart raced.

This memory he knew, instinctively. This was the moment he was pulled from his family, away from the security of his life. It wasn't so close to the memory before, but years later. His thoughts traveled to a small baby girl, the way she fit in his arms, the softness of her voice, cooing up at him as she moved her uncoordinated arms trying to grab his attention. Her eyes were so blue, deep like the ocean.. but that too, faded to darkness.

Luca blinked back to the chill of the cell, the pain of the hits he had taken. He never spoke, never uttered a word to the man, never made a sound as they pummeled his body. He had been there before, he knew how to take it, and not break. He didn't then, not in the time before, and he made a vow not to now.

The light from the afternoon sun shined in, giving a small rectangle of light to the opposite wall of the room. With a deep inhale, and some internal motivation, he moved the mat to that small space, hoping to soak up the heat.

And it worked, huddled in the blanket as the warmth began to grow from the rays that filtered in.

Under that thin blanket, Luca fell back into the dreamless sleep he had come to know and cherished the thought of those small glimpses of someone else's past.

CHAPTER 10

Noel leaned back against a lamp post outside the same building he had left Keira at nearly an hour and a half before. His mind was going in a million directions from all the information he had seen in his dad's private room.

He thought they could shift, and not only a little but into actual werewolves, something that had been lost centuries ago, according to the old family legends. Had his father gone off his rocker before his death? Had something he found at a dig triggered his obsession about the whole thing? There was no way any of them would be transforming into some hairy beast when the moon was full, that was just—

"Insane." He shook his head as he stuffed his hands down into his pockets. The chill in the air made the tips of them tingle and he turned his thoughts outwards to the goings-on of the people around him. Anything to distract him from whatever the hell was floating around in his head.

Like earlier in the more populated area of campus, Noel observed the way groups moved, all talking at once but seeming to understand the conversation. He saw the loving, cupid-eyed couples holding hands as they stared up at one another, not bothering to look where they were going. In fact, once or twice he held down a chuckle when one of the partners tripped over a root or forgot where the sidewalk ended and nearly landed on their ass in the grass.

But with all that was happening around him, what shook him completely back to reality was the phone in his pocket vibrating.

Holding it up to see the banner, Noel sighed. He swore with every bell he was getting some sort of update, all except the one he was waiting on from Juli. It was Ellie again, and he swiped his thumb along the home screen to see the full text thread.

Ellie: *What's with Keegan today?*

Guess Noel knew what he was doing on the way to the meetinghouse.

Noel: *It's Keegan being Keegan. I'll talk to him later. It's been a day from hell anyway.*

Ellie: *Why? What's going on?*

Noel: *Not really in the mood to talk about it right now.*

That was where the waiting game began. The reply bubble in the text went on, and on, and Noel rolled his eyes.

"What are you doing, Ell? Writing a book?" But a simple *"Okay"* was his only answer back from the younger sibling. "Unbelievable."

"What is?" Keira's unexpected appearance made him jolt, quickly tucking the phone away as he turned toward her, smiling.

"I guess it's a Summerford family's bad day."

"Keegan?"

"No, actually. That was Ellie, but she's worried about him."

"You are too, I can tell." She slipped her hand into his and the two headed off to their next stop. "He's not handling the change well, is he?"

"None of us do, but with him...it's his anxiety. He hates it." Noel didn't want to talk about Keegan. He certainly didn't want to start down the road of questions about how he spent his free time between classes which meant it was time for a subject change. "So, how was creative writing?"

"Don't say it like that," she giggled as she gave him a little nudge.

"Like what?"

"Creative writing is a very important class, Noel."

He grinned at her, loved to get her riled up, even if it was to get away from his own thoughts. "I know. I know." He pulled her to a stop, wrapped his arms around her and kissed her softly, trying to peck away the pout on her lips. "I'm sorry, I didn't mean to pick on your writing class."

She narrowed her eyes at him, pretending to be offended, but it didn't work. Two more kisses and she was smiling up at him. "How was history?"

"Ancient." He yawned out, hoping she didn't ask for the topic of the day, but he slipped away from her, took her by the hand and pulled at her gently. "Come on, I'm starving."

"For what? We had food before class."

His smirk told her everything she should have needed. "You know how they have that reserved space in the library?"

She stopped dead, getting him to turn. "Yeah?"

He dug down in his pocket and pulled a small key out, one with a plastic tag. "I kinda forgot to return the key."

Keira giggled as he waggled his brows at her, tugging her along, before she went willingly with him towards the library building. They had thirty minutes before their last classes for the day started.

"Control Headquarters - Chicago, Illinois"

Drake held the handset to his ear, his expression blank as he let the alpha on the other end growl into the phone. He stood in front of several large screens surrounded by men and women at desks behind and around him. On a loop, video from different angles covering the private airstrip played on repeat.

The time stamp on them was just before nine p.m.

Those around him continue about their day, unaware of the drama about to begin between him and the Summerford Pack Second, but he wasn't worried about them, he was worried about the man on the other end.

"Where's *my* alpha?" repeated in his ear and Drake smiled, finally breaking that cold facade.

"They were supposed to contact *you*, Gus, not your little intern," Drake grumbled, that smile fading as he addressed his old comrade-in-arms. "Stay calm and I'll tell you what I have."

"Well, they didn't contact me. It's been well over the allotted time for any kind of contact, Drake. Don't make me reach through this phone and—"

"Easy, Lieutenant," he let the title roll off his tongue, reminding Gus of his old position, and at his silence, Drake continued. "If you're ready."

"Tell me what I want to know."

"Well." He cleared his throat, grabbed a remote and took in the screens, following their order. "Looks like they were ambushed. Juli never got on the plane. Her assistant is dead, along with three of her detail."

"What the— Why weren't we told sooner?"

"Watch your tone, Alpha. I work for the World Council, not for you, and my friend died protecting *your* Pack Alpha."

Silence filled the line but for only a few seconds. "Forgive me."

The screens before Drake showed the same thing. A man, the one believed to be in charge, had his back to the camera ninety percent of the time. There were no absolute shots of his face. The car they arrived in was also positioned so there were no clear visible markers, no plates, and no way of determining the make and model.

"Just tell me she's not dead." Gustaf's words were pleas for any good information, but Drake didn't really have any, he only had one thing that might give him some hope.

"She's been taken."

In the meeting room, halfway across the country, Gus's eyes went wide, and he felt his world spin as his face went pale, in shock at those words on the line. The cell slipped from his hand, clattering on the floor as he reached out to brace himself against the wall. There came a pause, a stillness in the room before he shook it off, and straightened, suddenly becoming the poster child for composed and emotionless.

Fogerty rushed for the phone, scooped it up and put it to his ear, letting the man on the other end know what was going on before he disappeared into a corner away from the quiet alpha.

Gustaf turned to the council in front of him, to the six that still sit waiting on news, and he stood at the head of the table, eyes on them but not seeing any. He only saw Juli in his mind, her smile, her light, and he whispered; "Alpha Summerford is missing."

The sound in the room erupted as the members of the council began throwing questions at him, but he just stared at the spot before him. His fists clenched, pressing against the wood, and his eyes flashed a bright red, before he turned and left the room, headed for the office on the right.

Fifteen boys and girls stood in a circle, all facing inward on the polished gymnasium floor, dressed in the blue and gold uniforms of the Collins Junior/Senior High School. All but Keegan.

There was no way he was getting into those ugly blue shorts, not with the way they barely kept *anything* private on the football player he was trying hard not to look at. Daniel was standing directly across from him, and Keegan couldn't afford the distraction, not with O'Donnell around.

He wore the shirt though—hurrah for school spirit—and that was only because of the deal he had made with Hebert to raise his attendance, the shirt or nothing. He was perfectly fine with the black joggers he wore. They were loose enough, and they had deep enough pockets for his cell and his keys, two things he was never without.

Okay, maybe he wasn't really offended by the shorts, at least not on Daniel, which was probably because it was becoming harder and harder to ignore the man across from him. He could tell by looking at the jock that he wasn't the only one affected by the proximity of the other.

Pack members had this weird thing, though Keegan was pretty sure it was a myth, or at least he *had* been pretty sure it was one until he met Daniel without the constant scent of his teammates overriding his own.

True mates were a thing, at least a thing of legends and bedtime stories, almost like the whole prince/princess mythology Juli had told Ellie when she was little.

"One day you'll meet your Prince Charming."

Well, for people like him it was a little bit like that, but more like smelling something that you loved—like fresh baked pie—and having it amplified ten-thousand times, making you want it no matter where you were or how many times you smelled it.

His dad didn't do a great job of explaining it either, but Keegan got the point. The thing was it wasn't one sided. That person, that *mate* would feel the effects too, and they'd be drawn to each other.

Keegan hated it.

Hated being what he was, being attracted to him—no, wait, he didn't hate that part at all—most of all, he hated it happening during school. Which was why he never even noticed Coach O'Donnell—the heavy set, balding douche wearing the too tight shorts with a bright red whistle around his neck—moving up behind him until his voice broke through the haze, and Keegan straightened, his muscles tightened, and fear set in.

He was four students away, hands behind his back, eyeing over the crowd. “This week starts our track try-outs. I expect every single one of you slackers to be there, and I expect your best performance.”

Even with the panic building in him, Keegan shook his head, he couldn’t keep his expression neutral. He despised the man more than anything, and there was a reason for that, a reason for the absences and the panic, and that reason was stepping closer.

“It’s been a while since we were in the championship, so this year *will* be different.”

Keegan’s heart thumped painfully against his chest as the nasty, old body-odor scent of the man got close enough to drown out Daniel, and he could feel the heat of him at his back, crowding in on him. His whole body stiffened, ready for something, anything, but all he could do was curl his hands into fists, locking his eyes on the dark ones across the room as Daniel took one step forward.

Keegan’s clenched jaw and obvious tension triggered something in the alpha, a need to protect so strong he wanted to tear the old man apart, but a minute shake of Keegan’s head held him back. Mates were funny like that. The anger rose in him, his lips curling up, as he fought to control his breathing, even locked where he was.

“We lost our top runner when Summerford graduated. Since then, well, this team’s been crap.” O’Donnell leaned in, blowing against Keegan’s neck. The rancid scent of coffee tainted with whiskey was the only thing he could smell, and he cracked his neck if only to try to move away. It was the whisper that got Keegan. “I expect you to be a good boy,” and that pause meant exactly what Keegan feared, “and fill your brother’s shoes.”

Keegan let that smirk roll up on his lips. His survival instinct told him the more of a sarcastic asshole he was, the faster they’d leave him alone, so it was his go-to, but that didn’t mean it always worked.

“I have no intention of being near a pedo like you.” He knew it was useless; he had been trying to get away from this guy for years, and this was his last-ditch effort.

O’Donnell grabbed him by the back of the neck, squeezing tightly as Keegan stiffened in his hold.

The threat of danger broke the spell Daniel was under, but before he could take more than one step, Greg held him back, grabbing his arm and digging his fingers in.

"What are you doing?"

Daniel turned his glare on him, but Greg wasn't pack, he was human. He didn't understand. "You're seeing the same shit I am, man. Don't pretend you're not."

"It's Summerford," and whatever Greg's logic was, it didn't make Daniel's irritation at his friend any less. He yanked his arm away, feeling the scratch of Greg's nails on his skin. "Probably mouthed off and was just asking for it."

"You're a real piece of work." Daniel turned to him, chest to chest, but something in the air had him glancing at Keegan.

There it was again. That small, almost nonexistent shake of his head meant just for him, and Daniel couldn't believe what he's seeing. Keegan's not moving, not putting up a fight, not yet, and he didn't want Daniel to either. He shifted, bumping Greg with his shoulder as he turned to watch what was going on across the room. His eyes flared a bright red, something Keegan instantly picked up on, and the smirk on the beta's face fell.

Daniel stood in disbelief, wondering if anyone closer was going to make a move, but they all shifted, moved away, pretended not to notice, and the pleading look in his eyes was for Keegan alone.

The hold on his neck tightened, causing Keegan to wince at the feel of it, knowing he would probably have bruises later that he'd have to explain to Noel...*if* his brother was paying any attention, and he was usually good at cornering him, so he needed a good excuse.

"Don't take that tone of voice with me, boy!" And the smirk was back, because that was just the tinder he needed to spark the fire again. "You don't know how much influence I have in this town!"

He turned his head just enough to look the coach right in the eyes with his own bright gold and locked on. There was fury there, an anger that he held back because he wasn't going to jail for this guy.

"And you don't know how fast my mother could have your balls if you don't take your hands off me."

O'Donnell held the stare for a moment more before he smirked, a dead to rights creepy smile that could only betray his true intentions, and shoved Keegan forward, causing him to stumble a step or two before he righted himself.

He turned, head held high, and studying the coach as he continued his way around the class, but he was barely holding it in. His chest rose and fell in rapid succession. The breaths he took were not nearly deep enough to keep his head from spinning and his body shook with adrenaline.

HIs golden gaze faded to hazel as he scanned the group. No one was looking at him, no one even acknowledging what just happened, not one. Except Daniel.

The creeper's voice faded off into incoherent babble, at least to his ears, as Keegan blinked, holding back every emotion, even the ones he wanted to show, the fight he wanted to get into. He inhaled slowly, taking in the scent of the man across the room, drowning out the rancid body odor and whiskey that he felt crawling on his skin, and with one more look, he turned and walked out of the room.

Gus paced the office, shook his head, clearing his thoughts, and the angry red he knew was in his eyes. He could see the haze around his vision and no matter what he wanted to do; he knew it wouldn't accomplish anything.

He dug out his cell, tapped angrily on the screen, wishing the people who took what was his would feel it as much as the screen, and finally put it to his ear. It only rang twice before connecting.

"Marcus," the monotone voice on the other end answered.

"Get me Willard."

"He's out to lunch."

Gus stopped dead in his tracks. "I don't give a flying fuck if he's out to lunch put him on the damn— Hello?"

The line went silent, and he pulled the phone away to make sure the line hadn't disconnected, but the minutes were still counting. He only waited a few seconds before it connected again.

"Hello," the gruff man on the other end grumbled.

"I need something."

"Alpha, my apologies. Marcus is a useless twit. What can I do for you?"

"Like I said, I need something."

"I'm working as fast as I can to get the info you need on the beta—"

"No, it doesn't have anything to do with him."

"Then what?"

"Video surveillance of the Council's private air strip at Chicago Midway."

"Video—"

"Yes, video surveillance. Chicago Midway." Was everyone he dealt with an idiot, or was it just the moon?

"Personal or pack related."

"Don't ask stupid questions, just do it now!"

"I can have it to you—"

"Now, Willard!"

"Okay, but it's going to take codes I don't have at the moment, give me fifteen."

"As soon as you can."

"Do I contact you directly?"

"Yes."

"I'll call you back."

Gus ended the call, closed his eyes and dropped into one of the lounge chairs under the window. He drew in through his nose, and released it slowly, before running his palm down his face. With a sigh, he scanned the room, eyes going over every inch of the office, taking in things that belonged to the current Pack Alpha, including the family picture that hung on the wall.

"Oh, Juli." He shut his eyes tightly, counted silently to five before he looked around once more. "What the hell did you do?"

The phone in his hand vibrated, and not just once, but continuously until he flipped it over to look at the Illinois number. With a scowl, he brought it up against his ear. "Segal."

"It's Drake, we got disconnected."

"No, we didn't."

"Really," the man on the other end huffed, his voice filled with humor, probably trying to get the alpha to relax. *"Figured you pulled a pansy ass move and probably fainted, so I decided to call you back."*

"Fuck off, Drake," but his comeback didn't stop the smile on his lips. "Just tell me what I need to know."

"Is this line secure?"

"You called my cell, so, yes."

He sat forward in the chair, elbows to knees as he held the phone and waited for news, any news of what might have happened.

THE DOOR CREAKED, and a tray slid in, pulling Luca back to his new reality, causing him to freeze at the sound of it. The light had shifted, he was no longer in the warmth, but the steam that came from the tray wasn't something he could ignore. He crawled to it when the door was firmly shut, crawled on hand and knees across the loose dirt beneath him and leaned over the bowl of what looked like stew.

In a moment of hesitation, he wondered if it was poisoned, but it was fleeting as he grabbed the small, three-inch stick of bread and used it as a spoon to start scooping up the hot mess. It worked, even if it burned his mouth, but the feeling of the mixture hitting his stomach had him pausing.

It showed how long he had been without solid food, the way it hit him like a rock, and he curled into himself, letting it settle for a minute before he slowed down his rate of consumption. He needed to take it easy, let one mouthful go down at a time and breathe between each until there was nothing left of the stew but the chunks of meat and vegetables.

He used his fingers for those, not the first time he'd gotten the gritty taste of dirt with a meal, and he wasn't about to complain as he chewed thoroughly before swallowing. He had managed to finish without it coming back up and sat back on his heels if only to savor the feeling of being full. It was then that he noticed the bottle of water, snatched it up, and quickly huddled back in the corner.

He was silent, still, and listened.

"I'm opening the door. You move, I'll shoot you," came an unfamiliar voice from the other side.

Luca had no intention of moving let alone answering, but the door opened after a minute, and filled with the silhouette of a larger man. His flashlight came up, landing on Luca while he bent down and grabbed the tray. It was a tense moment before the light went off, the tray disappeared, and the door closed once more.

Time passed by in the silence, and Luca finally twisted the top off the bottle, raised it to his lips and gulped down several mouthfuls of the warm liquid. He was lucky it wasn't still cold, and he knew it. The cramps from the sudden shift would have brought up everything. He pulled the bottle away, knowing he needed to save it, take his time with it, and screwed the cap back on.

He was in the current of the air now, so moving was the only option. He grabbed the blanket, made his way gingerly across the room, and curled up once again in the corner, wrapped in the growing warmth of his own body.

Noel slipped into the still empty auditorium from the lower door. English Lit was the last class of the day and had at least ten minutes before anyone else found their way to it. He had left Keira at her room in the next building over and just had to get through this class before he could head home.

The schedule gave him about an hour of downtime before he had to head to get his siblings, but at this rate, he was just going to call the day a loss and skip it. He felt good, better than he had all day, however, there was just something under his skin that was gnawing at him.

With his keys still in his hand, having swapped out books at the truck, Noel made his way up the steps, only to stumble halfway to the row he claimed as his, his hand going to the back of the chair beside him. He managed to steady himself, unsure why he tripped in the first place, his fingers suddenly went numb, and the keys slipped away, falling between two of the seats on the other side of the aisle.

As he reached for them, a sharp, stabbing pain shot through his skull, doubling him over as he used the palms of his hands to press against his temples, hoping it would dull it some. His jaw clenched tightly; gums achy with electrical zaps that just went straight to his temples.

His hands cramped, forcing them away from his head as he curled up on the wide step, groaning in pain. He could see an outline of his vision, the orange halo around everything told him that his other side was showing, but no matter what he did, he couldn't blink it away.

The clenching of his jaw made the lower part of his face feel tight and he opened it wide, hoping to stretch it out, maybe dull the ache just a bit, but the only thing that did was bring the tearing sensation in his gums to the forefront. He ran his tongue along his teeth, feeling the way his canines descended, lengthened, and winced at the taste of blood in his mouth.

And just like that, as fast as it began, it was over.

Everything was gone. There wasn't any ache, any pain, not even a haze. The only thing left was the taste of copper, and exhaustion that ran through every muscle. His hands loosened, his body relaxed, his jaw unclenched, and Noel laid back on the step. Even his keys, which he swore were several feet away, were sitting right next to his fingertips.

He snatched them up, ran a hand over his lips, checking his palm for blood. Nothing. He turned his hand, feeling the phantom weight of his fingertips and he noticed there was definitely blood under the nail plate. Taking a moment to collect himself, to wait for his heart to slow, he debated on texting Gus, or even Keira, before he pushed to his feet, shaking.

With ragged breaths, he grabbed his bag, forced himself up the rest of the way and made it to the door, before he slipped out of the room. The door banged loudly behind him, echoing in the silence of the hall.

To hell with English, he was going home.

The locker room was empty and silent except for the light steps made by Keegan's sneakers. The metal and concrete room wasn't even the sanctuary he needed to process what the hell had happened. But, he couldn't be near people, not with how volatile he felt, with the anger boiling inside him.

He paused in front of a locker, not even his, just some random number with some random kid's things inside. He didn't care. He really didn't. He stood before it, fists clenched, eyes golden, heart racing and every little thing O'Donnell had ever said to him came racing back into his thoughts.

He bared his teeth, raised a fist, and slammed it into the medal door. The loud crack against the solid door drowned out the pain that shot through his knuckles, but it felt good. Really good. Tucking his chin to his chest, Keegan drew back again, other hand braced against the frame and let it fly. Four more times. And with each hit of his fist against the locker, the screams that were trapped inside him released, louder and louder with each hit, until he stopped.

He didn't move, at least not for a moment, catching his breath, feeling the adrenaline pumping through him take over, but his eyes moved over the dented locker. It had pushed in enough to see the contents, but the lock hadn't broken, and the hinges hadn't cracked.

He placed that bruised hand against the other side, bracing himself as the world around him tilted just a bit, and slowly he leaned his head down, skin to the cool metal, above the blood-spattered drops. The silence continued, one heartbeat, two maybe, but was broken by the slamming of the locker room door against the concrete wall as it swung open forcefully.

Keegan didn't bother moving yet, not as the boys started to file in. He didn't care if he never moved, at least until that familiar scent fills his nostrils.

Daniel stood there, frozen, eyes on the blood, on the damage to the locker, and it shifted when Keegan rolled his head to the side—if only to look at him—to the blood on his knuckles. Neither moved, not towards each other, but Daniel unknowingly created a wall between the man in front of him and the rest of the class.

Keegan inhaled, nostrils flaring, and raised his head, glaring at the jock. It was something meant as a challenge, but when it went unanswered, he grabbed his bag from the bench and headed for the door, towards Daniel. His shoulder knocked against him as he passed.

Daniel turned, eyeing after him as the door slammed shut. His wasn't the only confused expression in the room as others gathered around the dented locker, gazes locked on the now closed door, but it was the only one focused on the blood that dripped down the destroyed metal.

THE SOPHOMORE hallway was always full of gossip, so much so that most of the time Ellie didn't even need to wait to get home to figure

out what kind of trouble Keegan had gotten into. Most of the kids there would tell her whatever she needed to know. The problem was, it was more of a game for them, like taking bets on what he'd do next, she was almost happy it was his last year.

Except she wasn't happy about it at all.

She loved her brothers, but with Keegan it was more intense. She liked knowing what he was doing, *how* he was doing, which apparently wasn't hard to find out. She knew his schedule inside and out and also knew that his most hated class had ended ten minutes ago.

She feared for him, and Noel. She knew what they both were going through, even when they thought she wasn't even looking. When Noel left for a month to visit their Nan and Pops, she wasn't as deceived as they believed.

The calls he made home didn't come from Vermont. His care packages that their mom sent out weren't addressed to any town she recognized, and when he came back, he wasn't just a little off, he was drugged. And she knew why. Keegan wasn't the only one watching the lake that day.

She closed her eyes to the noise, to the voices, and to any inkling of what might have to do with a certain Summerford as she stood in front of her locker. It took a long moment of trying to find her patience before she found the strength to work on the combination and swap out the books she needed for the next class. She only had one class left, one more and the day would be done.

It was Reagan that threw off her concentration when the red head sidled up beside her, a smile a mile wide on her face, and waited until Ellie relented to say anything.

"What?" and that was said with a side-eye and a scowl.

"So," the grinning girl started, brows raised. "I heard a rumor."

"Is this like that telephone game where I have to pass it along to someone else without screwing up what you said?"

"What?" At least she could knock Reagan off a little bit, which was fun. "No."

She brushed it off as if the snarky comment wasn't meant to

make her stop the gossip and stood up on her tiptoes only to look down the hallway.

Ellie knew just where she was looking.

Mitch.

He caught their gazes, going from one to the other before turning back to his locker. They continued to observe him, like he was something to be studied, and he could feel it on his back as he slipped books out of the bag and into the locker before doing the opposite with new ones... slowly.

He was stalling.

His gaze went to Ellie and her alone as he closed the door, this time turned right in her direction.

Ellie froze, turned away quickly, and went back to her books. She knew the moment Mitch walked away, because Reagan was back on her feet and boring a hole in the side of her head, a Cheshire cat grin on her face.

"Okay." Ellie gave up. "Tell me."

"Your brother almost got into a fight this morning."

"You came to tell me about my brother?" The girl before her nodded, excitedly. "Old news, I already knew."

"Dammit!"

Ellie closed the locker, slipped her backpack on and both girls headed the opposite way than Mitch. Reagan is hopping.

"How much candy did you have?"

"Did you know he also punched a locker?"

That did stop her. "What? When?"

"About twenty minutes ago, ten maybe? Heard it was all dented up and bloody."

"Why is my brother the topic of conversation? Isn't everyone supposed to be fascinated by jocks or at least the swim team? Why Keegan? Also, I don't care." She glared, frustration running through her.

Reagan stopped in the middle of the hallway. "Why?"

"Because Keegan is a big boy, and not my problem." She whipped around towards the classroom again.

"Oh," was the only response she got before she saw Reagan turn and walk away.

Ellie debated for a moment, pulling the phone out of her hoodie pocket, and stared at the text thread to Noel. She had already texted him about him twice. She couldn't do it again. Slipping the phone away, she headed for her seat, making it just in time for the bell.

CHAPTER 11

"Control Headquarters - Chicago, Illinois"

Clearing the room, Drake's eyes are on the screen, the phone beside him on speaker, and he waited patiently. When he was the only one standing there, he leaned against the desk, crossing his ankles and arms, and completely relaxed.

"They're gone, we can speak freely." He didn't expect the man on the other end to give a shit anyway. Gus spoke his mind whenever he wanted, no filter, never had one, but the permission to do so seemed to put him at ease. "The details are still sketchy on some things."

"Just tell me what you know so I can go back to these jackasses and give them something. Her kids will be here shortly, they're going to want to know where their mother is."

Drake nodded, understanding the need for information, especially for the kids. Tom talked about the Summerford children all the time on their poker nights when Drake was home on pack land, so he felt the connection to them, and could sympathize with the trauma of already having lost their father.

"Summerford and detail arrived at one of Midway's private airstrips at approximately 9:23 p.m. They exited the vehicle and headed for the plane." Drake's eyes were glued to the screen as a car came screeching into the lot, window rolled down, angled so that the only view they had was the tip of the gun as it peeked out and fired. "It took less than five minutes, start to finish, before they had her in their custody. The detail did the best they could to defend Alpha Summerford and her man, but in the end failed."

Gustaf sighed over the line, and Drake paused to give him the time to take it all in.

"According to surveillance, the man went down first—"

"Doug Payne," Gus offered, getting a silent nod from the man.

"Then two of her detail ahead of them, closer to the aircraft, followed by Tom." He paused, preparing for the backlash the next little bit of information would get from the Pack Second. "It's believed that the plane wasn't staffed.

"What?" Milder than he thought but it might just be that he hadn't quite— *"What does that mean?"*

"They had someone on the inside." He turned towards the desk, looking right at the phone. "They knew when she was coming."

Gus paused, he didn't answer, he didn't move, there was just something in those words that sparked a fire in him that if he did either at that moment, he'd burn the whole world down. He placed both hands against the desk, lowered his chin to his chest and closed his eyes tightly.

"And we have no other details?" He clenched his jaw so tight that the pain zipped through right to his temple before he realized what he was doing and tried to relax.

"None." Drake's response held nothing in the way of remorse or

sympathy, but Gus knew he was just doing his job, it wasn't personal.

"Thank you."

Drake faced the screens, with the video paused on Juli's red eyes, the way she held herself, not showing any fear as the gunman approached. She wasn't dead, that much he knew, one angle showed the dart being plucked from her neck by the alpha while she was still conscious enough to do so, but after that, everything went blank.

"Thank me when we get your alpha back safely. The WC isn't going to be impressed if we lose another Summerford alpha. One's enough."

"Her children will be less impressed, and probably out for blood."

Drake smirked at that; he had met the middle one. "Alexandru was a good man, the best informant we had. If those kids are anything like him, they'll probably have her home before we have a clue."

"We can only hope," and those words were said with a smile on his face, Drake could hear it in his tone.

"I'll keep you informed."

Drake reached down and hit the button, disconnecting the call before he turned back to the screen and rewound the feed, back to the beginning, and the fact that there was something definitely wrong with the way it all went down. He was missing something. Something important.

Gus found himself in the chair behind the desk, hands in his hair as he propped himself up just to stare blankly at the keyboard.

There was no one on the plane? It wasn't staffed? They had given them enough notice to have a pilot ready, to have someone there as a second body. The Cessna was a five-person plane, there would have been an extra seat if it was just Juli, Doug, and Tom, but someone would have had to do a once over.

Nothing about this made any sense.

The problem was the six people sitting out in the meeting room and what to do with them. Not only that, but the kids would soon be on their way, and how the hell was he going to explain this to them?

Keegan's vision narrowed, filtering out everything but his destination, and even that was haloed with gold. His heart raced, his knuckles finally started to hurt, but the voices in his head, the ones he knew were fake, but persistent, encouraged him to lash out.

He needed to avoid that at all costs.

He squeezed his eyes tight, finally turning just under the bleachers, facing the fence, forehead to the metal as he laced his fingers through the chain-link. His chest shook as he released a lungful of air before dragging one in, something he repeated several times before the warmth of tears streaked down his face.

That's all he needed was for someone to see—

The sound of footsteps approaching had him tense. He was vulnerable, back to the world, but he didn't have the strength to turn around and face him, not *him* of all people. Those steps came to a halt not more than three feet behind him, just out of arm's reach, and that was good, good for both of them.

The scent of his cologne, the way it mixed with his skin, and the heat from the sun, hiding just under the hint of anger and fear nearly stopped Keegan's heart.

Daniel... Afraid? That wasn't—

He slowly opened his eyes, focusing on the dying patches of grass under the bleachers, the way the dirt around them was littered with wrappers and cigarette butts.

"I'm gonna fucking kill him," Keegan whispered, hoping that at least acknowledging the jock would ease that strange scent on his skin.

"While I agree," and his tone, the nonchalant way Daniel worded it, had Keegan huffing past the anger. "You probably shouldn't go announcing your plans."

He tipped his head back, the glare of the sun hitting him right in the eyes, but the warmth on his face had the tension slowly easing. "Go away."

"No. Look, I'm sorry I didn't stop—"

"Yeah, so am I."

The light touch of the alpha's hand on his shoulder had Keegan whirling around to face him, those bruised and bloody knuckles swinging, but Daniel, just a bit faster than the beta, grabbed his wrist, stopping it inches from his face. The low growl of a warning and the flash of gold from the smaller senior only had Daniel smiling.

"Been flashing that gold a lot, something you wanna tell me?"

"I'd like to break your nose."

The way he stated it, pretty matter-of-factly, wasn't a threat at all and Daniel knew it. He released his wrist and grabbed his shirt, holding it tightly in his fists as he pressed him back against the fence, crowding in on him like he had in the library. Daniel knew what it would do to the beta, how he would react to it, but he was betting it was something Keegan needed, and it was answered by a scowl.

"I'd like to see you try." The low, sultry answer was punctuated by the alpha red in his eyes, and Keegan shook under that glare, but he balled his fist up yet again, raising it to strike. "Easy, little beta." Keegan shifted against him, pushing out with his chest, his hips, testing the limits of his range, but he wasn't fighting to get away, just seeing how far Daniel would let him. "Key." That was a warning. "Come on—"

"Let me go," he whispered, almost pleading, but Daniel just shook his head curtly. Keegan's hand unclenched, relaxing enough to uncurl his fingers.

"Ain't gonna happen."

"Oh, yeah?" Their eyes are locked in a game that neither intended to lose, as his body shook, preparing for some sort of sympathetic response. "Whatcha gonna do, Alpha?"

Daniel licked his lips, biting down on his tongue just enough to remind himself to be gentle, especially when Keegan threw out the alpha card. "There's so many things I want to do to you." He traced his features with his eyes, needing nothing more than him. "Again."

In a motion of surrender, Keegan raised both hands, palms towards the man as everything in him let go, slouching against the fence, but his words were full of hatred, not towards Daniel, but the situation he had just been in. "Go ahead, take what you want. You didn't finish in the library."

The low gravelly tone of his voice was almost convincing, but Daniel scoffed instead. "You know, you're kinda hot when you're angry." Keegan's hands dropped as he glanced away, taking in the field, making sure they were alone, letting Daniel hold him up. "So much hotter when you're needy."

"Cut the shit, Payne." He bowed off the fence as he glared at him, pushing right into Daniel, testing his limits again, but the alpha didn't budge. In fact, he slammed him back against the metal, listening to it rattle under the force of it.

"I'm not playing."

"Danny." It was the whisper of a name they only used in private. "I can't." Daniel backed up, creating a hair's width of a space between them, scanning over his expression, trying to get a lock on his emotions. "I wanna hurt him. He just makes me so—"

"Are we talking about O'Donnell or Noel?" It was an honest question; the kid had been back and forth all day.

"My brother isn't the problem." He gestured towards the gym before grabbing ahold of the alpha's wrists, trying to pull his hands away, but he wasn't letting up and Keegan's eyes brimmed with tears. "I just want him to leave me alone."

He gave into the beta's touch, leaning in, gently rested his forehead to his as Keegan's eyes closed, and the tears fell. "I know. And he will, trust me, he will but you have to breathe. You have to stop hurting yourself." His answer was a simple shake of his head, as his anxiety intensified, the fight or flight kicking in. "It's not that hard, Key, just take a breath—"

"I can't do this," he spat. "Not anymore."

"Us?"

"Hide."

"You don't have to." Daniel pressed in, putting all his weight, as much as he felt was safe against him, and let his lips connect with the man's, letting the warmth and solidity of it calm the shiver that flowed through him.

Keegan pushed at him, hoping to get him to back off, to leave him like everyone else, but Daniel didn't move, he just continued lavishing him with soft kisses, light caresses, until Keegan gave in. He dug his knuckles into Daniel's collarbone, one last ditch effort before he opened his hands and cupped his face, thumb going over his cheeks as he pulled him in.

The kiss deepened as Keegan let go, the push of his protest turned into sobs of submission as his tongue swept across his lips, asking for entry, and Keegan let him take over. The hold on his shirt loosened, slipping one hand up to the back of the beta's neck before giving a gentle squeeze and his kiss softened.

His dark eyes focused on his face as he backed away, both melting into each other's arms, but Keegan had yet to open his eyes, taking in the way the back of Daniel's hand caresses over his skin.

"Come home with me."

Keegan bit down hard on his bottom lip, eyelids cracking just a bit to rest on him. "I can't."

"Because of this?"

"No." His fingers search for contact. On his neck, his cheek, under the collar of his shirt, Keegan was constantly moving, needing it. "My mom's coming home, there's a meeting—"

"Paige told me. I should have known something more was going on with you, I should have—" Daniel backed away, running his hands down over his chest as he straightened his shirt, tugging on the bottom hem as he reached Keegan's belt. His eyes shifted there, to the small patch of light skin showing, and he rolled his shoulder, taking two steps back. "I shouldn't have done that this morning."

The noise from the beta is more of a *pfft* than anything before he rolled his eyes and snatched his bag from the ground. "It's okay."

Daniel grabbed his arm, stopping him from going anywhere. "It's not okay. I can't keep doing that to you."

"We had an agreement. It's not like I didn't expect it."

"An agreement," Daniel barked, with a smirk. "That agreement came from a stupid guy who didn't have a clue how he felt after—" He yanked Keegan around to look him in the eyes. "I didn't know what I was feeling when school started, not about this, not about you." Keegan shrugged off his hand before turning away. He didn't want to hear this, not now, but he couldn't run, not when Daniel pressed against his shoulder. "I do now."

His eyes scanned over Keegan's profile, watching the way his lips twitched, the emotions that he went through, and he ran his knuckles gently down Keegan's cheek, swiping away the tears with his thumb.

"We're going to stop, I'm... I'm going to stop what happened this morning."

Keegan's smirk, his coping mechanism, was right back on his face as he turned to look at the alpha, keeping his body poised to run. "You gonna tell your jock friends you're fooling around with me?"

"That's not what I meant."

"Yeah, I figured."

"Keegan, I don't want to hurt you anymore."

"Then, you know, just keep doing this." He leaned in quickly, kissing him softly on the lips before he backed away, brows raised, waiting for backlash, but it never came. "Besides, it's not so bad, sneaking around, is it?" He gave just a small brush of his fingertips across Daniel's lips, as if to wipe away the kiss.

"You just said you didn't want to hide."

He mulled that over for a moment, giving a nod in agreement. He had just spoken those words in the heat of the moment but now— "I don't know what I want."

And without further preamble, he walked away, leaving Daniel to stare after him.

Daniel took a moment to gather himself, to not give into the frustration Keegan always left him with in school. It was like the kid was giving him whiplash, but it only made him want him more knowing he wouldn't be left hanging, but dammit, if the beta— He clenched his fist.

He didn't want to be that typical alpha. One who could be an asshole and overbearing, and authoritative enough to change his voice pattern, to make Keegan give him what he wanted. But the thought of tying him to a bed to get him to sit still for five minutes was starting to look like a really good idea.

He growled, swung out with his fist, and hit the fence, rattling it so hard it echoed down the line.

Noel barely made it into the driveway, missing the tail end of the Jeep by a fraction of an inch before he had it in park and stumbled out onto the asphalt. His head pounded, his vision blurred and while juggling the keys to the house, he tripped up the front steps. He needed some place quiet, dark, and cool.

Once in, he made his way towards the back of the house, down the hallway past the den, and both bedrooms, before turning left to the basement door. Yanking it open, he barely managed to flip the switch, giving the concrete room below a dull yellow glow. Both hands on the railing, he took his time going down, one step after the other praying that he didn't slip and bang his head against the hard floor.

Once both feet were on solid ground, Noel made his way around the staircase, away from the washer and dryer before him, and ducked under the low-hanging pipes until he found himself in the very back of the basement to a wooden door and the finished game room that took up most of the space.

It was darker back there, especially once he slipped into the room and closed it behind him. The only natural light streamed in through a twelve-by-twenty-four-inch window at the top of the wall, just under the beams of the floor above. He didn't bother with the lights, not even to find his way to the old couch that was pressed up against the concrete wall under the window and he flopped down on it, grabbing the well-used pillow encased in some itchy fabric. He tucked it under his head and let his eyes close.

There was blessed silence for a moment, a stillness in the air until he suddenly sat up, grabbed his phone from his pocket, and opened a thread, one labeled "siblings." He didn't have long; he just needed a few minutes.

He hit the little microphone at the bottom for voice-to-text and sighed before recording. "Stopped at home, see you at 2:30."

He sent it off with half-closed eyes and slipped into the blessed darkness of exhausted unconsciousness.

Keegan moved through the quiet halls. It was amazing that he got anywhere in school with the number of classes he skipped or slipped out of, but today was just one of those days where sitting locked in a concrete box was just not something he could do.

At the moment, he was making his way towards the Senior/Sophomore connection. The part of the hallway that separated the classes but connected the school buildings into one giant maze. The Juniors had one too, but that was on the other side, this... this one led to one specific thing.

His sister.

He skidded to a halt the moment his phone went off and pushed back into the small alcove that the bathroom door created to frantically dig it out of his pocket, trying to avoid the cuts on his hand, holding his breath for what might be on the screen. He hadn't heard from his mother all day, had once from Ellie, not unusual, but this could be anyone.

When the screen lit up, he was surprised to see a text from Noel. The obviously voice-to-text message was supposed to read one thing, that much he was sure of, but what was written was something completely different. Good thing he could speak Summerford.

"You don't usually go home." He opened the thread, ready to text back, but looked up just as O'Donnell and Hebert started down the hall. He ducked into the bathroom, put his back to the wall, and listened closely for them to pass by.

He didn't have time for texting when he had places to be. He'd see his brother at two-thirty.

He scooted out of the bathroom, glanced in both directions and headed for the door with his hands tucked into the pockets of his jeans. He always made himself look innocent, backpack over his shoulders, a little hair in his face, slouchy shoulders, it made him look smaller, more docile for those who didn't know him, which was something that never happened considering he was the topic of most school gossip circles.

Slipping through the double doors, he came up on George, the old security guard that monitored the cross-section, and gave him his best innocent grin. He liked the old man, and apparently, for whatever reason, the guy never gave him trouble. He dug into his back pocket as he approached and smiled.

"Afternoon, Keegan."

Fidgeting with the paper he pulled from his pocket, Keegan handed it to the man behind the desk. "Hey, George, living the life?"

"Can't complain." Well, he could, but Keegan was pretty sure no one would be listening anyway. With a gentle hand, George took the paper and looked it over. A legitimate looking forgery of a hall pass to the guidance counselor office. He wrote it almost every single day, so he wasn't really worried about this one *not* passing inspection. "Come to check in?"

With a neither-here-nor-there shrug, Keegan held out his hand for the pass. "You know how it goes."

Without so much of a blink of hesitation, the old man gestured down the hall. "You know where it is. No wandering."

"Thanks, man." With a smile and a salute, he stuffed the paper away and headed off down the hall, except once he was away from George, and could navigate freely.

He paused in front of room 126, slipped up to the window, and peeked in.

Three rows of desks lined the room across, going four back with two students each. Ellie sat in the front row, closest to the window and furthest from the door, but she was constantly peeking up at it between writing notes.

Keegan remembered the reason he started to sneak around, to protect her from the shadows, to never let on that while she was his sibling, he couldn't care too much, at least, not to let it show.

He was almost three when she was born, though their birthdays overlapped enough that most people thought there were only two years between them. He was fascinated by the tiny new thing that made weird noises at strange times of the night.

Her crying never bothered him, even when she wailed for attention, to be fed or even changed, but it called to him, had him up and out of bed in the wee hours of the night, slipping into her nursery even before his parents knew either of them were awake.

He would pull the ottoman from the rocking chair to the crib and climb up, just to see her better, and somehow reached up to turn on the toy above her head. It never soothed her, not until Keegan started to hum along with it, then the crying stopped, and her eyes landed right on him.

The first time it had happened was when she was barely two months old. Her nocturnal whines had shaken him out of a deep sleep and panic had risen in him at the thought that she might be hurt, so he ran right to her, and reached through the bars on the crib just to hold her tiny hand. At the touch, she stopped and held on, even the flailing movement of her limbs seemed to ease, and she looked at him.

"You mine, sissy," he would whisper to her. "I protect you."

No matter what, he would find his way to her.

She was almost a year old when things turned, when his protective streak got the best of him. They were playing in the backyard, the three of them and friends, and he was chasing her, as he always did, her giggle lighting up the world around him, but it was Noel's friend Sam that had the world come crashing down.

Looking back, he was pretty sure Sam didn't mean it at all, but when he barreled into her, trying to catch the frisbee that Noel tossed, and knocked the little girl to the ground, all Keegan saw was red. He attacked without warning, punching and scratching at Sam, yelling at him about hurting his sister and all the while Noel was trying to move him, to get him off, but Keegan, even then, was a force all his own.

It took Alexandru to remove him, and while the soon-to-be Pack Alpha was stern, his voice when he spoke to Keegan that day would never be forgotten.

He couldn't do that. He couldn't attack people for no reason. He couldn't hurt other kids. What provoked him to do that? And when Keegan answered, it wasn't a good enough reason. Sam hadn't intentionally hurt her, and Ellie didn't need him to fight her battles, for him to protect her.

That was the day that things turned, that all eyes were on him every moment of the day when he was home. They watched him, stopped any excessive play before it even began, reminded him to keep his hands to himself, that she was smaller than he was. It was the day that Keegan felt singled out.

It was the day, the very first time, he felt different, and he hated it.

He stepped back, let Ellie go—but not too far—shrunk in on himself, held in the anger. It was the wrong thing to do.

It came to a head two years later when he couldn't hold back anymore, couldn't control the monster inside of him, and an innocent game between him, Sam, and Noel, turned ugly again. He's not sure what triggered him, what sparked that need to protect himself, but he knew Ellie was nearby, so close to Sam as the boys ran around the yard. He had that flashback to her falling, to her crying, and Keegan grabbed a bat.

Everything else was a blur.

Sam wasn't hurt, the bat never got that close, but he remembered the people, the women they brought in to talk to him, and he remembered seeing the worried look on his parents' faces.

He snuck into Ellie's room for the last time that night, as he had every night, watching her sleep for only a moment, to make sure she was breathing. He needed to see that she was peaceful, and safe, and after that he shut it off again, stepped out of that room, and closed the door forever.

Keegan wasn't supposed to care that much, he wasn't supposed to be that protective. His sister wasn't supposed to be his to watch over, so he didn't. He let her go.

Ellie knew who to look for and what time it was. Every day, the light tickle at the back of her neck would flare up and she would search for the familiar feeling of pack, of family, and it never failed.

She would catch him looking in, eyes locked right on hers, before scanning the room and settling once more. Today she straightened, not enough to catch anyone's attention but just enough for Keegan to know he's been seen. She knew he would need it after everything that she had heard about his day so far. To make sure she was where she was supposed to be.

It was a strange concept to her, why he did what he did, but Paige had explained it once, and apparently it was a beta thing. He was a protector, even if he was an asshole most of the time, and what he considered his was his highest priority.

She had seen him sneak down the hall to Noel's room, especially after the whole lake incident, and silently peek in on his brother, but it was usually followed by him grabbing his keys and heading out the door, so she thought at first that he was making sure he wouldn't be seen. After a while, though, the relief she saw in his eyes the few times she purposely made an effort to catch him was right there before it was masked, and he barked out a sarcastic remark.

She never told him she knew any of it.

Ellie lifted her fingers from the desk, a little wave in his direction before she quickly grabbed the pencil again, still not letting him go until she saw his fingers in the window, just a tiny wave back, and then he's gone.

With a smile on his face, Keegan pressed his back to the wall, and closed his eyes, relief washing over him, before he glanced around, making sure the coast was clear. He only needed a moment anyway, then he pushed off the wall and headed out the door at the end of the science wing.

Outside, the air was a bit chillier than he remembered, but then again, the last time he was fuming, hopped up on adrenaline. Now, he was calm, almost happy. He found a spot at the edge of the small green and plunked himself at one of the picnic tables. His eyes went to the sky, getting lost in the way the clouds moved before he inhaled deeply, taking in the light scent of snow in the air. It was almost hypnotic, but it got him to open up, to feel relaxed enough to speak.

"She's fine, Dad," he whispered to the clouds. "I checked on her like I told you I would every day." He laughed at it, at the fact that this was what he did with his fake counselor time. He went out and talked to his dad. It was therapeutic in a way. "Noel doesn't know. Mom doesn't know. We have our own set of rules, right? Keep Ellie safe, make sure Noel doesn't do anything stupid, do the best I can." He paused at that one. "Do the best I can," he repeated, the smile fading from his lips. "Am I? Like, do you think Danny's it, Danny and Paige? And this fucking school?"

The sounds of nearby birds filled the air as Keegan nodded, and behind him, the bell rang, cutting the tranquility of the moment.

"Okay, that's it. School's over".

Gus paced, his arms crossed, eyes narrowed at nothing, but he could feel the presence of the six in the room, standing around waiting, mingling and mumbling between themselves. Rollins was the one that interrupted his stride, stepped in front of him and blocked his way.

It took more control than he wanted to admit keeping the red in his eyes from staying past the first few seconds, but he did it. "Now is not the best time."

"Yes, but we should really discuss your beta problem."

"If you moved him, he's not a problem."

"You said you couldn't send him back because you believed him to be a missing beta. Which beta? From which pack? My associates haven't been able to get much out of him. In fact, nothing at all."

That brought on the red. "Keep your lackeys away from him. He's injured enough as it is. There's no need for an interrogation."

"Then why not keep him in the general population?"

Gustaf pinched the bridge of his nose, stemming off the headache, or at least hoping to before he glared at Rollins. "He's supposed to be at the medical center, Rollins, what did you do with him?"

"He's exactly where you told me to put him, Alpha."

"Fine, and while it's none of your concern what I do with members, his safety and that of those around him is a priority."

"In that case," the beta smirked, "I'll have him moved."

"You'll leave him be until I give the say so."

Rollins gave a slight bow, tilting his head to the side to expose his pulse, an old practice that Gustaf hated.

"Anything you wish, Alpha." Gus gave a frustrated sigh and turned to the table. He leaned his fists against it, as Rollins stood to his side, eyes still on him. "You will tell me who he is as soon as you find out, won't you? I can't police the land if I'm out of the loop."

"Yes, of course," but it was said with a dismissing tone. "The children should be arriving soon."

"With his mother missing, does Noel know that he becomes temporary Pack Alpha?"

"The boy knows the laws."

"Yes, but an inexperienced alpha, even that of the bloodline, leaves us open for any number of enemies to come in."

"This will be a temporary issue."

"You seem so certain."

Gus turned to face him; eyes narrowed on the smug man. There was something untrustworthy in his expression, something he was hiding. "And you seem... guilty."

"Not at all, Alpha. I'm merely concerned about the long-term possibility of—"

"It would be in your best interest to stop while you're ahead."

"Duly noted."

It was Gervais, who had overheard the entire conversation, who spoke up next. "What do you intend to tell them?"

His eyes focus on her, and the other four members of the pack council, the concern in their eyes. "The truth."

And just like that, the murmurs of the group rose again.

Noel sat up quickly, head swimming from the rush, and he glanced around the basement. His alarm hadn't gone off yet, but he knew it was close to time. Pushing to his feet, he snagged the phone from the table and made his way out of the room, up the stairs, and towards the door.

He paused only for a moment to scan the house, something didn't seem right, something felt... off. Instead of leaving, he headed back towards his room, passing the basement door, and pushed it open. Nothing was out of place, nothing had been touched from where he had left it that morning, but there was a strange vibration in the air.

With a sigh, he pivoted—the very wrong thing to do—swayed a bit, and went back down the hall, stopping in the kitchen only to grab a banana, and then he was out the door.

Once settled behind the wheel of the truck, he started it up and shifted into reverse just as the phone in his pocket vibrated.

"Shit." He hit the brakes just as he hit the end of the driveway and dug the phone out before it stopped ringing, and with a quick two taps to the screen, he dropped it into the cupholder.

"Hey," Keira's voice smiled over the speaker.

"Hey, Kay, sorry I bailed."

"Are you alright?"

Noel finished backing out, yanked the truck into drive, and

headed down the road, now navigating by memory. “Migraine hit during English Lit, nearly had me on the floor, so I stopped at home for some meds. All good now.”

“You sure?”

“Yeah, totally.” He hated lying but there was no way she was going to understand him hallucinating shifting into a mythical beast on the stairs of the auditorium. He wasn’t sure he even believed it. “Hey, I’m headed to get the kids, can I call you back? Looks like there’s traffic.”

“Absolutely. Let me know how the meeting goes and say hi to your mom for me.”

“I will. Love you.”

“Love you too.”

His whole demeanor changed the moment the line disconnected, and he slammed his hand against the wheel. “Dammit!”

He leaned against the front of the brick building, eyes going over the waves of students, and got lost in the normalcy of it, at least until Paige slipped into his view. His usual smug smirk grew into a wide smile as she placed her hands on his chest and leaned in. It was like Daniel all over again, but with soft curves and perfumed skin. He absolutely loved that position.

She curled into him, placing her head on his chest as he wrapped his arms around her. He dipped his chin, lips going to her hair, and took in her scent for just a moment, letting the world go quiet again. It wasn’t until she pulled back, her eyes trying to capture his, that he sighed. His eyes flitted to the group of football players and that smile faded.

They stood near the parking lot and there in the middle of them was Daniel, scanning the crowd only to catch Keegan’s eyes.

At that point, there was no hiding the fact that he *was* looking, but Keegan turned away anyway.

"I wish the two of you would quit playing around." Paige's scolding voice had him glancing back at the jock, and the pretty blonde his arm was around, which only had Keegan scratching his head.

"Not gonna happen." His amused reply had Paige stepping back.

"You know what you two have is not a bad thing."

"It is. Being a beta and wanting an alpha, wanting him?" He pushed her away, gently, before yanking his bag from the ground. "Kind of a bad thing."

"I just don't understand how. Your designation doesn't dictate who you have feelings for or who you're attracted to."

"My mom might." He took a moment before he turned a hesitant glance in her direction. "He asked me to come home with him. Told me that he couldn't hurt me anymore."

"And you walked away, didn't you?"

"Don't I always?"

"You could stop."

"No," he laughed, "I don't think so, you know that's just not me."

Paige stepped up behind him as he moved to walk away, wrapping her hand around his arm and yanked him to a stop. He rolled his eyes as he turned to look at her. "I know loving him doesn't make you love me any less, Key—"

His eyes instantly went back to Daniel, but the soft feel of her hand had him turning back.

"I don't," he whispered, denial right there in the forefront. "I don't love him."

"You do, and you need to figure it out before it destroys you from the inside."

Out of the corner of his eyes, he saw Noel pull up and park, idling in the lot. He'd never been so happy to see the dumpy, old truck before and he leaned in smiling.

"I have to go; Mom should be getting in soon."

"I know. If you need me, you know, for after—"

He kissed her softly. "I'll call you later."

With a sigh, and not a moment to reply, Paige stood there as he walked away. She only observed for a second as Keegan moved towards the truck, catching Daniel's eyes before the man quickly looked in her direction and Paige shook her head.

The two of them were really starting to get on her nerves.

CHAPTER 12

Noel's timing couldn't have been more spot on. He had rushed out the door, hoping to make it, but pretty sure he was going to be the late one after telling his siblings—no, not telling, drilling it into them—that he would be there precisely at two-thirty. His episodes during the day not only drained him but made his head spin and the brain fog was nearly unbearable. Still, the small state of near unconsciousness he managed to get in had definitely helped clear some of it.

He always found it strange, even after two years of this routine, to watch them both in their elements. He didn't remember his "after school" because it was so different from this. He went straight to the track to stretch and warm up, but this whole hanging out waiting, that never happened for him. He purposely didn't have an off-season. He made sure he had a sport to lean back on at every turn. He had plans and knew exactly how to get them. Until he didn't.

Sports was going to be his in for UMass because that was his dream, that university. He had hyped it up to his parents, mentioned it at every turn and when it came time to send in his application, he had nailed it, interview and all. However, the local community college was a free ride with his parents working there. All the way to graduation.

So that's where he started, hoping that after two years he'd have enough credits to transfer over, and he did. His grades were top of his class, it should have been easy, a piece of cake to make that change, but then that one life-altering day hit, and everything went out the window.

They were down to one income, his mother's, and with the pack leadership shifting to her, he felt his dreams slipping away. He was an alpha, and in the pack, it was part of his job to take care of the younger ones.

Noel didn't blame his siblings for it, not in the slightest. He didn't hold them accountable at all. However, there were times that he wished he was back in those hallowed halls, roaming from class to class if only to make sure what he had heard had happened today didn't continue.

He put the truck in park, but let the thing idle, keeping the heater going to help block out the chill running through his veins. He glanced down at the phone on the dash still empty of notifications from his mom, or updates on her whereabouts, and he thought to himself about how this would be just like her to think it would be a happy surprise to them by appearing out of the blue. It was par for the course, this lack of communication, but as Keegan approached from the northern part of the building, striding right past the gathering of jocks, he knew he needed to keep that to himself because the look in his brother's eyes was dangerous.

He hid the jolt that flashed through his body the moment the door swung open, creaking on old door hinges that someday Noel was going to have to replace. His eyes went to his brother the moment his bag was tossed on the seat beside him, and Keegan climbed in, slamming the heavy metal behind him.

They stared at one another, hazel against blue, and Noel could feel the buildup of tension throughout the cab. Keegan's glare was clearly a challenge, something about it just begged Noel to say the wrong thing. Noel just waited to see the shift in him, the way he relaxed in the comfort of the cab. It only took a moment with Noel not backing down, but his shoulders slumped, and Keegan suddenly looked away.

"You didn't have to steal my keys. I could've easily met you at the hall." Noel's scoff had him giving his older brother a side glare before shaking his head. "Such a dick!"

"Really? Gus made it pretty clear that all three of us needed to be there. I wasn't taking the chance on you disappearing again." Noel knew the moment it was out of his mouth that he had triggered his fight response as the smirk rose up on the beta's lips. It came off as defiant, but Noel knew better.

"You know, I could've just hotwired it and said screw it." It was good to know he had that skill, but Noel said nothing, just let him go. "Gone to school myself, or skipped, but it's Mom," and his eyes turned to bore into Noel's. "And she hasn't been home in a week—"

"Three days," he huffed, "tops."

"I'm not going to fuck that up, too. Pack or not, it's just the four of us now."

He had a point, but Noel only responded with a nod before letting his eyes focus on the movement outside the cab. The quiet made his skin tingle, igniting an itch beneath it, and while Noel wanted to ignore it, he couldn't. He spoke instead.

"Something's got to change, Key. The sneaking out. The sneaking in. Mom's Pack Alpha, it's not good for her image." Noel honestly couldn't give a shit about anyone's image, but it was a thing for him to lecture Keegan about it. Strangely enough, the younger one usually responded better to the whole "you're being disrespectful" aspect of things if worded right. There was something in his makeup that just snapped in place when that tone was used.

"Not like I ran off to Vegas on a full moon—which, by the way, is soon—and got mated."

Noel whipped his head around for that one, his eyes wide as he stared in Keegan's direction in full disbelief at that statement.

Keegan laughed loudly at the shock on his brother's face, clearly amused by it.

"That's not funny!"

"Kinda is."

"Not even a little." He huffed and looked away.

"Maybe a little." The last response was quiet, as if he had finally settled into the seat, let go of the day, and let his brother's presence ease the anger in him. "You should try to relax." Noel rolled his eyes because, of course, Keegan would be a pain in his ass today. "You're not Pack Alpha yet, live a little."

He wasn't even sure what to say to that because the annoying little brother was right. "Mom's counting on me."

"Bullshit." Keegan rolled down the window, propped his elbow on it, and huffed. "You know, ever since Dad died, you've been on this." He wasn't sure how to put it. "Streak."

"A streak?"

"Yeah, you used to be fun." His hazel eyes landed on Noel's profile. "Now, you're just an asshole."

He was, there was no use denying it, so they sat in silence for a few moments before he could even look at Keegan.

"I just feel like Mom needs as much help as she can get, you know? Like I'm not doing enough to take anything off her shoulders."

"She doesn't. She has Gus, she has the council. Dad would have wanted you to be a kid for a little while longer, not take on the role of "pack" anything." He gave a small shrug and did a once over of the crowd. "That's *why* she has Gus."

"So, what? Joking about running off and eloping should be what I spend my time doing? Jumping out of windows? Stealing cars?"

Keegan's gaze settled on his, a harsh glare that, while it would shake anyone else, never even bothered Noel. For just a second his beta gold shined through before it faded, a small warning of how on edge Keegan was.

"I *never* stole that car, Noel!" His barked words suddenly lowered, along with his eyes. "Tanner did, and you know it."

Noel turned away from him, giving him a moment to get it together, and settled on the cars flowing out of the parking lot. It was the guy in the number "17" jacket that caught his attention, and the way the boy walked across the lot with his eyes on Keegan even as he moved.

"What's with that guy?"

"What guy?" But he saw the moment Keegan followed his line of sight, right to the jock, just for a second before he looked away, rubbing his knuckles.

"The one you're not looking at."

"He just a stupid jock."

"Hmmph," and the sound was meant to be just another way to say *"yeah, right"* but it set Keegan off, making him fidget in his seat.

"What now?"

Noel let his eyes settle on his brother again. "He's the one you were fighting in the hall this morning?"

The growl that rumbled from the beta nearly vibrated through the cab. "Ellie's a little snitch."

"She's just looking out for you."

"Sure she is."

"So, is he? The one?"

Keegan shook at that question, or maybe just the words before he gave a shrug. "It wasn't even a fight, words mostly. Hebert stepped in before it got to that point and, yeah," Keegan scowled, "hands to myself, Dad."

Noel grabbed his wrist, holding it up as his brows raised, almost in a silent *"explain this,"* taking in the blood and broken skin before meeting Keegan's eyes. "Sure looks like it."

"Trust me, if that was his face, he wouldn't be standing there looking so pretty."

"Locker then?"

"You know—" He snatched his hand away, cradling it against his chest. "I get the whole protective big brother vibe you're trying to put on, but please don't. And yes, it was a stupid locker. Better than his face."

There was something in Keegan's voice that had Noel grinning, a softness when he talked about the boy, and Noel couldn't help it. "But he's just a dumb jock, right?"

"Piss off."

That was when he really noticed it, when his heightened senses finally kicked in, coming down from the overload of earlier. Keegan's scent had shifted to... something.

"Key," and that was very gently spoken, "I'm really trying here, but you smell like—"

"Just because you have the nose of a wolf, doesn't mean you have to scent every emotion coming off someone!"

Noel raised his hands in surrender. "I just—"

"Nothing, you just nothing. It's fucking annoying, and it's invasion of privacy. Learn some personal space." Keegan slumped back in the seat, suddenly, as if all the fight had gone out of him, and he shrugged. "He's just a dumb asshole anyway."

"Okay," Noel nodded, slipping just a few inches closer to his own door. *Personal space.* "Okay, we'll leave it for now."

"Thank God."

Silence filled the cab, and they were comfortable in it, both looking out at the dissipating number of Juniors and Seniors, knowing there was only five minutes before the rest of the school was released. Noel stole glances at Keegan, saw the way the tension ran out of him the more he was surrounded by the familiar scent of family.

But something from earlier that day had him breaking the tranquility. "There was a protest on campus today."

"Yeah, there's a few starting up here, too." Keegan kept a quiet, couldn't care less attitude front and center as if he wasn't bothered by it at all.

It did nothing for Noel's protective side, though, as the hair on the back of his neck stood up. "That shouldn't be allowed here."

"It's not like it's gonna matter. The school's small, and the population of pack members is higher than you think." Those hazel eyes landed on Noel. "Nothing's gonna happen."

"It does matter. All it takes is one slip-up from *any* pack and we're moving targets. You have to be careful, Key."

"You're delusional." He rolled his eyes, crossed his arms over his chest and looked away.

"Probably. Doesn't mean I'm wrong."

Keegan gave him a quick glance and a nod. "I'll be careful."

"That's all I ask." Noel sat forward as the bell echoed in the air. The door to the Freshman/Sophomore side opened and Ellie stepped out.

Ellie scanned the parking lot, spotting Noel's truck without any issue before she shivered against the cold. The day's taken on a chill she wasn't ready for, but she was happy to have it done. Mitch had managed to sneak away without giving her the opportunity to check on him, and Reagan had happily skipped to her bus, which left her alone and praying that this meeting went well. She just wanted some quiet because her head was killing her.

However, Paige walking in her direction told her that her prayers were about to go unanswered. It's not that she didn't like the omega, in fact, she got along pretty well with her, but she was the only one of that designation she knew and a little over-the-top sometimes. Worse than that, she was Keegan's girlfriend, so she knew *everything* about their family.

With a mumbled *"just great,"* Ellie headed for the truck only to meet Paige on the sidewalk.

"Hey, Ell." Her greeting was soft, as if she were approaching a wild animal, but Ellie figured that dealing with Keegan gave her the impression that all Summerfords were that way.

"Hi." Her tone wasn't as friendly, but that didn't deter the blonde.

"So... Keegan's been having a day." Ellie rolled her eyes, tired of all of the BS, and started to walk away but Paige blocked her path, hands up. "Wait," she pleaded, which had Ellie pulling the books in her arms closer to her chest. "I didn't come over here to talk about him. Bad segue. I wanted to know how you're doing?" Not one for words, Ellie just shrugged. "That good, huh?"

"It's been hard on all of us." She hoped her lack of empathy would have this conversation over as her hand went to the back of her neck, rubbing at the pain there, but the concern on Paige's face told her *no such luck.*

"I'm not asking about all of you, just you."

"Fine." She waved her off but lowered her tone. "I'm fine. I have a bit of a headache, so I'm sorry for being a bitch. No," she giggled. "I have three different kinds of headaches, two that live in my house, and one at the base of my neck that won't go away."

The look of concern on Paige's face didn't do anything for the thoughts of what it could be that had run through Ellie's all day, but she still took a step back as the omega came closer.

"Where?" Ellie handed her the books, making it easier for her to lift her hair and turn, showing her the exact spot on the back of her neck. There was no use describing it, she couldn't put into words what she was feeling anyway. The omega took a moment to look before Ellie dropped her hair and held her hand out for her books. "For how long?"

"A week now, maybe." Paige offered the novels back just as gently as she did everything else, and Ellie took them happily. They were her security.

"I don't think that's just a headache."

"Well, wouldn't it be great if I finally presented now that she's home?" The scowl on her face apparently had Paige smiling. It was great that her discomfort amused the omega. "I'd be okay with getting this over with."

It was contagious the way Paige grinned, the way her eyes sparkled, and Ellie couldn't help but smile back.

"That would be great." She pulled Ellie into an awkward hug, which only confused her more since she wasn't sure what to do with it. "Call me if it gets worse. I have a few ideas that might help."

Ellie nodded as Paige stepped back, smiling like a weirdo, waiting on the nod that she gave before she walked away without another word. Ellie shook her head, watching the girl disappear around the building.

"No wonder Keegan's dating her, they're both so weird," she whispered to herself as she headed for the truck.

KEEGAN'S EYES weren't on Ellie. They were on the way Paige had disappeared from sight, and even with how keen he had been watching them, he didn't have much warning before a moderately full backpack was tossed in through the window, landing on his lap. Keegan huffed, glared at Ellie, sliding over closer to Noel as she opened the door and climbed in, dropping the heavy books in her arm to the floor.

"Hi," she whispered.

"Hey," they responded, in unison and with the same tone, something unusual enough for her to stare at them, curiously.

It was strange to watch the two of them shift uncomfortably under her gaze, but there was something about the air in the truck that made her wonder about what they had been talking about prior to her arrival. Shaking it off, she slammed the door closed as Noel put the old truck in gear and headed out of the parking spot, turning away from them.

"How was class?" Noel's deeper voice invaded her daydreaming and she scoffed at him.

"It's school, Noel." Her tone was a near perfect match for Keegan's as far as *"give me a break"* was concerned and he smirked just a little. "It's boring and dumb."

"Like people," Keegan added

"Like people," she agreed.

"What did Mitch do now?" The older one teased, but it got him what he wanted, a very animated display of dramatic arm waves before she threw them up in the air and crossed them, huddling back in the corners.

"Ugh! Boys are so stupid! No offense."

"None taken," Noel laughed but it was Keegan's "no argument here," that had them exchanging a grin.

"He's trying too hard."

"Boys always try too hard," Keegan whispered, and that caught Ellie's attention.

"Know from experience?"

Keegan glared at her. "Shut up, you little narc! Thanks for ratting on me, by the way."

"If it gets all the way down to the Sophomore floor, then I have to report it."

"Who says?"

"Dad."

Keegan bumped into Noel as he turned towards his sister, but the older one managed to keep the truck straight even with the shifting body in the middle seat.

"Okay, guys, that's enough!"

"Dad's not here!" The growl wasn't threatening, it was painful. "Stop telling on me."

"Dude," Noel's voice caught his attention, getting him to sit back. "You're eighteen, own your shit." At the stoplight, Noel leaned forwards, eyes on Ellie. "And Ell, I don't need to know everything that's going on. There's nothing I can do about it anyway."

They fell into silence, an easy one that lasted for a few seconds before Keegan raised his right arm, fingers curled into a fist and held it just off his leg between them. Noel smiled when Ellie hesitated for a moment, looking over her brother's profile before she rolled her eyes and bumped the back of her fist against his.

And Noel's smile slipped away, hoping the peace between the siblings was enough to hold down whatever was growing in him.

THE PARKING LOT to the meeting house held eight familiar cars and that had Keegan sitting forward, hoping to get a better view because some of them he recognized but the ones he didn't— It just made his hackles rise.

"What's going on?"

"Don't know." Noel slipped the truck into the space furthest away from the building, and easiest to get out of, before putting it in park. "Gus just said Mom called a special session."

"That we have to be here for?" Ellie's worried voice had him back on edge.

"I guess." He shut off the car, glanced at the two of them as they exchanged glances before looking to Noel for guidance. "Come on."

Noel slammed the door as Keegan and Ellie slipped out, meeting him at the front of the truck.

Keegan's eyes were still on the unfamiliar vehicles. "I don't get it; we've never had to be here before."

Ellie inched closer, her arm rubbing against his. "Maybe it's because of the whole summit thing."

"Maybe." Noel wasn't getting a good feeling about it either. He needed a subject change and quickly. "Hey, Ell, have you had any problems with people?"

"I always have problems with people, because... people."

Keegan grinned at that, he knew it all too well, but Noel slipped up on the other side of her, put his arm around her shoulders and gave her a gentle squeeze.

"I know, but I meant any problems with them being prejudiced against you?"

Ellie scoffed. "Why? No one even knows what I am. Yeah, they know I'm pack, but not which designation. I don't even know what I am yet."

"She has a point." The middle one shrugged as he reached out to touch a BMW with a new wax job. Noel rolled his eyes at Keegan but focused on Ellie.

"Don't worry," he rested his chin on her head for a moment before letting go. "It'll happen soon."

With a sigh, he headed towards the door, his siblings not far behind.

Gus looked up as the door opened and Noel stepped in, eyes scanning the place before he moved, holding the door for Keegan, who walked proudly after him. Ellie wasn't far behind, taking in all the pack leaders in the room as the oldest glanced up at the clock on the wall.

"3:00 p.m."

Noel could feel the power in the room, the different mix of the men and women that fill the space, but he wasn't fooled by them. He knew how the pack council was formed, the way the highest-ranking member of the largest family was chosen, giving a voice to the area they live in, but he also knew that they didn't seem to care if that person was a scumbag or not. His eyes landed on Rollins, the need to kick him out flowed over him. He didn't trust him, never had.

Gustaf straightened, hand raised to Rollins who shifted to step away from the table and waited for the doors to close behind the children. The conversations around the room, the muddled voices of the others, came to a quiet halt, leaving the room filled with tension. Noel took a moment, looking over them all, before his gaze landed on Rollins, who only responded with a smirk.

Something was wrong. Something was going on that Noel couldn't seem to pinpoint. He could feel the way Keegan shifted to his left, just a step behind, pressed against his back, like he was ready to jump, and Ellie... her uncertainty of the situation was in her scent. He didn't like it; he needed to protect them even if it was from their own pack.

Gustaf slipped around the table as the rest of the council stayed perfectly still while he approached. He debated on how to do this, how to ease the pain of what he was about to tell the three of them. There was only one way he could think of, so he gave a slight bow and whispered, "Alpha."

That got Noel to stand at attention. It was ingrained in them, something in their DNA that made that part of them recognize submission, but Noel didn't understand this at all.

Gus moved, closing the space between them as Keegan reacted nervously. Ellie's gaze went from one alpha to the other, hoping there had been some sort of mistake, but when Gustaf bowed again, she knew, deep inside, they were about to get handed some terrible news.

"Stand up, stop bowing." And he did so but his eyes didn't rise to meet Noel's. It made the younger alpha's heart race. "Gus, what's going on?" The anger in his voice was shadowed by fear, and this got the man in front of him to look up. "Why are you—" That was when he noticed the absence of one member: of the most important members of this council. "Where's my mother?"

In the darkness of the windowless room, huddled on the cot in the corner, Juli struggled with a restless sleep. No one had been in the

room at all, hours had passed and yet she was left alone. Her head pounded from the drugs, but that wasn't the reason she groaned in pain.

Her eyes were clenched shut, much like her fists, and the only thing she could see behind her closed lids was the flash of gunfire, the way it echoed across the night, and the sounds of the casings ticking off the cement as they fell.

She ducked behind Tom again, feeling him push her to protect her, but she also felt the moment the bullets entered his body. The way the man bucked as he went down. Doug's dead body lay prone on the tarmac, eyes wide open, staring at her with two shots to the back.

She stared right into Tom's eyes as the blood dripped from the side of his lips and she tried to scoot away. She couldn't move, not when the shadows loomed over her. It wasn't how it happened, but she could see the gun in *his* hand, the way it pointed right at her heart. A real gun, not the tranquilizer. It was deadly, meant to kill, and the sound of the shot fired off had her sitting up on the bed.

Her eyes are bright red, her heart pounds against her chest, only for a moment before they roll back, and drift shut.

The Pack Second's eyes go from Noel to the siblings behind him. "Come with me."

"What? No, what the hell is going on?"

"Noel?" Ellie stepped up beside him, her hand slipping into his as she pressed against his arm.

"It's okay," he whispered, hoping to reassure her, but Keegan had a different take on the situation.

"It's not okay." He growled, drawing Noel's gaze to him. He was angry, a default setting when he knew something was out-of-place, and his eyes were bright gold. He stepped closer, blocked by Noel's arm across his chest, but it was his glare that kept Keegan in place. "Something's wrong, I can smell it. There's fear in the air. From them." His gaze, haloed in that golden color, went over the six others in the room before he locked it on Gustaf. "Answer him!"

Rollins stalked forward, angered by his tone. "Mind your manners, beta!"

Keegan growled, a deep rumble that vibrated against Noel's arm, but the fingers twisting in his shirt held him still which did nothing for his mouth. "Make me, old man."

"Keegan," Gus snapped. "That's enough!" He blocked the view between them, getting the angry teen to focus on him, but his eyes were on Noel. "We should speak in private."

"The council was called here by my mother, Gus. You can say whatever it is in front of them, can't you?"

"It might be better if—"

"Why are you addressing me as alpha?"

"Noel—"

"Answer me!" Those words were an order, a tone that was filled with power, something none of them had ever heard before, and Gus's brows furrowed at it.

His light eyes locked on Noel, stepping forward only to place his hand gently on his shoulder, feeling the way Noel tensed under his touch. The moment Gus connected, he was able to see all of what Noel had gone through that day, all of the shifting emotions.

To his left, Keegan clenched his fists, taking in the way his brother bristled from the touch, instantly on edge, and he tried to keep it in, but it wasn't working, not anymore. The skin that had finally started to heal over the slit knuckles opened, as his fingers dug into his palm, and the blood dripped to the floor.

Ellie moved closer, free hand going to Noel's arm as her eyes shifted to Keegan, filled with worry, but Gus saw it, noticed their collective stance and removed his hand, holding both up as a sign of surrender.

"Something's happened," he whispered, gaze flitting between the three before landing on Noel. "Your mother's missing."

"No," Ellie whispered, full of disbelief. "No, you're lying."

Keegan shook his head. "How? Are you sure?"

Noel raised his hand, silencing the two to collect his thoughts, but his sister was so tuned into them both, she voiced the question running through his head. "Why aren't you out there looking?"

Gus lowered his head, eyes still on Noel but he ignored the youngest Summerford for the time being. "Noel, you're the acting Pack Alpha by bloodline rights of succession."

"How?"

"You should know the pack laws!" Rollins snapped, which had Keegan bristling, but Noel ignored him.

"I am well aware of my duties." His voice held that power still and Noel could see the man shiver out of the corner of his eyes. "It would be wise to shut your mouth." He ignored Rollins after that, focusing on the Pack Second in front of him. "How did she go missing?" His arm was firmly across Keegan's chest again, but his gaze, growing ever brighter with each passing second, was locked on Gus. There wasn't an answer yet, but Noel was determined to get one. "Where is my *mother*, Gustaf?"

"We don't know."

Ellie's knees weakened, barely holding her up as she leaned into her brother. Keegan's anger grew, and with a low, deep rumble that no human, or pack member had been able to accomplish, he let out a warning. Noel released his shirt, only to hold up his hand, visible to Keegan but not the others, and he felt him stand down even with his eyes filled with that unnatural glow.

"Tell me what you *do* know."

Gus turned to the room, giving the six members a simple nod, and waited as they began to exit the meeting room.

"Wait!" Keegan barked, getting all of them to freeze. He was antsy, and now had Gus's full attention. "Where the hell was your goon squad?" The beta's eyes rested on the alpha. "You were supposed to protect her." Noel was barely winning the battle of holding him back, but it was becoming apparent that Keegan wasn't going to hold off much longer. "Where, Gus?"

Rollins took it upon himself to move closer—the very wrong move with the angry brother tucked behind him, right into Keegan's eyeline—but his focus was on Noel. "Control your beta, Alpha."

Noel glared at him, eyes golden and slowly growing darker, pissed off beyond anything he had ever felt. No one spoke to Keegan that way, and yes, he was *his* beta, his to order. Not Rollins'. Gustaf sent his own glare in Rollins' direction, which had the beta tilting his head in submission.

"I meant no disrespect. However, this is not the time nor place for childish blow-ups."

Noel shifted this time, placed himself fully in front of Keegan, protectively and focused in on the Head of Security. "My beta has every right to be upset." His voice was low, almost void of emotions. "And if you ever speak so casually about him again, I'll have you removed from pack lands."

The council leader shifted his gaze from Noel to Gustaf, waiting on a reply, on a defense, but getting none, he nodded, eyes to the floor as Noel moved closer to the table. Gustaf came up to his right as Keegan remained to his left, reaching back for Ellie's hand. She wasn't hiding behind them; they had put up a wall to protect their youngest member. Rollins hadn't moved.

"Now." Noel drew in a breath, standing straight, gaze going over the remainder of the people in the room. "Does someone want to tell me what the hell happened to my mother?"

"Calm down." Gus shifted to the side of the table, taking in the three of them.

"Calm down?" Noel chuckled, spying the others slipping away, and he waited for the six to leave the room, slinking away to the shadows. He released Ellie's hand as he placed his fists on the wooden tabletop, blue eyes hard and unyielding. "You just told me our Pack Alpha is missing, and you want me to *calm* down?"

It was Keegan that reached out this time, coming down from the emotions that had run through him. There was just Gus, no one to protect Noel from now, and Keegan needed to focus on his brother. His hand rested on Noel's arm, feeling him vibrate with something other than anger, but it was quickly shaken off.

He stood straight, unsure of what to do next, but Noel's eyes rested on him, an apologetic frown on his face, and Keegan got it. It's not that he didn't appreciate the touch, the comfort, but Noel was about to blow, and he didn't want Keegan to feel it.

With his stare back on Gus, Noel lowers his voice to a whisper. "Tell me everything."

Gus gestured to the office, this time with no immediate need. "Come with me."

Noel chanced a glance at Keegan, then one at Ellie before following, his siblings not more than three steps behind and his mind went back to the simple rules his mother repeats every time she left, and the last, the most important one.

Noel rolled his shoulders as he stood in the doorway of his parents' office, filled with their things, their faces and his golden eyes shifted to a bright orange. This time he didn't blink it away, he just stared.

Juli made it the rules, and Noel intended to honor them all, especially the last. Above anything else— Protect the pack.

CHAPTER 13

THE DOORS to the meeting house swung open with force, banging against the iron stair rails. The growing darkness of the mid-December evening made it nearly impossible for Noel to track Keegan's movements down the steps and out into the parking lot where the Honda and truck sat quiet and cold.

He found him though, down towards the back of the lot, where the old town cemetery met the browning grass of the lawn, pacing like a caged animal ready to spring. He was furious, Noel knew that, and he wasn't about to pin his brother down, especially with the scent of anger that flowed from him. It was like smoke from a burning building, almost suffocating, so he stopped on the other side of the truck bed, away from him, letting him have his time.

Keegan pulled out his phone, the screen lighting up the scowl on his face as he flipped through his apps to find his text messages. He hovered on Paige's name, wanting to reach out, wanting a distraction from this holy hell, but he hesitated. It was then that he noticed his brother, and in that instant, as he looked towards the truck, his eyes sprang to life with a vibrant gold.

"Leave me alone." The tone of it wasn't anger, but fear and Noel knew he couldn't.

He raised his hands, moving around the bumper to close the distance. "Keegan—"

He expected the boy to rush him, to throw a punch. He never expected the teen to raise his hand and close his eyes. "Don't. Just don't." His words were just above a whisper, but Noel heard them clearly. "Okay?"

Noel inhaled, expanding his chest, but he also shoved his hands down in his pockets, leaving himself open for attack, something that had Keegan questioning, before he exhaled.

"I wish I could just let you go; I really do." Two steps closer, smaller than before, but still closer. "But I need you."

The barking laugh from the beta echoed in the night. The meetinghouse wasn't on a main road, it was on the corner of a crossroad, on one of the original travel ways the settlers used when the town was founded, something now almost completely abandoned except for the houses spattered around the woods.

"You need me? That's rich." Keegan turned to face him, his phone still in his hand. "For what? Backup? To be your little token beta? Stand by your side while they crown you alpha?"

"No, that's not it at—"

"Hard pass," he snickered. "'Cause you've seen me, right? I can hold my own."

That's it, that did it. Noel didn't hold back this time, he moved forward, right into Keegan's face, hands balled into fists, and his eyes flickered orange.

"What the hell did he do to you?" The force of those words held the same power as the last time Noel used the voice inside where he basically made every other person come to a standstill, and Keegan blanked.

The smirk fell from his face, the fear dissipated, turning to confusion at the question. "What? Who?"

"That stupid jock? What did he do to you?"

It didn't take but a moment for Keegan to recover from that question, for the anger to cloud the other emotions that his whole body went through, and while he should have backed off, Keegan bared his teeth instead.

"He didn't *do* anything. It's just—" That quiet pause had the tension in Noel's body easing, to see his brother duck his head, look down at his hand, and the blood that had once again dried. He wanted to reach out, but he held back, waiting on Keegan. When the hazel eyes of the man before him met his, Noel was taken aback. He never gave in that quick. "It's been a really bad day."

"Yeah." Noel unclenched his fists. "That seems to be going around."

"It's O'Donnell—"

"What's he bothering you about now?"

He saw the fight that Keegan's going through, the gambit of emotions that showed in his expression, in his eyes before he lost the courage and shrugged. "Forget it. He's just a douche."

When he didn't make a break for it, Noel laid a gentle hand on his shoulder, feeling the shiver under his touch. "Key—"

It was quickly shrugged off as he stepped back, that sarcastic smirk back on his lips. "I said forget it. Whatcha follow me out here for anyway?"

"Don't do that."

"Do what? Huh? Don't push aside everything? Don't act like nothing's wrong? Don't fly off the handle?" He was doing a lousy job of that anyhow, might as well make a point with it.

"That's not—"

"Blame it on the ADHD, right?"

Noel was the one confused now. "What the hell, Keegan?"

"I *said*," he huffed, "forget it."

"I don't think I can now."

"Well, I have... So, let's move on. What do you want?"

He's quiet for a moment, taking in his brother like he's recovering from whiplash and the way Keegan can turn it on and off. He rubbed his head, shrugging before he spoke again. "I need your help."

Keegan started to move, like pacing was the only way to not bolt, but he didn't go too far from Noel. "Doing what?"

That had Noel smiling. "Really? Come on, Key, you're smarter than that."

"Yeah, well, some would beg to differ. So, quit fucking around and tell me straight out what you came out here for."

"Okay." He put himself in front of the beta, halting him in his tracks. He needed his attention, his full attention, and locked his eyes on him. It wasn't a contest, he wasn't starting a fight, and he wasn't fighting for dominance either, he needed him present. "Okay, enough of the destructive stuff."

"No one's being destructive, Noel! Get over yourself and stop projecting," but Keegan *had* stopped, and his muscles were yelling at him to move.

"What?" He hadn't seen that coming.

"Listen." He crossed his arms over his chest. "If anything, it's you, okay? You're the one being destructive. You went to Dad's office—

"How the hell—

Keegan laughed. "Did you completely forget Mom had that security system put in after he died? The one that notifies *all* of us when that door even creaks?" Noel *had* forgotten, hadn't even thought of it, and he caught off guard. "Okay, well, maybe you forgot. You forget a lot of things."

And the whiplash was back because, "what the hell's that supposed to mean?"

"Me, you asshole!" Keegan snaps, his arms going wide. "You forgot me!"

"I would—"

"Never? Yeah, I know." He tented his fingers over his nose, pinching the bridge of it as he turned away, putting his back to his brother.

Noel stayed quiet for a moment, just to see what he would do before he spoke again. "Remind me."

Keegan debated for a moment, his hands came down, before he let his head tip back, and he turned around once more, facing him. "When Mom leaves, you follow the rules, and that's good. I get it, but..." He took a minute to shrug before their eyes met. "Did you ever think that the rules are a crock of bullshit?"

With a shake of his head, Noel huffs. "They keep us safe."

"No!" Keegan steps back, his fists clenching, trying to keep it in. "No, Noel, they keep us in line. Nothing about them keeps us safe!"

"Then talk to me, tell me how to fix this."

"You could start by—" He stopped, eyes going to the ground as the memories of the day flash back to him.

O'Donnell's behind him, leaning in close, crowding against him. His sweaty, meaty hands on the back of his neck, squeezing, his nails digging in. He could see the creepy smile the asshole wore as he gave him a shove forward. He could hear the sound of the locker, the way it echoed as his fist connected with it. The sight of blood on his knuckles and the concern on Daniel's face when he saw him.

It all came back, all rushing at him as his heart started to race, and he clenched his jaw trying to push it down, trying to shove it away, but it's Daniel's weight against him, the way he crowded him against the fence that had his fingers slowly uncurling, and brought back the ability to look at his brother.

"It doesn't matter," was all he whispered.

"It does." Noel shook his head, trying to get him to see, to talk to him. "It matters to me."

Keegan let the moment of silence drag on for a little longer. "I wanna drop out."

That wasn't what he expected. "Of school?"

"No, dumbass, out of book club. Yes, out of school!" The smirk rose again at the quiet pause. "Not what you were expecting to hear, was it? Nah, didn't think it would be."

"You have half a year left."

Keegan shrugged. “Then I want to remote. I can’t—” He huffed, trying to keep calm to explain this. “I can’t be in that building anymore.”

There had to be something Noel wasn’t seeing, but taking in Keegan’s stance, at the way his body was ready to run just standing there with him, with the one person he should feel safe with, he knew what he had to do. “Okay.”

The shock on the younger brother’s face was comical. “Wait? That’s it? No fight?”

“You said it wasn’t the jock, but obviously, something is going on if you want to quit, so.” Noel didn’t know how to approach this any other way. “Okay.” But he could see the way Keegan began to rev up because he thought it was too easy. “On one condition.”

“Of course, you’re just like Mom, always something, some sort of—”

“I’m going to need you to do what you do best.”

“What? Annoy the hell out of you?”

“No.” He crossed his arms, spreading his stance just a bit as if this wasn’t the biggest thing in the world. “I’m going to need you to break into things. Mainly, Mom’s computer.” He saw the smirk turn into a smile, a wide, troublemaker smile that went right to Keegan’s eyes, as the request sunk in. “Good?”

“Yeah,” and that smile can be heard in his voice. “All good.”

Noel patted him on the shoulder before stepping away, and he was almost to the bed of the car before he noticed the lack of movement behind him. Glancing back, he saw the man still standing there, eyes focused on the gravel.

“Coming?”

“In a minute.” He pulls his phone from his pocket, waving it at him, “gotta make a phone call.”

Noel got it; he knew his brother too well to not know that Keegan had his own tools for this. He left him there, headed back into the building to check on Ellie, because with the way Keegan left, he could tell she was upset.

Keegan dialed out, put his phone to his ear, and waited for his brother to disappear inside as it rang.

ON HIS WAY IN, Noel was shocked to hear a familiar voice. He hadn't realized that Rollins had stayed behind, but just outside the small kitchen door, one that hadn't yet needed to be replaced and was as thin as a sheet of plywood, he could hear the conversation going on.

The first few things he mumbled were too low for Noel to pick up clearly, but he was certain he heard his mother's name. He closed his eyes, thinking back to his father's study and that paper in the private room, and concentrated on the man behind the wall. Everything filtered in, the hum of the lights above them, the drip of the water in the bathroom sink to the left, and slowly, as he focused in more, the small snippets of the conversation grew louder.

"Yes, she's gone." Noel's heart raced. "No, they don't know where she—"

The frequency around him grew higher, and Noel found himself pressing his hands against his ear. He couldn't get it to stop now that it started, causing his stomach to turn, but Rollins' voice was still coming through.

"—Is in charge. No, he's just a stupid kid. I'm telling you; the Summerford Pack is vulnerable."

The buzzing took over, blocking out everything else, becoming unbearable. Noel doubled over, moving his hands until the thickest part of them was almost painfully squeezing his head. His vision began to grow hazy as the world started to spin. He couldn't do it anymore, it was too much, and he bolted for the bathroom.

He barely made it to the stall before vomiting up everything he'd eaten for the day. The nausea that rolled through him forced everything up, sucking the energy out of him. When he finally had a chance to sit back, he's pressed against the cool concrete wall, and caught his breath, unable to move.

Whatever that was, he never wanted to do it again.

DILLON'S EYES were glued to the TV, to whatever show happened to be playing, not that he had a clue because he was pretty sure it was in Japanese. He hadn't even bothered to put on the subtitles, just watched it for the content, which made *no* sense to him whatsoever.

He needed a distraction with all the questions Detective Wells had asked him about Alesha that morning, shaking him from a blackout sleep. He was still in disbelief, still in the mindset that Lesh would call him and tell him it was some sort of joke, or that she was running off with some dude she had scoped out on the internet, all things he had told the cops.

He just needed not to think about the bad side of it. So when the phone on the nightstand beside his bed practically vibrated off as it rang, he put the show on pause and yanked it off the table. He knew who it was going to be, no two ways about it. He knew Juli was coming home, and that Keegan probably needed a night of debauchery to recover but when he answered, putting it right to speaker, what he got was something completely unexpected.

"Hey, Key, what's going on, man?"

"I need you to do something for me." No hello. No *what's happening*. Just... that?

"Did you get arrested again?" The scoff on the other end told him not to even bother asking, which only served to make him more curious on what his little cousin was up to. "Okay, anything, just stop with the suspense."

"You cave too easy," the beta chuckled, but the mystery of the call was short lived. *"Can you go to my house, through the back garage door and up to my room?"*

"Dude." He sat up on the bed, eyes narrowed at nothing. "You want me to break into your house?"

"No! There's a key by the washer. I need you to get my laptop."

Dillon swung his legs off the bed, grabbed his jeans that were haphazardly discarded on the floor among just about everything else he owned, and paused. "For what?" But the silence on the line told him Keegan wasn't about to give details yet. "Never mind, it doesn't matter." Because usually Keegan's silence meant it was probably illegal. "Let me just..."

He yanked on his shoes, hopped out into the hallway as he buttoned his jeans. Stopping in the kitchen, eyes right on the key rack, he paused.

"There's one problem."

"How can there be a problem? You haven't even left the house yet?"

Dillon glanced around at that, ducking down to check under the table, and behind the microwave before he straightened, curious. "How did you know that? You know what, never mind." He gazes longingly out the window at the Jetta parked quietly in the driveway, untouched and unloved. "The problem is my license is suspended and my mom has the car keys. Joan and I are not going anywhere."

"Totally forgot you named your car Joan Jetta," Keegan mumbled. *"In fact, I wish I hadn't remembered that at all, thanks. The Jeep keys are hanging on the hook in my kitchen. Take those, bring it here. I really need that laptop."*

With a growl at his cousin, Dillon yanked on his coat and headed for the garage door in the kitchen. He made his way down the steps and about two seconds away from running towards the Summerford house when his eyes landed on a bike just sitting there. He really hated bikes.

"Man, you owe me big time for this."

"Just get the laptop, please."

Dillon pressed the button on the side panel, and paused as the garage door slowly opened, suddenly realizing one thing.

"Did you just say please?"

"Fuck off, Dill!" The growl was back in his tone, and Dillon found himself smiling.

"That's more like it." He took hold of the handlebars and made it out onto the driveway only to pause again. "Hold up, are you talking about *the* laptop?"

"Know where it is?"

Dillon grinned, full of mischief, and hopped on the bike. "Sure do."

KEEGAN LOOKED up from the spot he had been focusing on while leaning on the bed of the truck. His gaze went right to where Noel was as he stepped out into the doorway, hands in his pockets, waiting.

"Good, bring it here, and text me when you pull up. I'll come outside." He disconnected the call, slipped the phone away and headed into the meetinghouse behind his brother, who had headed in as soon as Keegan moved his way.

KEEGAN PAUSED in the main room causing Noel to stop a moment after. It was as if he realized his brother wasn't getting any closer. He put his hands on his hips, Keegan licked his lips, biting down as he struggled. The indecision to enter the room or not was right there reflected in his eyes. Noel saw it, he understood it, but he also knew if Keegan didn't go, he'd regret it.

"Hey," Noel stepped up beside him, not cutting off his entrance or exit in any way and took a minute to just look over his profile. "Come on."

"No," he gave a small shake of his head. "I don't—"

"You honestly don't think she wants you to stay away, do you?"

His hazel eyes darted from Noel to the room. "Yeah."

"She's our baby sister, Keegan. There will never be a time when she won't want you there for her, even if you don't make a single sound."

He chuckled at that because there were days when Keegan was really good at being the broody, silent type, but he still wasn't moving towards the room. "I can't— I don't know how to help her if she's afraid."

"You don't have to help her," Noel grinned. "This is Ellie, right? The one who decided that she was going to teach herself to ride a bike without training wheels alone because she didn't want anyone to see either of us helping her out. The girl who raced a bike down the road with no chain because she knew she could stop it on her own?"

"The one who jumped from the top of the swing set because she thought it was easier than climbing down." Keegan outright laughed at that memory, but it faded the minute he thought of the aftermath of that, of how angry he had been because he *hadn't* been there to help her. "Yeah, she's badass, but she's never had to deal with Mom disappearing."

"And neither have we, so, we're in the same boat." Keegan's eyes went wide at that turn of phrase, something Noel waved off. "I know, bad choice of words, but can you imagine what we can do if we stop pushing each other away and start leaning on one another. Last summer would have never happened if I just talked to you."

"Well, I wasn't exactly an open book either." He crossed his arms, closed his eyes, and shook his head. "You really think she wants me in there?"

"I can't believe you think she doesn't." He rested his hand gently down on his shoulder and gave it one good squeeze. "Come on. I need you, I told you that outside, and I *know* she needs you too."

"Okay." He glanced at his brother one more time, dancing on his feet, nodded to himself as if that was going to move his feet, and pushed himself in the direction of the room.

The door to Keegan's bedroom slowly creaked open, letting the light from the hallway spill in before Dillon knocked it open wider, and flicked on the switch. He stopped dead, eyes rolling as he shook his head.

"Jesus, kid, clean your shit once in a while."

He didn't bother to kick anything out of the way, just headed straight for the closet on the furthest end of the room. He pushed the left folding door open, crouching down carefully to make sure he wasn't going to kneel on anything—like some forgotten candy bar—and reached in, shoving the clutter away.

He ran his hand down the wall, waiting to feel the telltale bump of the hidden panel, and smirked when his fingers hit it. He felt along the edges until he could use his nails to grasp the sides of the panel, popping it out of place.

There, tucked in the foot-high cubby was a thin laptop bag. He placed the panel aside, then reached in, slowly pulling it from its hiding spot. Just to be certain, he sat back, placed the bag on the floor and unzipped it, opening it to find the silver laptop—expensive looking tech with no logos—and a small hard case of USB drives.

He quickly closed the bag, replaced the panel, and with it tucked under his arm, headed out of the room. If Keegan wanted him to actually take *this* out in public, he wasn't fooling around getting it to the source. There wasn't anything on it that could pin Keegan for any wrongdoing, but the power and the programs on this one little unit — Well, there would definitely be questions.

Moving through the kitchen, he stopped at the keyholder, looked over the ones left, knowing that some of them were just keys. They didn't belong to anything drivable anymore, a few were to the "toys" in the shed out back, but the Jeep keys with the green bottle opener attached were what he was looking for. He snatched them off the hook and headed out the door, right for the machine in the driveway, leaving his bike behind.

He slipped in, a little worried that the hardtop hadn't been put on the machine yet, but the flimsy plastic half doors seemed to work okay. Keegan's way of thinking was a little strange for just about everyone to follow. He placed the laptop down where it would be safe, on the floor of the passenger's side, started it up, and headed out down the road, praying he wouldn't get caught.

Gus looked up from behind the desk, eyes going right to Keegan, who looked a little on the pale side, but when Noel gave a slight shake of his head, he said nothing about it. Noel stopped at the water cooler, grabbed a cup and filled it as Keegan headed for the second lounge chair, eyes on Ellie.

The oldest of the three covered his smile with the cup, and the pretense of drinking as Keegan whispered softly to his sister, dragging her attention from the book in her hand. The way she looked up at him, the relief in her eyes at his nearness, made his heart flutter. He was glad he convinced him to come in, but the closeness was short lived when his phone went off and Keegan brought it over close enough for Ellie to read.

"It's Dill." He rubbed his hand across his lips, giving his sister a pleading look, hoping she'd understand.

"Is he all right?" He nodded but didn't explain. "What's going on?"

"He's outside. I asked him to pick something up for me from the house, to bring it here." The two were eye-to-eye now, the others in the room didn't seem to exist, even with Noel's watchful gaze on them. "I promise I'll be right back, but we need this."

"It's your laptop, isn't it?" There was no judgment in her voice, no weird accusing tone that he had heard from so many other people, and he bit down on his bottom lip as he nodded. "Go get it."

"What?" He barely contained the shock as he sat back, wide-eyed.

"Is it gonna help with Mom?" Again, he nodded. "Go get it."

"Okay." He slowly rose, his hands rubbing on his thigh. "Um, Noel will stay here with you."

"I got this." She grinned, and that just sealed it there. She'd be okay, she wanted him there, she wasn't afraid of him. People were always afraid, but not her. "Go."

Keegan smirked and bolted from the room, slipping past Noel without so much as a word.

Noel saw the moment her smile faded, and worry set in. "What?"

"He's really scared."

"I know." He just didn't know what he could do to help him except give him something to do. "I know you are, too."

"Except I know we're going to get her back," she shrugged, and of course, she had faith in them, she always did. "I'm not so sure he does."

"He will, we just have to work together."

"Where's he going anyway?" Gus asked, and both Noel and Ellie raised a brow, eyes on each other and smiled, but shook their heads, refusing to answer.

They knew Keegan was about to do what he did best.

DILLON TAPPED on the steering wheel, the engine still running, but the radio was silent. He hated the meetinghouse. There was just something creepy about it—besides the woods at the back and the old cemetery that most of the trees hid from the road—something about the building itself always set him off. So, he was completely thrown and totally startled when the passenger's door was ripped open, and Keegan grinned up at him.

"You scared the shit out of me, man." Dillon placed a hand over his heart, leaning away from Keegan.

"You really have to come up with another name besides *man*." The beta laughed as he scooped up his laptop from the floor. "But thanks." He held it up for just a second before tucking it under his arm. "I owe ya."

And that struck Dillon just as strange as the *"please"* from earlier, and he cocked his head to the side, scanning over the hazel eyed beta. "What's going on?"

Keegan waved him off. "Bullshit stuff."

"Enough to need that? Enough to have you bring it *here* of all places. With Gus inside."

"How do you know Gus is in there?" Dillon rolled his eyes and pointed at the Honda as if it weren't completely obvious. "Oh," he smirked. "Well, this," he held the bag up, "might just change everything." He stepped back, hand on the door, and gave his Jeep a once over. "Get home safe. You can take her; I'll ride home with Noel."

Yet another shock. "Now I know something's up, you hate your brother."

"I don't hate my brother." Keegan rubbed his temple.

"It's okay if you do. I don't like mine."

"Yeah, but Jordan's a fuckwad, so... there's that."

Dillon scoffed as he put the Jeep in gear. "Text me later."

Keegan was about to walk away but glanced back over his shoulder. Something Noel said stuck with him, something besides the *"I need you"* that he spouted earlier, and Keegan sighed.

"Hey, Dill." He cleared his throat, uncertain on how to be that person, the one that showed a softer side to people outside his zone. "I'm sorry about Alesha."

Dillon glared at him as if he were some foreign being that just dropped in from another planet. "Ah," he had no idea what to do with this new *thing*. "Thanks." He scratched at the back of his head. "I'm sure she'll be just fine. She's... she's tough."

Keegan nodded, completely out of his league, and he patted the door, going back on the smirk he always wore. "Not one scratch, dude."

Dillon scoffed, gave him the middle finger as he let off the clutch, pressing on the gas. The Jeep lurched forward getting Keegan to slam the door shut. He stepped back to watch the Jeep leave the lot, kicking up stones.

He inspected the bag, knowing that everything he needed would be right there at his fingertips, and made his way into the meeting house, closing the door tightly behind him.

"Rollins' Residence - 5:34 p.m."

Somewhere in the darkness of the house, a door clicked and scraped open, pulled against the rug beneath it. From the hallway, Mitch turned the corner into the kitchen, rubbing his eyes as he headed straight for the fridge. The only illumination in the room was the yellow glow from the light just above the stove, which threw everything into shadows.

Mitch stretched, opening the freezer first, dressed in sweats with "Collins High School" written down the side in gold, and a tee-shirt loose enough on him to be comfortable. There was nothing in it that he found at all appealing.

He leaned down, grabbed the handle to the fridge and yanked it open. The light from inside illuminated the kitchen, giving his eyes a bright glow as he dug into the back to find what he was searching for. Junk food of any kind.

A low moan had him standing straight, eyes wide, as he scanned the room around him, but there was nothing but the sound of the wall clock ticking. He shook his head, feeling overworked and probably a little on the "overstudied" side. Turning his attention back to the food, he reached for the back, knowing there was a slice of chocolate pie hiding in its usual spot.

That moan echoed through the house again.

He wasn't imagining it. He slowly stood, pie going to the counter as he closed the fridge, and his eyes landed on the basement door. He was pretty positive now that he wasn't hearing things and made his way towards it in sock-clad feet, keeping his movement almost silent.

He reached out, hand on the knob as that moan came again, louder this time and definitely coming from the basement. He yanked the door open, peering down into the darkness. He hated the basement, especially the stairs. It was dark enough that they disappeared about halfway down, as if nothing existed after that point.

He flicked the switch on just inside the doorway, illuminating the rest of the way down, but it was unfinished, with spaces between and every horror movie he'd ever seen, mostly with Ellie, came flashing back to him. It didn't look safe at all. The light at the bottom of the stairs flickered and his heart started to race.

They were totally discussing her love for the macabre when they got together again.

The painful moan, a little louder this time, followed by a rough cough had him moving but not down the steps, not yet. He left the door open, turning towards the counter. He grabbed a large knife from the block before he set it down, and yanked open a drawer, only to fish through a mess of random things to find a flashlight.

Holding his breath, he clicked the end, and let the relief wash over him when it lit up, but he did it three or four more times before he's satisfied that it actually worked. Scooping up the knife, he turned, armed with both that, and headed down into the semi-darkness.

When he hit the bottom step, he swung around, letting the beam go over everything there. An old washing machine, empty boxes, and shelves with things that no one was ever going to look at again.

The floor was nothing but cold concrete and the socks are no match for the chill that ran up from it. He was a little pissed that he didn't think of grabbing a jacket since it was always colder there than anywhere else in the house, but he pressed on, hugging himself the best he could with the sharp object in his hand. He didn't even know why he grabbed it; it wasn't like he was going to find anything more than a mouse in the place. Even then, he was pretty sure his cat probably took care of that too.

In the back, along the furthest wall, was a large, heavy door, wide enough to be considered the size of a walk-in freezer but made of wood. The sign that graced it wasn't "root cellar" or "wine cellar," it was "keep out," but the opened Master Lock was screaming for him to come in.

He paused, debated for a moment, and swung the flashlight around to check behind him. The moan was absolutely coming from beyond the door this time, and he didn't wait. Mitch slipped the lock off and swung the door wide.

Inside was nothing but darkness, and cold as hell. He shined the light in, illuminating the long hallway before him. "What the hell?"

Cautiously he stepped in, moving into the darkness. He couldn't believe it, Ellie was right. She always thought there was a weird feeling at his house, especially under the patio out back, but he never thought it would be this.

The floors were nothing but loose dirt, and he was close with the walk-in freezer part. It was so cold he could see his breath, but he pushed on, flashlight going over the multiple, heavy, wooden doors that lined each side, all with a small window at eye-level.

He needed to know what these were, so he stopped at one, and slowly pulled it open. Thank God it was empty inside, at least, from what he can see by the small light he's holding. There was a cot and a pot. It smelled like death, and he quickly stepped back, closing the door.

With his heart now racing, and his respirations uncontrolled, he moved on. He wasn't sure why he was continuing, there couldn't be anything good at the end of this, but when he came to a cross-section, he didn't believe what he was seeing. The hall opened to the left, showing him another door, one that would lead out to a bulkhead. The bulkhead to his house!

He was shocked still for a moment, imagining every horrible thing he could about this place, but it was a hoarse cough that got him spinning to the right, to another endless looking hallway with no doors in sight.

He moved towards it, as if "curiosity killed the cat" was now the very definition of his death, well, that and hypothermia, but not three doors down, he stopped again. A loud clank came from just beyond the last door on the right. He needed to know now, couldn't stop what was coming next, and he pressed his ear to the door.

Two more coughs, the shuffle of movement, and Mitch stepped back. He was scared, shaking, and pretty sure he's about to let out a zombie hoard, but he slid the lock, the shriek of it against the rusty metal was ear piercing but he had to see.

Pulling it open, Mitch stuck the light in first, then his head when nothing moved.

Luca's body had frozen, more so out of fear than the icy temperatures in the cells, but his eyes were locked on the way the door slowly opened. *Don't move, don't speak, don't fight.* It was all his brain could tell him as the light hit his eyes. The pain from it seared through his head, but he didn't make a sound, just wrapped the blanket tighter around himself, huddling low, and raised an arm to block out the beam

His eyes, in response to it, shined with a bright golden hue.

The light suddenly left, the door slammed shut, and the sound of retreating footsteps echoed in the night.

Luca closed his eyes, tears streaming down his cheeks, as he pulled the cover over his head, praying he survived the night.

Mitch slammed the "keep out" door shut, replaced the lock, and didn't stop until he hit the kitchen floor, literally. His dirt crusted socks slipped on the linoleum and sent him skidding across on his ass, tossing the knife. It slid under the table, lost under the baseboard register.

He got to his feet, trying to catch his heart as he stripped off the socks, and ducked into his room. With the door closed behind him, Mitch leaned against it, trying to figure out what the hell he just saw, but he couldn't even—

He snatched his phone off his desk, but only after locking his door. He knew where Ellie was, at the meetinghouse, he knew she's busy, but this was just—

He opened the thread, quickly typed out *"we need to talk,"* and sent it before he slid down to the floor, hands in his hair.

"Jesus Christ."

CHAPTER 14

Noel could see both siblings from where he stood behind the desk, going through the papers spread out on it.

Keegan paced along the back wall, the only spot with room to do so in the office without knocking into anything, but close enough to the windows that if he needed to, he could open one. His laptop bag was sitting right in plain sight, and while Noel remembered when he was given the device, he knew by looking at it, at the protective way it sat, that there was much more to it now. Keegan wasn't going far from it.

Ellie took up one of the lounge chairs, her eyes on her phone as she clicked away on something intense. Noel was positive she wasn't texting, not with the way her thumbs moved over the keyboard, but it was the look of full concentration on her face that gave it away completely. She was looking up something, and pretty deep into her research.

That brought him back to Gus, who stood in front of him, the three feet of hard mahogany between them was the reason he hadn't reached over, grabbed the alpha and shaken him until he rattled. That and the fact that he needed more answers They had talked before, when the members were dismissed, but not about everything, not about what to do next.

And that was where they stood now, waiting on Gus's contact to call back, waiting for Drake to do something in Chicago besides sit on his ass. Just waiting.

"They don't have a clue? Not a single lead?" He stopped shuffling the papers, they weren't doing anything but keeping his hands occupied anyway and rested his fists to the wood. Keegan's grumpy voice huffed a "*useless*" from the direction of the windows. "Not helping, Key."

That had the beta halting in his tracks, arms crossed, scowl on his face. "Oh, I'm sorry. I didn't realize I was supposed to be helpful." He turned his gaze from Noel to Gus, narrowing his eyes on him. "And what kind of half-assed operation is this council running when you can lose one of your members that fast?"

"It wasn't the council—"

"Right," he huffed.

"Keegan!" Noel rubbed his forehead, hoping to not have to tie the kid down. His brother was trying to provoke the Pack Second, and Noel didn't have time to keep separating him from other people. Just as fast as his attitude arrived, Keegan was waving him off, going back to pacing and Noel shook his head. He had no idea what to do with him.

"It's fine," Gus spoke low, eyes on Noel now as he let the frustration wan. "We're all on edge. But what I do know is this. Mr. Payne sent a text when they arrived at the plane. Your mother also sent a text to you, but... After that it was radio silence. Drake confirmed that Tom didn't make it and that your mother was taken."

"And Doug?" Both alphas shifted towards Keegan, at the pain in his eyes, but Gus only shook his head. "Shit."

The look of uncertainty, of what to do next rose on the beta's face, getting Noel to press for anything more. "That's your confirmation?"

"That's as good as we've got, Alpha."

"*Stop* calling me that! My mother is not dead. I am not Pack Alpha!" It was like a button was pushed from that title alone, and Noel swept the papers from the desk in front of him. They scattered across the room like morbid confetti, and the only thing he could do to gather himself was take a breath.

He pressed his fists to the wood again, curling his fingers in against his palm this time so he could feel the prick of his nails. He needed to see that he wasn't imagining this and squatted down behind the desk, hiding what he was doing as he opened his hands. Under the nail beds, the tips of black claws peeked out, as blood started to pool along the cuticle.

He stood straight, put his back to them and shook it out. Trying to ease the pain, he flexed his fingers as he stretched them wide, as if he were fighting a cramp, but he didn't turn around yet, not until he was sure.

"How the hell did you lose her?" He could hear that power in his words, the vibration that had everyone listening earlier, and behind him Gus stiffened, but didn't answer. He whipped around, eyes bright, and right on Gus. "Tell me!"

Keegan took a step towards him, only to have Noel raise his hand, just enough to be seen, but it halted his steps.

Gus cleared his throat, shaking off the effects. "There's no description of the car or the people who took her."

Noel's eyes were on his brother, the way he frantically clenched and unclenched his fists, and his worry was now only on him.

"Do you need to go?" His only response is a slight shake of his head, and the fact that he started pacing again, which brought Ellie into his sight. "Ell?" It was as if they were mirroring the other with the "no" response before she turned back to the phone. Noel let those responses wash over him. They weren't running. Not yet. "Wonderful." He settled on Gustaf again. "What's your next move?"

"I really don't—"

"You keep referring to me as alpha, start treating me like one. What is your next move?"

"Drake has our best people tracking her phone and any electronics she might have had on her when she got to the airport, but—"

"They'd make you take them out at security." Noel picked up a pen, twirling it in his hand, anything to keep busy but he looked to Ellie. She was still on that phone, and he realized that something was wrong. He moved from behind the desk, slipping up beside her, not blocking Keegan's path at all and gently touched her shoulder. "Anything?"

She glared up at him. "Hacking a pack line isn't as easy as you think."

No wonder she looked frustrated. He gave her a quick smile and rubbed her shoulder. "Keep going."

He headed back to the desk, but this time it was to the front to lean on it, lowering the volume of their conversation, not that anything could be kept from his siblings.

"There has to be something we missed." It was the pause in Keegan's steps and the look on his face as he stared at the lamp in front of him that had Noel's attention. "Key?" The beta's eyes snap up to his. "What is it?"

"They'd make them take all of them out of their pockets, off their person."

Ellie glanced up at her phone. "All what?"

"Her stuff, her electronics. Phone, laptop. I don't know, Fit Watch? Anything metal or with an electronic signature."

"Right." Noel thought he was following the train of thought. "If she went through security."

Keegan pointed at him, wiggling his finger. "Exactly. Safety protocols, all that."

"We already talked about that."

But that got Ellie to pipe up. "Right, most TSA checkpoints would."

"And they'd scan it, but if you were taken." He was mumbling now. "They'd ditch it, right?"

Noel pinched the bridge of his nose. Keegan's trains of thought were like fifty on the same track headed for a collision course with a brick wall, they just had to wait until they collided to get an answer. "Keegan, you're rambling."

"I know, I know." He centered himself. "This is all an "if," but she didn't go through security."

"Why not?" Ellie was all in now, which was usually the thing that happened when Keegan started throwing out conspiracies.

He snorted, like he was happy he was the only one in the loop. "Mom had a private jet. Would have driven straight to the strip. Never even got out of the car at the gate."

Noel got it now. "No passing through the TSA gates."

"No collecting two hundred dollars." Keegan pointed at him again, this time with a nod. "Which means either she still has them on her—"

"Unlikely if no one can track her," the youngest added.

"Or they took them off and ditched them somewhere. Probably destroyed them beforehand."

"Not making this any easier," Noel whispered, his confusion completely apparent in his expression.

There was a look on Keegan's face that he couldn't place, not until he spoke again. "But it does."

Noel sighed; this was not getting him anywhere. "I know your mind is like an escape room but pretend you're speaking to a swarm of third graders."

"It's simple," Keegan shrugged. "What about her ring?"

Noel was stumped. He stood there in silence waiting for more, but suddenly got it when Keegan stepped closer. With one swipe, Keegan had that bag in his hand, and he'd already unzipped it.

"Their wedding rings?" Ellie apparently had no clue as to what was going on.

"Mom and Dad always said we were the ones that got them if they died." Noel crossed his arms, he never really thought of that. "Those rings were pretty unique."

"More like ugly as hell." Keegan laughed, moving towards the desk as he opened the silver top on the fifteen-inch screen. Noel locked eyes with his brother as Keegan raised his hands in surrender.

"Okay, I'm out of the loop, what's going on?" Gus glanced at all three, at the way they all had the same expression but said nothing else.

"What if they're that way for a reason?" Noel's response had Keegan grinning.

It was Ellie's scrunched nose that had Noel smiling. "You'd wear gaudy jewelry for a reason?"

"No," Keegan whispered as Noel shifted to the other side of the desk, right beside him, fingers on the keyboard of his mother's computer and with one quick look at Keegan, who only replied with a shrug, he started typing. "You hide something in gaudy jewelry for a reason." Three times, three incorrect passwords, and Keegan was about at his wits end. "What the hell's the password?"

It was Ellie that walked over, pushing Noel aside as she squeezed in between her brothers, and leaned over the keys. Like lightning, her fingers sailed over the keys just for a second before she stood and gestured to the "Welcome, Juli" screen. Both boys' eyes were on her as she walked back over towards the window, plopping down in the lounge chair.

"How—" Noel was floored, exchanging looks with Keegan before focusing on Ellie. "How'd you do that?"

Keegan laughed, actually laughed before he shook his head. "She's the favorite, remember?" But that was when Keegan locked his fingers together and stretched his arms out, smirking as he hip-checked Noel. "Okay, my turn."

He slipped into the chair behind the desk, brought his own laptop closer, connecting the two together with a small purple wire before he slid Juli's back and opened the screen on his own with a blurred series of codes. He was totally unfazed by the fact that Noel peered over his shoulder as he worked.

It was Gus that wasn't sure what was going on as he stepped closer to the table. "What are you going to do?"

Keegan looked up with a wicked smile on his face. "I'm gonna hack into Mom's security system."

Noel smiled proudly. He knew what his brother was capable of, seen some of his handiwork too, but the shock on Gus's face told him the Pack Second had no idea just how skilled the kid was.

This was going to be fun.

MITCH HAD MANAGED to pull himself off the floor and make his way back towards the kitchen even as his body still vibrated from everything he had seen. There was a man. In his basement. What the hell was that? He couldn't even wrap his mind around it, not really, but he hadn't heard from Ellie, and wasn't even sure *what* to do next. One thing was certain, he couldn't let his dad know he even had a clue.

The headlights of the car reflecting on the wall had him moving, scrambling to the cabinets to get the bowl, spoon, and cereal out. He grabbed the milk and set himself up, even put the box and carton away before the main door opened and closed with some force.

He tried his best to look relaxed when Tobias entered the kitchen, even scooping a large spoonful in just to keep his mouth shut as the man eyed him over, headed for the coffee pot.

"Thought you had homework," his gruff voice always had Mitch on edge. Tobias had never touched his son, or his wife, but Mitch always felt that threat was so close to the surface. He hated walking on eggshells around him and now he knew why. He could feel it.

He gave the best nonchalant shrug he could and finished most of what was in his mouth before he answered. "Got hungry."

He pointed at the bowl. "Soup or cereal?"

Mitch hadn't noticed how far away his father was until he glanced up. Tobias was nearly across the kitchen.

"Oh. Cereal," Mitch mumbled.

He was waiting for the lecture on how it was dinner time, but it never came. The older Rollins simply moved towards the fridge, grabbing the milk before setting it on the counter. Mitch watched with interest as he grabbed the Fruit Loops from the counter and poured himself a bowl, standing on the opposite side of the island, but he didn't miss the way he glanced at Mitch's bare feet... dirty, bare feet.

"What happened there? Your mom's going to have a fit if you tracked dirt in the house?"

Mitch looked down, wiggled his toes, and shrugged. "Lacey got out when I put out the trash from my room. Had to chase her around the backyard."

"Your cat never goes out."

"Which is probably why it was so easy to get her once she realized where she was," Mitch smiled, making the comment as lighthearted as possible, hoping to ease his dad's suspicions.

It took a few moments of silence, but the old man scoffed. "Must have been pretty funny to see."

"Yeah," he grinned. "She figured out grass in December is far from warm."

"How was school?"

Mitch glanced up as Tobias stuffed a spoonful of the colorful circles into his mouth, eyes still on his son. "Boring. Fire drill about lunchtime, but other than that—"

"Good. Remember what I said about that Summerford girl. You don't need the distractions."

He could only nod, there was no sense in arguing with him, but he couldn't keep quiet. "She's not a distraction. She's just a friend. I have plenty of friends, Dad." Mitch picked up his bowl, turning to head out of the kitchen with it still half full, but he gave a glance to the basement door before settling on his father. "If anything's a distraction, it's this whole extracurricular thing you suddenly have me on."

"Getting you into college is going to save you a lot of trouble as a beta, Mitch."

"A lot of things could save me from being a beta, Dad, like having a life, having friends that I can count on. Not going into the security field. We aren't defined by our designation, not anymore. Times are changing."

To say the shock on Tobias's face was thrilling and more than fulfilling would have been an understatement but with what he now knew about his father, there was no way he was following in his footsteps.

Mitch had to get in touch with Ellie or Gus soon. That guy wasn't going to survive in the cold for too much longer.

NOEL HAD MOVED out of the office, giving Keegan the privacy to do what he needed with the laptops. The sound of the ticking on the keyboard was grating on his nerves and the space had started to close in on him.

Gus was standing at the end of the table, eyes going over the folders of the missing pack members again, something that Noel had started to see as normal since those folders were always there, and Gus was always searching them.

"What are you looking for when you go through them?"

Gus stood up quickly, shocked back to the real world by the sudden presence beside him, and he drew in deeply, grounding himself.

"Clues," he shrugged, eyes following his fingers over the edges of the folders. "Some of these are decades old, others are weeks, but there has got to be some common ground. Your mother has the other half, a few personal to the pack, to us, but these are the ones that have fallen through the cracks. These are my reminders."

"Why do you do this to yourself?" Noel never understood that part, why Gus was alone at his age, more married to the position than anyone he had ever met. It was like there was something driving him.

"I'm not doing anything, just my job."

"Gus, you should be out there having a family, not taking care of us, watching over us twenty-four/seven."

He smiled at him, actually smiled as he shook his head. "You are my family. You, your mom, your brother and sister. You're all I need right now and watching over you is kinda what I live for."

"Can I look through them?"

Gus gathered up the folders, pulling them away from Noel. "No."

He wasn't sure why that was so absolute, but Noel wasn't letting it go. "I can help."

"You are helping," he gestured towards the room. "You're doing *your* job."

Noel turned to see Ellie walk out of the office, her bag on her shoulder. She had snuck out to the truck after things had calmed down, and Keegan had come back in, swearing up and down that she had homework to do. It was the uncertain way she was looking at him that had him curious. "What's up?"

"I have a paper due." Her tone was light, but just like everything else, she was straightforward. "All my notes are on my Google docs at home."

"Can you do it on your phone?" He didn't want her out of his sight, he wanted her close, but the glare she gave him told him he wasn't going to win this one.

"If I want my eyes to go crossed, sure." There was a hint of Keegan in those words and Noel rolled his eyes. At least Gus seemed amused by the banter.

He gave a quick glance in the older alpha's direction for some sort of guidance, but Gus merely shrugged. He wasn't getting between the two of them. Noel dropped his head back, gaze going to the ceiling, counting mentally down from ten before he looked at his sister.

"I don't know if I'm comfortable with you being alone."

"Fair," she agreed, but crossed her arms. "Though, you forget I have the combination to the safe, and I know where Mom keeps the taser."

He nearly choked at the serious way she presented her facts, but it also made him smile because she wasn't giving up and she wasn't giving into the fear. "Okay, then...would you like me to bring you home?"

"Please."

With a minute shake of his head, Noel stepped away, headed for the office to grab his keys. Ellie watched after him for a moment before she turned back to Gus. She knew he was looking at her, checking her over for any signs of the state of her emotions, but the slight tilt of her head and the raise of her brow was what finally got him to speak.

"Are you okay? I know the boys have—"

"Please, don't treat me like a child. I understand what's going on." Those words were harsh, and she hadn't meant for them to come out that way, but she knew someone was going to start babying her at some point. She had been through enough in the last year to see the signs.

"I'm just offering support, Ellie."

"I'm not alone, though I can see how all of you think that."

"Hey, however you deal is your thing, I just—"

"I know. I'm sorry." Letting her arms drop to her side, she stepped closer, giving him a small smile. "I just don't want to be coddled. I know I'm sixteen and I should be doing other things, living a little, going out partying. But this is me, this is how I deal." She reached out, slipping her fingers around his for just a second before she let go. "I have friends to lean on."

Noel's return to the room broke the tenuous silence between them, as Ellie stepped back, pulled her jacket tightly around her and waited he held up his keys and gestured towards the door. With one last look in Gus's direction, Ellie followed him out into the night.

THE STREETLIGHTS PASSED LIKE BEATS, lighting up the interior of the cab for only a second before darkness took over again, an almost hypnotic pattern that had Ellie lost in her own head even on her phone. She was typing out notes, hoping the voice in her head would give her the words needed to accurately spell out what she wanted to say.

"You okay?" Noel's whispered words caught her attention, bringing her eyes up from the night mode phone. She gave him her usual glare, not something meant as anger or to be rude, it was just how she looked when she took in the situation.

"I'm not weak." However, she wasn't sure why she felt so defensive about everything.

"I never said that, just asked." Noel focused on the road, counted out his breaths as he settled, trying to push down that protective side.

"Why is it that when Keegan gets quiet or paces, you guys find it normal, but when I do, suddenly there's a reason for concern?"

"You don't think this is reason enough? Ell, you never growl at me like this." She opened her mouth to protest but was quickly silenced by the slight raise of his hand. "Don't deny it, you *are* growling, and you never do."

"I have a headache," she finally admitted. "And it's only getting worse. Mom's missing and I can't seem to crack this code to get in and track her phone."

"Is that what you've been doing?"

"Up until we left, yes."

"I thought we said they'd probably got rid of it?"

"But when and where might be a clue." This grabbed his attention. He hadn't really thought of that. "If they didn't find it at the airport, maybe they tossed it somewhere else."

"Like on the road?"

"Somewhere between Midway and wherever they took her."

Noel got it; he understood her train of thought. As he pulled the truck to a stop at a red light, his fingers tapped against the wheel. She hadn't said another word to explain, and he was too wired to leave it alone.

"So, if it's on, can we track it?"

"Essentially. There's that whole "Find my phone" app, or even whatever cell towers it's tracking at for signal."

"What if it's not on?"

"Still could."

Noe glanced at her, a little confused just as the light turned green. "I'm not following."

"We can trace it back to its last location." She shifted in her seat, turning towards him more, her eyes right on him. "Think of it this way, the last tower it hit should be the last place that comes up on the app. It will at least give us a direction."

"Huh, you and Keegan really have a knack for this whole hacker thing." His smirk set her off in a weird way, getting her to sit back and look out the window.

"Funny." She crossed her arms, sighing. "It's not so much hacking when she has it on all our phones. It's just a matter of getting into the server to find the location."

She picked up her phone again, opening the notes, and slipped back into her work, only to look up again when Noel pulled into the driveway, and put the truck in park.

"Want me to walk you in?"

Ellie swung the door wide, grabbing her books and the backpack before she slipped out. "No." He chuckled at her straightforward answer. "But thanks."

She slammed the door without waiting, headed up towards the front entrance, but glanced down at the bike that sat on the grass, and took in the fact that Keegan's Jeep was missing. It was the squeaky sound of Noel's window rolling down that caught her attention.

"Hey, Ell." She stopped just short of the steps and turned. He was practically leaning out the window, arm over the door. "We'll find her."

She gave him the best smile she could, dug her keys out of her pocket, and waved before heading up to the door. The rumble of the truck as it backed out was the last thing she heard as she closed the door.

In the foyer, she flicked the lights on, and locked the deadbolt. She was alone in the silence, or what had been silence which was broken by the bird whistle on her phone. She rolled her eyes, almost praying that it wasn't one of her brothers, but the annoyance slipped away at the text on screen.

Mitch: *Ell, come on. We need to talk.*

Apparently, that wasn't the first time he had texted that night using almost the same words, so there was an urgency there, something she needed to reply to.

Ellie: *I thought we weren't supposed to talk after school?*

The reply bubbles went on for a moment after she hit send, waiting on the next line from him.

Mitch: *He can go to hell, and you really need to hear this.*

She bit down on her lip, her mind going in a million different directions as she pondered her reply. She really needed to get that paper done and with all that went on, did she really need another mystery on top of the news from today? And why was she so calm about all of it?

She plopped down on the bed, crossing her legs as she tucked the phone in the space between her knees and cradled her face in her hands.

"It would also be awesome if this damn headache would go away," she mumbled, fingers rubbing at the back of her neck, just as the phone went off again, this time more of a cat call than a bird, and curiously, she picked it up. "Ugh! What now?"

There, in the small banner that ran across the screen, was her brother's name, alerted by the specific tone. Clicking it with her thumb, her eyes went over the quick text.

Keegan: *Not gonna ask if you're doing okay, but...*

Ellie rolled her eyes. It's not that she didn't want to answer him, but— She flipped back to the conversation with Mitch.

Ellie: *Is this a 911?*

The response she got, while expected since his dad was home, was a little abrupt and very unnerving.

Mitch: *Tomorrow. GTG.*

With a sigh, she placed the phone on the bed, got up and made her way towards the dresser, taking out pajamas. Changing didn't make her feel any better, and the thought of a shower seemed somehow tedious and more tiring than the damn words she needed to get down, so with a flop down on the bed, she grabbed her phone, and growled as she replied to Keegan.

Ellie: *I'm fine. I thought you weren't going to ask?*

The painful rumble in her stomach suddenly reminded her that dinnertime was slowly slipping by. She shook her head, wondering if she should just take the points off and not finish the assignment, but the thought of the leftover pizza in the fridge had her up and moving towards the kitchen.

Keegan: *Didn't think you'd answer.*

She yanked the door open, grabbed the pizza box out and set it on the counter, debating on whether to even heat it up, but responded instead.

Ellie: *Find anything?*

She grabbed two slices, not really wanting to hear his answer, and dropped them on a sheet of paper towels that she pulled from the roll, just as the phone whistled again.

Keegan: *Nada.*

That couldn't be right, Keegan was an expert.

Ellie: *At all?*

Of course, his response was classic Keegan.

Keegan: *That's what nada means. Gotta go back to work. Don't eat all the pizza.*

She glanced from the phone to the two slices on the counter, and back. That was just a little weird. She stuffed the phone away, grabbed the slices from the counter, and headed out of the room before she quickly backtracked and grabbed a soda from the fridge.

It was going to be a long night.

It was late, Paige had just gotten home maybe a half hour before, which wasn't anything new for her schedule mid-week, but it had been a very trying day.

After Keegan left, and Ellie had told her about the headache, Paige couldn't get her mind off anything but the Summerfords, which just irritated her to no end. She got Keegan, they had been together for a while so worrying about his flip flop personality was par for the course, but Ellie? How did she not know that the headache was the first sign of her presentation? Where the hell was Juli, and did she even have a clue what came next?

Stepping into her room with a towel wrapped around her, still irritated even after the shower, she couldn't stop the racing thoughts, so, of course they just got worse when her screen lit up. The phone had been tossed on the bed when she entered the room, along with everything else she had been carrying, but now it was filled with Keegan's name as a text banner filled the screen.

She made a grab for a tee-shirt—one of his no less—and pulled it on along with a pair of loose shorts before she dropped down on the bed and grabbed the phone. One simple word was all he ever sent in the beginning.

Keegan: *Busy?*

And while she expected his text, there was just something about it that had her worried. He never asked anything, just told her "outside" or "coming" to indicate his intentions, but "busy?"

Paige: *Just got out of the shower. You okay?*

The uncomplicated response made her heart race.

Keegan: *No.*

She sucked her lip in, trying to figure out how to reply to that because the wrong one would push him away when he really needed to be pulled closer, but the bubbles were going again, and it took all she had to wait.

Keegan: *Can I see you tonight?*

Okay, there really was something going on. She typed out her response, a simple "yes" but just as her thumb went for the send button, there was a knock on her door.

Unimpressed at the lack of privacy—because this knock could only mean one thing—Paige swung it open, and her mother's judgy once-over conveyed everything Paige wanted to know.

"You're not sexting on that, are you?" It wasn't even a motherly tone, it was completely accusatory, and Paige rolled her eyes, walking further into the room. "No Keegan tonight." This had Paige looking but not answering... or denying. "Your father's coming home early, and I don't need him to find that boy here."

"There's nothing wrong with him!" She knew that was the reason her dad didn't like him, because he was convinced that Keegan was some sort of sociopath.

It was her mother's raised hand that got her to stop her protest. "I like Keegan, you know that, but your father—"

"Is a hypocrite and wouldn't understand. Got it."

"I'm sorry, honey. I know his— I know Juli's gone, and I don't mind him here when she's away, just not tonight."

Paige knew her mom had grown up with Juli just like Paige had known Keegan forever and while her tone was her wanting to keep her daughter safe, she hated that he had to stay away. "Okay, Mom."

"Thank you." She stepped in, gave Paige a quick kiss on the forehead, and backed out of the room. She paused at the door, hand wrapped around the handle and gave a fleeting smile. "Goodnight, sweetie."

"Night," Paige whispered, watching as she closed the door and brought the phone back up, erasing the "yes" and replaced it with "no." She hit send before she could change her mind, but she couldn't leave him. There was something going on and Keegan needed *someone.*

She dialed out without a second thought and brought the phone to her ear.

"Paige?" Daniel's words were huffs, and while she was curious, she really didn't want to know what was going on.

"Are you busy tonight?" Her eyes slowly moved to the nearly full moon outside her window.

DANIEL SAT down on the workout bench, grabbed a towel from his bag, and placed his elbows to his knees as he looked around the empty gym. Why did he know this was coming? He wiped his forehead, closing his eyes.

"What did he do now?" He let the frustration out in his tone because two hours of working hard on weights and cardio had done nothing for the feelings that Keegan had left him with that afternoon.

"I'm not sure, but if he texts or calls, please go to him. He needs one of us and my hands are tied."

"But you don't know what's going on?" He took a swig of the water beside him before running the towel over the back of his neck.

"If I could guess, it would have to do with that meeting, but he never asks if I'm busy, just shows up."

"Yeah, that doesn't sound like him." Daniel glanced up at the door, at the muffled sounds of people outside it and cleared his throat. "Okay," and there was an audible sigh, one that told him she was relieved. "I'll answer, but I gotta go."

"Sure."

He tapped the screen, tucking away the phone, just as Greg and Pat stepped into the room. The dark-haired, human boy—Daniel refused to see him any other way after the gym fiasco—smirked at him as he and Pat headed for the weights. Greg stopped in front of him, looked over his shirtless chest, and shook his head.

"Bulking up?"

Daniel shoved his towel in the bag and stood, gripping the handles, and headed for the door. "Fuck off."

"Hey!" He stopped at the call, knowing that Greg wasn't too far behind. "You can't seriously be mad at me for that shit still. I didn't do anything."

"That's right," he snapped around, staring at the jock in front of him. Pat seemed to fade into the background as Greg met his gaze. "You did *nothing*. You just stood there and blamed *him*, said he probably deserved it. So, like I said, fuck off."

"Why are you up on him? Got a thing for the low life?"

Daniel grabbed him by the shirt, twisting the fabric in his hands as he got right in his face, eyes red in anger. "Look, I don't need to validate myself to you, but until you know the loss of someone you love, don't go around throwing shit names like that. You don't know what he's been through."

"And you do?" Greg had the audacity to laugh.

"Yeah," he narrowed his eyes, lowered his voice, and dropped the man as fast as he had gone at him. "I do."

He turned and stomped out of the room, leaving Greg just a little confused, heading straight for the parking lot.

He could see the end of that summer in his mind, the way Keegan backed him against the abandoned Snack Shack in the silence of the beach, empty because it was only five in the morning. He was manic, on edge, even with the moon slowly sinking in the west, but Daniel only raised his hands, keeping them in sight to ease the beta's anxiety.

"You can't tell anyone!" He snapped him forward then back against the weather-worn wood again. "Promise me, Danny, promise."

"I can't," Daniel only swallowed hard, whispering out the words. "I don't want to."

"You can't tell anyone," Keegan's growl was full of pain. They had been doing this for nearly a month since the first time, sneaking out to meet up, to see one another without the judgment of others but now summer was coming to an end. School started in a week and Keegan was terrified. His eyes rimmed with red, the fear in them obvious as he tried to control the tears welling up in his eyes. "They'll—"

"They'll what?" He pushed away from the structure, into the hold, wanting to just pull him in. "They'll judge us? Whisper?"

"They'll try to hurt me." The words slipped from his lips, void of emotion, and Daniel saw the mask come up, something terrifying to see. His hazel eyes slipped to green, and his pupils constricted as his face paled, but all he did was blink. "You don't know them."

"Who?"

The grip on his shirt released and that hand that had been holding him against the wall slipped away. Keegan backed up. There wasn't a smirk on his lips, or mischief in his gaze, there was just—nothing. Daniel couldn't let him disappear. He reached out, snagged his sleeve and pulled him back into the shadows.

"Who, Keegan?"

"You know."

The problem was he really didn't know anything except what he saw every day when they were in school, and very rarely did it have to do with the middle kid. Everyone worshiped the ground Noel walked on, the championships he had won, but Keegan was the one in the shadows, ignored, unknown, until—

Daniel shook his head. "Wait, that's you?"

His grip tightened. He had heard of the team hazing a beta, locker room stories of five against one, but the ending was never clear. They boasted about how they started it, how bruised and beaten he was but they never explained the marks they carried, the obvious beatdowns they had gotten, chalked it up to rough play on the field.

"Answer me!" His voice grew deep, gravelly, as his eyes blazed red. Keegan stared blankly at him, not even registering the way Daniel pulled him in, one hand slipping around his waist as the other released his shirt and pressed against his cheek, but he nodded, just a slight tilt of his head that had Daniel shaking. He leaned in, letting his forehead rest against Keegan's and he closed his eyes. "Let me protect you."

"No way." There was the laugh, the confidence that he had it under control, and while Daniel thought he would struggle to get out of the hold, Keegan melted into it, hands slipping up his chest to hook behind his neck. "You can't protect me because I don't need it."

"I'll keep them away." He brushed his lips against his, feeling the beta's breath warm against him and he shivered at the difference between the outside world and the man in his arms. "I promise."

"Sure, Alpha," the reply was soft, inviting. "I believe you."

The memory faded into feelings. The simple feelings of needing to be in his arms.

Daniel ran his hands over his head, scratching at the back of his head as he sat in the darkness of his car, the engine on, music off, waiting. He wasn't going home, not with the phone call from Paige replaying in his mind. He was just going to wait, and if he didn't hear from him soon, he was going to find him.

He'd always find him.

In the darkness of the small windowless room, where the shadows of solid things were just outlines, and the pain of her injuries reminded her that she was alive, Juli sat tucked in the corner facing the door.

Waiting.

The only thing she could see was the red halo of her vision, and the only sound came from the even thump of her heart.

CHAPTER 15

Noel debated, as he sat at the light by Cafe West, to go straight back to the meetinghouse, or turn left onto Bourne Street to make his way towards Keira's. While it should have been a no-brainer to just head back, he didn't. In fact, he didn't even head towards his girlfriend's but went straight and then his first right. It wasn't a street he knew well, but he knew where it led.

Gate Thirty at the Quabbin Reservoir.

This was the place he had spent the most amount of time alone with his father, where they had time to talk about everything. Alexandru would take him there on hikes, "guys hikes" was what he would call them, and for the longest time it had been him and Keegan going, until the middle one suddenly stopped participating.

It continued to be a way for Noel to let everything go, to let nature in, and to get a hold on himself when he was going through his presentation. It was where he learned to run, and tonight, under a cloudless, moonlit sky, he ran again.

Jeans were a little too constricting to get a good speed, but he did his best. Parking the truck in the small lot just outside the gate, Noel had pulled on a beanie, stripped off the light jacket he had thrown on in the meetinghouse and popped his earbuds in. The music on his phone was the same as the night before, something with a beat, something he could get lost in, and he moved, starting off slow as he disappeared down the tree lined dirt road.

There was something primal about running in the woods, something he cherished, bringing him back to his roots. He thought about the notes in Alex's office, the ones about the werewolves, about his family, and he wondered if that was why? Did he feel this way because he was just that? A monster that took the lives of men during the full moon.

He made it to Keystone Bridge, breathed in the night air, and paced in the loose dirt that covered the top of the man-made arch. Below him, flowing swiftly from the recent rains, the river reflected the light above, giving his world a strange upside-down view and Noel thought back on the last time that happened on a night just like this.

It was senior year, the winter before graduation. He and Keira were fighting, and he was out on the bridge alone. This time though he was sitting, legs hanging over the edge, swinging as he sat there with a bottle of whiskey, the kind that would do some internal damage if you drank too much. As it was, Noel wasn't even feeling the buzz and he was a third of the way through the bottle.

That was when he heard the snapping to his right, from deep in the darkness of the wooded trail. He hadn't expected to find anyone out there, so when they moved out into the moonlight, Noel did his best to stand.

That was when the booze hit him, and he wobbled too close to the edge. Strong hands gripped his shirt, drawing him back further onto the bridge and away from his perch on the edge. He knew the face he stared into, knew the smirk and the bright blue eyes that seemed to glow in the moonlight.

"What the fuck are you doing out there?" Adin Michaels growled, snagging the bottle from Noel's hand. "Smart." He raised his brow as he raised the bottle. "You know people are going missing, right?"

"What do you care?" Noel teetered, still not steady on his feet, which was probably why Adin hadn't let go yet.

"I don't." He shoved the bottle back at him, hitting him right in the chest, but he kept his hold. "Come on."

He tugged on the coat, and while his feet betrayed him, following with stumbling steps, Noel growled. "Let go."

"Wow." Adin came to a halt at the edge of the dirt, where the ground finally met the bridge and dropped his hand. "You really are the asshole everyone says you are." He crossed his arms over his chest as he stared down Noel. They were the same height, almost the same build, with Adin's chest being just a little wider, and neither moved, at least not until Adin scoffed. "You can't stay out here by yourself."

"Why not? No one asked you to come out here."

"You're right." He smirked, like he knew all of Noel's little secrets. "The Quabbin is neutral ground, I'm completely in my right to be out here, just like you...and you can't even stand straight right now."

"And that makes you, what? My hero?" Noel shook his head, eyes on the bottle as he tried to unscrew the cap, something Adin tightened to the point of it probably never coming off again. "What the fuck, man?"

"You don't need any more."

Noel dropped the bottle, stepped closer, pressing his chest against him and let his anger show in his eyes, baring his teeth like he was about to bite him. "Who the fuck do you think you are to tell me what I don't need?"

"You're an alpha, Summerford, get your shit together!" And he wasn't sure why that snapped him back, why he relaxed, or let the gold fade, but he did and took a cautious step back. Both turned their gaze away, taking in the shadows of the trees. "My aunt used to come out here."

"So." Noel sat down in the middle of the path, done with being on his feet.

Adin only shook his head, plunked beside him, and pulled a knee up as he looked around. “You asked why not? I’m telling you why you shouldn’t be out here alone. My aunt went missing from here.”

Noel knew about the missing members, two or three here and there, but he never knew anyone who actually lost a relative. His gaze went to Adin, who stared at anything but the man beside him.

“M’sorry,” he whispered, blinking away the haze that the alcohol created. “They’re trying to figure—”

“Yeah, I know.”

The only thing that filled the night for a few quiet moments was the sound of crickets and birds. Mid-March was strange in New England. Sometimes the only thing you could hear was the wind, other times it was like spring all over again. The “Indian summer” weather was in full swing on that night, and the nocturnal animals were completely confused.

“What are you doing out here? For real?” Adin’s voice pulled Noel from the daydream he had slipped into.

“Girlfriend.” Noel nodded, and the world spun. “We had a fight.” He shook his head, again, the wrong thing to do. “I don’t know. It was... stupid. She has all these plans and mine are completely different.”

“Yeah, I have one like that.”

“One?” His eyes were on him now, unsure and curious. “You make it sound like you have more.”

The smile that rose on his lips was mischievous, more of a Keegan smirk than anything and Adin shrugged. “I do.”

“Jesus,” he chuckled. “Sometimes one is more than enough for me.”

“Yeah, they’re not all serious. Actually,” he paused; brows tight as he thought for a moment. “None of them are, truthfully.”

Noel scoffed, not judging but definitely impressed. “I don’t want to be an alpha.”

It was Adin’s turn to scoff, but it slowly turned into a laugh. “Man, that sucks.”

“What?”

"You can't change who you are, Summerford. Your designation is what it is. The only thing you can do is hope to accomplish something with it."

"I'm too drunk for philosophical shit."

"And I'm not drunk enough." He leaned back on his hands and stared up at the stars. "I'm a beta."

"I know, I can feel you." Noel mirrored him, but instead of bracing on his arms, he just let himself fall back on the dirt.

Adin didn't know if he wanted to laugh or cringe. "You can feel me?"

"Yeah, alphas can feel..." His eyes rested on Adin as his hand did a sweeping motion towards him.

"I didn't know that."

"Don't you have an alpha nearby?"

"Nope," he gave a quick shrug. "Family of all betas and omegas. The closest I get to alphas is the guys I play with on the team, and they don't go spilling shit like that."

"Oh." Noel let his hands rest on his stomach. "Both parents in my house are alphas, my brother's a beta, just finished his..." He wasn't even sure what to call it now, but Keegan didn't change much from before, just got a little bit angrier.

"I get it."

A stillness settled between them, and Noel let his eyes close as it washed over him, at least for a little bit until he felt the pain of knuckles digging into his ribs. "You can't stay here, Summerford. Let's go."

"What?" He growled, wanted to just pull the covers over his head, and sleep for a little longer, but then he remembered he wasn't even home.

Blinking, he found himself looking up at the star-filled sky, and to his right was Michaels, still sitting where he was, staring off at nothing. A chill went through every part of his body, like the temperature had dropped twenty degrees and he forced himself up.

"Why are you still here?" He didn't mean for it to come out angry, but it did, and Adin raised a brow, scowling.

"Well, I could leave you here, watch the news in the morning that you had fallen into the river and cracked your thick skull, but my fingerprints are on that bottle and I'm sure my sneakers left marks somewhere around here." He got to his feet, dusted off the back of his jeans, and reached down, grabbing Noel's arm before getting him up vertical. "Where's your keys?"

"What?"

"Does drinking make you deaf too? Keys!" When Noel just stared at him, a little unsure, Adin stepped closer and started digging through his pockets. Noel did his best to protest, trying to push him off but it wasn't any use, scowling at the beta when he stepped back, truck keys in hand. "Not gonna let you kill someone either, let's go."

The hike back to the truck was a long one, with Noel tripping over everything, rocks, branches, the air, but they made it. Adin kept his word; he drove him home. He didn't remember much after the beta had dropped him off, but his truck was in the driveway the next morning.

Watching the river now, the way the moon looked wavy in the water, Noel fought to remember why he hated the man. Why the very presence of him on campus had set off the other side of him. Maybe it had something to do with the rest of the year, the races, or the football games. Noel was the kicker for the Collins team, only faced Adin a few times on the field but Michaels had a knack for injuring players.

Or maybe it was just his mom's rules and Keegan was right, he just played along like a good soldier.

He clenched his fists, looked down the dark trail and debated on going, but with a sigh, he turned back towards the trail entrance and his truck. He needed to check on Keegan, to get out of his own damn head, and find his mother.

Noel stopped in the kitchen when he slipped into the meetinghouse. He knew how his brother operated, loved his caffeine while he worked, and from the look of the cold, empty pot, he hadn't had enough. Instead of starting it, he grabbed a bottled water from the fridge. It was nearly ten, he didn't need to be hyped up.

He moved through the hall, passing Gus who never even looked up from the work he was doing, and went straight to the room, only pausing in the doorway. Keegan sat behind the desk, earbuds in, eyes glued to the screen, typing away. He'd drown in it if he let him. Once he got into it, he had a hard time getting out, and maybe coffee wasn't the best idea.

He knocked, catching his attention as Keegan sat back, shut off the music and rubbed his hand down his face before pressing the heel of his hand into his eyes. His hair's a mess, which meant he was tugging on it, a usual reaction when things didn't go his way, but Noel had seen that kind of thing before, where Keegan actually had bald spots from it, and he stepped closer, placing the bottle down.

Keegan glanced at it only for a second before his eyes went to Noel's. "Thanks."

Noel sighed, watching him go back to the screen. "Sure."

He didn't move, just stood there patiently, waiting on the exact response he got, which was a low rumble from his brother.

And without looking up, that growl became words. "Can I help you?"

"We should call it a night." He didn't want to, but there was still school, and a kid that might not be so easy to pull back if he let him just go with it.

Bright gold eyes stared up at him in shock. "What?"

"Home?"

It was all he could suggest, but it got Keegan up on his feet, placing both hands on the desk for only a moment before he slammed both laptops shut. “No! Not a chance in hell, man! Mom’s out there somewhere.”

“And I want to find her just as much as you but this...” He gestured towards Keegan’s unkempt self, with the dark green flannel undone, his wrinkled shirt, and the wild look in his eyes. “This isn’t going to help, so pack it in. You have school tomorrow.”

“Like hell, I do.” He rounded the desk, standing eye to eye, as much as he could with the height difference, and rolled his shoulders, but Noel didn’t move, didn’t even blink. “This is bullshit, Noel! Not even alpha for a day and you think you can order me around?”

Noel took a step back, prepared for this kind of reaction, and raised his hands, giving him space. “I’m not going to argue with you, Key. Mom gave strict orders, and you know how that goes.”

“Strict orders, my ass! I’m staying home tomorrow, and I’m coming back to crack this.” He moved in, closing the space so there was only a hand’s width between them. “You’re not going to stop me.”

Noel wasn’t going to argue either, he got what he wanted, him *away* from the computer, but Keegan bumped his shoulder on the way by, letting him know exactly how he felt about it. He calmed himself, turned and leaned on the desk.

“Fine.” That one word had him pausing in the doorway, hands clenched, as his body stiffened, ready for a fight. “But listen, the rest of the pack can’t know what’s going on.” The only answer he got from that was a long sigh. “Tell me you know. That they can’t know Mom’s gone.”

He whipped around, anger in his expression, but there was something in his eyes, desperation maybe, fear? God forbid, hope?

“Then get me a solid lead on her. Tell him,” pointing out towards the main hall, “tell him to show you the tapes, to let you in on everything, because I’m pretty sure they’re leaving something out.”

“I can’t do that either. Not tonight. I can’t let you get so deep into it that you get lost, and you do that. You get obsessed.”

Keegan dropped his head, pressing his chin against his chest, and his fingers twitched as he released them. "All right."

Noel blinked like he had just seen something he didn't quite understand. "All right?"

"Yeah, I'll..." He stomped his way back to the desk, grabbed his phone and wiggled it at Noel. "I'll go see Paige, or something." It was a good excuse, even knowing he couldn't. She had said no, but Noel didn't need to know that. "I'm sure she'll let me in."

"Good. That's good."

"But." And there it was, his finger coming up to point at Noel, to get right in his face. "Tomorrow you're not going to stop me. Say it."

"Okay." He didn't want to agree to that, but he had to do something. "Okay."

Keegan turned, snatching his coat off the chair in front of the desk, and walked out of the room, leaving Noel there a little confused, and a lot worried.

KEEGAN MADE it through the room without Gus even muttering a word, but as he slipped out the door into the night, he stopped just to take in the cold night air. The clouds had rolled in covering the moon, sending the lot into near blackness.

He took only one step down, stopped his body from running, and sat down on the top step. With a sigh, he pulled his phone from his pocket and stared at the screensaver, fingers rubbing against his palm as he debated for a moment before opening the text to "Bye Boi."

Eyes closed, breathing even, he gave himself a second to center before he typed the words out, watching them appear. "*Need you. Usual spot?*"

It only took a second for the bubbles to appear, to start moving as he bit down on his lip and the reply popped through.

Bye Boi: *You okay?*

Keegan rolled his eyes, fixating on the streetlight before he replied. "*No.*"

Bye Boi: *15.*

He put the phone down, tented his hands over his nose, and exhaled into them. His whole body shook. He needed this but he needed his brother off his back.

Stuffing his phone away, he slipped back inside the building.

Gus looked up from his paperwork when Keegan stopped beside him, still a few feet away, and fidgeted. He had been mumbling as he shuffled around the papers at the end of the table. He couldn't sit, could barely stay still, but the boy's silence and shifting was getting under his skin.

He was about to yell, but looking into those worried hazel eyes, it faded. "What is it, Keegan?"

"Can you," he shifted again, like his clothes were uncomfortable. "Just tell Noel I went home instead of—" Gus's bright blue eyes, the way he stared had Keegan's hackles up, it always did because he felt judged. "Just tell him I walked home."

"You actually going home?" He gave him a slight shrug and a shake of his hand. "Gonna go meet your girl?" Keegan ducked his head, taking his gaze away. "Nah, you're gonna meet your alpha boy." The fear in Keegan's eyes was evident, front and center, and he swallowed nervously, waiting for it, but Gus waved him off, before he got this fond look in his eyes. "I remember my first alpha."

"But you're an alpha?" He was thoroughly confused. He knew it happened, hell, his parents were both alphas, but there was a fine line between what they had and all-out war on the home front. Most alpha pairs were like oil and water.

"Might be," Gus laughed, "but I never said I was a saint." That nostalgia was strong, and Keegan wrinkled his nose as the scent. "She was—" Gus cleared his throat, went back to shuffling his papers and addressed him without looking up, trying to keep the blush on his cheeks hidden. "Go on, have fun. Just remember to sneak back in before your brother has to wake you up."

"Thanks?" He mumbled and dashed for the door.

Gus smiled, but it faded as he looked over the missing persons reports on his desk. Maybe he shouldn't have let him go on alone.

NOEL LET the chair recline back, still warm from his brother using it for the last few hours, and he dropped his head on the rest behind him. Keegan's nervous scent, the way it took over the room, was strangely calming, surrounded by the little knickknacks and pack photos. Each wall had something, each shelf was filled with small, framed photos of families, most with children.

There were ones of Rollins, with Mitch and his wife Debra. The Whites, O'Leary's, but Noel didn't concentrate on those. He seemed to focus on the small lamp in the corner, and the buzz that filled the room.

It was getting brighter, almost blinding, and the noise was deafening. He clenched his jaw in pain, pressed his hands to his temple and squeezed his eyes shut, which did nothing for the light around him.

He's suddenly outside, the air filled with a slight chill, and the scent of some strong incense. Noel glanced around, taking in the crowd dressed all in black, and Juli beside him. Keegan to his left, on edge as usual, but he had Ellie's hands clasped gently in his as she wrapped her arms around him.

In front of him is a mahogany casket, covered in beautiful flowers. The banners of "Father," "Son," "Alpha," are gently wrapped around the bouquet. At the head of it, the pastor stood, a man he remembered from his childhood, but couldn't place. His mouth moved, but the only sound he heard was the humming coming from all around him.

His hands clenched as he focused on the casket, on the sound of fire crackling, the scent of burning rubber, and underneath it a strange smell he knew was flesh. The sudden sting in his palm, a jolt of pain that zipped through him as he scanned the crowd before looking down, uncurling his fingers. Four, crescent-shaped wounds on the palm of his hands bloomed, and his nails and skin became covered in blood.

His hands started to shake, a light sheen of sweat beaded on his forehead, and his breathing picked up, uncontrolled. Stuck in a panic, Noel leaned in towards his mother.

"I'll be right back," and then he was gone, disappearing through the crowd.

He made his way through the cemetery, still dressed in a suit, but it was as if the sun had fallen behind midnight clouds, everything went dark. The only thing lit is the old stone crypt that he stumbled towards. He leaned against it, letting it hold him up as he pressed against the cold stones.

He brought his hands up, watching the blood leak from the wounds, dripping down his arm, and he closed his eyes tight, blocking out the hum as it grew louder. He just needed a minute to calm down.

His heart thumped against his ribs, painful and strong, and Noel found himself back in the office, eyes on the ceiling. There was no noise, and the lights were dimmed. He swallowed back the bile and the feeling of his stomach rolling, the same reaction that had been happening all day.

"What the hell is wrong with me?"

Ellie sat up in bed, eyes glancing around the room. The house is still quiet, her brothers weren't home yet, but there was something, some sort of presence there.

She slipped from the comforter, grabbed the thick book that had taken space on the nightstand table and made her way towards the door. She never closed it when the boys were out, it was just a thing she wasn't comfortable with, but she was also glad she sprayed the hinges because there was no sound when she opened it wide.

She slipped down through the hall, following the feeling, the tug at her core, and made her way into her parents' room. It was chilly. Juli never liked the heat turned up when she wasn't home, thought it was a waste of energy, but this wasn't a natural cold, there was something about it that didn't sit well.

Ellie lowered the book, looked at the shine of the moon through the window and blinked at the bed, where she saw her dad standing. Alex was strange, almost see through, but he held a book open in his hand and he was scanning the pages.

She startled as his eyes came up to meet hers, and he gave a small smirk, ignoring the fear in her eyes as she took a step back. Behind her, the sound of bickering grew as her brothers' voices drew closer, and she backed up against the doorsill, to watch as Keegan stomped towards his room, Noel right behind them.

The argument was over a book, or something that had to do with one, but before she could figure it out, the vision faded, and she turned back to her father. Alex hadn't moved, his gaze was back on the book in his hand, but that changed as well when he picked his head up, as if his name had been called, and he closed it.

She watched with a strange fascination as he set the book down on the stand and moved right for her, disappearing before he took three steps, but that book remained.

Glancing around in the slowly fading light, Ellie moved towards the nightstand, eyes going over everything in the room until they landed on the title of the book. "Cei Dintre Noi."

"Those among us?" Ellie whispered, but as soon as the words

flowed, she found the vision fading and once again she was sitting up in bed.

The door was exactly how she left it, the book on the table beside her hadn't moved, and her phone sat black and silent. She didn't bother looking at the time, she just turned over, closed her eyes and hoped to fall back to sleep again.

It came surprisingly easily.

Just off into the woods along a stretch of farmland filled with rows of stalks sat an old woodshed, one that Keegan's headed straight for. The stalks themselves had been cut down to about six inches after Halloween, barely leaving cover for the small building. It wasn't far off the beaten path, and less than a ten-minute walk from not only his house, but the school and meetinghouse as well. This has been Keegan's hideout for years, anything to get away from his family when he was having a hard time, and they've never found it, no matter how hard they looked.

He had originally been camping out in the old vault where they kept the bodies in the winter in the cemetery next to the meetinghouse, but he had been found there too many times to keep going back, and Noel had a knack for pinpointing his scent from pretty much every place in town. He was pretty certain that the scent of the stalks and the fertilizer was what threw his bloodhound of a brother off his trail for so long, covering up his anger and anxiety. Now it wasn't just a place to get away and calm down, it was a place to meet up.

He stopped just for a moment outside the door and looked it over. The twenty-by-twenty shack was pretty sturdy, had two small windows, one beside the door, and one on the back, so it was easy to see the lantern light from where he stood.

With a deep breath, he reached for the handle, clicking it down with his thumb before he pushed it open.

The soft glow lit up the mainly wooden walls of the small building. There's nothing much in there, a few old wooden crates for chairs and tables, some mounted shelves that hold strange little treasures from over the years and the air is filled with the hum of the electric heater that warmed the space.

It was weird to have electricity all the way out there, but they—being the kids who used it way before Keegan ever found it—had managed to figure out a way to wire it in, but only for the heater, the lamp was still a battery operated one, but worked just as well.

Keegan let out the worry he was holding as he listened to the latch close behind him before locking the deadbolt, ensuring the world stayed outside, and his eyes moved across the room to the alpha sitting on an old mattress set, something much newer than expected.

Daniel hadn't looked up yet, but he was smirking as he sat against the wall, one leg sprawled out on the mattress, the other set off the bed with his foot on the floor, with his phone in his hand. He looked comfortable, not at all uncertain, in his jeans and tee-shirt. The varsity jacket he had worn all day was gone, cutting away the separation of their school "cliques."

Keegan shivered at the sight of him before turning towards the window. He yanked the old, tattered towels across, blocking out any way to see in, before he moved towards the edge of the mattress. Daniel put the phone down, his attention right on Keegan, as the beta knelt down at the furthest corner of the bed, before shifting to the middle Daniel sat up, coming away from the wall.

The beta crawled up the bed, hovering over him as Daniel scooted down to lie back. Nose to nose without touching any other way, he held back until he couldn't anymore and settled his hands on Keegan's waist, tentative but tender, slipping just under the hem of his tee-shirt.

"You sure this is okay?" His dark eyes locked on those hazel ones as he held off the memories of the way Keegan reacted earlier that day. He didn't want to scare him or do anything to set him off with that experience so fresh in his mind.

Keegan bit his lip, tilted his head just a little and brushed his lips over Daniel's. It was soft, almost nonexistent, just to see what happened next. The alpha didn't tense, didn't pull back.

"Better than okay," he whispered as he sat back, getting Daniel to chase the kiss he promised.

His fingers reached for that green button-down, taking it in his grasp as he held on, now pressed chest to chest with the beta, and gently pushed it off his shoulders, dipping down to kiss along his neck.

Keegan gave into the touches, his lids fluttering closed as he let the shirt drop behind him before he ran his fingers along Daniel's arms until he reached his shoulders. Shivering, Daniel wrapped his arms around Keegan's waist, fingers splayed along his back, hot against his bare skin under the shirt and Keegan let out a small sigh.

"Tell me what's wrong," he pleaded between kisses along his exposed shoulders.

In a sudden rush of movement, Keegan pushed at him, breaking his touch from his neck as he hovered above, hands locking him to the mattress.

"Don't go all alpha on me, Payne." Keegan scoffed. "I don't need it from you."

"Really?" Daniel teased but could plainly see the worry in Keegan's eyes.

The way the beta shook told him he definitely had his attention even while he frantically grabbed at the bottom of Daniel's shirt. He sat up again, letting out a low, possessive growl as his shirt seemed to disappear, and Keegan stilled at the noise.

"On second thought." He was breathless, pupils wide with desire, and Daniel could scent just how much he *needed*. "That might be kind of fun."

Daniel smiled, wrapped his arms around his waist, and flipped him down on the blanket, pinning him beneath him. He knew what it did to the beta, knew how it grounded him, kept him present and he was going to use that to his advantage because it was in his nature to provide for him.

With a flash of red, Daniel leaned in and kissed him deeply, pulling a moan from the man under him.

NOEL SAT FORWARD, pushing the chair away from the desk as he rested his elbows on his knees. He needed a break, needed to sleep, and ran his hands through his hair.

Without warning, the pain hit again, and the sound in the room amplified. His hands blocked it out, but only so much as he pressed them tightly against his head. His stomach turned leaving white spots behind his lids.

"Gus," was the only thing he got out, but it was muffled like he was underwater. He tried to sit up, to push back in the chair, but the room started to spin, and he put his head between his knees.

The noise canceled out everything, even his own heartbeat, just before the world spun and went black.

Only seconds passed before the rush became almost too much when he opened his eyes. He was now outside, the sun was up, the skies were blue, and in the driveway was a familiar black car. Noel made his way down the steps, away from the front door, a familiar feeling of deja vu flowed over him.

Tom stood by the rear door, smiling as he approached, but before he could say anything, the front door opened again. Juli walked out, dressed in business casual, making her way down towards the car, with her purse in hand.

Noel smiled at the way she adjusted her jacket, trying to get it to feel comfortable before she finally got fed up, and grinned up at him.

Standing between Tom and the door, she tossed her bag in before taking Noel's hand.

"You sure you don't want Gus to come over?"

He remembered this now and shook his head. "I think I can handle the two of them for a week, Mom. We're not babies anymore."

"I know." She reached out to touch his cheek, worry and pride in her eyes. "I swear it's only for a week."

"I know, I have the itinerary."

"You remember the rules, right?"

It was the first time she went away after Alexandru died, the first conference without him, and Noel did his best to smile. "They're etched into the back of my eyelids."

"Smart ass!" She kissed him on the cheek, hugging him tightly.

For a moment he hesitated, before hugging her back. It was only a month or so after the lake incident, after his therapy started, and while he seemed confident to her, he was terrified of being alone. "I learned from the best."

She backed away, holding his shoulders. "You learned from your father."

"Like I said," the smile fell. "The best."

Juli let him go, slipped into the car, and gave him a small smile as Tom closed it behind her, before moving towards the driver seat. Noel stepped back as the window rolled down and the car shifted into reverse.

"I'll be back in a week," she repeated, reassuringly, and the only thing he could do was nod.

As the car backed out and drove away, Noel raised a hand, waving before he felt his heart sink and the anger bubble up as the world blurred.

He was suddenly aware of the lack of spinning. The warmth of the sun had been replaced by the chill of the office, but there was no humming, and the light didn't hurt his eyes.

He grabbed for the desk, fingers refusing to work at first, but he finally was able to bring himself up to his feet, his legs shaking from the exertion. He took a moment to look around before clicking off the desk lamp, sending the office into darkness.

His legs worked better than he thought they would by the time he walked out of the office, pulling the door shut behind him. He took a moment though, to lean against it, gathered his thoughts and finally turned towards the meeting room.

He could see where Gus stood leaning over the table, the same folders that had graced the tabletop when he came in were now spread out in front of him and he could tell, even from a distance, that whatever was going through the alpha's head was not good.

His scent was tinged with smoke, the sign of anger, like a fire raging out of control, and he approached with caution, something the other man in the room noticed as he stood, bright eyes dancing as Noel stopped. With a huff, Gus grabbed the chair and sat down, elbows going to the edge of the armrests while he laced his fingers together.

"Taking your own advice and going home?"

Noel scoffed, like that was the worst idea in the world and continued making his way to the table, eyes scanning over the folders.

"Maybe. Might stop by Keira's on the way." He pulled out a file, looking over the eight-by-ten photo attached to one side. He knew he had already asked about the cases, but he really wanted to pull an answer from him about the extent of it. "What are you working on?"

Gus snapped back to his feet, gathered up the files and pulled them away, trying to hide what he was doing. "Nothing you need to be concerned about."

He knew right then that it was a hopeless quest and dropped the file.

"You know what," he nodded, "maybe with everything going on, I'll just go home, check on Ellie."

"That's a good idea, they're going to need you."

He smirked, shaking his head.

"Keegan would beg to differ." He rapped his knuckles on the table twice and headed for the door. The worried voice from across the room had him pausing.

"Don't give up on him."

With his eyes on Gus, Noel shrugged. "I would never do that, he's my brother."

"I know, but I also know that you don't seem to notice how much of a hard time he's having."

"We all are, we all *have* been. That's not a reason for him to—" He stopped, just stopped, raised his hands in surrender, not sure of what he was going with, but he took a moment to rethink it, calmly. "I know his diagnosis, Gus. I've been dealing with him since the moment he came into the world screaming, but damn— Something has to give."

The older alpha made his way towards the end of the table, leaned back against it and crossed his arms and ankles, a way to seem relaxed, which instantly put Noel at ease. "He's trying to figure himself out."

"You know." One breath, two... "He's not the only one with things going on. Trying to sort through shit."

"This about your eyes?"

That stunned him for a moment, wondering just what he meant. Did he know about the weird shifts, the blood under his nails, the orange halo when his eyes glowed? He shook it off and scowled. "What? No! I don't care about what color my eyes are. I am who I am. Red, gold, puke green, it doesn't matter. I'm still an alpha, I know that."

"Right." He rubbed his fingers across his brow. "But your brother doesn't."

"Why are we talking about him?" It was a straightforward question, one that deserved a straight answer, but Gus just moved back to the head of the table.

"He'll tell you when he's ready, but just," he narrowed his eyes on him. "When he does, be gentle."

Noel waved him off, shook his head, and walked out of the building.

EPILOGUE

Noel stomped his way down the steps, turning just after the bottom one to make his way down to the parking lot.

"Be gentle," he thought to himself, digging his keys from his pocket. *"That should probably be something we're teaching him."*

Noel reached his truck in record time, the air outside had changed to a bitter cold that made him shiver, and goosebumps rose on his arms. He fought with the key for a moment before he yanked the door open and stilled.

The wind, just the way it moved through the trees, caught his attention, and Noel found himself slowly turning towards the cemetery.

A low, mournful sound, almost like a deep howl, came from somewhere powerful, flowed over the night breaking the rustle of what was left of the leaves that hung on high branches. He circled, trying to pinpoint where it was coming from, but it seemed to be everywhere.

And then it stopped just as suddenly as it began.

The hairs on the back of his neck rose as his eyes landed on the movement of shadows within the trees, and the clouds shifted to cover the light of the moon, drowning everything in darkness. His heart raced, eyes turned blood red, and he quickly climbed into the cab, slamming the door behind him.

The old truck started up with a rumble, canceling out everything else around him. Red brake lights lit up the forest as he stepped on the pedal and put it in reverse with a quick flash of white. His headlights popped on, and the truck rolled off the gravel lot, disappearing down the road.

On the wind, came another sound, closer, deeper, searching, before the wind picked up and swallowed it down.

Gus looked up as a quiet howl breached the inner walls of the meetinghouse, pulling him once again from the files. He stood, unsure of what he just heard and made his way towards the pair of windows that faced the parking lot and the woods.

Curiousness had taken over, not something he was keen on admitting, and he placed both hands on the glass, blocking out the light from behind him. There's nothing out there but darkness, shadows casting shadows that create more shadows, and Gus stepped back.

He grabbed the cord beside him, yanked it gently, and lowered the blinds before stepping away to check the emergency exit door. A sudden shiver went through him, like a ghost walking by, as he made his way back to the table.

The file on top, the reason he had pulled them away from Noel so quickly, was Luca's. His medical records and the photos taken to document his injuries were open, front and center. He couldn't scar the kid like that, not after what he knew Noel had witnessed with Alex, so he pulled them away.

He should have explained.

But how, when he didn't even know what the hell was going on himself? Lost in Luca's eyes, as the beta stared into the camera, Gus sat down hard in the chair, his hands going to his hair. He needed to find out what the hell was going on, and he needed to do it fast.

KEEGAN SAT UP, sweating heavily, eyes adjusting to the darkness, but he didn't wake up on his own. It was a call in the night. Daniel was still asleep beside him, curled up on his side, with his arm draped over Keegan's waist. There was something out there, Keegan could feel it.

He slipped out of bed, hugging his arms against the chill that filled the small shack. The electric heater fought to keep them warm, to keep the sudden drop in temperature outside from getting in, but Keegan didn't even notice. He headed straight towards the small window directly across from the bed, the one facing the empty corn field, and pushed the curtain aside.

His eyes were wide as he watched the moon peek out from behind the clouds, took in the way it lit up the barren field that stretched before him and the low sound of a howl filled the night.

That's what he heard, that's what woke him up. It was a cry for pack, the sorrowful sound of loneliness, and Keegan quickly dropped the curtains, stepping back. His eyes bright gold against his will.

"Keegan?" Daniel's gruff voice was rough with sleep, and Keegan shook off the gold, moving back towards the bed before he climbed into the warmth of the man and the covers.

He curled up against him, let his arms hold him tight, and the body heat pushed the cold away, but there was something out there, and Keegan couldn't close his eyes.

Luca vibrated from the drop in temperature, his body running on fumes, and the cold was winning. He didn't even care anymore. He was freezing, he was tired, and he was giving in.

But he could feel it in his bones, the sudden ache that came with the sound of the wolf's howl. He clenched his jaw, gripped the blanket tight, and let his eyes grow wide and gold as he stared up at the moon through the small, barred window.

The pain in his stomach doubled him over, even as he fought against it, and the heat rose within him taking over. He wasn't cold anymore. He was angry and shaking for another reason now, but the moment a second low howl came through, that anger faded, and he sank back, a tear falling from his eye as he slipped into unconsciousness.

Her bright red eyes scanned the room. There was something out there, something calling her, and Juli began to pace. She needed to get out, to get to her kids, to go to Gustaf. There was something wrong, she could feel it in her bones.

The lock on the door clicked, causing her to ready herself, and even as the light flooded in, the only thing she saw was red.

To be continued...

LIES

THE PACK BOOK TWO

Stunned by the news of their mother missing, the three siblings find themselves at a turning point. They can't continue the way they're going, divided while hoping for change, and they finally realize that working together makes them stronger.

As they begin snooping around, looking into what they believed were the ordinary lives of their parents, the Summerford children realize one thing. The amount of lies and falsities that surround their family and hometown is immeasurable. However, it becomes abundantly clear that it's not just the older generations holding things back, but they themselves, as the truth about their own lives begins to unfold. There comes a point where nothing can be held back.

In order to survive what comes next, they must let the others in. One way or another, the truth needs to be told.

Made in the USA
Middletown, DE
13 August 2024

58625160R00177